"For Ensign Sato, translation is as much an art as a science. . . ."

The doctor went on. "It involves intuitive reasoning as well as the collation of a learned body of knowledge. And her fear, quite simply, is that when the Xindi cut into her brain, they somehow damaged her ability to reason in that manner."

"You've told her that isn't the case though," the captain said. "That there was no damage to her brain."

"I told her I believed that to be the case, yes."

"And what did she say to that?"

"She asked if I was certain."

"And you said . . ."

"Fairly certain was, I believe, my exact response."

Archer's exasperation must have shown on his face. Phlox hurriedly continued.

"The fact is captain, that for all we know about how the human brain functions, there is still a great deal that remains a mystery. The Xindi may very well have damaged Ensign Hosh's ability to synthesize knowledge in certain ways. I frankly have no way of knowing for certain."

"You're not helping me here, doctor."

Phlox frowned. "I thought I was being very helpful."

— STAR TREK —
ENTERPRISE™
·ROSETTA·

DAVE STERN

**Based upon *Star Trek*®
created by Gene Roddenberry
and
Star Trek: Enterprise
created by Rick Berman & Brannon Braga**

POCKET BOOKS
New York London Toronto Sydney

This book is a work of fiction. Names, characters, places and incidents are products of the author's imagination or are used fictitiously. Any resemblance to actual events or locales or persons, living or dead, is entirely coincidental.

An *Original* Publication of POCKET BOOKS

POCKET BOOKS, a division of Simon & Schuster, Inc.
1230 Avenue of the Americas, New York, NY 10020

STAR TREK is a Registered Trademark of Paramount Pictures.

This book is published by Pocket Books, a division of Simon & Schuster, Inc., under exclusive license from Paramount Pictures.

ISBN-13: 978-1-4165-0956-1
ISBN-10: 1-4165-0956-9

First Pocket Books printing February 2006

10 9 8 7 6 5 4 3 2 1

POCKET and colophon are registered trademarks of Simon & Schuster, Inc.

Manufactured in the United States of America

For information regarding special discounts for bulk purchases, please contact Simon & Schuster Special Sales at 1-800-456-6798 or business@simonandschuster.com.

With thanks, once again, to Margaret Clark,
Donna O'Neill, and Scott Shannon at Pocket.

Messrs. Feinstein, Weisler, and Spector
over at Amherst.

And the good people past and present—
Paula Block, Mike Okuda,
Rick Berman, Brannon Braga, Harve Bennett,
and Gene Roddenberry—at Paramount.

HISTORIAN'S NOTE

The events in this book take place between December 27, 2254—while the Orion women were passengers on the *Enterprise* ("Bound") and January 19, 2255—when a xenophobic group tries to stop the formation of an alliance between Earth and several alien governments ("Demons").

ONE

On the bridge of the *Starship Enterprise*, on the edge of uncharted space, Captain Jonathan Archer tensed in his command chair. A speck of silver flashed on the main viewscreen.

The cacophony of electronic signals sounding around him surged in intensity: at the science station to his left, at weapons, directly behind him, at auxiliary communications to his right.

They were coming.

"Same vessel, Captain." That was his science officer and second-in-command, Commander T'Pol, Vulcan, one of only two nonhumans serving aboard *Enterprise*. She looked up from her viewer, straightened, and stood. "On intercept course."

"Confirm that." Reed at tactical spoke. "Picking up an energy buildup in the aft section of the ship, Captain. As before."

Archer nodded grimly. "As before"—as in the two other times they'd encountered this ship. When the energy buildup was a prelude to weapons fire. As in they had about half a minute before said fire occurred again.

"Mister Carstairs." Archer spoke without taking his eyes off the viewscreen. "Any change in their signal?"

"No, sir." Ensign Carstairs was at his right hand, at the aux com station, handling routine communications duties, so that Hoshi—Ensign Hoshi Sato, *Enterprise*'s com officer—could concentrate on translating that incoming alien signal. The captain forced himself not to look in her direction. Hoshi was working; even without seeing her, he could picture her in his mind, seated ramrod-straight at her station, head cocked slightly to one side, listening to the alien signal. Let her work. If she had something to report she would tell him.

"Captain?"

"Mister Carstairs. Speak."

"I'm picking up something coming from the lateral sensor array."

"Something."

"Very faint. Very regular, though. Could be a signal, could be noise. I'd need to divert some processing power to filter out . . ."

"No. We need that processing power for the UT. All of it." Hoshi answered before Archer could, and now he did turn to look at her, and found that the picture in his mind had been exactly right. She sat exactly as he had envisioned her, listening, seemingly oblivious of the frenzy of activity around her.

Excepting, of course, that she wasn't oblivious at all.

"It'll keep, Ensign," Archer told Carstairs.

"Fifteen seconds to weapons range, Captain," Reed said. "This would be a good time to . . ."

"Do nothing," Archer snapped. "Travis, maintain course and speed."

"Aye, sir," Reed and Mayweather both said, almost simultaneously.

Reed wanted permission to bring their own weapons on-line. Archer wasn't going to give it to him. He'd briefed the captain earlier this morning; telemetry from their last encounter showed a potential weakness in the alien vessel's defense systems, one Reed thought he could exploit.

But Archer didn't want to send any mixed messages. *Enterprise* came in peace. He would not assume an offensive posture under any circumstances. He didn't want to fight; he wanted permission to enter what the aliens obviously considered their sovereign space. He wanted to talk to them. Hard to do that at the moment, though. Considering.

Again, he forced himself not to look back at Hoshi.

"Weapons fire," Reed said, and a nanosecond later something streaked by the bridge, light flashed, and the entire ship shuddered.

Archer frowned. That felt closer than the other times.

"Same weapon as before," T'Pol announced, bending over her viewer. "Charged particle rays, transmitted as two separate beams, sources join at target point to produce explosive effect akin to a molecular disruptor."

"It might be my imagination," Archer said, standing. "But that felt a little bit closer than last time."

"Not your imagination at all, Captain." T'Pol spoke without moving. "It was closer. One hundred meters off our port nacelle."

"One hundred meters." That was Trip, behind him. His chief engineer let out a long, slow whistle. "That's pretty close."

"That it is."

"Might not be a bad idea to charge the hull plating, sir," Trip said, stepping up alongside his chair. "Just in case."

"We've been over this, Trip," Archer said. "We don't want to send any mixed messages."

Trip smiled. "Just a friendly reminder."

"Noted."

"They're charging weapons again, Captain," Reed said.

" 'Cause as much as we don't want to send any mixed messages," Trip continued, "the odds of us eventually being able to communicate with these people greatly increase if we're alive."

"I got it, Trip, thanks."

The alien vessel filled the viewscreen before him. This was the third time in as many days that they'd encountered the ship. For all its weaponry, it was small—maybe a quarter the size of *Enterprise*. Clean lines—utilitarian, functional, more like an Andorian ship in that respect than, say, a Klingon or Vulcan vessel. No structures for ornament or effect. Not a warship per se either, though they obviously had their share of weapons.

"Sensor readings coming in, sir," T'Pol said. "Biosigns, roughly a half-dozen humanoids, Minshara-class atmosphere characteristics—difficult to distinguish among them, a number of what I would call sensor artifacts . . . some kind of protective field perhaps."

"Same as before, in other words?"

"Yes, sir, same as before. No additional data."

"Weapons fire," Reed interrupted.

Another flash of light, and the ship shuddered a second time, even more strongly.

An alarm sounded.

"That felt like a hit," Reed said.

"Negative," T'Pol said. "Disruption occurred one

meter off the port nacelle." She paused a second. "Reading significant scorching and overheating in surface thermal components."

"Damage?"

"None I can detect."

"Rerouting signal to auxiliary conduits, just in case." That from Trip, already back at the engineering station. "Like I said, that's some damn fine shooting."

"Assuming they meant to miss again," Archer said.

"I believe that to be the case, Captain," T'Pol said. "Correlating data from our previous two encounters with the alien vessel, I've detected a pattern to their weapons fire."

"Go on."

"Our first encounter, they fired twice, targeting coordinates fifteen hundred, then one thousand meters off our position. Second encounter, coordinates five hundred, then two hundred fifty meters off. This encounter, one hundred meters, and then one meter off."

Archer nodded. Trip spoke.

"Not much margin for error next time, sir. Sure we don't want to charge the hull plating?"

Archer hesitated, and then, almost of its own volition, his head swiveled in Hoshi's direction again.

She looked up at the same time, almost as if she'd read his mind, and shook her head.

"Nothing. There's no pattern to the signal. Each pulse is different from the preceding one. Entirely different waveforms, each time. Makes no sense. How can you construct a language like that?"

The question was rhetorical. *A good thing*, Archer thought, because he had no idea how to answer it. Hoshi had come to the captain's mess last night for dinner, and started to explain how she was attempting to translate the signal, frequency analysis, linguistic theory, applications to underlying brain structure, on and on and on. Archer had kept up with her until dessert, a good forty-five minutes, but then she'd started in on some of the more esoteric theories about language acquisition, application of Chomsky's principles to first encounters, and he'd had to stop her, completely lost.

After that, they'd talked about water polo for a while.

"Captain, additional telemetry coming in." T'Pol was bent over the viewer again. There was an edge to her voice; Archer had an ear for the subtle variations in her tone, at least. She sounded excited. No, strike that. "Excited" was too strong a term. Interested, perhaps.

"We're picking up variations in electrical activity throughout the alien ship," she continued. "Fluctuations in their power grid. The configuration of the grid itself . . . appears to be changing."

Archer frowned. He looked over at T'Pol, and then back at Trip, who had his head down and was making frantic adjustments to his own console.

"The shape of the power grid is changing?"

"Yes."

"Is that . . ." He frowned again. "That's not possible . . . is it?"

"No." She continued to stare at her viewer.

"Damn peculiar," Trip said. "But it looks like that's what's happening, all right. Here. Take a look."

Archer walked to the engineer's station. Trip's console showed a 3-D model of the alien spaceship, thick white lines representing the ship's exostructure against the black background of the screen. Thinner green lines pulsed within the white ones—the ship's power grid, a sensor-generated map tracing the electrical energies coursing through that superstructure.

"That's how the grid looks now." Trip drew his index finger down the middle of the screen. A solid blue line appeared, splitting the image they were looking at in half. He keyed in a series of commands, clearing the right-hand side of the screen, shrinking the image till it fit whole in the left, then bringing up a second, similar image to fill the right-hand side of the screen.

Trip pointed to the image on his right. "That's how it looked before."

Same ship, same white lines, but as the captain looked at the two of them side by side he saw instantly that the network of green lines—the power grid—was vastly different. "Could they be rerouting power?" Archer asked.

"No. We'd pick up residual energy traces. This," Trip pointed from one image to the other, "it's like they rewired the whole thing. Physically laid new conduit in seconds. Which—like you said—isn't possible. At least not with any ship I know."

"Which is why I am attempting to recalibrate the sensors," T'Pol said. "We may have incorrectly compensated for the alien ship's defensive shielding."

"That could account for a certain degree of error," Trip said. "Not enough to explain this, though."

"So how are they doing it?" Archer asked.

"That's the sixty-four thousand dollar question, all right," Trip said.

T'Pol looked up from her viewer. "The what?"

"Colloquialism," Trip said, and smiled.

T'Pol frowned. She seemed to be on the verge of commenting, but Reed interrupted her.

"They're charging weapons again," Reed said.

Malcolm's hand hovered over his console; Archer debated giving the order he knew his armory officer was waiting for, charge the hull plating, stand their ground, make the alien vessel react. Truth be told, he was as tired as Malcolm of running away from this particular vessel.

Their first encounter had come the day before yesterday, with *Enterprise* a week out of Barcana Six, skirting the edges of known space. The Vulcans had been out here, the Andorians too, Tellarites, a few others, so they had a rough idea of what to expect, but it was very, very rough. Archer had wanted to fill in the blank spots on their charts, wanted to see what was beyond the edge of those old Vulcan maps. Just as they'd been about to stop skirting the edges and actually enter unexplored territory, though, they'd picked up the alien signal, followed in short order by the alien ship, and then the warning shots. The delineation, Archer assumed, of the aliens' territory. The statement "This far, and no farther."

Zefram Cochrane's words from the inaugural ceremony of the warp-five complex came to mind, and Archer smiled wryly to himself.

No boldly going allowed around here, the captain thought.

"All right," Archer said, taking his seat again. "No sense in finding out how close that next shot's going to be. Full stop, Travis. Back us off at impulse—slowly—along our previous course. T'Pol, let's take another look at those old Vulcan charts, see what else is out here."

"Captain?"

That was Hoshi. Archer turned to face her.

"We're not giving up, are we, sir?"

"Giving up? No. But there's no sense in banging our head against this particular wall right now."

"Sir," Hoshi began, and there was a world of emotion in that single word—anger, frustration, disappointment, and a few others the captain couldn't name, "I can—"

"I know you can. I know you will." Archer held her gaze a moment, and offered another encouraging smile; what else could he do, after all?

"Keep at it," he said. "I want to come back this way."

"Yes, sir," Hoshi said finally, and turned crisply back to her station once more, and began to work again. She would keep at it, Archer knew, keep at it till she translated that signal, no matter how long that took. The captain knew what the rest of the crew was only beginning to realize, that there was steel behind Hoshi Sato's delicate facade.

Archer walked back to the situation room: T'Pol was there already, a three-dimensional map of the space surrounding them projected above the table she stood at.

"Barcana Six," T'Pol said, pointing to a small dot at the very top of the galactic plane, in the corner of the projection closest to her, "and our current position." She indicated a spot a little farther away from the corner, and down toward the center of the projection.

They spent the next few minutes discussing alternative routes through the sector—the alien ship, by its actions, had effectively claimed a significant portion of the space they were now in as their own—eventually settling on a route that took them back toward the apex of the galactic plane, and on a course ninety degrees starboard of their current heading. The captain had Malcolm and Trip join them, and they were in the middle of refining the course, taking into account reports from Tellarite survey logs suggesting the presence of scavenger ships—possibly even Klingon pirates, a narrow arm of what the Empire claimed was their sovereign space extended into one of the nearby sectors—when Hoshi interrupted.

"Excuse me—Captain? The noise Mister Carstairs was picking up earlier?"

"Go on."

"It's definitely a signal. Sounds a little like Thelasian to me."

"Thelasian?" Archer returned to his seat, his officers taking their regular stations as well.

"I think so, sir. Running it through the UT now."

Archer frowned. "What do we know about the Thelasians?"

"Very little," T'Pol said. "One of the oldest recorded spacefaring civilizations in the quadrant. Exact point of origin unknown, sources suggest dwindling population numbers."

"They run a lot of the trade guilds."

That was Travis. He continued without turning, his attention focused on the helm.

"A lot of the guilds that deal with outlying areas of the quadrant, at least. We had occasional dealings with them on *Horizon*."

Horizon was the cargo freighter Travis had been born and raised on, the freighter his family owned, which—after his father's recent death—was now commanded by his brother, Paul.

"Definitely Thelasian," Hoshi announced. "Some

kind of alert message—wide-range transmission. Not meant for us specifically."

Archer nodded. "On speakers."

She nodded back, punched in a series of commands on her console. A crackle of static, and then—

". . . all ships within range of this message. Remain clear of coordinates . . ."

—another burst of static, as the UT struggled to keep up—

". . . reports of numerous unprovoked attacks by unidentified vessels. Sector-wide task force forming to deal with these attacks. Respond on this frequency. Message repeats. First Governor Maxim Sen, Thelasian Trading Confederacy, to all ships within range . . ."

Archer signaled Hoshi to cut off the signal, and was about to have her respond as per the message's directions when he noticed something odd.

Travis's hands had fallen away from the helm.

"Travis," the captain asked. "Something wrong?"

The ensign took a good five seconds before responding.

"Sir, did that message—was that—did he say Sen?"

"Sen. Yes."

"Maxim Sen?"

"That's what it sounded like to me. Why?"

"Sen. Maxim Sen." Mayweather shook his head. "Sonuvabitch."

Archer almost fell off his chair. In the three years the captain had served with Travis, he'd never, ever heard him curse before.

"Ensign?"

Travis spun about in his chair quickly. He seemed to be, as far as Archer could tell, blushing.

"Sorry, sir. It's just that—"

"It's all right. You know him, obviously."

"Know him? Well, I couldn't really say that I know him. But know of him. Know who he is? That, for sure, Captain. That for sure."

Trip was suddenly at Archer's side again.

"Sounds like a story waiting to be told, sir."

"And how." The captain stood. "T'Pol, take over here, if you would. Trip, Travis . . ."

Archer headed for the ready room.

TWO

Inside, he gestured toward the room's other chair, and then toward his helmsman.

"Have a seat."

"No, thank you, sir. I'm fine like this. Captain, I want to apologize again for the language I used before, I just—"

"It's all right, Travis. We're all grown-ups here. Now—Governor Sen. The Thelasian Trading Confederacy. Explain."

"Especially the sonuvabitch part," Trip added.

"I'm guessing this has something to do with *Horizon*," the captain said.

"Yes sir."

"And Sen was involved?"

"Sen and a lot of money." Travis fell silent for a moment; Archer could sense the anger building inside him again. The captain exchanged a quick glance with Trip.

"Travis . . ."

"It's a long story, sir."

"We've got time." The captain had told Hoshi to hold off on responding to Sen's message until he'd had a chance to talk to Travis. T'Pol had triangulated the message's point of origin: a small planet a day's journey away, in what the Vulcans had called the Procyron system, which meant *Enterprise* was well out of their sensor range. Sen wouldn't know they were here until they wanted him to, which was just the way Archer wanted it for now.

"Sit," Archer said, again nodding to the chair.

Mayweather reluctantly settled himself into it.

"Where to begin," he said, leaning forward and clasping his hands together. "I guess with the certification, when the Cargo Authority gave us clearance for the Morianne-Deneva run. That was a big shot in the arm for us financially." Travis paused, and shifted position, craning his neck so he could catch the captain's eye. "Morianne is—it's the gateway to the old Allied Worlds systems. Huge trading market."

"I know Morianne. Go on."

"Well . . . the trading post there, Prex Morianna—that's run by the Thelasians."

"I didn't know that."

"Yes, sir. The Morianne take their cut, but the Confederacy's in charge. They run the guilds, the docks, everything. Which didn't mean much to us at first, the big deal was just getting clearance to go there, to Morianne—it meant dozens of new trading partners. A whole new market for the goods we handled, and goods from dozens of new worlds to import as well."

"When was this exactly?" Trip asked.

Mayweather turned again to face the commander. "Maybe thirteen, fourteen years ago. Paul was turning twelve then, I remember, so . . ." He frowned, and thought a minute. "No. It's more like seventeen years ago now. Wow. That's hard to believe."

"Time flies," Archer said. "Seventeen years ago. So you were . . ."

"A lot younger. And not much use to my father, I can tell you that." Travis smiled. "That was the year Paul and I set up a laser-tag course in the aft cargo bay. Spent pretty much that whole year doing nothing but that— didn't matter what the cargo was, we were climbing all over it, setting up obstacle courses, that sort of thing . . . not too smart in retrospect, considering."

Mayweather turned again toward the captain, to include him in the conversation, the ensign shifting in his seat one more time, at which point Archer suddenly realized (or more accurately, remembered) that the ready room was intended as a place for quick, private conversations/communications, for decision making, for his own quiet contemplation.

Long stories, perhaps, were better told elsewhere.

Travis cleared his throat.

"Before you get started again," the captain said quickly. "Anybody here hungry?"

Travis was; Trip wasn't, and neither was Archer, but they all went to the mess hall anyway. Eleven hundred hours, still an hour before shift change and the lunch rush, so the place was deserted, as Archer had counted on. He and Trip got coffee and took seats at a table along the far wall, while Travis waited for a sandwich.

Trip took a sip from his cup, and shook his head.

"I gotta cut down on this stuff."

The captain studied his friend. "Late night?"

"Early morning. Hess is still sick, so third shift is short a man. Woman, in this case. I've been picking up for her on the back end. Got up at zero-four-hundred today."

"Ouch."

"Ouch is right." Trip took another sip. "You know what else? I walk on the bridge the last two mornings, and Hoshi's already there. Looking like she's been there all night."

"Really?"

"For a fact. Captain—don't know if you've noticed, but she's pushing herself mighty hard these last few days."

"I'm not worried about Hoshi," Archer said. "She can handle it."

"I know. It's just that . . ." Trip pursed his lips, shook his head. "She seems a little obsessed with this particular translation. Maybe you ought to talk to her—tell her to relax a little."

Archer bit back the first reply that came to mind—nobody ever died from a little hard work—and nodded.

"I'll talk to her," he said, and he would, though he might not exactly phrase things the way Trip had—"relax." He didn't think Hoshi would listen to him if he said that anyway. The captain suspected she'd take a break when she'd done what she set out to do, and not a second earlier.

"Sorry, sir," Mayweather said, joining them. "Didn't think that would take so long."

Archer told him not to worry, not to rush: Trip took up the conversational slack while Travis ate, bringing the captain up to speed on a few ship-related matters, and a few more personal ones. When Archer noticed that Mayweather was finished, though, he put the conversation back on track.

"Okay Travis. Let's get back to your story. Governor Sen and the Morianne-Deneva run."

"Right." Travis took a deep breath. "Okay. So Morianne—we did a handful of runs out there, at a month and a half each way from Deneva, but they were good runs, sir. Very profitable. Not only did we find new customers for the ore the Authority required us to carry, but we made contacts with a whole new group of traders, people from all over the quadrant. Not just representatives from different mining consortiums, either—we're talking Shandeeki painters, Dondran arms merchants, the Maszakian engineers, and of course, every transaction we made"—here Travis paused—"we dealt with representatives from the Thelasian Trading Confederacy."

"Including Sen, I'll bet," Trip said.

"No. Not right away. He wasn't part of the government then—at least I don't think he was. I got the impression he was more of a freelance guy then—just a trader. Whatever he was, though, I remember him coming on board *Horizon*, all of us getting introduced to him before he and my father went off to talk business. The upshot of which was we took on the second leg of a delivery contract they had, for a private customer back on Deneva. A shipment of high-end solar panels, which they loaded onto *Horizon* the next day in a dozen duranium reinforced, tamper-resistant cargo pods. Those pods—I'd never seen anything like them before. Or since. Built like tanks. Hit 'em with a small nuke, probably wouldn't even scratch the paint. Seemed that way anyway."

"But something went wrong," Archer said.

Mayweather nodded. "It sure did. We got to Deneva, and no sooner had we requested permission to dock than two CA ships pull up alongside, come aboard, and without so much as a by-your-leave confiscate the pods."

"Because . . ."

"Well, it took a couple weeks for us to find that out.

A couple weeks of my father knocking on almost every door at the Authority, calling in favors, getting down on his hands and knees and begging. Finally he got the story—part of the story, anyway."

"Let me guess," Trip said. "Those cargo pods weren't really full of solar panels."

"Oh, there were a few panels in there on top, for show. We checked them out before we signed off on delivery from Sen. But underneath . . . well, we never found out exactly what was underneath. But from the hints my father's contacts at the Authority dropped, we're pretty sure there were weapons. Some pretty powerful weapons."

"Sen was running arms," Archer said.

"Someone was," Travis said. "He denied any knowledge of the shipment's contents as well."

"You didn't believe him?" the captain prompted.

"I didn't know what to believe. My father, though—he had his doubts, that's for sure."

"Okay, I get all that," Trip said. "So what happened next?"

"Next." Travis frowned. "Next, we tried to get our money back."

"Your money." Archer frowned. "Explain."

"We bought the cargo from Sen—and the contract to supply that cargo to the customer along with it. Without the cargo to sell . . ."

"You were out the money."

"Yes, sir. And it was a pretty big chunk of money."

"Where was the customer in all this?"

"We never found that out either. My dad thought that they might have gotten arrested too, but it's also possible they heard about the trouble we had and just decided to take off. Which left us going back to the Thelasian authorities back on Morianne for some kind of restitution."

"What about the Cargo Authority?" Trip asked. "Seems to me they would have a vested interested in getting involved—considering where the arms were going?"

Travis shook his head. "The CA didn't want to rock the boat with the Confederacy, Earth being the new kid on the block and all."

Archer almost smiled. He knew that feeling a little too well himself.

"So what'd you do?" Trip asked.

"Well, the first thing we did was head out on the Morianne-Deneva run again. We needed money, and the only way to get it was to keep working. So my dad stayed focused on that. We all stayed focused on that. We took on live cargo—which is very profitable but very labor-intensive, if you couldn't guess. A lot of that work—feeding, cleaning, exercising . . . that fell on me and Paul, which put a stop to the laser tag for a while. Meanwhile, my father worked on trying to find someone in the Confederacy to talk to. To complain to—about the money, and about Sen. He had to meet with the Confederacy representative, begin some kind of a formal appeals process. Petition for a portion of our money to be returned. We left Morianne that first time, thinking we made progress, but . . ."

"Let me guess," Trip said. "Next time you came back, they had no record of your filing an appeal."

"You got that right," Travis said. "No matter how many times we filed, how many times we tried—"

"You never got the money back," Archer supplied.

"No, sir, we didn't and that's another reason why I'm—"

The mess hall doors opened at that instant, and Doctor Phlox walked in. He caught sight of the three men, and made a beeline for their table.

"Captain. Gentlemen. Commander T'Pol told me I would find you down here, sir."

"She was right. What's on your mind, Doctor?"

"A few things. The Thelasian Trading Confederacy, for one. I understand we've made contact with them?"

"That's correct. We were just talking about the Thelasians, as a matter of fact. Travis here was telling us about an encounter he had with them, when he was back on *Horizon*."

"I too have history to relate regarding the Thelasians, sir. Do you mind . . ."

Archer nodded to the chair next to him, and Phlox sat.

"Please—continue with your story, Ensign," he said to Travis.

"Not much more to tell, sir. We have an open appeal with the Confederacy. Last I heard . . ." He shrugged. "Well, it was more of the same."

The captain nodded. There were some other things he wanted to say to Travis, chief among them that no matter what Sen had done seventeen years ago, the man was apparently the head of the Confederacy now, and they would have to treat him with the respect due that office. They meaning everyone aboard *Enterprise* but in particular Travis, and that whatever issues he had with Sen regarding the past, he'd have to put them on hold.

"All right, Ensign. Thank you. Doctor . . ."

Phlox nodded. "My experience with the Thelasians. I dislike, of course, speaking ill of anyone, but in this case, I will make an exception. The Thelasians—and I speak of the Confederacy now as an institution, not necessarily of the people themselves, who of course must be judged as individuals in their own right, I want to be clear on that . . ."

He looked around the table as if he was waiting for a response.

"You're being very clear, Doctor," Archer said. "Go on."

"You should take great care in dealing with them, sir. They can be most unpleasant people. Untrustworthy. The one I dealt with was a real . . ." The doctor frowned, and thought for a moment.

"*Garkohuda,*" he said, or something like it. "*Teyaneema Garkohuda.*"

Archer looked at Trip, who looked at Travis, who shook his head.

"Which means . . ." the captain prompted.

"In the human vernacular? The closest analogue, I believe, would be son of a bitch."

Trip burst out laughing. Archer, unable to help himself, followed a second later. Travis turned away from the table, his shoulders shaking.

Phlox looked confused.

"I don't believe this is a laughing matter, gentlemen."

Archer got control of himself and explained why it was. Then Phlox went on to relate a horror story concerning a delayed shipment of antibiotics to a Denobulan colony that instantly sucked any remaining levity out of the room by the time he was finished talking.

"I'm getting a fairly good picture of the kind of people we're about to deal with here," Archer said after the doctor finished. "But we'll be on our best behavior anyway."

"Our usual charming selves," Trip said.

"That's right. Travis . . . ?"

The ensign nodded. "Of course, sir."

"Good. Doctor," Archer said, standing, "thanks for your input. Gentlemen, let's get back up to the bridge and—"

"Excuse me, Captain," Phlox interrupted. "Before you go—there is another matter I wanted to speak with you on as well. If you could spare a moment . . ."

The doctor looked serious about this matter too, whatever it was. "Sure. Go on, Trip, Travis. I'll catch up to you in a minute."

The two men left. Archer sat back down.

"What's on your mind, Doctor?"

"A matter I've been concerned with for some time now," Phlox began. "It concerns Ensign Hoshi."

THREE

There were fifty-seven pulses altogether in the alien signal. Each pulse was of a different wavelength. There was no apparent mathematical relationship between the individual wavelengths, nor between any groupings of wavelengths that she or the computer could come up with. Each wavelength was discernible as a discrete audio frequency; the entire pattern of fifty-seven pulses took approximately twelve seconds to listen to. The first time she heard it, it sounded like a continuous burst of static. At the end of her shift that day, Hoshi forwarded it to the workstation in her room. She listened to it several dozen times before going to sleep that night, hoping to hear something, she wasn't sure exactly what, some kind of pattern that might provide a way in to a more regimented translation effort. By the end of that time, she could hear a distinct tune to the signal. She listened to it countless more times over the next two days; somewhere in the midst of all that repeated listening, she realized she'd memorized that tune. And even as she worked on more typical approaches to the signal's translation—frequency analysis, physical mapping of the waveforms, experimental substitutions of local language clusters for each of the coded pulses—she continued to hear it sounding in her head. She was fairly sure she dreamed it last night;

she definitely woke up to it this morning. She heard it even now, sitting at her station on the bridge. She decided that maybe she'd been hearing it a little too often.

It was starting to sound like one of those old Elvis Presley songs her mother always used to play.

"Ensign. Ensign Sato. Are you with us?"

Hoshi looked up. T'Pol stood next to her, wearing the closest thing to a frown she'd ever seen on the Vulcan's face. She'd obviously been talking to Hoshi for quite some time now.

"I'm sorry ma'am—what?"

"I asked if you had searched the database for alternative Thelasian dialects—we'll want to program those into the handheld translators in anticipation of any contact with the Confederacy."

"No, ma'am, I haven't done that yet. I'll get on it right away." Hoshi felt herself blushing. T'Pol had asked her to do that a few minutes after the captain, Commander Tucker, and Travis had left the bridge. Half an hour ago now, she saw. And what had she done in that half hour? Nothing, except sit and think, and listen to the signal in her head. She should blush.

She should also, Hoshi realized, have taken the initiative and done what T'Pol had suggested on her own. That was part of her duties, after all—facilitate interspecies communication. Not a job she was doing particularly well at the moment, either.

Time to get back to it, Hoshi thought, and swiveled to the UT substation to do as T'Pol had suggested.

The Vulcan was still standing over her.

"Commander?"

T'Pol lowered her voice. "Are you quite all right, Ensign?"

"All right?" Hoshi frowned. "I'm fine. Frustrated, but fine."

T'Pol continued to look at her. Hoshi felt like a specimen under a microscope.

"I noticed you came on shift early this morning."

"I did. I came on early yesterday too. Stayed late last night, and the night before that as well." Hoshi kept her voice calm as well—as calm as she could, anyway. "I just want to get that signal translated, Commander."

"So do we all. And I'm sure you will succeed at that task—I fully share the captain's confidence in your abilities. When, that is, you are functioning at the full extent of those capabilities. I do not believe that you are doing so at present."

"I'm fine."

"You are frustrated, Ensign. I understand."

Hoshi nodded. Of course she did. T'Pol had been right there with her for most of the last seventy-two hours, working not only on the alien signal but on several versions of *Enterprise*'s standard hail message— greetings, we come in peace, we have no designs on your territory/resources/personal possessions—for broadcast to the aliens. T'Pol had worked with Hoshi and Carstairs on translating that greeting into every language in *Enterprise*'s database, and even a few that weren't, ones that the Vulcan and Doctor Phlox knew only smatterings of. The team had made looped greetings of those messages that cycled every eight point six minutes, that had been broadcasting ever since 0100 ship's time last night, ten and a half hours. The aliens never responded to any of them.

"However," the Vulcan continued, "you must allow your body and mind to recuperate so that you can function optimally. You have already been on duty for the length of standard shift—an hour beyond that, in fact. Mister Carstairs." T'Pol motioned him forward. "Please take over for Ensign Sato."

As he rose from his seat at the aux station, T'Pol lowered her voice again so only Hoshi could hear.

"I suggest you take a break from this particular task for the next few hours. If you wish to return with the third-shift crew and work then you are free to do so."

"I don't want to take a break."

T'Pol nodded. "I understand. I am not offering you the option."

The Vulcan turned her back and returned to her station.

Hoshi took a deep breath.

Temper, she told herself. *Temper temper temper.*

Carstairs was standing over her.

"Hoshi?" he asked tentatively.

Hoshi tapped the console in front of her with her fingertips. Tap, tap, tap.

"Take over," she said quickly, standing and heading for the lift.

The second the doors closed behind her, she drew back a hand and made ready to punch the wall. She barely—just barely—held herself back. Instead, she started counting to ten—always a good calming technique. Center herself, regain a sense of equilibrium. Maybe she should hit the gym as well—get the blood flowing again. Except what would she do once she got it flowing—go back to her room and sit? Maybe she should rest instead; even though she didn't feel it now, she knew she was tired. Maybe she should do what T'Pol had suggested—nap until third shift, hit the gym, and then hit the bridge. Get the best of both worlds then, mind clear, body relaxed, refreshed and ready to work. She might even be able to work straight through third shift and into her own regularly scheduled tour . . . unless T'Pol got it in her head again to put a limit on the number of hours Hoshi worked. Which she just might—actually, what she would probably do would be to tell the captain that Hoshi was pushing herself too hard and let him set those limits. *So never mind the gym,* Hoshi thought. What she needed were results.

Maybe she should go back to the UT lab and work there.

The lift doors opened.

"Ensign?"

T'Pol stood in front of her, and for a second Hoshi thought that somehow the Vulcan had beaten her down to the crew deck.

Then she realized that she hadn't even left the bridge yet, that she'd just stood there in the lift without moving for the past—what, half minute?

A wave of exhaustion swept over her.

"What are you doing?" T'Pol asked.

Hoshi smiled—even to her, it felt forced. "Didn't mean to hold up the lift. I was just trying to decide where to go."

"Your quarters. You are obviously exhausted."

"I'm a little bit hungry."

"The mess hall then would seem an obvious destination."

Hoshi opened her mouth to protest again—what exactly she was going to say, she wasn't sure of—but T'Pol spoke first.

"I shall accompany you there."

"No," she said quickly. "That's not necessary."

"Perhaps not. But it is necessary you rest, and

regain your strength. Your focus. We agree on that, do we not?"

Hoshi nodded reluctantly. "Yes."

"Good. Then I trust you will make either the mess or the crew deck your destination, and not return to the UT lab to continue your work." Without waiting for a response, T'Pol took a step backward, allowing the lift door to shut again.

Hoshi glared at the space where the Vulcan had been, then started the lift toward crew deck.

Okay, so T'Pol was right. She needed to rest before tackling the alien signal again. But translating that signal, that wasn't the real problem, that was only a symptom. An ungodly difficult symptom, perhaps, but a symptom nonetheless.

The real problem, she was afraid, went deeper then that.

The real problem was in her mind, or rather, with her mind. What had been done to it.

The real problem was the Xindi.

Archer frowned. "You said there was nothing wrong."

"Physiologically, there is nothing wrong. There was no damage to the underlying brain structure." Phlox, who in between relating his recent conversations with Hoshi had decided to eat lunch, took a bite of his sandwich before continuing. "My instruments recorded no loss in synaptic firing efficiency, no measurable deficiencies in either short- or long-term memory function."

"But . . ."

"But psychologically . . . Captain, what Ensign Sato went through was a highly traumatic experience."

"Of course it was a traumatic experience. Those

Xindi bastards put parasites in her brain. How could it not be a traumatic experience? But it hasn't affected her performance in the slightest. She's still . . ."

Archer's voice trailed off as he saw the expression on Phlox's face.

"Has it affected her performance?"

"She worries that it has."

Archer frowned. "Is this just over the last few days, or . . ."

"Mostly over the last few days, though there have been other occasions."

"She's said nothing about this to me."

"Well. For one thing, she did not want to worry you."

"If it's affecting how she does her job, she should have told me. You should have told me."

"As I am now doing. Though I must tell you, Captain, in my opinion her performance has not been compromised in the slightest. However, my opinion is not what matters in this instance. Ensign Sato's does, and she has . . . concerns."

"Go on."

"We have had numerous discussions recently on the nature of her work. What exactly is involved in successfully translating an alien language. Fascinating discussions, though I must admit much of the material is beyond my comprehension."

"You're not alone there."

"In the course of those discussions, I came to the realization that for Ensign Sato, translation is as much an art as a science. It involves intuitive reasoning as well as the collation of a learned body of knowledge. And her fear, quite simply, is that when the Xindi infested her brain, they somehow damaged her ability to reason in that manner."

"You've told her that isn't the case though. That there was no damage to her brain."

"I told her I believed that to be the case, yes."

"And what did she say to that?"

"She asked if I was certain."

"And you said . . ."

" 'Fairly certain' was, I believe, my exact response."

Archer's exasperation must have shown on his face. Phlox hurriedly continued.

"The fact is, Captain, that for all we know about how the human brain functions, there is still a great deal that remains a mystery. The parasites may very well have damaged Ensign Sato's ability to synthesize knowledge in certain ways. I frankly have no way of knowing for certain."

"You're not helping me here, Doctor."

Phlox frowned. "I thought I was being very helpful."

The com sounded. "Bridge to Captain Archer."

That was T'Pol.

"Excuse me a minute." Archer walked to the nearest companel. "Archer here. Go ahead."

"We have been contacted by the Thelasian Trading Confederacy."

"What?"

"We have been contacted by the Thelasian Trading Confederacy."

"How . . . I thought you said they couldn't find us."

"I was wrong. Their sensors are obviously more sophisticated than I allowed for."

"They contacted us specifically?"

"Yes, sir."

Archer sighed. So much for leisurely planning. "All right. Is Trip up there yet?"

"He is just now coming on duty."

"Have him and Travis brief you on what we just talked about. I'm on my way." Archer shut the channel and turned back to Phlox. "We'll have to continue this discussion later, Doctor."

"Yes, of course."

He turned for the door, hesitated, then turned back to Phlox. "You think I should talk to her? Hoshi?"

"I'm not certain. The problem really is one of self-confidence—the ensign doubting her own abilities. And the best way, of course, for her to cure those doubts is to successfully solve the problem before her."

Archer nodded. It was up to him, of course, was what the doctor's answer (or lack thereof) really meant, which was fine, but he really didn't have time at the moment to decide. Right now, he had to get up to the bridge, and talk with Travis's old friend Governor Sen. Should be interesting.

"Captain."

Archer, halfway to the door, turned around again.

"The Thelasians," Phlox said. "Remember. *Garkohuda. Teyaneema Garkohuda.*"

This time, the captain didn't laugh.

"Yes, Doctor, I got that," he replied, and left the mess hall.

FOUR

Enterprise was the ship's name, painted in ridiculously large letters on the primary-hull surface alongside a group of numbers that represented some further kind of identification specific to the species homeworld, a Minshara-class planet on the outer rim of the quadrant called Earth. That name had rung some kind of bell with Sen, and after perusing the records Roia had found for him, detailing the Confederacy's previous encounters with the species, he realized that he himself had, years ago, been involved in several transactions with them. Said transactions had occurred on some of the more remote bazaars, Karrus Prime, Prex Morianna, X-17, none of which had made any sort of lasting impression on Sen, probably because none had been especially profitable. Worth more attention were *Enterprise's* recent whereabouts, in particular an extended trip into the D-4853 anomaly, referred to in several databases by the unlikely name of the Expanse, as well as (and here Sen took special notice) its involvement in the ongoing Vulcan-Andorian conflict, which indicated to the governor that despite their relative youth as a species and lack of technical sophistication, these humans, as they referred to themselves, bore watching.

Jonathan Archer was the captain's name, and that too rang some kind of bell with the governor, but there was nothing beyond that name in the primary database. Sen had Roia forward the query to some of the more specialized information brokers, and then sat back at his desk.

The humans had still not responded to his signal.

"Roia," he said, and the voice—or, rather, what his brain perceived as a voice, thanks to the simulation program—came back immediately through the implant:

Governor.

"They are receiving us?"

Undoubtedly, sir.

"They have a reason for not responding, then." Sen wondered what it was; most likely, they were busy searching their own databases for information on the Confederacy. *Just taking them longer,* he thought, and no wonder. Humans had nothing like Roia; at their current rate of technological development, it would take them a good hundred years to build something similar.

Roia was a software agent Sen had designed for his use on becoming viceroy of the Coreida Sector. The agent was named after a female who had never, ever done as he requested, and so it gave Sen particular pleasure to be able to have this avatar, which he'd given the voice of that same female, at his constant beck and call. Childish behavior, he knew, but then Sen had a problem when it came to people who refused to do as he said. He wanted to grind them into dust.

"Let's send a second transmission, Roia. Open channel."

Open.

"*Enterprise*, this is Governor Maxim Sen of the

Thelasian Trading Confederacy. Repeating our previous message—we have fixed your position, estimate your course parallels that of a vessel similar to those that have attacked ships traveling this sector of space. Be advised you exercise extreme caution in any encounters with said vessel, also ask that you forward any records of said encounters to Procyron for analysis and collation. Please respond *Enterprise*. Message ends. Loop that, Roia. Continuous signal till they do respond."

Yes, sir. A reminder, sir, the Defense Council is awaiting your presence in the Upper Solarium.

"Of course." The weekly meeting. Normally he hated this part of his job—meeting with the military commanders, most of them mercenaries hired to protect shipping routes, with little loyalty to the traders who paid them—but he had been pleasantly surprised by the speed and efficiency of their response to this crisis. They had not only set up convoys to escort the most valuable shipments through the areas of space in question, but today were proposing a further refinement of the armed offensive they had presented to Sen last week. An offensive that would involve not just Confederacy ships, but vessels from over a dozen other worlds that had been affected by the unwarranted, unprovoked attacks on Confederacy trade routes. Representatives of those worlds were in the Solarium now as well, making Sen's own presence there necessary.

But there were things he had to do first.

He had Roia instruct the steward to prepare his lunch and bring it to the meeting room, estimating his arrival there in nine minutes. Then he had her cause a short in the automated system feed, which disabled the government recording systems, thus providing complete and total anonymity to his actions. He quickly reviewed the status of his personal accounts and then shifted funds into those accounts from several trading consortiums he'd set up under the authority of the governorship. Wholly legal consortiums.

Wholly illegal transactions.

He was seconds away from completing his work when the implant sounded.

Governor.

"Roia."

Enterprise is responding.

Sen thought a moment. Talk to the humans first, he decided. That would be brief, and perhaps germane to the Council meeting. "Tell the Defense Council they'll need to wait—five to seven additional minutes. Is my lunch ready?"

Yes, sir.

"Have it brought here." Sen finished transferring the money—now his money—and had Roia bring the systems feed back on-line. There would be a gap in the records, but he'd already had Roia circumvent the security protocol so it would never be noticed. Not until it was too late to matter, at least.

"Open a channel to *Enterprise*."

Open. Visual and audio are available.

"Give me both." Sen enlarged the viewer, and positioned his chair so that *Enterprise*'s captain would see not just him, not just the governor's office, but the whole of Tura Prex's skyline behind him. The scale of the megalopolis, the sophistication and beauty of the construction. It would impress upon the humans their relative unimportance in the scheme of things.

The viewer activated. The bridge of a spaceship appeared. Several figures were visible, some sitting, some standing. Humans. Now he remembered the race. Bipedal, large eyes, very expressive faces . . .

There was a Vulcan too. A female. Interesting.

Sen's eyes lingered on her a moment, then were drawn to one of the humans—a male standing in the center of the bridge. The captain, undoubtedly. Captain Archer.

He was young, Sen saw. Very, very young. Just like the race. Young, most likely immature, and most certainly at a disadvantage in interactions with any older, more sophisticated species.

A thin smile crossed the governor's lips, and then he spoke.

"Captain Archer, I presume?"

One thing Travis hadn't mentioned about Governor Sen.

The man looked like death warmed over. Actually, "warmed over" was not the right term. The right term was just the one word "death." Governor Sen looked like death. His face was the face of an Egyptian mummy—wrinkled, shriveled, ancient. And, incongruously enough, smiling.

Never judge a book by its cover, Archer thought, forcing himself to return Sen's smile.

"And you must be Governor Sen. I am Jonathan Archer of *Enterprise*—and thank you for your warning, sir. Though I'm afraid we may have already encountered one of the ships your messages spoke of." The captain went on to briefly relate their experiences of the last few days.

"You're lucky to have escaped unscathed, Captain.

The attacks are often quite deadly. There have been numerous fatalities over the past year."

"No idea who they are?"

"No."

"Or the reason for the attacks?"

"They are clearly attempting to establish territorial boundaries," Sen said. "The territory in question, however, is largely Thelasian, or has been established by treaty as neutral space."

"I see," Archer said, making a mental note to have T'Pol brief him a little more thoroughly on races with any sort of territorial interest in this sector. Not that he didn't trust Sen, but given what Travis had told him about the man . . .

Well, he didn't entirely trust Sen.

"I would appreciate you forwarding on specifics of your encounter with this ship," Sen said. "We can take your raw sensor data."

Archer was about to agree to the governor's request when he realized that the raw sensor data would not only provide Sen with the information he was asking for, but would also give him a fairly good idea of *Enterprise*'s sensor capabilities. And the ship's maneuverability. Their standard defense postures. Maybe he was being paranoid, but that was not information he wanted to share at the moment.

"We'll put together a report for you," the captain said.

"Thank you." Sen's smile remained frozen in place. He seemed genuinely pleased.

It'd be hell sitting across from this guy at a poker table, Archer thought.

"As I mentioned in our message, Captain, we are currently planning an offensive against this species, designed to eliminate any future attacks. Representatives from several races in this sector and surrounding ones are meeting on Procyron now to finalize those plans. Meanwhile, I want to assure your species, and any others aboard your ship"—at this Sen's eyes went briefly to T'Pol—"that the trade routes are open and safe, and will remain open and safe."

Archer frowned. "That's important of course, Governor, and I may be speaking out of turn here, but talk of any sort of major offensive seems a little . . . premature to me."

"How so?"

"These aliens, whoever they were, were nowhere near as interested in hurting us as they were in defending their territory. They had several . . ."

"It is not their territory," Sen interrupted.

"Of course. Excuse me. What they *perceived* as their territory. I was just going to say that they had several chances to damage our ship, and were quite careful not to."

"There have been encounters similar to yours," Sen said. "But there have also been, as I said, other, far more destructive incidents. My belief is that the nature of the encounters are shaped by the individual commanders aboard these ships. Their temperament."

"As well as the temperament—and actions—of the vessels they encounter, I would think," Archer said.

Sen eyed him suspiciously.

"You seem to be trying to defend this species, Captain. Is there a reason for that?"

"No. Not trying to defend. To understand. Which reminds me—we also received a signal from this vessel," Archer said. "A repeating message we were unable to translate. We'll include that in our report as well."

"It's undoubtedly the same message sent in previous

encounters. We have, as of yet, been unable to translate it either."

"It seems to me that should be your first priority, Governor. Establishing communications so that you can determine what it is these aliens want."

The smile remained frozen on Sen's face, but this time something in his eyes changed. Archer decided then that not only would he not want to play poker with the governor, he would not like to have him as an enemy. That something in Sen's eyes looked to the captain like anger. A great reservoir of anger.

"Again, forgive me if I'm speaking out of turn," the captain added.

"Of course." The anger in Sen's eyes was gone as quickly as it had come. The governor regarded him coolly. "You have some interesting views on the proper conduct of interspecies relations, Captain. Let me offer you some advice: In our long experience as a spacefaring civilization, we Thelasians have found that nothing is as important as the safe maintenance of neutral travel corridors. And in this sector of space, the maintenance of those corridors is the duty of the Confederacy. I would ask you to realize too that not every ship is able to defend itself as well as yours. Most vessels lack the variety of armaments you carry—your phase cannons, photonic torpedoes, and the like."

It took a great deal of self-control for Archer not to react to that statement.

How in the world had Sen obtained that kind of detailed information on their weapons systems?

"Our weapons are a tool of last resort, Governor. Far better to avoid their use altogether, wouldn't you say? To make communication—not conflict—a priority?"

"This conflict, I remind you, was not of our initiation. But I admire your ideals, Captain. And your courage in expressing them. Unfortunately, the universe does not deal with idealists kindly. You humans will learn that, I'm certain. Over time."

"I hope not. Our ideals are a large part of who we are."

"Forgive me if I've upset you, Captain. I didn't mean to—how did you put it—speak out of turn?"

"I'm not upset. And you're entitled to your opinions, of course."

"Of course. Our differences are what make interspecies relations so often . . . interesting." Sen leaned back in his chair. "I'm afraid I have to end our conversation at this point, Captain. I have another appointment. In the interim, I look forward to receiving your report, and, of course, you are welcome on Procyron, should you desire to visit. Sen out."

The viewscreen went dark before Archer could reply in kind.

"Sonuvabitch," Trip said.

The captain nodded. "Condescending sonuvabitch."

Impertinent twit. Sen hadn't been this angry since . . .

Well, since Roia. And that was, what—seventy years ago now? Eighty?

The implant sounded.

Lunch is here. Defense Council awaits your presence.

"Defense Council will have to wait." He needed, Sen realized, to calm down. He would eat first. "Apologize again for me. I will be another ten minutes. Have Colonel Yusa start his presentation. Send the transmission to the viewer here."

Yes, sir. Response from Teff-Langer Conglomerate

on your query re: Captain Archer. Multiple references available.

Well. That was fast.

"Show them to me."

They are quite expensive to retrieve in full, Roia said, quoting him a price.

Sen didn't care. He asked for all of them. The viewer began filling with text. Sen ate as he read. He couldn't help but be impressed. Again, for a youthful species, for a relatively unsophisticated species, Archer and his ship had managed, somehow, to be in the thick of a great many things. There was more information on their involvement in the Vulcan-Andorian conflict, more on their travels within the so-called Expanse, and with a race known as the Xindi, who Sen had never heard of before. And then some information on Archer alone, courtesy of the Confederacy's representatives on Qo'noS, which Sen, as he read, recognized as the source of his initial feeling of familiarity on first hearing the captain's name. He had seen this report before, months before in fact, and taken note of it, due to the not-inconsiderable sums of money mentioned. There had been no possibility of obtaining that money back then, though, so it had not remained uppermost in his consciousness. But now . . .

Things with Qo'noS were different. Everything, in fact, was different.

Sen finished his lunch then, and considered the possibilities as he made his way to the solarium.

FIVE

First shift ended. Second shift began. Archer
retreated to his ready room, where he found a number
of items on his workstation, awaiting review. First
was the report for Sen on *Enterprise*'s encounter with
the alien ship. It was as innocuous as he'd asked for.
He made it even more so, removing references to
some of Hoshi's translation efforts, and then forwarded it to Carstairs for transmission.

Next was a summary from T'Pol of what little
information she'd been able to find on the
Thelasians. Sen hadn't lied about one thing: they
were an old race. T'Pol had found isolated mentions
of them almost as far back as the beginning of
recorded galactic history, contemporaneous with the
Allied Worlds and the Barreon, and their mutually
self-destructive war. She referenced one source that
claimed the Confederacy was the legitimate succes-
sor to the old Allied Worlds, which caused the captain to raise an eyebrow. No extant civilization had
ever claimed any sort of direct linkage with the Allied
Worlds, or the Barreon for that matter. Archer called
up that source, and read through it for himself. He
wasn't convinced. There was a lack of specificity with
regard to dates, a lack of detail with regard to planetary coordinates. Interesting stuff, though. T'Pol had
found it in the Vulcan database, but the original

source wasn't named. Could it be Vulcan? Not likely; compared with the Thelasians, even the Vulcans were a relatively young space-faring species. The Confederacy had already been up and running for centuries before Surak was even born.

There was also a note from T'Pol at the end of the summary, saying that she was in the process of obtaining more current information on the Confederacy: she hoped to have that information to Archer shortly.

And then there was another transmission from Procyron. From Sen's office. A more formal invitation to visit the planet, and to attend some sort of conclave taking place there two days from now. A conference regarding the aliens that had attacked *Enterprise* and so many other ships; a chance to be the first humans to see the great capital of the Thelasian Confederacy, Tura Prex, and for the two of them, Archer and Sen, to continue the conversation they had begun.

The invitation had an entirely different tone to it than his previous conversation with Sen. Why the sudden spasm of inclusiveness, of interest in humans and himself, Archer wondered. The captain didn't quite understand it.

The com sounded.

"Tucker to Captain Archer."

"Archer here. What is it Trip?"

"You standing me up again?"

"Standing you up? What . . ." All at once, he remembered what. "Dinner. Sorry—I forgot."

"I figured as much. Just been sitting here, talking about the right way to fry a chicken with Chef. You want to reschedule?"

"No." The mention of fried chicken made Archer's

stomach growl. He hadn't eaten since breakfast. "I'll be down in five."

"I'll be here. Out."

Archer entered the captain's mess to find his chief engineer seated in front of a cheese plate. Chef was there too; Archer asked him to fry up a chicken however he thought best, sat, and told Trip about Sen's invitation.

"So are we going? Procyron?" Trip asked.

"Can you see any reason not to?"

"Beyond the fact that the guy gives me the creeps? No."

"Then we're going." Archer called up to the bridge, and had Travis lay in a course. "Be a chance, maybe, to get a peek at those sensors of theirs. The ones that let Sen figure out what weapons we had."

"I've been thinking about that," Trip said. So had the captain. The second Sen had signed off, that had been the topic of a spirited discussion around the bridge. Consensus had narrowed it down to two distinct possibilities; the first being that the Confederacy's sensors really were so powerful that they were able to ascertain *Enterprise*'s weapons complement all the way from Procyron, the second that they'd used remote sensor stations to augment the reach of their equipment. Trip had argued for the latter, making the case that along long-established trade routes such as the Confederacy claimed, it would make sense to have such stations. He and Malcolm had started a sensor sweep to look for such stations as the captain had gone off duty.

"See," Trip pointed with a cracker, "how in the world does Sen know we have a phase cannon? We never charged it, we certainly never deployed it—"

"Like we were talking about—some very powerful sensors."

"And some awfully good analysis, to be able to pick out one hunk of metal from all the others surrounding it."

"Okay. So . . . how did he know?"

"Ah." Trip sat back with a smile. "I'm thinking somebody just told him."

"Somebody told him? All the way out here, somebody told him about us?"

"Yeah."

"No. How is that possible?"

"You read T'Pol's report, right? These guys have been around forever—the Confederacy. Trading with every race in the galaxy. Trading every commodity under the sun—including information."

"Information on us, you mean?"

"Bingo."

Archer frowned. Was that kind of information about *Enterprise* readily available? His first thought was no; it was a big galaxy, they were one small ship, they were an exploratory vessel, they didn't fire their weapons all that often. Except when they did—

The Xindi. The Vulcans. The Andorians.

"Maybe," he said. "But think about this: How did they know ask about us in the first place? How did they know we were out here at all?"

Trip's face fell, and then, an instant later, brightened again.

"Okay. That's where these remote sensor stations— or the powerful long-range ones on Procyron—come in. They got a visual ID on us, and then they did their research. Just like T'Pol did on them."

Could be, the captain thought. Except that if Trip was right, they had a lot more databases to draw from. He wondered what other kinds of information might be in them.

Chef came in with the chicken; conversation stopped for a few minutes as they ate. Before it could resume, the companel sounded.

"T'Pol to Archer."

"Archer here. What is it?"

"I have additional information on the Thelasians for you."

"Trip and I are in the mess. Come on down."

"I don't wish to disturb your dinner."

"Don't worry about that. We'll be done by the time you get down here."

They were indeed done when she entered; done save for a small piece of chicken on Trip's plate. He stabbed it with his fork and held it out to T'Pol.

"This is Chef's recipe. You gotta try it."

"It is animal flesh."

"Well . . . yeah." Trip smiled.

She raised an eyebrow.

Archer set his napkin down on the table. "You have something for us?"

T'Pol gestured to an empty chair opposite Trip, on the other side of the table. "May I . . ."

"Of course."

T'Pol sat. She clasped her hands together on the table in front of her. "I have just spoken for the second time today with a member of the Vulcan Council. My first conversation with this person was a request for information on the Thelasian Confederacy—a very brief conversation. Our second talk was considerably longer. This person relayed to me the substance of a conversation they had with a third party regarding the Thelasians. Said third party is nominally a member of the Vulcan Cultural Exchange Commission, but in reality . . ."

"A spy," Trip interrupted.

"Just so."

The captain sighed. Spies. Information brokers. Untrustworthy trading partners.

He longed for a good, old-fashioned first contact.

"This is highly sensitive information," T'Pol said. "My source on the Council was reluctant to allow me to share it."

Archer nodded. "Of course. I understand that. Go on."

T'Pol looked to Trip.

"Yeah, yeah. Doesn't leave this room. Speak."

She looked from Trip to Archer. "As a functional institution, the Confederacy is dying."

"Dying?" The captain sat back in his chair. "That is sensitive information."

Trip let out a long, low whistle. "And how. Your source is sure about this?"

"Yes. The actual disintegration is predicted to begin occurring within a short span of years, though the crisis has been building for several decades. You have read the summary I prepared previously?"

"Yes."

"We both have."

"Then you know that the Confederacy—though not a formal political entity—controls both this sector and several surrounding ones through the enforcement of various trade duties and military alliances. However, strategic pressures—technological developments, expansion of other races into the afore mentioned sectors, an overall increase in intragalactic trade—have weakened that control. There have recently been numerous instances of trades taking place without Confederacy sanction. Sen's selection as governor was apparently a mandate to try and restore order to the process. According to this source, he is widely perceived as a man not averse to the use of force."

"Why does that not surprise me?" Trip said. "We sure we want to go to this place right now?"

Archer ignored him. "What are the practical consequences of the Confederacy's disintegration?"

"Unknown. Much of the territory they control is not familiar to us. We have no way of telling how critical their presence is in those areas. Within the parts of space we do know—the territories closer to the Barcana Sector—the effects are expected to be minimal. Trade will continue, of course."

"The Confederacy just won't get its cut anymore."

"Correct."

"So Sen won't get his cut anymore." Trip smiled. "Couldn't happen to a nicer guy."

Archer frowned. "I can think of one possible negative effect that your source didn't mention. These attacks, like the one that happened to us—if the Confederacy collapses, that may lead to more of them."

"We have only Sen's word that the aliens are aggressively expansionist," T'Pol said. "We do not know what their true intentions are."

"No," Archer agreed. "Not yet we don't." He told her then of his decision to go to Procyron, and then added, "Brief Travis on the substance of what we've discussed, if you would. I'm going to want him in on the landing party. Hoshi too."

"Ensign Mayweather I will talk with immediately.

Ensign Sato . . . I would prefer to brief her tomorrow, on shift. I have sent her to her quarters for the day."

"Oh?" Archer asked.

"She was working too hard," T'Pol said.

The captain frowned.

"Told you so," Trip said.

SIX

Procyron was old. Very old, and very, very dirty.

Part of that was because of the sky, of course; what they'd first taken for cloud cover was now revealed, halfway down to the surface, as pollution, a brownish haze that dulled everything, the streams and lakes that came into focus as the shuttle descended, the bright light of Procyron's sun as it sank beneath the horizon, and most of all the city they were fast approaching. Tura Prex was a mega-megalopolis; that was the only way that Archer could think of it. Its towering structures spanned what had to be dozens of kilometers in either direction, but he'd actually mistaken it for a geologic formation from a distance, that was how completely the pollution obliterated the normal gleam and sparkle you would expect to see given the size of the city. What truly impressed Archer, though, was that, according to Sen, it was only the third-largest city on the planet.

Procyron—Procyron Seven, actually, but as the other six planets in the system were nothing more than balls of rock, too close to Procyron's sun to permit establishment of any sort of colonies, this world was the only one that rated a name—was a Minshara-class planet somewhat bigger than Earth, surface area split almost equally between land and water. Four larger landmasses, dozens of smaller ones, including the one they were currently gliding over. Gliding over fast, rapidly approaching Tura Prex.

The console beeped.

The captain looked down at his instrument panel (the viewscreen was useless, the cloud cover was so thick) and frowned.

"Proximity warning," he said. "Multiple readings."

"I'm on it." Travis, next to him in the pilot's chair, eased their speed. The ship hiccoughed.

"Commander Tucker was right. Controls are a little sluggish," he said.

Archer nodded. Trip had told them the shuttle was overdue for maintenance, which he had been trying to get around to for a week, but because of Hess being out . . .

"Six ships." That was Malcolm, manning the console behind him. "Heading right for us."

They were coming fast, ridiculously fast.

"Weapons, sir?" Reed asked.

"Not yet," he replied. "Let's give them a chance to stop."

Which they did . . . a scant fifty meters short of the shuttle. A split-second later the cloud cover broke, and the dots on the panel became small ships arrayed in space around them. Half a dozen ships, each approximately the size of the shuttlecraft, but far more streamlined in construction. Pointed. A lot of sharp edges. A lot of what looked to him like weapons emplacements.

"No life-signs. My guess is those vessels are under computer control. Remote control," Malcolm said. Which explained their ability to start and stop so fast—g-forces were not a factor to worry about when there was no crew.

"Plenty of weapons, though," Reed continued. "Phased energy sources, multiple warheads . . ."

"Got a signal coming in," Hoshi, the fourth—and final member—of the landing party, spoke from the back of the small ship, alongside Reed. "Thelasian standard. These ships are our escort; we're to follow the lead one down to the planet's surface."

As she said that, one of the ships broke formation, and dropped like a stone toward ground. At a nod from the captain, Travis followed.

Tura Prex rapidly took shape before them.

But even as they finally got close enough for the captain to pick out individual structures, the ship in front of them veered sharply and disappeared into a gap between two huge towers at the edge of the city. The shuttle followed and, after a series of sharp turns and one very near miss with another of the automated craft, lurched downward and came to a sudden stop.

Travis sat back from the controls and exhaled noisily.

"That was not fun."

"But we're down," Archer said. "Nice work. Hoshi, let *Enterprise* know we're down."

"Ah, I wouldn't say down exactly, Captain."

That was Malcolm.

Archer looked at the control panel more closely and saw what he meant.

They weren't actually down on the ground at all. They were still almost a thousand meters above the planet's surface.

The captain followed Reed out of the shuttle and onto a docking pad—a relatively small docking pad. Ships—most of them just like the one they'd followed here—flitted above. They flitted below, too—far, far below. Little dots that could have been people or could have been other kinds of ships moved beneath them as well.

Malcolm pointed toward a walkway—not much wider than one of the corridors aboard *Enterprise,* perhaps ten meters long—leading from the pad into the nearest building.

"I assume we're to take that."

"I assume so," Archer said.

Travis clapped Reed on the shoulder.

"It'll be fine. Just don't look down."

Hoshi eyed the path nervously as well. Archer walked around the edge of the docking pad, and tried to get a better look at the city below. A gentle force-field pushed him back from the edge.

"Safety feature. Wouldn't do to have our guests tour the city that way, would it?"

Archer turned. A man was coming down the walkway toward them. Actually, the walkway was moving, carrying him in their direction. The man wore a blue and green uniform, held something that looked like a padd against his chest, and was smiling.

He stepped off the walkway and onto the docking pad.

"I'm Gemel Prian. On behalf of Governor Sen and the Thelasian Confederacy, welcome to Procyron."

"Thank you. Jonathan Archer. I'm captain of the *Enterprise.* These are members of my crew Ensign Travis Mayweather, Lieutenant Malcolm Reed, Ensign Hoshi Sato."

"Welcome, all of you." Prian bowed to each in turn. "I want to apologize on the governor's behalf—he wanted to be here to greet you personally. Unfortunately, he was called away on urgent business."

"I understand, of course," Archer said. "Should we return another time, or wait for him, or . . ."

"No, no, I'm sorry, I'm not being clear. The urgent business the governor had to deal with—it concerns you as well." Prian's smile of welcome disappeared. "The entire Trading Confederacy is meeting now, in the Assembly Chamber. You're to come as well. If you would follow me . . ."

Prian stepped back on the walkway. Archer and his crew followed suit.

For the next five minutes, they were conveyed— slowly at first, and then faster—through the city. Past, around, and sometimes even through tall gleaming spires, between huge dirty-orange buildings, each the size of a starship, and finally through a short tunnel of gleaming metal before emerging into a large, bright, open space, dominated by three tall towers directly in front of them, ringed by a half-dozen shorter buildings.

Hundreds of people were walking back and forth within that space—no, "people" was the wrong word, "beings" was more accurate, because though the vast majority of them were humanoid, the variety of races Archer saw at a glance made the Xindi Council look homogeneous by comparison. Insectoid, reptilian, non-carbon-based, aquatic, some in environmental suits, some practically naked, and not a single species the captain recognized.

It made him realize, all over again, how big the galaxy was, and what a small portion of it Starfleet had explored.

"This is the government complex," said Prian, stepping off the walkway, which Archer only now realized had come to a stop a few seconds earlier. "We walk from here."

The captain stepped off too, and followed the Thelasian, who seemed to have an uncanny ability to pick a hole through the crowd, in the direction of one of the three towers. The Trade Assembly," Prian informed them, pointing—which was, Archer saw, slightly different in appearance from the two towers flanking it: more windows in its surface, a more impressive entranceway (in front of which Archer noticed quite a number of humanoids in similar uniforms—guards?), and atop it what looked to be a clear glass dome.

Archer shielded his eyes and squinted upward to study that dome further, at which point he realized they weren't outside at all, they were in fact underneath a much larger version of the dome atop the building, in an entirely self-contained atmosphere. The dirty, rust-colored sky they had flown through in the shuttle was barely visible through its surface, which was inset with a number of small bright light sources. Ships—they looked identical to the ones that had escorted them down to the planet's surface, albeit, the captain thought, somewhat smaller—buzzed above them, and Archer saw now that atop the other two buildings were what looked like weapons emplacements as well, and the funny thing was, those weapons weren't pointing up toward the sky, as he would have expected, but down, toward the ground.

Food for thought, given the briefing on the Thelasians' internal political troubles T'Pol had given them.

Archer glanced behind him and saw Malcolm's eyes focused in the same place.

At that instant, a woman—humanoid, yellowish

skin—stepped in front of Prian and began yelling at the Thelasian.

Prian nodded once, then again, the picture of understanding, and began talking as well, obviously trying to calm her down.

Archer couldn't understand a word they were saying. He turned to Hoshi, who already had her translator out and was entering data.

"Interesting angle on those guns, wouldn't you say?" Malcom had stepped forward and spoken quietly in the captain's ear.

"Absolutely," Archer replied.

"What I also find interesting," Malcolm went on, "is how far away from here we had to land. The number of ships they had escorting the shuttle."

"Not to mention the roundabout path we took to get here," the captain said. "I'm not sure I could find my way back if my life depended on it."

Malcolm held up his padd. "I think I could help in that regard, sir. Should it become necessary."

Archer caught a glimpse of a small video still—the image of the path before them—realized that Malcolm had been surreptitiously recording their journey through the Prex, and smiled.

"Excuse me, Captain."

Archer turned to see Hoshi, frowning at the UT in her hands.

"Nothing, I gather."

"No, sir. I get one cluster that could be a name—probably the governor's name, if I had to guess—but besides that . . ."

"All right. Keep at it." He offered a smile of encouragement, to which Hoshi gave a rather woeful nod in return. He could imagine her frustration—particularly given what Phlox had told him earlier—but this was neither the time nor the place for a pep talk.

"Forgive the interruption," Prian said, and Archer saw that he and the yellow-skinned woman, who had stepped out of their path and was now deep in conversation with two other females from her race, had finished their business. "This way, please."

He led them up to the Trade Assembly's entranceway—past an awfully substantial armed detail—and into an elevator, which bulleted upward the second the doors closed behind them. A moment later, the doors opened again, and they walked through another armed detail and into a huge assembly hall that the captain thought at first was open to the sky, then realized was in fact underneath the dome he had seen earlier from outside. Light—much brighter than the natural sunlight that had shone through the shuttle windows coming in—poured down from above.

Then, suddenly, people poured down as well. Aliens, of all different varieties, all the species they had seen outside and then some, coming toward them, jabbering all at once, looking angry and impatient. Archer got a brief, better glimpse of the Trade Assembly—they had entered onto the lowest level of the hall, which was stepped like an Earth-style auditorium—before the crowd reached them and they had to give way, backing up till they could go no farther, till the captain felt the wall that served as the closed end of the half-shell-shaped structure at his back.

"Very enthusiastic greeting," Malcolm managed.

"I don't think it's for us," Archer said.

Prian had his hands up in the air, and was practically shouting, struggling to be heard. The captain managed to turn just enough to catch Hoshi's eye.

She had the UT padd pressed up against her chest and her neck craned in what looked like a very painful position.

"Sen again, I think," she said, reading off the screen. "That's it."

Archer nodded. That didn't surprise him. Everyone was obviously looking for the governor. He and his crew were just caught in the middle.

"Let's get out of here," he said, turning his head and waving Malcolm forward. He wanted to get himself and his crew to a place where they could at least hear themselves think, maybe even have a conversation without shouting.

He lowered his shoulder and pushed forward. The crowd gave way.

The crowd pushed back.

Archer found himself slammed back up against the wall.

"Oof." He frowned, took a deep breath, and readied himself for another try. "On my count: one, two—"

He felt a hand on his shoulder. Malcolm.

"Easier this way, sir." Reed nodded to his left. The captain saw Travis and Hoshi, backs pressed tight to the wall, sliding away from Prian and the mob crowding Prian.

The captain nodded and joined them.

"This place is a madhouse," Archer said, jamming himself in between one particularly large yellow-skinned humanoid and the wall. "It's like the 602 Club on St. Patrick's Day."

"Worse," Malcolm said.

"What do you mean worse?"

"I doubt there's a bartender like Ruby waiting on the other side of this crowd," Reed said.

Archer smiled.

A hand clamped down on his wrist, stopping his progress.

The hand was blue.

"Pinkskin," a voice said. "Your kind are far from home."

Archer looked up and found himself staring into the scarred face of an Andorian officer.

"Oh joy," Malcolm muttered.

SEVEN

The Andorian officer was named Quirsh. Nominally a sergeant, he was now in command of his planet's trade legation to the Confederation, and had thus adopted the honorific "ambassador." It didn't suit him. Quirsh was perhaps—with the exception of the few Tellarites she'd encountered—the most undiplomatic being Hoshi had ever met in her life.

Right now he and the captain were arguing—or rather, Quirsh was arguing and the captain was trying to guide the conversation down a different path—over *Enterprise*'s intentions here on Procyron. Quirsh insisted that the Andorians had been trading with the Confederacy for over a decade and thus, under recognized interstellar conventions, had a right-of-first-refusal monopoly on certain commodities coming from this sector of space to the more traveled paths within the Alpha Quadrant. Archer kept trying to tell him they weren't here to trade at all, they were here because their ship had been attacked, and he kept trying to work his relationship with Shran into the conversation too, telling Quirsh about the alliance the two of them had helped engineer between their two races, but Quirsh wasn't buying any of it, not the bit about why *Enterprise* was here and certainly not the rapprochement between their two races. He'd apparently heard little of those events out here, and what he had heard he'd chosen not to believe.

The captain and the Andorian didn't need her help understanding each other, so Hoshi had her UT focused on one of the aliens haranguing Prian—a yellow-skinned man who looked to her to be of the same race as the woman who'd stopped Sen's deputy outside the Assembly. The machine was making note of similar syllabic clusters, assigning them arbitrary meanings from a list of possibilities in its data banks, and testing those meanings in sentences. Hoshi was doing the same thing herself, albeit in a less rigorous, more instinctual fashion. It seemed as if they'd be able to translate this language, which was good, as failing the captain twice in one week would have been too much for her.

Though she supposed she'd better get used to failure. The deeper into space they got, the more often it was likely to occur, at least according to Doctor Teodoro, who'd taught a seminar at the Training Institute on this very subject. An advanced seminar, fourth year, very exclusive, *Toward a Universal Translator: Alien Grammars and the Limits of the Possible*. Hoshi had been one of only five people admitted to it.

Lately, she'd been thinking about that seminar a lot. About the first day of class, when Doctor Teodoro had walked in punctually at 9:00 A.M., ramrod-straight (a military bearing, Hoshi knew now, that came from Teodoro's own career aboard one of the earliest Starfleet survey vessels, where the then Ensign Linda Teodoro had served as both linguist and armory officer), and brought the display screen on the far wall of the room to life, and typed in:

Universal Translator = Impossible

before sitting down in her chair at the far end of the long, oval table her students were gathered at.

Hoshi remembered looking at the screen, looking around the table at her classmates (Bei Quajong, Donal Rafferty, Jerome Hegler, Simone Tam, whom she'd spent more time with over the last few months than her own family) for their reactions, and then looking back at Doctor Teodoro, who sat back in her chair, stone-faced.

Hoshi couldn't tell what she was thinking. Neither, apparently, could anyone else. No one said a word.

"Okay, linguists. 'Seminar.' " Teodoro looked around the table. "The word means what?"

"Small group of people meeting to exchange ideas," Donal shot back.

"Right. And that right there," she nodded toward the board, "that's my idea. What's yours, Mister Rafferty?"

"I think you're right."

Teodoro shook her head. "First day of class, and you're kissing my ass already?"

Hoshi stifled a laugh. Donal blushed.

"No, sir. Ma'am."

"Doctor is fine here. In this context. So why do you think I'm right?"

"Structure. Chomsky says—"

"Ah." Teodoro held up a hand. "Your own words."

Donal nodded. "Human language is a function of species-specific brain structure. Grammars are phenotypical expressions of underlying genealogical . . ."

Teodoro shook her head again. "Mister Rafferty. Class. We won't be talking like textbooks in here, all right? Everyday language. Pretend I'm a politician. Or an admiral."

Everyone laughed.

"Not funny," Teodoro said. "These are complex concepts. You have to be able to make them understandable to the layman—to the people who you'll be working with, and asking to support your research. And if you are lucky enough to be out there—out in the field—"

She nodded up, in the direction of space, at the same time focusing her attention on Bei, whose desire to serve "out there" was already a running joke among her classmates and apparently the Institute's faculty as well.

"—you'll have to explain why polarizing the hull in the face of an alien vessel that's just charged weapons is likely to be seen as an offensive action. Are we clear on that?"

Nods around the table.

"Good. So Mister Rafferty . . . would you like to continue?"

Donal did. He did pretty well at laying out Chomsky's theory of universal grammar, which had floored Hoshi the first time she encountered it, when she understood that what the man was saying was that human language was an innate capability, like a dog's sense of smell or a bat's ability to echolocate. It wasn't learned; it came naturally. And what followed from that . . .

"So is everyone with Mister Rafferty?" Teodoro asked. "We all—humans—can learn each other's languages because they're all basically the same. They've been the same since we climbed down from the trees. Stone Age language, and our language—things, actions, modifiers. There's no difference in form whatsoever. There's been no evolution of language from then to now. But an alien language . . . that's going to be like nothing we've ever encountered in our lives."

She looked around the room again, and waited.

"We all agree, then?" She pointed at the board. "Universal Translator equals Impossibility?"

"No. I don't agree." That was Jerry. "We've already got a good start on a Universal Translator. There are over sixty alien languages in the database already."

"Those come courtesy of the Vulcans. Besides—is that a translator, or a giant dictionary?"

"Practically speaking—does it matter?"

Hoshi cleared her throat and spoke for the first time.

"We haven't really encountered any aliens yet," she said.

Teodoro swiveled in her chair to face her. "Ah. Ms. Sato, yes? Go ahead."

"Vulcans, the people from Alpha Centauri, the Rigelians—for our purposes, they are us. Bipeds, toolmakers—"

"The Preservers," Max said.

"Legend," Teodoro said dismissively. "Not backed up by biology. But Ms. Sato's point is still a valid one. What is going to happen when we meet up with an alien race that doesn't have two arms and two legs, and doesn't think like we do, doesn't organize concepts the way we do? Maybe it doesn't even use speech. What then? How can we put its vocabulary into a computer?"

There was a long silence then.

"We can't," Hoshi said finally.

"That's right. We can't." Teodoro looked around the table once more, meeting the gaze of every student before rising from her chair and walking to the board.

"It's impossible. A Universal Translator is impossible," she said, touching the screen with her forefinger.

"That's one starting point for all our discussions this semester, people. Here's the other."

She returned to her seat then, typed something very quickly, and punched in a key. The display changed to read:

Universal Translator = Necessity

And at last, Teodoro smiled.

"So as you all can see, we have our work cut out for us."

Which turned out to be an understatement if ever there was one. By the end of the semester, Hoshi and the class had mastered not just the work of pioneering human linguists like Chomsky and Pinker, Weisler and Feinstein, but the Vulcan theorists as well. They'd also successfully translated more than two dozen additional alien languages (rough data supplied courtesy of some of the more adventurous Starfleet—and civilian—explorers). And yet . . .

By the end of the semester, Hoshi, like everyone else in the class—like Teodoro herself, too, Hoshi suspected—remained torn. Was a true Universal Translator possible? What they had now was nothing more than a giant dictionary, as Teodoro had pointed out. And there were limits to that dictionary's effectiveness. Limits she and *Enterprise* had just smacked into pretty hard: The nonrepeating signal. The fifty-seven coded pulses.

And again, despite the here and now she found herself in, her present circumstances, which included any number of races standing right in front of her, races whose languages she could and should be attempting to incorporate into the UT's database,

Hoshi's thoughts went back to that alien signal, and the ship that had broadcast it. To the aspect of the situation she found most puzzling—and perhaps most troubling—of all.

Enterprise's scans of the alien vessel had detected half a dozen humanoids aboard, working in a Minshara-class atmosphere. The scans weren't as detailed, as precise as T'Pol would have liked, but for Hoshi's purposes they were more than enough. The aliens were bipeds: two arms, two legs, gross anatomical structures very similar to those displayed by most other humanoid races *Enterprise* had encountered in her travels so far. Close to human—close as, say, Ambassador Quirsh over there. The LMUs—language meaning units, the base concepts that most bipeds shared, I, me, you, eat, sleep, etc.—should have been similar as well. So the language should have been relatively easy to translate. And yet it wasn't.

Or maybe it was. Maybe the real problem was her, or rather, what the Xindi did to her. To her brain. Maybe all that mucking around in there had messed things up, and now she'd never be the same again. Maybe she should give Carstairs a crack at the alien signal. Maybe he'd have better luck.

Maybe she should just go back to Earth, teach grade-school Japanese for a living. Write a book about her experiences: *My Years In Space.*

She could call it *Toward a Universal Translator: Alien Grammars and the Limits of Hoshi Sato.*

The UT beeped. It had just finished translating the language of the yellow-skinned man yelling at Prian, Hoshi saw. Well, at least all her programming efforts weren't fouled up. She studied the display.

The yellow-skinned man's name, she learned, was

Aloran, his race was the H'ratoi, he was in fact their ambassador to the Thelasians, they were part of the Confederacy, obviously, perhaps the most important member race next to the Thelasians (at least in the ambassador's opinion), and they'd just lost contact with two more of their ships, and what was Sen going to do about it? When could they speak to the governor, where was he? Why was he avoiding them again?

Prian waved his hands helplessly.

"What do you have?"

Malcolm was leaning over her shoulder.

"He," Hoshi said, indicating Aloran, "wants to know where Sen is. His race has been a member in good standing of the Confederacy for a long, long time. Practically forever. They deserve special consideration. He deserves special consideration. Why hasn't Sen met with him? Doesn't the governor value their contributions to the Confederacy? And so on, and so on, and so forth." She shrugged. "And you?"

"Doing a little eavesdropping." Reed nodded behind him, in the direction of the Captain and Ambassador Quirsh, who were still going at it, having moved away from the larger mass of people crowded near the front of the Assembly Hall and taken up position in one of the aisles a few rows back. "Found out a few things. Some you might be interested in."

"Oh?"

Reed nodded. "The Andorians have been attacked twice. First time, the ship was heavily damaged, currently being repaired by the Thelasians, for what—if I heard correctly—is a ridiculously exorbitant fee."

"No surprise there."

"No indeed. The second attack occurred two weeks ago. This time, the Andorians weren't so lucky." His expression turned grave. "Sixty-nine out of the seventy people killed. Ship destroyed. The dead included the entire trade legation, which explains how a nincompoop like Quirsh became ambassador."

She nodded.

"The lone survivor, by the way? Her."

He pointed in Quirsh's direction, toward an Andorian female standing by herself, apart from the others. Tall, thin, intense-looking, radiating—though Hoshi couldn't quite say how—a "do not disturb, don't mess with me" air.

"First Technician Theera," Malcolm said.

"Technician?" Hoshi shok her head. "She looks more like a security officer than a technician."

Malcolm turned to her and frowned.

"No offense intended," Hoshi said quickly.

Reed smiled. "None taken."

"She just has that air about her . . ."

"She's a linguist, actually," Malcolm said.

"What?" Hoshi raised her eyebrows in surprise.

He nodded. "Yes. And if I heard right, she's managed to translate a portion of the alien signal."

Hoshi's jaw dropped.

At that instant, the murmuring around her trebled in intensity, then turned into a full-fledged roar. The crowd surged forward.

She turned, and saw that Governor Sen had entered the Trade Assembly.

EIGHT

The governor paused in his tracks, taken aback for a second by the noise.

The bodyguards closed ranks around him.

Roia tied into the security system and alerted him to the number of mercenaries in the hall—fourteen—whose ID chips marked them as experts in unarmed combat and thus as potential threats to his safety, at the same time giving him their approximate locations. Sen fixed those locations in his mind as he took in the entirety of the hall before him—the delegates and soldiers and merchants and pilots and ambassadors crowded together in the aisles, pressing forward toward him, shouting out his name and various epithets in any number of languages.

The governor sighed, and almost turned right back around.

God, he loathed democracy.

All this meaningless, extraneous ceremony and chatter. A significant waste of time, devoted to—what? Really, what was the point? Why pretend that everyone was entitled to an equal vote, that everyone's opinion deserved equal weight, that decisions should be made by majority rule? What nonsense. That wasn't the way the world worked. Individuals made decisions; deliberative bodies . . . deliberated. He hated the hypocrisy displayed by some of the

Confederacy's newest members, the ambassadors and trade legates who insisted on ratifying every decree coming from his office, every new tariff and/or fee he tried to impose. Had they spent a lifetime working in the Guilds, learning the mechanisms of the marketplace, knowing how to read the subtle signs pointing toward commodity shortfalls or surpluses? No. Did they know which races needed coddling, compromise, and which responded only to force, or the threat of punitive financial action? No. Should their assessments, then, of relevant situations, of crisis points, hold equal weight to his?

The suggestion was ridiculous. Laughable. Clearly, they had no business telling him how to run the Confederacy. He would certainly never dream of interfering in, say, the Szegedy's internal political situation; he didn't know the historical background behind those conflicts, anymore than he knew how to make Maszakian breakfast stew. It was not his area of expertise, so he deferred to those who knew better. Let them do their jobs. As he should be deferred to so that he could do his. Deferred to without the need for this ceremonial nonsense—deferred to completely and immediately so that quick, decisive action could be taken. That was how things got done.

People would know that, Sen thought, *if they bothered to study history—if they were able to look at it dispassionately, free of idealistic, ideological bias.* Great civilizations, great accomplishments arose from the doings and actions of individuals. It was true here on Procyron, it was true on H'ratoi Prime, it was true all across the galaxy. True even on a relative backwater like Earth, whose history he'd been reading up on last evening, again courtesy of the Teff-Langer Conglomerate. Was there ever a better example of one individual triggering change through his own, ungoverned initiative than the young king Alexander? The melding of cultures he'd brought about? Not in Sen's opinion. Earth, in fact, was full of such figures, Green and Gandhi, Mao and Madison, Julius Caesar and yes, even Jonathan Archer, whose list of accomplishments at such a relatively young age was practically Alexandrian.

Sen's eyes swept the hall now until he found the human captain, in conversation with a blue-skinned alien—an Andorian. That was right; the two races were relative neighbors, at the moment arguing about something. Arguing quite vociferously, in fact; the Andorian's body language indicated potential violence. Should he have the guards intervene before the conflict escalated? It wouldn't do to have the captain damaged; the price would quite likely go down if he was damaged. Although perhaps, Sen thought, he was misreading the signals.

"Roia," he subvocalized. "Humans and Andorians. Summarize relations."

She did so. Sen was surprised to learn that despite what he was seeing, the two races had just entered into a tentative alliance. What was more, Archer had played a pivotal role in shaping that arrangement. Another accomplishment for the history books by the young captain. Considering what Sen had planned for Archer, though . . .

It was more than likely the Earthman's last.

"Governor?"

Sen found himself looking directly into the face of one of his bodyguards. Kuda. The captain of the troop.

"Of course," he said smoothly, realizing at once that the man had been standing there for some time, waiting for Sen to move forward. "Go."

Kuda nodded, and spun on his heel and strode forward, followed by his troop, who were all tied in directly (through the security network) to Kuda's central processing system, and so moved in direct lockstep with their leader, clearing (none-too-gently) a path for Sen to the stage. The governor climbed the short flight of steps onto it, nodding to Prian as he did so, who acknowledged the governor with a grateful smile. Sen saw the H'ratoi massed all around his assistant; those people simply would not accept the slightest loss on any of their shipments, a trait that the trader in Sen admired as much as the governor in him abhorred.

Sen raised his hands in the air, palms faced forward, and the crowd quieted.

"Thank you all for coming. Please—be seated. And forgive the delay . . ."

"Do you have news of our ships?"

Sen looked down and saw that same H'ratoi, the one who'd been harassing Prian, their ambassador—Aloran (unprompted, Roia quickly provided his name)—staring up at him. His first instinct was to order the man ejected from the hall. In the old days of the Confederacy, the glory days, no one would have dared to even exhale loudly when the first governor was speaking, and if they had presumed to interrupt, they would more than likely have been thrown not just from the hall but from the top of the building and none present would have lifted a finger in protest. But, of course, these weren't the old days anymore, and the H'ratoi were not only one of the

Confederacy's oldest (and most important) members but supplied a significant portion of the manpower and equipment necessary for the protection of the trade routes. H'ratoi—even ones as bothersome as the ambassador—had to be tolerated. In the name of defense. In the name of democracy.

Sen favored the man with a slight smile.

"Ambassador. If you'll allow me to briefly . . ."

"Do you have news?" the ambassador repeated, cutting Sen off, glaring up at the governor with impatience.

It was all Sen could do not to stride off the podium and throttle him.

"Yes," Sen said, in as level a tone as he could manage.

"And . . ."

"It's not good news, I'm afraid. We have confirmation of the attack."

The hall erupted again. Voices shouted for details, voices shouted in anger, eyes glared at Sen and at the uniformed generals—the Defense Council—assembled at the side of the podium. The Pfau delegate behind Aloran punched the air with her fist, and yelled something incomprehensible. Behind her, the Palisan representatives huddled together and shook their heads vociferously. A few rows back, and to the governor's right, the Conani shouted Sen's name, demanding to be recognized, to be allowed to speak.

And in the same row, but farther to the left, all the way to the left, the human captain stood impassively, arms folded across his chest, a guarded, watchful expression on his face. Sen watched as Archer's eyes swept the hall, assessing what he saw, and an instant later the captain leaned over and whispered something into the ear of the human next to him, who nodded. Sen found himself wondering if Archer saw the assembled delegates the same way he did. A mindless, unthinking mob. Rabble. He wondered what the man thought about democracy. More than likely, the captain shared the views of most of the other Earthlings Sen had been reading about last night, viewed representative government as the ultimate evolution of the political form. No wonder they were a backwater.

He signaled again for quiet and, when he got it, went on to place the enemy's latest assault in context, quickly summarizing the attacks to date—how and when they had taken place, the total damage incurred broken out in monetary units and in lives lost (substantial), the Confederacy's current state of knowledge regarding the attackers (minimal)—before finally returning to a discussion of the latest incident.

"Two days ago, one of our *Kenza*-class cargo transports left Procyron heading toward the Rina declension lines, escorted by two H'ratoi fighter vessels. This morning, while attempting to transit the nearest of those lines, they were attacked." He locked eyes with the H'ratoi ambassador again. "I'm sorry to report the convoy was destroyed. All cargo, all ships, all hands . . . lost."

The crowd erupted again. Sen struggled to be heard over them.

"I had summoned you here to consider what sort of action we should take against these intruders. Against these recurring attacks. It is my feeling that this latest vicious, unprovoked assault dictates only one response."

Sen leaned forward on the lectern, quieting the

angry crowd with that single movement, and cleared his throat.

"Members of the Confederacy, we have been reactive for too long. You elected me to take a stand against these intruders, and it is now plainer than ever that we must make that stand a firm and unyielding one. As at Coreida . . ."

A roar of applause from the crowd at the mention of Sen's most famous triumph, where as viceroy he had indeed been responsible for stopping a series of unprovoked attacks on the Confederacy's ships, though not exactly in the way people believed.

". . . we must meet force with force. We must defend our freedoms, and the freedoms of those who stand with us. My friends, war is the one—the only—answer to these unprovoked assaults."

A larger roar this time. Shouts for blood.

Democracy.

"This very morning, in emergency session," the governor continued, "the Defense Council voted—a unanimous vote," Sen smiled at the memory of that, thank God for the military mind, at least they knew the virtues of chain of command. The generals had simpy rubber-stamped the action he recommended, less than seven minutes, certainly, from start of the meeting to dismissal, "to declare war. I now ask the Assembly's authorization for that action. If voting delegates will please move to your stations . . ."

"We need no formal vote!" the H'ratoi ambassador bellowed, turning to face the crowd. "Our course of action is clear. Fellow delegates, all of those in favor of granting the governor a similar declaration . . ."

He didn't even need to finish his sentence. The crowd erupted in a single, unanimous roar.

"And opposed?" the ambassador prompted.

Not a single voice. Not a sound, a whisper of discontent.

Sen bowed slightly, and smiled.

"Thank you, Ambassador. I am happy to see the Confederacy so united. I want to assure you all—the Defense Council and I have been deliberating potential retaliatory strategies at some length these last few weeks, and we . . ."

"Excuse me."

Sen frowned.

Jonathan Archer stood in the center aisle, in a spot that had somehow miraculously cleared for him, and took a step closer to the podium.

It was almost as if the crowd had given way for him. Ridiculous, of course. They didn't even know who he was.

"Forgive the interruption," the captain continued. "My name is Jonathan Archer. I represent Starfleet and the planet Earth, Alpha Quadrant. I just wanted to introduce myself, say a few words." He looked directly at Sen. "With your permission, of course, Governor."

Sen nodded. What else could he do, after all?

Democracy.

"Of course, Captain. Please . . ."

"Thank you." Archer turned his attention to the delegates, allowing his gaze to sweep the hall once. "My ship was recently attacked as well, so I understand completely the Assembly's action—the anger being expressed here. The desire for revenge. I just wanted to say that during our encounter with one of these intruders, they made repeated attempts at communication before firing on us. I'd like to suggest that if we can decipher those communications, we will not only have a better idea of their motivations," scattered hissing at that, Sen knew most of the delegates didn't care a whit about the intruders' motivations, all that concerned them was the cargo and the lives that were being lost, "but also an advantage during any future conflicts, that being the ability to understand their ship-to-ship communications and quite possibly transmit some false—and strategically misleading—information to their vessels."

The crowd, all at once, fell completely silent.

Sen nodded silently to himself. Transmitting false and misleading information...he should have thought of that himself

"I know our friends the Andorians here," Archer continued, indicating the blue-skinned delegate he had been standing next to previously, "have made some progress along those lines. I believe, in fact, that they've even managed to translate a portion of the alien signal."

A murmur of surprise at that news—which Sen had deliberately been keeping quiet—buzzed through the crowd.

"Am I correct in this assumption, Governor?" Archer asked.

All eyes turned toward Sen.

"Governor?" the H'ratoi ambassador prompted.

Sen cleared his throat, nodded, and coughed before speaking, solely to give himself time to calm down, to not betray the rage that was pouring through every fiber of his being.

He forced a smile. "Well. In part it is true. Captain," he said to Archer, "I wish you had talked to me before sharing this news publicly. I have been consulting with the Kanthropians," he gestured toward a group of a half-dozen Mediators seated to his right, clad in the characteristic brown robes of their order, "and have delayed making any announcement pending their evaluation of the data."

"Please. Forgive me if I've spoken out of turn," Archer said.

"Not at all," Sen said. "I understand your motives completely."

The two men locked eyes.

Insolent pup, Sen thought.

"Governor." That from General Jaedez, the Conani representative on the Defense Council. Jaedez looked mad and Sen couldn't blame him. He'd kept knowledge of the translation—however preliminary—from them as well. No doubt Jaedez would express his displeasure more openly at the Defense Council meeting tomorrow.

Luckily, Sen wouldn't be there to hear it.

"What is this translation the human refers to?" Jaedez asked.

Sen sighed inwardly. Nothing to do now, of course, but to share the news with all.

He gestured toward the Mediators.

"Elder Woden. If you would . . ."

One of the Kanthropians stood and faced the Assembly.

"Any talk of a translation is premature, I must say. Certain data has been offered to us by the Andorians, and based upon that data, we have concluded that certain assignations of meaning may potentially be made, in particular one informational grouping which seems to us to correspond to—"

"Mediator. Can you get to the point, please?" Jaedez said. "What portion of the signal has been translated?"

The Mediator frowned.

"I hesitate to use the word 'translation.' Preliminary data is suggestive, rather than definitive. We must all bear this in mind as—"

"Mediator," Jaedez said again. "The 'suggestive' translation, then. If you please."

Elder Woden frowned a moment, then nodded.

"A single phrase. No more. The name of the attackers. Their species." The mediator paused a moment. "We believe they are called Antianna."

Once more, a buzz erupted in the crowd. "Antianna? Why were we not told? What else do we know about this race?"

"Please," Sen said, signaling for quiet. "We are of course making further translation of the signal a high priority. The Mediators are in charge of this effort, and I can assure you . . ."

"We have relevant information to share," one of the Maszakian delegates said, standing. "Data obtained by one of our ship captains during his last encounter with the aliens. We would gladly make it available."

"Thank you," Sen replied. "As I was saying . . ."

"We have information to share as well," Archer interrupted. "Similar data. And resources. I would like to offer the services of our translator," the captain gestured behind him then, toward a strikingly attractive female, whose features instantly reminded the governor of Roia's long-vanished physical counterpart, "who is eager to participate in any efforts to decipher the Antianna signal."

Sen stood a little straighter at the podium. For the first time that afternoon, his features formed into a smile of genuine pleasure.

"A very generous offer, Captain Archer," he said,

attempting to catch the female's eye. "Your eagerness to be involved is noted, and appreciated."

At that instant, the implant sounded—Roia prompting him with an update on the convoy's progress. They were on schedule for arrival this evening. A few minutes early, even, as they were just now coming in range of the first Baustin monitoring station, which Roia had temporarily disabled to permit their safe passage into Confederacy space. And there was still much to do to prepare for their arrival.

Time to bring things here to a close, he thought.

"Anyone with further data on the signal—or information to share regarding the Antianna—should contact the Kanthropians immediately. I thank you in advance for your cooperation in that matter, and for coming this afternoon." Sen smiled. "And I remind you all of the reception this evening at the solarium, to welcome those who have come from off world, who have so generously offered your services to the Confederacy in this time of need."

He bowed slightly, and nodded to Kuda, who instantly formed the bodyguards into a phalanx around him.

"Good afternoon," he said, and spun on his heel, and left the Assembly hall.

NINE

The captain had been swallowed up by a crowd of delegates, all anxious to talk to him. Hoshi had wandered off in search of the Andorian translator. Malcolm was going on and on about how well trained Sen's bodyguards were ("Look at the coordination . . . the way they move—no wasted motion whatsoever. Remarkable"), but Travis, frankly, wasn't paying all that much attention to any of it. He was too busy counting up the number of uniformed Thelasians he'd seen over the last hour or so, both inside (and outside) the Assembly. Dozens, at least. No, more like hundreds. Functionaries, escorts attached to each of the Assembly delegations, security personnel, maintenance workers . . . the Thelasian government was huge, obviously. The thought of how huge impressed him. Actually, "impressed" wasn't the right word, "disheartened" was closer to the truth. Maybe even a little depressed. The task he'd set himself last night, the task that had been okayed by the captain this morning, before the shuttle launched, the task of wading his way through that bureaucracy to find *Horizon*'s money, suddenly seemed impossibly big.

"Now, how do they do that?" Malcolm asked, interrupting his train of thought, and Travis, even though he knew the question was rhetorical, followed Reed's gaze to the front of the Assembly, where the last of

Sen's bodyguards were now beginning to exit, four at a time, two facing the left side of the hall, two the right, each pair marching in perfect lockstep with the other, while simultaneously scanning the crowd and keeping one hand on their weapons.

He had to admit it was an impressive sight. Unnaturally so, in fact.

"That's the sixty-four-thousand-dollar question, all right," Travis said.

Malcolm frowned at him. "The what?"

"They're chipped."

Travis looked around Malcolm to see who had spoken. He found himself staring at a very short, very pale, humanoid. Male or female, it was impossible to tell.

"Chipped?" Travis asked.

A second humanoid, identical to the first (a twin, perhaps?), leaned around that one and said again:

"Chipped." The second humanoid pointed to the side of its head. "Neural implant. All the guards have to have them."

"Have to be on the network at all times."

"When they're working."

"Of course when they're working."

"And tall. They have to be tall, too."

"Even when they're not working."

"Two point one two five meters. That's tall."

"Of course to us, anything above one-five is tall."

Travis looked from one humanoid to the other, heard the opening bars of "We Welcome You to Munchkinland" in his head, and tried hard not to laugh.

"I'm Lieutenant Malcolm Reed," Malcolm said. "This is my shipmate, Ensign Travis Mayweather. We're from . . ."

"*Enterprise,*" the first said. "Like your captain."

"That's right," Reed said.

The first little alien closed its eyes. They stayed close for a beat; then it opened them again, and said: "*Enterprise.* Initial warp-five-capable vessel, developed by Starfleet, headquartered Sol system, Planet Three, Earth, Level-Four Technological Development, Dominant Culture: Anglo-Saxon. Operations head: Admiral Robert McCormick. Form of planetary government: Representative democracy. Current head . . ."

"How do you know all that?" Travis asked, guessing the answer the second he spoke, which the little alien confirmed by tapping the side of its head and saying, "Chipped. Networked."

Travis and Malcolm exchanged glances.

"And who are you?" Reed asked. "What race . . ."

"Poz," the first said, interrupting.

"Verkin," said the other.

"We are Bynar."

"Were. Not anymore."

"Now we're freelance."

"Broke the network."

"Hopped a transport."

"Stowed away."

"And here we are."

The two looked inordinately pleased with themselves.

Malcolm held out his hand then. The two Bynar stared at it.

"It's a human custom," Reed said. "A way of greeting one another. Shaking hands."

He showed them how to do it.

"Interesting," Poz said.

"Poor hygienic practice," Verkin said. "No worry for

us—cross-species infection rates are minuscule—but among members of your own race . . ." The alien's voice trailed off, and it shook its head. "Bad habit."

Malcolm frowned.

"So these bodyguards," Travis said. "They're tied in to a network, so they're all getting the same commands . . ."

"At the exact same instant," Poz said.

"Makes sense, I suppose," Reed said, frowning, clearly uncomfortable with the idea.

"Critical response situations demand instantaneous communication and informational clarity," Poz said.

"Why waste time with words?" Verkin said.

"And the chip provides this communication?"

"Direct thought transmission."

"And occasionally, more," Verkin said.

"Unsubstantiated," Poz said.

"The Straz case," Verkin said.

The two glared at each other.

"More?" Travis asked. "What do you mean more?"

The two aliens continued to glare at each other.

"Hmmphhh," Poz said.

"Hmmphhh," Verkin concurred.

"There is conflicting evidence," Poz went on. "However . . ."

"However," Verkin nodded.

"Some believe the technology has been taken a step further. That there are now chips which, once implanted, allow not just for thought transmission but actual control of a subject's movements."

"Control?" Travis shuddered involuntarily. The idea of someone putting a chip in his head, taking charge of his movements . . .

"The concept is simple enough. The interface is

extended deeper into the brain structures. The implant overrides conscious thought decision."

"There are rumors," Verkin said quietly, leaning forward, "that First Governor Sen has used the technique on some of his more recalcitrant political opponents. A form of punishment. The Separatists have made this charge on several occasions."

"The Separatists." Reed and Travis looked at each other. "Who are they?"

This time, it was Verkin who closed his eyes for a moment, accessing the network, and then opened them again.

" 'Separatist.' Commonly used terminology for members of an underground political movement that came to prominence over the last half-decade throughout the Thelasian Confederacy. Name arises from the core of their political belief system, that the Thelasian race must seek independence from the larger trade organization that at present governs all aspects of their lives, before the inevitable collapse of that organization threatens fundamental political stability."

Inevitable collapse, Travis thought. Based on what T'Pol had told them, that sounded about right.

"Sen did not appreciate their point of view."

"Not in the least."

"He had the group outlawed."

"And Straz . . ." Poz shook his head. "Terrible thing."

"Straz?" Reed frowned. "Who's Straz?"

"Their leader."

"Former leader."

"Made the mistake of criticizing Sen before the Trade Assembly. Taken to task in a private meeting with the governor."

"Now a minor functionary in the Intelligence corps."

"Very minor."

"And a strong supporter of the governor's."

"Very strong."

"Word to the wise," Poz said, leaning closer. "Your captain should watch what he says."

"Who he says it to."

"Or he may end up the same way."

Malcolm nodded. "I'll take note of that."

Hoshi fought her way through the crowd surrounding Captain Archer to the Andorians, who were all clustered together, arguing (what else?) among themselves and with every other delegate in speaking distance. All, that is, except Theera, who still stood apart from the others, looking completely detached from the proceedings.

Hoshi took a moment to study her before approaching.

She was tall for an Andorian—one hundred seventy centimeters, at a guess, and lean—sixty kilos at the most. Built like an athlete, Hoshi thought, a runner, except that she stood with a certain stiffness—like someone not really comfortable with her own body. Her skin was a dark, uniform shade of blue. Her hair was clipped short, to the nape of her neck. Her uniform looked brand-new—the dark brown coverall sharply creased, the black sash that ran from her left shoulder down to her waist spotlessly clean and shiny.

There was a scar on the brow ridge just above her left temple—vaguely circular in shape. Hoshi wondered if it was a souvenir of the alien attack. Correction, the Antianna attack. That put her in mind of the signal. Which of the fifty-seven pulses that she hadn't been able to make heads or tails of Theera had managed to assign meaning to? Why was it a tentative translation? She had a lot of questions. Time to start getting some answers.

She cleared her throat.

"Ensign Sato. You desire something?"

Theera had spoken without turning. Hoshi was too surprised to respond for a second.

"Yes, I—how did you know my name?" she finally managed.

"The ambassador has briefed us on your starship. Your personnel." Theera did turn to face Hoshi now. From this angle, the scar was practically invisible. "I assume you seek information about the translation."

"You read my mind," Hoshi said, offering a small smile.

"I did not."

Theera's expression didn't change.

"No," Hoshi said quickly. "You read my mind— that's a saying we have. Humans. It just means that you're exactly right. That's what I was thinking."

"Obviously," Theera said, and then before Hoshi could respond, continued, "I suggest you speak with the mediators. They have all relevant data."

"I plan to. But I was hoping that I could talk to you as well. I'm a little confused by what Governor Sen said. Has there been a translation or not?"

"The Mediators can answer that question better than I."

"But it's your work they're building on."

Theera shifted uncomfortably. "Yes."

Hoshi waited for her to say more, for further explanation. None was forthcoming.

That was odd.

"Can you tell me at least which of the pulses you were working with?" Hoshi asked. "I'd been looking at the first half-dozen most closely—arbitrarily assigning meanings to some of the smaller forms within each wave, looking for some kind of pattern . . ."

Theera was shaking her head. "Again—I would suggest talking to the Mediators."

"You could at least tell me whether or not it was one of the first half-dozen pulses," Hoshi said, allowing a little of the exasperation she felt to come through in her voice.

"Which of the first half-dozen," Theera repeated, and at that moment their eyes met, and Hoshi had the most ridiculous sensation that the Andorian didn't have the slightest idea what she was talking about. Ridiculous, of course. The Andorian clearly must have spent as much time as Hoshi with the signal; how could she not know which pulse she'd been focusing on?

Hoshi pulled out the handheld UT module she was carrying with her. "I have the signal in here," she said. "If it would help to hear . . ."

"Human."

Ambassador Quirsh, standing in the row in front of them, had turned around to face the two of them.

"What are you doing with my translator?"

"I was—"

"Hoping to steal credit for our achievement?"

"No, I . . ."

"I forbid you to converse with her," the ambassador—or rather, the legate, though actually, of course, he was the gunnery officer—said, drawing himself up straighter.

Hoshi put the handheld back in her pocket.

"Ambassador Quirsh. We're all working toward the same goal here," she said. "We're all trying to find out the reason for these attacks. To understand what the aliens want. I don't see how sharing . . ."

"Humans and Andorians? Working toward the same goal?" Quirsh wagged a fat blue finger in her face. "That is a laughable suggestion. Laughable." As if to prove his point, Quirsh actually started laughing then.

Some of the other Andorians immediately joined in.

"Ha," another snorted.

"Ha, ha," said a third.

Quirsh kept wagging his finger. Hoshi felt the urge to snap it off and hand it back to him.

"May I remind you of events at P'Jem?" she said. "The Vulcan monastery? Weren't we working toward the same goal then? Making sure the treaty terms between yourselves and the Vulcans were honored?"

Hoshi was referring to one of *Enterprise*'s earliest missions, when Captain Archer had discovered an illegal Vulcan listening outpost hidden beneath a monastery on the planet P'Jem. The post's exposure—and the subsequent destruction of it and the Vulcan monastery—had convinced the Andorians (in particular, Commander Shran, their leader) that the humans were not simply Vulcan lackeys, and had been the start of the current rapprochement between the two species.

"P'Jem," Quirsh snorted. "Your captain has shared with me the fairy-tale version of what happened at P'Jem. Claiming that he was responsible for the exposure of the outpost."

"That's exactly what happened."

"More likely the Vulcans knew our heroic comrades had discovered their secret. More likely they commanded your captain," here Quirsh jabbed with his finger again, "to pretend to turn against them, to befriend Guardsman Shran in the hopes of worming his way into our confidences."

"That's simply not true," Hoshi said.

Quirsh glared at her. "Are you calling me a liar?"

Yes, Hoshi thought.

"Of course not," she said, gritting her teeth. "But I'm certain a careful review of the events at the monastery . . ."

"Everyone getting along all right?"

She felt a hand on her shoulder, and turned to see Captain Archer standing alongside her.

"Your subordinate," Quirsh said, "has insulted me."

Hoshi glared. "With all due respect, Ambassador, that's simply not the case. I was merely stating that P'Jem—"

Quirsh threw up his hands. "P'Jem again? Are we never to hear the end of this?"

Archer's hand tightened ever-so-slightly on Hoshi's shoulder. "Ambassador, I apologize for any misunderstandings between you and my translator here. The important thing, of course, is not what happened at P'Jem, but what happens here. What we can accomplish if we work together. Building on the efforts of your translator."

The captain smiled at Theera, who—Hoshi saw—had taken a few steps back from the group. Establishing her boundaries again.

She nodded her head toward Archer, in recognition of the compliment, but said nothing.

"Hmmmff," Quirsh said, somewhat mollified.

"Perhaps you are right. However, we have turned all our data on the Antianna signal over to the Kanthropians. As I believe Technician Theera made clear, you should speak with them."

He glared at Hoshi, who forced herself to smile in return.

"Of course," she said. "Forgive any intrusion on my part. I'm simply anxious to complete the translation."

Quirsh continued to glare, as if he didn't believe her for a second.

Finally, the Andorian turned and nodded to Archer.

"Good day to you, Captain," he said, and swept toward the chamber exit, the other Andorians trailing in his wake, Theera among them.

As soon as he was out of earshot, Hoshi turned to the captain. "Sir, I did not insult him. I was just . . ."

"I know, I know. The man's an idiot. Soon to be replaced, never fear. But until then . . . we'd better play nice. This is not the time for any sort of incident."

"Yes, sir," Hoshi said, knowing Archer was thinking about the scheduled interspecies peace summit back on Earth, in less than two weeks' time. The Andorians, the Tellarites, the Vulcans, almost a dozen species in all would be gathering to discuss spheres of influence, trade agreements, self-defense pacts, and the like. It was a project near and dear to the captain's heart. In fact, Hoshi didn't think it would be stretching the truth too much to say that the conference wouldn't be happening without Jonathan Archer's efforts. So she would be nice to Quirsh.

Even if it killed her.

"Talk to the Kanthropians," the captain said. "I guess that's what we'd better plan to do then."

"Yes, sir. I gather they're some sort of interspecies

mediators. When we get back to *Enterprise,* I'll request a meeting with their representatives. See if I can't . . ."

Archer was shaking his head. "We're not going back to the ship tonight."

"Sir?"

"Change in plans. We've been invited to a party."

"A party?"

"Governor Sen's reception."

"But I thought . . ." She frowned. "Didn't he say that was for the delegates?"

"And now . . . us."

"Why the special treatment?"

"Not quite sure," Archer said. "Something to think about, though—wouldn't you say?"

"I would," she replied, adding it to the list she'd been compiling in her head of things to ponder, just underneath the fifty-seven pulses, the Antianna sensor readings, and Theera's puzzling behavior.

TEN

The humans had accepted the invitation, Prian reported, and were even now on their way to the guest quarters the governor had provided. Sen signaled his acknowledgment through the implant and, that part of this evening's plan taken care of, activated the e-stat privacy protocol and directed Roia to disable the systems feed once more, to begin transferring the last of the monies from the consortiums into his private accounts.

While waiting for her to do so, he spun in his chair, and looked out the window at the city beneath him. His gaze went automatically, unconsciously, to the shopping bazaar, the very heart of the Prex, the center of his world for the last century and a half. He would be sorry to leave it; those streets held memories for him, memories of his youth as a vendor for the Dalok silk combine, of the twenty years he'd spent as an arms merchant for the Shandreeki smugglers, of the decade, only recently past, when he'd visited it as a returning hero, the viceroy of Coreida, the avenger of dozens of ambushed cargo ships.

Lately, of course, his visits there had been greeted with much less good cheer—when he'd gone in with a troop of bodyguards, in search of Separatists, or to collect the taxes that had fallen delinquent. Some chided Sen behind his back, he knew, for playing the part of tax collector when he had an entire bureaucracy charged with that task, but the governor felt it important to make a statement, to set an example. If he allowed a merchant within plain sight of his office to mock the Confederacy tariffs, if he did not personally skin such delinquents alive . . .

Of course, in the end his actions had mattered little. Trading, and the tax receipts it generated, was down five percent this past month. Sen had managed to cover the shortfall by slapping a small surcharge on some sales, and transferring contingency monies from elsewhere in the budget to meet operating expenses, but this was the fourth month in a row revenue had been down, and the trend, his advisors assured him, was going to continue. There was nothing he could do to reverse it.

The Confederacy, they told him, was on the verge of bankruptcy. Sen quickly realized he had a choice to make then, and—just as quickly—had made it.

Roia signaled him; the funds were in his account. The systems feed had been reactivated. *Enterprise*'s crew had arrived in their quarters and were beginning to use the terminals there to access the public information archives.

Sen tied into their separate uplinks so he could monitor their activities.

He was primarily concerned with Archer—the only one of the four, he saw, whose uplink to the archives was inactive. No matter. He took care of the most important thing first, had the system make note of and tag the captain's biosigns so that Sen would know his exact whereabouts at all times. That done, he activated the visual monitor, and saw that Archer was simply lying on the bed assigned him. Not sleeping—his eyes were open—but thinking. Contemplating. Sen nodded his silent approval; that was just what he would be doing in Archer's position. Considering the facts, among which were certain to be puzzlement at his invitation to the reception—his inclusion in the Confederacy's affairs at such a high level. Archer had to be suspicious. The odds that he would be able to figure out Sen's true motives, however, were infinitesimal.

The governor switched the monitor to the next room, and smiled.

He was looking at the female. The linguist.

Her uplink was active. She was querying multiple databases within the archives for information on the Mediators, and their work with the Antianna signal. He thought briefly of tying into her connection, coming to her rescue, as it were, with additional information, but reluctantly decided against it. Better not to alert the humans as to just how extensive his surveillance of them was. He would have his chance to talk to the female tonight, at the reception. Perhaps (he allowed himself a small smile of pleasure) even do more than talk.

Roia notified him of an incoming signal, from the Qo'noS convoy. He asked her to wait one moment while he checked in on the other two members of the *Enterprise* crew. One was, oddly enough, viewing historical records of previous trading activities between the Confederacy and Earth cargo vessels—harmless enough activity, while the other was—

Sen frowned.

The other member of *Enterprise*'s crew, a slightly built dark-haired man, had somehow managed to access construction blueprints of the guest quarters, and was in fact on the verge of discovering how extensive the security/monitoring systems in that building were.

The governor immediately disabled his access to those blueprints, and after briefly considering (and then deciding against) sending a lethal electric shock back through the uplink to eliminate the little man as a concern altogether, had Roia flag his biosigns as well, so that the restrictions on his access to the system would follow him no matter where he went on Procyron. It was a difficult protocol to initiate, she informed him, one that would occupy a considerable chunk of her remaining processing power. Sen told her to do it anyway, adding that she need maintain the protocol only for the next few hours—until the governor was no longer planetside. That done, he closed the monitoring system, and activated the communications uplink to the Qo'noS convoy, shaking his head as he did so. First Archer, and now the dark-haired man . . .

These humans, he thought. *Too clever by half.*

The screen before him wavered, cleared, and displayed the image of the convoy's commander.

"Governor Sen."

"Commander. Welcome."

"You are ready?"

"I will be. In approximately five hours."

"And you have the access codes?"

"I do."

"And the human?"

"I'll have him then as well."

"Excellent." The commander smiled, displaying a set of stained, yellowing teeth—some of them rather sharp-looking. He looked, the governor thought, not so much happy as . . . ready to eat.

Sen smiled back. "And you'll have the currency?"

The commander grunted in the affirmative, managing to look somewhat insulted in the process.

"Five hours," the commander repeated. There was nothing more to say after that, and rather than chatter on like so many of the Confederacy's members, the commander simply closed the channel.

Brevity, Sen thought. *Very refreshing.*

He rose from his seat then, and went to prepare—for the reception, and certain other events set to occur simultaneously.

Hoshi heard Malcolm swear, once, then a second time. Footsteps sounded, coming from his room into hers.

"Damn thing just kicked me off the system."

She turned away from the monitor. "What?"

"I was . . ." Reed shook his head. "Never mind. Can I use yours for a second?"

Hoshi shrugged, and got up from her chair. She'd just been going in circles the last few minutes anyway, accessing the same pieces of information over and over again, albeit through different links. Some of it interesting, some of it not. There was very little—almost nothing—on the work the Mediators had done on the alien signal; no surprise there, considering what they'd said regarding the preliminary nature of their work. She had found a treasure trove of information on the Kanthropians themselves. They were, literally, mediators, they spent their time traveling about the galaxy, or this part of the galaxy, anyway, trying to broker peace between warring parties, or find common ground in disputes of all kinds, commercial, territorial, military . . . A lot of their work involved linguistics as a matter of course. There were multiple references within the system that called them "the most well-trained, gifted translators in the quadrant." Hoshi looked forward to talking to them—perhaps tonight, if they were at Sen's reception, certainly tomorrow, if not.

The most interesting information she'd found, however, had to do not with the Mediators, but Theera—First Technician R'shee Theera, of the Andorian Science Service, posted to the Andorian *Cruiser Lokune* for the past two years. Theera's work during that time had focused on something called the Universal Translator Project, which was described as "an attempt to move beyond dictionary-based translation to the development of a machine intelligence that could actually parse speech for linguistic concepts."

Shades of Doctor Teodoro, Hoshi thought, and then: Theera and I should have a lot to talk about.

Except that—based on their recent encounter—she wasn't sure any sort of conversation between the two of them was going to happen.

Reed cursed again.

"Still nothing?" Hoshi asked.

"No." He frowned. "Where the hell did it all go?"

"Where did what go?"

Hoshi turned and saw the captain standing in the doorway to her room.

"The data I was looking at," Reed said. "It was on my screen a few minutes ago and all at once . . . the system just shut down. When I got back on again . . . it was gone."

"Gone?" Archer repeated.

"Without a trace," Reed said. "As if it never existed

at all. I thought perhaps it was a problem with my terminal, but . . ."

"Sensitive data?"

"Well . . . yes, I suppose you might say so."

"Would the governor say so?"

"Without a doubt."

It was pretty clear to Hoshi what had happened. "They locked you out."

"That seems the most likely explanation," Reed said, turning in the chair to face her now. "Although to do that, they'd have to be . . ."

Archer's communicator sounded.

"Hold that thought," the captain said, and opened a channel.

"Archer here."

"Captain?" It was Commander Tucker. "Thought you'd be heading back right about now."

"That was the plan. But something's come up," the captain said. He started to explain—not just about the reception, but about the credit chits Sen had given them to shop with and the guest quarters he'd provided. The quarters were an act of generosity—four bedrooms, each twice the size of the captain's quarters aboard *Enterprise*, along with an elaborately furnished common room that could have comfortably held the bridge and the ready room with space to spare—that Hoshi had found it difficult to understand up until just this moment, that is. As the captain continued talking, Reed stood and left the room. He returned holding his padd, and showed Hoshi the display screen. It read:

Can't talk here being monitored

She nodded, took the padd from him, and typed in a message of her own.

Reed looked at it and smiled.

Trip and the captain, meanwhile, were still talking.

". . . still want to get that shuttle back up here— sooner rather than later."

The captain frowned. "Tomorrow isn't soon enough?"

"I got the manpower tonight, Captain. Can't say as I will then."

"Sir?"

All three of them—Hoshi, Reed, and Archer— turned as one. Travis stood in the doorway.

"I can take the shuttle back up."

Archer frowned.

"What about the reception?" he asked.

"What about *Horizon*'s money?" Malcolm chimed in.

Mayweather smiled.

"I found something," he began. "In the Thelasian archives . . ."

"Ah," Hoshi said, cutting him off, and holding the padd so that Travis too, could see it.

He frowned.

"Trip," Archer said into the communicator. "We'll get right back to you."

"Sir?"

"We'll get right back to you," the captain repeated. "Out."

He closed the communicator, and turned to the others.

"I have an idea," he said. "Let's go shopping."

ELEVEN

It turned out that the money was, in fact, precisely why Travis wanted to get back to *Enterprise*.

While looking through the Thelasian archives, he'd found (to his surprise) an entry on *Horizon*. A badly outdated entry, one that listed the ship's top speed as warp one point five, its captain as Paul Mayweather (Paul Sr., Travis's father, dead almost a year now), but did, in fact, make reference to a petition filed on Morianne more than a decade earlier. The problem was, only a ranking office of the *S.S. Horizon* could access those records. So Travis needed to find his family's ship. And to do that . . .

"I need to be back on *Enterprise*," he finished explaining.

Before the captain could respond, Hoshi interrupted.

"We might be able to find a com station down here," she said. "In fact, considering the extent of the Thelasian trading network, you might even have a better chance of finding *Horizon* through their facilities."

"Then they'll know what he's up to," Reed interjected. "Better off doing the search through a secure network."

"How secure can any network be around here?" Hoshi asked.

Malcolm nodded. "True enough."

"People." The captain stopped in the middle of the street. "All interesting points, but you ignore two things. Number one, we're supposed to be at this reception in just a few hours. So if we're going to take advantage of the governor's generosity . . ."

"I don't really need to go shopping for something to wear, sir," Hoshi said. "My mother sent a dress to me for my birthday last year. Very formal. I'm sure it would be appropriate."

"And number two," the captain continued, ignoring the interruption, "Trip really needs the shuttle back on board *Enterprise*. So if you want to go, Ensign . . ."

"Aye, sir."

"Good. Then you're dismissed. Tell Trip I will speak with him after the reception."

Another nod, and Travis left them then. The three of them then split up, each taking a handful of the credit chits Sen had given them, making plans to rendezvous back at the guest quarters in another hour. It took Archer longer than that, though, to find something he thought suitable: first, he was recognized by an assembly delegate who began badgering him on the importance of safe travel corridors, then he got completely turned around and wandered down a portion of the Prex that was given over to currency speculators. Then he ran into Malcolm—who he suspected might have been following him the whole time—who promptly began haranguing the captain for permission to bring one of the MACOS, or even Chief Lee, planetside to help with security, given that Sen's intentions were now—more than ever—suspect. Eventually (after a few futile minutes spent trying to convince Reed that his worries were misplaced, that nothing untoward was going to happen tonight at the reception, there were simply going to be too many people there), the captain ordered Malcolm to go find himself something suitable to wear.

Archer waited until he was gone, and then continued his own shopping, at last finding something that not only looked appropriately formal but fell within his price range.

He returned to the guest quarters to find Hoshi waiting for him, as excited as he'd seen her in a long while.

"You found something good?" he asked.

"Yes, sir," she said. "A private language database. Bought seven new languages for the UT, including one with conditional verb forms. Conditional verb forms." She shook her head in amazement. "I've never seen anything like it. The language is called Vendorian, and apparently the people—"

"Vendorians, yes. Interesting. But I was asking about the party. If you found anything to wear?"

Hoshi frowned. "Well . . ."

The captain shook his head. "You'd better get back out there then. The reception starts in another hour and a half."

Hoshi didn't move. She cleared her throat. "The thing is, sir, database access time was quite expensive."

"How expensive?"

She smiled weakly.

"You spent all the chits?"

"Yes, sir. But there's that dress my mother bought me. I was thinking I could have that beamed down."

The captain sighed. "All right. Let's see what we can do."

But it wasn't as simple as all that. They had to have clearance to use their transporter beam. Had to talk to the right people, and Archer couldn't find Prian to smooth the way. The person he was speaking to told the captain to stand by. Time passed.

A chime sounded.

"That's the door," Hoshi said. "I'll get it."

She did. The captain overheard talking, and then the sound of the door closing.

Hoshi came back carrying a box. There was a note on the top of the box.

"It's addressed to me," she said, reading off the card. "Hoshi Sato. Compliments of Governor Sen."

Hoshi opened the box. She reached inside and pulled out a single piece of red cloth, which she held up in the air.

"It's fabric," she said. "Some kind of stretchy fabric."

"I think it's a dress."

"It's too small to be a dress."

"It's a dress."

"Probably another piece in here," she said, and started digging around in the box.

There wasn't though. Just a pair of ridiculously high heels.

"It's not a dress," she said again.

"Go try it on," Archer said.

"Sir . . ."

"Present from the governor," he said. "We don't want to insult the governor."

She sighed, and went into the room she'd been assigned.

Five minutes on, by Archer's reckoning, she hadn't come out.

"Everything okay in there?"

Silence.

"Hoshi . . ."

The door opened, and the first thing that registered on Archer's consciousness was that it was a small piece of fabric indeed.

The second thing was that his communications officer was a very attractive woman. He'd known that intellectually, of course, but it hadn't really struck him before. It struck him now.

Like a ton of bricks, it struck him.

Hoshi looked at him, and then down at the ground.

"I don't feel comfortable," she said.

"You look wonderful," Archer told her.

She glanced up at him and smiled.

Archer returned the smile, remembered who had given her the dress, and frowned.

Right then the door to their quarters opened, and Reed walked in, holding up a box.

"Found something that looks remarkably like an old-style Navy dress shirt. Now some might think this a bit too flamboyant, but my feeling is, when you've got it . . ."

His voice trailed off as he caught sight of Hoshi.

". . . flaunt it," he said. "Your mother bought you that?"

She glared. "No, my mother did not buy me this."

He looked even more confused. "You bought it?"

"No!"

"It's a present from the governor," Archer supplied.

"Sen."

"Yes, Sen."

"Governor Sen." Reed still looked confused. "Why is he buying Hoshi a dress?"

The captain was wondering that himself.

"Why don't we get changed," he suggested, "and go find out?"

She didn't have to wear the dress, Archer had told her. If she was uncomfortable (which, of course, she was). But Hoshi could read between the lines of what the captain was saying. Sen would be insulted if she didn't. And the captain wanted Sen in an expansive, joyous mood. A talkative mood. Insofar as such a thing was possible. So she wore the dress. And let her hair down. She looked like a different person. Ready for a party. The captain looked ready too: he had purchased something akin to an old-fashioned tuxedo, with a vest instead of a coat jacket, an open-collar shirt. He looked, Hoshi thought, dashing. As for Malcolm . . .

Well, his "Navy dress shirt" was blue and white, as garishly loud as she'd expected, and if he gave her any more grief about her outfit . . . she was going to give it right back.

The reception was being held at the solarium. An elegant-sounding word, which (Hoshi knew) was derived from the Latin, originally referring to a Roman water clock, circa second century BC, though the latter-day, more common (and here, more apropos) definition of the word was a glass-enclosed porch or living room—a sun parlor.

This sun parlor, however, was at the very top of the tallest structure she had ever seen in her life. A building that reminded her more than anything else of the old Space Needle back on Earth, a single slim, towering building that tapered off to a point so high up into the sky as to be invisible.

A handful of H'ratoi, also dressed to the nines, shared the elevator ride up to the top with them. Hoshi was gratified to see that one of the females had on an outfit that made Sen's gift look like an overcoat.

It was a long way up. A long ride. Hoshi spent the time wondering if the Kanthropians would be there. If they'd be any more forthcoming than Theera regarding the work they'd done on the Antianna signal. Wondering if Theera's work tied in to what she'd been reading about this afternoon—the Universal Translator Project. Most likely, though, the Kanthropians wouldn't know anything about that. She'd have to talk to Theera regarding the wider implications of this translation. She wondered if Governor Sen could help her get to the Andorian—get Theera to talk to her. Probably. She wondered what she'd have to do to make that happen. Nothing she wanted to think about too hard. And speaking of Sen . . .

What was going to happen when she saw him tonight, which most certainly she would? What should she say to him? Thanks? She'd already sent along a message to that effect after deciding to wear the dress; the functionary who received it assured her he would pass the missive along directly to Sen, though he also intimated that the governor would be most appreciative if Hoshi relayed her gratitude in person. That conjured up a whole new series of images that made her want to find the shuttle and head back to *Enterprise* as fast as the little ship could carry her.

She shuddered involuntarily.

"Cold?" the captain asked.

He held out his vest to her.

"No. Thanks." She smiled. "Just wondering what the party'll be like."

The elevator slowed, and came to a stop.

"It'll be a formal kind of thing is my guess. Fairly quiet," he added. "You remember Captain Hernandez's swearing-in ceremony?"

Hoshi grimaced. "I remember all right."

"Something like that," the captain said. "Sedate."

"Somnambulent," Hoshi responded, as the elevator doors opened, and they were struck by a sudden wall of noise and heat and light.

The solarium was the size of a small concert hall. It was jammed tight with people.

"Sedate," Reed said, standing aside to let the H'ratoi pass.

Archer frowned. "Or not."

The captain told them to mingle, so off she went.

Except after forcing her way into the heart of the crowd, Hoshi barely had enough space to stand, much less start a conversation. Her guess, the solarium was half the size of the Trade Assembly, and crowded with about twice as many people.

Nonetheless, she started pushing her way through; she met Tellarites and a Vulcan (a member of the Cultural Exchange Commission who, she learned in an abbreviated conversation, had known T'Pol's mother), Maszakians and Pfau, and a very tall, very rude Conani delegate, who lectured her on the foolishness of attempting to negotiate with terrorists such as the Antianna. She also passed by (but did not exchange words with) Ambassador Quirsh, who glared in response to her tentatively offered smile. Fine. She didn't need to talk to him anymore. Who she needed to speak with were the Mediators, except that nowhere in the entire room did she see anything resembling a brown robe. Maybe they weren't coming; they didn't, based on what she'd seen of and read about them, seem like the partying type.

She mingled a bit more.

Eventually, she reached the outer edges of the circle-shaped space, where the crowd thinned slightly, and she turned to take in the room as a whole. It was a breathtakingly beautiful structure; the walls—transparent to the stars outside—curved gently upward, forming a dome whose apex was perhaps thirty meters above the floor. The elevators were directly under that apex; she saw now that the elevator shaft continued upward to the very top, to a second, much smaller room, whose floor was made of the same transparent material as the walls and ceiling. There were at least a dozen guards in that room, which was empty otherwise. Probably some kind of private meeting room, an office.

She turned away from the party then, and looked out through the glass, out over Tura Prex. A sea of lights swam beneath her—far, far beneath her. The stars in the sky seemed closer. Some of them, she realized, were ships. Patrol vessels, most likely, similar to the ones that had escorted them down to the planet's surface earlier. She wondered just how high up they were here.

She turned back toward the part again, noticed a horseshoe-shaped line of tables partway across the room. Food. Drink. Might as well, since she didn't seem to be doing much good here otherwise. She made her way toward the closest table. A man in a dark blue coverall stood behind it. As she approached, he smiled at her.

"Nice dress," he said.

Hoshi smiled back. "Thanks." She picked up a glass of something off the table—something blue—and sniffed it.

"Hold on a minute," the man said. "Before you drink . . ."

He ran a scanner of some sort over her and looked at the results.

"It's safe for you. Well, relatively safe. As far as intoxicating beverages go." He smiled. "Two of those, you'll certainly be having a good time."

Hoshi frowned. The last thing she needed to be right now was drunk. On the other hand . . .

She could stand to relax a little bit.

"Bottoms up," she said to the man, and took a sip.

Her throat burned. Her eyes widened, and watered.

"Bottoms up?" the server asked, frowning.

She held up a finger. One minute.

"Colloquialism," she managed a second later. "It means good health. Cheers."

"Ah."

"So what is this?" she asked, holding the glass up.

"Romulan ale. You like?"

Hoshi swirled the drink around. Swirl, swirl, swirl. She felt a little swirly herself.

She felt, for the first time in what seemed like forever, like she was starting to relax.

"I like," she said, and raised the glass to take another sip.

Then, out of the corner of her eye, she saw another shade of blue. Blue skin. An Andorian. Theera, standing a few tables down. Hoshi saw brown as well. Two Mediators standing next to her. The three of them seemed to be arguing about something.

Hoshi set her glass back down on the table, and went to find out what.

The captain had gone searching for, and after some effort found, the Maszakian delegate who had spoken up that afternoon in the Trade Assembly. The two of them had retired to the edges of the crowd, to talk in as quiet—and private—a place as could be found in the solarium.

"Sen represents the last gasp of the old Thelasian autocrats," the Maszakian—whose name was Yandreas—said. "He does not understand how the universe has changed around him. The Confederacy no longer holds a monopoly on the interior quadrant markets. Species such as yours, Captain, have pushed past the warp barriers that kept them confined to their immediate stellar neighborhoods, and dependent on the Confederacy's ships for the goods of the larger galaxy."

"And Sen—and these autocrats as well—they're not willing to change?"

"Whether or not they are willing to change matters little," Yandreas said. "The facts are what they are."

"The Confederacy is in trouble."

Yandreas nodded. "Revenues from trading taxes and surcharges have fallen dramatically over the last few years. There is great concern among some of the larger interstellar financial consortiums. The viability of some of the outlying Thelasian posts is in question. In fact," the alien looked around to make sure no one was listening, and then leaned closer, "I would say the viability of the Confederacy as a whole is in question."

No surprise there, Archer thought.

"It would seem to me," the captain began, framing

his words carefully, "that what happened in the Trade Assembly today—the declaration of war—may impact on that viability."

"How so?"

"War is—among other things—a commercial enterprise."

"Are you suggesting that the governor deliberately started this war?"

Archer let the words hang there a moment before responding.

"Not . . . necessarily. But he doesn't seem to be trying too hard to avoid it, does he?"

"He was elected to deal with these attacks, Captain. As he dealt with the problems at Coreida."

"Yes," the captain said. That was the third time today he'd heard the word. "I've heard a lot of talk about Coreida. But I've yet to hear exactly what happened there."

"It's a long story," Yandreas said.

"Well." Archer smiled. "The night is young."

The Maszakian frowned. "Excuse me?"

"Figure of speech," Archer said. "It means we have plenty of time."

"Ah." The Maszakian nodded. "Very well then," he said, and began his story.

Archer leaned closer, so as not to miss a word.

Immediately on entering the room, Malcolm had pushed his way through the mob and staked out a spot near the edge of the party, where he could watch what was happening. Captain's orders be damned, he had no intention of mingling or taking the temperature of the crowd, trying to figure out the relative strength/size of factions for and against Sen, who might be convinced to delay the war and who was determined to fight it. His job was security. Specifically, the captain's security. Already he didn't like the fact that the party was so crowded, and he had no backup. So he was going to watch Archer like a hawk. Not allow the captain to get too far away from him. And Sen. He was going to keep an eye on the governor as well.

Right now Archer was at two o'clock from him, clear across the room, at the very edge of the party. The captain was talking to one of the delegates from the Assembly. Pleasant, friendly, private conversation. Nothing to worry about there. Sen was at nine o'clock, almost directly to his left, the center of a large, boisterous crowd, a half-dozen of his bodyguards standing nearby. Close enough that Malcolm could see the expression on his face. Polite interest for the most part, and then, every few seconds, Sen's attention seemed to drift. Maybe it was just his imagination, but it seemed to Reed the governor had other things on his mind.

It would be helpful, Malcolm suspected, if he knew exactly what.

The governor was paying attention to two different conversations at once, the one going on in front of his face, the inane blather of the H'ratoi ambassador, and the one in his head, the one that Roia was piping in through the implant, a talk being picked up by the security monitors between the human captain and one of the Maszakian delegates, a talk that kept causing him to frown at inappropriate moments during the ambassador's pontifications.

Had he not been in such a public place, of course, he would have done a lot more than frown, he would have had the Maszakian thrown from the top of the tower, and the human—clearly the instigator in this instance—dismembered, then thrown from the top of the tower. But of course, there were other factors to consider at the moment.

"So do I have it? Your assurance?"

Sen blinked, and realized the H'ratoi had asked him a question.

"Your pardon, Ambassador. I was momentarily distracted—new arrivals." He waved a hand in the direction of the elevators, toward a group of nonexistent newcomers. The ambassador didn't even bother to turn. "What were you saying?"

"The Conani particle weapons—they are impressive, but have yet to stand the test of battle. I do feel that our phased-array disruptors offer the fleet a much more powerful—and reliable—weapon."

The ambassador continued at some length, going on and on about the history of the phased-array disruptor, managing to work in mention of the H'ratoi's numerous "sacrifices" over the last few weeks, and their deserved rights and the Confederacy's moral responsibility to acknowledge those rights, but what he really wanted, of course, was the Confederacy to force all ships in the armada to retrofit those disruptors. Sen had to struggle not to yawn. It was all of very little concern to him, the disruptors, or the particle weapons, the fleet, the war, the H'ratoi, the Maszakians . . . in a very short while, they would all be someone else's problem.

"Ambassador," he interrupted. "As you know I don't make these decisions on my own. But I do want to assure you that my position on these matters will be very clear to the Defense Council when they meet tomorrow morning."

Which was certainly true enough, as far as it went.

"I appreciate that, Governor," the Ambassador said.

"Of course. Now if you'll excuse me." Bowing, Sen took a step backward, and turned . . .

Only to have another figure step directly into his path.

He looked up to see General Jaedez blocking his way forward.

"Governor." The Conani towered over him. Glared down at him. "I wish to speak to you."

"Of course, of course."

"As I told your assistant earlier today, I desire to speak further with the Andorian. The translator."

Sen made a show of frowning. "I thought that meeting had been arranged," he lied. "Were you not contacted?"

"I received no communication from your staff."

"Terrible oversight," Sen said, though of course the oversight had been on his part, oversight to make sure no such meeting happened, at least not before his plans had been finalized, which they were now, so . . .

He subvocalized a request to Roia, who informed him that the entire Andorian legation, including the translator, was indeed present this evening.

"But one that is easily rectified," Sen continued. "I believe the translator is here this evening, in fact, if we are fortunate perhaps we can discover . . ."

He turned, and saw the Andorian right where Roia had said she would be.

What Roia hadn't mentioned was that with her, wearing the red dress, was the human female.

Sen smiled.

". . . exactly where she is. Ah. You see?"

General Jaedez turned and followed his gaze.

"I do," he said. "Thank you, Governor."

"Oh, please, General. Allow me the favor."

"Excuse me?"

Sen smiled. "I'll escort you to her. Make the appropriate introductions."

Jaedez nodded. "That's very gracious of you, Governor."

"Not at all. The pleasure will be mine." He made a show of bowing. "This way, if you please."

Hoshi stopped a few paces shy of the group and listened for a moment, trying to look inconspicuous. Trying to look interested in the food on the table in front of her.

"S-12 is near," one of the Mediators was saying. "A further series of interviews tomorrow . . ."

"No. I have to return to Andoria."

"We understand that. The interviews would delay your departure by a few hours at most."

"During which time I would miss my transport."

"There are courier ships aboard S-12. All have Type-Two FTL, so that the trip to your homeworld would actually be considerably shorter, should that prove . . ."

"What you request," Theera said, "is impossible."

"Not impossible. Quite possible. You are being unreasonable."

The other mediator spoke up. "We have talked with your immediate superior. Ambassador Quirsh. He assured us of your full cooperation."

"I have given you my full cooperation," Theera said, a touch of anger in her voice. "I've told you everything I know."

"Everything you are consciously aware of," the

Mediator said. "There may be more. There are certain procedures—"

"I have told you everything!" Theera said, much louder than before, loud enough that everyone within earshot—including Hoshi—looked up.

Theera visibly gathered herself, took a step back.

"I ask you," the Andorian said, in a much, much, quieter voice, "to leave me alone."

Hoshi frowned. What was going on here? Something to do with the translation, clearly, the Mediators thought Theera was witholding information of some kind, but what?

She walked up to the group and cleared her throat.

"Excuse me," she said.

The Mediators and Theera turned to face her.

"I'm sorry to intrude. I'm—"

"We do not require the services of a courtesan at present," the nearest—the younger—of the two Mediators said.

"You are dismissed," the other added.

Hoshi flushed beet red.

"I'm not a courtesan," she said.

"Indeed?" the first Mediator said, staring at her. At the dress.

Hoshi mentally cursed Sen for sending it, and herself for wearing it.

"I'm Ensign Hoshi Sato—from *Enterprise*. My captain spoke at the Assembly earlier today . . ."

"Ah. Captain Archer."

"That's correct."

"I found his proposal objectionable," the Kanthropian said. "Mediators do not perform their work in expectation of having it turned toward military purposes."

"I'm sorry?"

"Your captain's desire to use the Antianna language as a weapon in this war? To say the least, that does not meet with our approval."

Hoshi frowned. They were missing the point entirely. The captain had, of course, just been proposing that as a way of getting out the information to the Assembly, to let them know that progress on translating the alien signal had been made. But she couldn't very well say that to the Mediators, could she?

"I understand that," she said, choosing her words carefully, "but I can say on Captain Archer's behalf that should your work lead to a peaceful resolution of this conflict, that would be looked on favorably as well."

The Mediator took a moment to absorb those words, and then smiled.

"I believe I understand what you're saying, Ensign Sato."

"Good," Hoshi said, and from the look in his eyes, she thought he did, that he got what the captain's true purpose in speaking up today had been.

"Now, as ship's linguist," she continued, "my job is to find out more about the work that has been done to date on translating the signal. And to offer my assistance in furthering that effort."

The Mediators exchanged glances. The elder of the two cleared his throat.

"As Elder Woden made clear, our work at this stage is preliminary. No firm conclusions can be drawn."

"I understand. I'd still like to take a look at the data."

"It should be available shortly."

"Shortly?"

"Yes."

"Why not now?"

Again, the Mediators exchanged glances. "A decision to release our research can only be made by the full Mediation Council. I am certain it will be discussed at the next opportunity."

"When is that?"

"Soon."

"Soon." Hoshi frowned. "In case you've forgotten, war has been declared. I would think that would make sharing this kind of information urgent, considering that a successful translation could help save lives."

The Mediator nodded. "In theory, you are correct. In practice . . ." He looked right at Theera. "I can safely say that the Council will be hesitant to share data without the confirmation of certain facts."

Hoshi looked from one of them to the other, and wished she knew what, exactly, was going on here.

"And now if you'll excuse us," the Mediator said, bowing. "Ensign Sato, we will speak again, I am certain."

"Of course," she replied.

"Technician Theera." The Mediator turned to the Andorian then, and bowed as well. "We will speak further as well."

"You are mistaken," she said. "I am leaving tomorrow."

"We will speak further," the Mediator reiterated. "Good evening."

Without another word, both Kanthropians walked away, melting into the crowd.

There was an awkward silence.

"So you're leaving tomorrow?" Hoshi asked.

"Yes."

"Returning to Andoria?"

Theera nodded.

"We were there, a few months ago," Hoshi went on. "Our captain and Commander Shran . . . they went down to the ice caves. I saw some images—it's quite beautiful down there."

"Yes. It is."

"We saw the rings too. They were amazing."

Theera nodded again, but said nothing.

So much for establishing a rapport, Hoshi thought.

"Why is it," she asked, suddenly tired of dancing around the subject, "that no one wants to talk about this translation?"

Theera glared. "You'll excuse me," she said, and moved to go past Hoshi.

Hoshi took a step, blocking her way.

"What is it that the Kanthropians think you aren't telling them?"

The Andorian hesitated a second before replying.

And in that second, in her expression, Hoshi saw not just hostility, but fear.

"That is none of your affair," Theera said.

"Forgive me for stating the obvious, but I think it is. I think it's everyone's affair. Like I said, we're about to go to war. People are going to die. Or don't you care about that?"

The Andorian's expression softened.

"You do not understand," she said. "The situation is . . . complicated."

"Yes," Hoshi said. "I get that."

Again, Theera hesitated.

Then she looked over Hoshi's shoulder, and all at once, the expression on her face changed.

"Governor," she said.

Hoshi turned and saw Sen standing directly behind her. General Jaedez was next to him.

"Technician," Sen said, and then turned the full force of his gaze on Hoshi. "Ensign Sato." The governor smiled, and the skin on Hoshi's arm crawled.

"I see you received my gift."

Archer had heard enough.

He thanked the Maszakian for his time, and went in search of his crew. He spotted Malcolm, standing next to one of the refreshment tables. The lieutenant was sipping from a glass in his hand—something orange-brown in color. There was a table full of similar glasses next to him.

"I thought I told you to mingle," Archer said, picking one of the glasses up off the table.

"You did at that," Malcolm said. "I was just taking a litle break."

"Hmmm," He held the glass up to his nose and sniffed. A strong odor, but not an entirely unpleasant one. Reminiscent of some of the better scotches he'd had.

"Bottoms up," he said to Reed, putting it to his lips.

"Sir," the lieutenant said hurriedly. "It's rather strong, I would sip gently at first so that . . ."

But it was too late.

Archer's throat was already on fire.

"Auh," he said, setting the glass back down on the table.

"Sir?" Malcolm asked.

The captain gasped for breath.

He turned away from the crowd and coughed. He coughed again. His eyes watered.

"Captain? Should I seek medical assistance?"

Archer waved him away. He'd be fine. In a minute. He was sure of it.

Fairly sure, anyway.

The captain bent over and put his hands on his knees. Coughed a few more times, took a few deep breaths, and then stood.

"Wow," he said, shaking his head, trying to clear it. "What was that?"

"If I understood the gentleman over there correctly," Reed said, pointing toward a man in a black coverall—a coverall, Archer thought, that looked strangely like the tunic Malcolm had purchased—"it's some sort of a Klingon beverage. *Mot'lok*, I believe he called it."

"Klingon," Archer said, taking a deep breath. It was only fitting. His relationship with the Empire was not a friendly one—at least not at the moment.

They wanted him dead—or, more accurately, they wanted him alive, so that they could take a long time killing him.

Maybe, he thought, they were going to do it with *mot'lok*.

Sen introduced the general to the Andorian linguist, then maneuvered himself into a conversation with the human female. Hoshi. He escorted her to one of the refreshment tables, and offered her a drink. She refused. He offered her food. She refused that as well. The more he tried to do for her, the more resistant she was. Her eyes flashed fire.

His blood stirred. Sen was reminded, once more, of the long-vanished Roia. He wished he had more time; he would have taken the female to the Prex at Saleeas Optim, bought her a Keelan, plied her with the accumulated knowledge of a thousand years of

Thelasian civilization, delicacies from across the civilized worlds of the entire quadrant. As it was . . .

He checked in with Roia. Kareg's ship was close. He had less than an hour.

No time for subtlety.

"Did you enjoy the bazaar, Ensign Hoshi? The Prex?"

"I did."

"Remarkable variety of goods, from worlds that I don't expect you humans have been to before. You have warp-five capability, is that right? Places you won't get to for quite some time, at that speed. Sample the merchandise while you can. I'd be happy to advance you more credits, should you so desire. If there was any particular thing that caught your eye . . ."

She shook her head. "No."

"It is fortunate for you I had the dress, is it not? It looks marvelous on you. As I knew it would."

"Thank you."

The female appeared distracted. She was looking over his shoulder, Sen realized, back toward the Andorian linguist, and General Jaedez. He thought he could guess why.

"You're curious about the translation?" Sen asked.

For the first time, he saw the light of excitement in her eyes.

"Yes. Very."

He leaned closer to her. "I have access to the Kanthropian database. A personal keycode. Would you care to see the information in it?"

She leaned back from him. "I'd be very interested in that, yes."

Sen reached around her and picked up a glass off the table. A goblet, with a brown liquid inside that didn't so much slosh as ooze as he tilted the glass to one side.

"This is *kanar*," he said. "Marvelous drink. Quite safe for your species, I assure you. We have an expert medical staff—xenobiologists very familiar with your species. If I'm remembering correctly," and of course he was, as Roia was feeding him the information as he spoke, "this particular drink will act in a very similar way to alcohol on your blood chemistry. Provide a pleasant, harmless narcotic effect. Please." He held the glass out. "See for yourself."

"No, thank you. I'm less interested in the drink than in the database," she said.

"I admire your dedication," Sen said, and drank the *kanar* down himself. Very refreshing. He set the empty goblet back on the table.

"The keycode is in my office. A short distance from here. If you'd care to accompany me . . ."

She frowned.

"We pass by the Prex," he offered.

"I'm not much of a shopper."

"No shopping, no alcohol . . ." The governor shook his head, made an expression of mock displeasure. "What pleasures do you allow yourself, Ensign Sato?"

"Well . . ."

"Recreational sex?"

The female blinked.

"Recently, I picked up several new techniques from a courtesan of Rigleigh's Pleasure World. Mentally stimulating. Physically challenging. Perhaps you would care for a demonstration?"

The female changed color.

"Is that a yes?" Sen asked.

• • •

The captain set off again into the crowd. This time, Reed went too, staying with Archer long enough so the captain could see him "mingle" and so that he could see Archer safely eased into a conversation with delegates sympathetic to his own views. Translation, rather than war. Reed listened for a few minutes and then excused himself, ostensibly to get a drink but in reality to take up a position directly opposite his previous one, from where—again—he could watch the captain in relative privacy, without fear of interruption.

On his way to that new post, he spotted Sen, standing near Hoshi. Standing very, very near Hoshi.

He smiled. That would be, Malcolm knew, worth a few digs later on. But for now . . .

He stood back from the crowd, and watched.

Most parties, in his experience, had a rhythm to them. An ebb, and a flow. This one, he decided, was currently ebbing. It wasn't so much that people were leaving, but rather that they were not moving around so much. Staying in one place, as opposed to flitting about from conversation to conversation. It made the captain easier to keep track of—and Sen, too.

And it made the governor's bodyguards very easy to spot indeed. They were the ones standing around, doing nothing. Most wore the same blue and green uniforms as the ones he'd seen earlier in the day, but some were undercover—at least as undercover as they could be while at the party and not of the party. Stuck out like sore thumbs, they did

Reed decided that perhaps he'd better mingle just a bit.

He circled the edges of the crowd, joining in on a

conversation about weapons systems, which ones the Confederacy's war fleet was likely to use. He made a mental note of those systems he'd never heard of before—ion cannons?—before moving on to one of the refreshment tables, where he got another, slightly smaller glass of the *mot'lok* to sip from. He would have to watch those sips carefully. It was, as he'd warned the captain, strong stuff.

At the table next to him, one of the servers (a woman, dressed in an oddly ill-fitting coverall) set down an empty platter, and began filling it with food from the table. Reed watched her a moment, disturbed by the seemingly haphazard way she arranged the food on the plate, seeing it as his sister, who once ran a restaurant, would have seen it, as the mark of poorly trained staff, before turning back to his task. Archer and Sen (and Hoshi) were right where he'd left them. From this side of the room, he also noticed that the governor's guards were arrayed in a very precisely shaped circle around Sen (though the nearest ones stood a little farther from him now than before, probably to give him privacy while he spoke to Hoshi). If they were indeed all networked, as the two little Bynar had told him earlier today, he had no doubt they used that network to maintain formation precisely.

Might be a valuable tool after all, he thought. A neural implant. Especially for security. Though he was certain that neither the captain nor Travis, in particular, would agree with him. Reed had never heard anger in the ensign's voice the way he'd heard it earlier, when Travis had mentioned Sen's name. And speaking of the captain, and Governor Sen . . .

He looked up to check on their position, and at

that instant the server from the next table over wandered directly in front of him, blocking his view of the party.

"Excuse me," a man said, stepping up next to the woman. "I'll have one of those."

She smiled, and held the platter out for him.

He frowned.

"Serving utensils?"

Her smile wavered a moment, then came back even stronger.

It struck Reed as a particularly forced smile. An artificial one.

He frowned.

Little alarm bells were going off in his head.

"Oh how stupid of me to forget those," the server said. "I'll go get some."

But instead of turning back toward the tables, she headed off deeper into the party, still carrying the tray. Walking with determination. With purpose.

Heading right for Governor Sen, and Hoshi.

Reed set down his drink, and set after her.

When the female made it clear that recreational sex was not on her agenda that evening, Sen excused her from their conversation. He watched her go regretfully. Ah well. When he reached Qo'noS, there would be—from what he'd heard—argumentative females to spare.

The governor subvocalized a series of questions to Roia. He learned Kareg had moved into position, was awaiting his signal. The guards had prepared and cleared the upper solarium. The data caches in his terminals were clear as well—wiped of all potentially incriminating data. His credit accounts were full.

All was in readiness then. All that remained was to locate the human captain, and bid a final, fond farewell to Procyron. He would miss this place, no doubt about it.

He turned and saw a server heading toward him, carrying a tray. Drinks, he hoped. Perhaps even some of the *mot'lok*. That would be, Sen thought with a smile, only fitting, to use the Klingon beverage for a final ceremonial toast to his time here.

He stood in place, watching the server come closer and closer. Waiting.

Archer was not stupid.

He was well aware that Malcolm had spent the entire party watching him. Watching out for him, ostensibly. Fine. Part of him appreciated it, though he did resent the fact that Malcolm didn't think he could take care of himself. Part of him wished, though, that Reed had looked on this party as a bit of an opportunity as well—a chance to fulfill another aspect of his job as security chief, that being to do a little surreptitious research on the weapons systems other races in this part of the galaxy had. To talk to those races Starfleet was unfamiliar with, and get a sense of their offensive—and defensive—capabilities. It was only prudent for Admiral McCormick to have that information in hand.

Instead, though, Malcolm had spent virtually the entire evening clinging to the fringes of the party, nursing a drink. And to what end? Nothing was going to happen here; there were simply too many people. Too many guards, Sen's personal troop, in their blue-and-green uniforms, were everywhere. Archer thought there might be undercover guards as well. One particular H'ratoi he had noticed, in fact, had never seemed to be more than half a dozen meters away from him the entire evening. The captain wondered if Sen, too, was keeping an eye on him.

And speaking of Sen . . .

Archer had some things he wanted to say to the man. Not that he thought he could reverse the course of action the Trade Assembly had taken this afternoon, but the governor should know that there was considerably less enthusiasm for the war—and the diversion of resources it would cause—than perhaps today's vote had indicated. Archer wondered, perhaps, if the two of them might find a quiet place to discuss such things. The Kanthropian translation efforts as well—what else the Mediators' work might have revealed about the Antianna. He wondered if Hoshi had been able to find out anything in that regard.

He looked up and scanned the floor. There.

The governor stood—by himself, surprisingly—in the center of the room. A server was walking toward him, holding a platter of food held in front of her, a smile frozen on her face.

There was some sort of commotion going on just behind her, Archer saw. People shouting. A lot of angry faces. Someone was forcing their way through the crowd. A second later, the crowd suddenly flew apart, and a familiar face—a familiar body—came charging through.

Malcolm?

The server dropped the platter on the ground.

The smile on her face vanished.

Reed hurled himself through the air.

• • •

The woman reached across her body with her right hand even as he flew toward her, bridging the last few meters between them with a single jump. He landed on the woman's back, and she fell to the ground with a loud crack and an audible exhalation of air.

Her right arm and whatever weapon she'd been planning on using on Sen were pinned beneath her. But her left was free. She tried to use it to push herself over onto her side, to dislodge Reed. He grabbed her wrist with both hands and straightened the arm rather forcefully, then pinned it to the ground in front of her.

He became aware of figures standing over him. Blue-and-green uniforms. Sen's guards.

"She might have a bomb!" Reed said. "Get everyone back!"

The woman was cursing a blue streak at him, much of which the UT translated as nonsense phrases. At least, Reed thought they were nonsense phrases. He'd have to talk to Hoshi about it later. For now—

One of the guards knelt down and jabbed something into the woman's arm. She stopped cursing. She stopped moving. She lay still.

Reed's eyes widened in horror. He looked up at the man.

"What did you do?"

"Exactly what I ordered. Standard procedure in these cases." Governor Sen stepped forward, a look of absolute fury on his face. "Move back."

For a second, Reed thought about staying right where he was, about telling Sen exactly what he was thinking at that instant. *Wouldn't that do wonders for interstellar relations*, he thought.

He got to his feet, and stepped away from the woman.

The second he was clear, two guards drew weapons and fired. Reed thought for a second they were using laser pistols; the energy beams looked similar. But when the rays struck the woman, her body literally began glowing with energy. A faint blue outline of some sort appeared around her for a second. The blue turned to orange, then red.

The woman disappeared as if she'd never been there at all.

"Everything is fine," Sen said, turning in all directions, smiling—as false a smile as the woman who had just tried to kill him had worn—and speaking to the crowd. "The terrorist has been apprehended. Please—continue to enjoy yourselves. The night—as a new friend of mine is fond of saying—is young."

People looked around, unsure.

Sen walked into the crowd then, shaking hands, and accepting expressions of concern. Of sympathy.

The party, hushed into silence a moment before, gradually came back to life.

Reed felt a hand on his shoulder. He turned and saw Captain Archer standing next to him.

"Nice work, Malcolm."

"Sir." Reed shook his head in disbelief. "Did you see that? What that weapon did?"

Archer frowned, and shook his head. "Not the weapon, Malcolm."

"Sir?"

"Sen. It was what Sen did. He's a dangerous man."

Reed nodded, about to concur, about to suggest that perhaps he should have let the woman do the job she'd set out to and then apprehended her when all at once, the captain smiled. Another false smile.

"And here he comes now," Archer said.

Reed put on a smile himself, and turned to greet the governor.

He had never been in any real danger, of course. Roia had flagged the counterfeit staff person—no doubt a Separatist—Sen was sure Intelligence division would find a connection soon enough, they were already rounding up the usual suspects and from that instant on, the guards had a relatively clear shot, minimal collateral damage assured, anytime they wanted to take it.

But Sen had wanted to give the human—the dark-haired man, who'd spent the entire evening watching not just his captain but Sen—a chance to release some of his pent-up energy. To feel as if he were on top of the situation. To get him to relax, for just an instant.

Starting right about now.

"Captain Archer."

"Governor Sen. You're all right?"

"Yes. Fine. Thanks to your officer here."

"Lieutenant Reed."

"Lieutenant Reed." Sen repeated the man's name, and regarded him with a smile. "I owe you a great debt of thanks, Lieutenant. May I propose a toast?" Roia fed Sen an interesting tidbit of information through the implant then, and the governor turned toward the nearest refreshment table. "The *mot'lok* perhaps?"

The captain, like the female earlier, changed color.

"Something else," Archer said. "That's not my favorite."

Sen nodded. "Of course. It is an acquired taste. Like most things Klingon."

The governor smiled then, pleased at his own wit. At the glare in Archer's eye.

He snapped his fingers and a server approached (albeit with a bit of understandable hesitancy). They all ordered drinks.

Back to business, Sen thought, and lowered his voice. "Captain, I wonder if I might have a word with you. I've been thinking a bit about what you said earlier—at the Assembly."

Archer smiled. "Governor. It's like you're reading my mind."

Sen smiled back. "Oh?"

The drinks arrived. He and Archer made small talk. The dark-haired man—Reed—watched. Apparently, all the man's pent-up energies hadn't dissipated yet.

That wouldn't do at all. Sen subvocalized a command to Roia. A few seconds later, Kuda appeared.

"I need to speak with you," he said to Reed. "Regarding the terrorist."

Reed frowned, and shook his head.

"Could we do it later? I'm feeling a bit worn-out at the moment."

What an excellent liar, Sen thought. He subvocalized another command.

"Now would be better," Kuda said. "While your memory of the event is fresh."

"I'd really rather wait," he said, a little more firmly.

"Malcolm." Captain Archer touched his man on the shoulder. "Do it now, please."

The mask of false emotion Reed had been wearing dropped, and Sen could see the depth of the man's concern. His suspicion.

"Yes, sir," he said reluctantly.

"We'll be right here," Sen lied.

Kuda led the man off.

"He's a good man," Archer said again. "Occasionally overprotective, but a good man."

"He has your best interests at heart, I'm sure," Sen said. "Now about that word . . ."

"Whenever you'd like."

"I was thinking someplace more private, actually."

Sen drew the human's attention to the upper solarium, high above the main floor.

Archer hesitated a second.

"I'll have one of the guards notify your man where you are," Sen said. "If you'd like."

The captain shook his head. "Not necessary."

"Very well then." The governor smiled. "Shall we?"

The two men turned as one then, and made their way toward the central elevator bank.

Hoshi had circled the party twice, the first time to blow off some steam—recreational sex? Please—the second to look for Theera, to pick up the conversation that Sen's appearance had interrupted. She didn't see the Andorian anywhere.

On her third circuit of the room, she witnessed Malcolm save the governor's life, and saw Sen's would-be assassin murdered. The combined result of which was that she felt like stalking up to Reed and saying, "How could you?" Which was of course the wrong reaction; she should be congratulating him, except her stomach turned at the idea.

Maybe what she needed was another drink.

She stomped off to the nearest refreshment table.

"Any Romulan ale?" she asked the server.

"Sorry," he said, then smiled at her. "Nice dress."

A sound something like "grrrrrr" escaped her mouth.

"Whoa, whoa," the server said, backpedaling away from her, hands raised in self-defense. "I can go check. We may have more."

"That," she said, nodding, "would be a good thing."

"We must be very high up here," the captain said.

"Oh we are. Roughly five thousand meters above the planet's surface. Touching the edge of the planet's atmosphere," Sen replied.

Archer looked down, and then up. It did seem to him that the stars were brighter than the lights of the city below. One star in particular, in fact. A silvery white dot that seemed to him to be moving toward them. Probably one of those patrol ships they'd encountered earlier, while coming in on the shuttle.

He turned away from the window. Sen was standing over a large circular table that occupied the center of the room (the upper solarium, as he had referred to it), studying a display screen built into the top of the table. It was running a text feed of some sort, in a language Archer didn't recognize at all. Several languages, in fact, running down the screen in parallel columns. One of those languages looked to him like Orion, or a dialect thereof, which he'd had occasion to brush up on recently, a run-in with some slavers. It wasn't text, though, so much as numbers. If he was reading it right. Sen was deeply absorbed in the readout. Happy about what he was seeing. Archer wished Hoshi were there to interpret.

"Good news?" the captain asked, pushing aside one of the chairs that surrounded the table to get closer to the screen. As he did so, he noticed that the floor they stood on was now opaque, cutting off their view of the party below. Neat little feature. Privacy on demand.

"Very good news," Sen replied without looking up.

"I'm glad to hear it."

"Yes. The transfers have all cleared, and the routing data has all been erased."

Archer frowned. "I don't understand."

"It's not important. What it means is that we're ready to go."

Sen straightened. He held a weapon of some sort in his right hand, aimed squarely at the captain.

Foremost among the thoughts crossing Archer's mind at that instant was that he really had to learn to trust Malcolm's instincts.

"I thought we were going to talk."

"We will. At a leisurely pace. Quite soon, in fact."

Keep him busy. Keep him speaking, the captain thought, his eyes flickering around the room, searching for a weapon of some kind, any kind. He had one hand on the chair he'd pushed aside. He wondered how heavy it was, if he could grip it with both hands and throw it before the governor could fire. Not likely. Might be his only chance though.

"Care to tell me what this is all about?"

"Money, power . . ." Sen shrugged. "The usual sort of thing. Ah. Here we are."

Sen's gaze went to the window behind Archer. The captain turned and saw that same silver star he had noticed before, growing larger with each passing second. Coming closer. It wasn't a star at all, he realized, and turned back to Sen, opening his mouth to speak again.

The governor raised his weapon.

There.

General Jaedez, and Theera. And Ambassador Quirsh. Surrounded by a knot of uniformed Thelasians. Quirsh and Jaedez were talking, Theera stood by, looking distinctly uncomfortable.

Why, Hoshi thought, *did I have the feeling that the same conversation she'd witnessed was playing out all over again?*

She took a step toward the group, and someone touched her shoulder.

Sen, she thought, shuddering.

She took a deep breath and turned around.

Malcolm.

He smiled. "You and the governor getting along all right?"

She glared.

"Do not," she said, pointing a finger, "expect me to congratulate you for saving that man's life."

"I know," he said, frowning. His eyes went past her, scanning the room.

"I'm kidding," she said.

"I know," he said again, continuing to look all around.

"What's the matter?" Hoshi asked.

"Where's the captain?"

"I haven't seen him. Why?"

"Where's Sen?"

"Don't know. Don't care." The last slipped out before she could stop herself. Maybe, she thought, two Romulan ales were her limit.

"See if you can spot him," Reed said, ignoring her remark. "He's got to be here somewhere."

He looked to his left, and his right, and Hoshi did the same, and he looked over her shoulder, and she looked over his, and then he looked up and said—

"What happened to the floor?"

Hoshi looked up too then, and saw Malcolm was

right. The floor of the upper room, which had been transparent before, was suddenly opaque.

"Privacy feature," she said. "I wonder who's up there."

"I can hazard a guess," Reed said. "Come on."

He took her arm.

"Where are we going?" she asked.

He pointed upward.

There was a sudden flash of light, and a noise like the end of the world.

TWELVE

Hoshi opened her eyes.

She was in a small, dark, dank cell. It smelled of something terrible. Something alien, something awful, something that made her skin crawl, made the veins in her forehead ache and pound with remembered pain, something that—

Xindi.

"Oh God," she said, getting to her feet. She knew where she was now. Aboard the reptilian ship. After they'd stolen her from *Enterprise*, beamed her right off the bridge. That sort of thing wasn't supposed to be possible, Trip had assured them of that. Except here she was. Again.

The door hissed open, and the reptilian commander walked in.

Governor Sen was next to him.

"It's a dream," Hoshi said out loud, though of course it had to be a dream, the reptilian ship and commander were dust now, dead all these months.

Unfortunately, that didn't matter at the moment.

"We were quite impressed with your linguistic abilities," the Xindi said, just as he had all those months ago, when they'd tortured her and put who knows what kind of parasite into her brain to make her give them what they wanted, when they'd ruined her innate, God-given ability to—

"That—and your dress," Sen added, and Hoshi realized she was wearing the red outfit the governor had given her.

"This is a dream," Hoshi repeated. "It doesn't matter what you say. What you do. None of this is happening."

Sen and the Xindi looked at each other, then laughed.

"Then you won't mind if we . . ."

The reptilian commander smiled and held up a weapon, the same weapon, she knew instinctively, he had used to inject the parasites into her brain earlier.

Dream or not, she wasn't going through that again.

Hoshi sprung from her seat and shoved past the two men, running out into the corridor. An alarm sounded. *Enterprise*'s alarm. The call to battle stations.

She looked around. She was aboard her own ship.

"Hoshi!"

She turned. Captain Archer was running toward her.

"The Antianna. They're attacking! We need that translation!"

All she could do was shake her head.

"I'm sorry, sir. I'm so sorry."

"You don't have it yet?"

"No."

"Hoshi." Archer's shoulders sagged. "You let me down. I trusted you, and you let me down."

"Yes, sir. I let you down."

"I'm going to need a new translator," Archer said. He looked past her and smiled.

Hoshi turned and saw Theera.

"I have the information you need, sir," the Andorian said.

"Yes." Archer nodded. "Go ahead."

Theera frowned. "But I can't tell you."

The captain frowned back.

The nearest bulkhead exploded. Archer hurtled through the air, crashed into a bulkhead, and lay still.

Hoshi turned away—

And almost ran right into her mother.

"Remember this one?" her mother asked, and started singing the fifty-seven-pulse signal. She stopped, and started, stopped and started, more times than Hoshi could count.

"It was a big hit for Elvis. Got it yet?" her mother asked.

"No," Hoshi said. "No I don't understand."

Her mother frowned, and shook her head.

"Kids. You think you've done a good job with them, and then something like this happens."

Before Hoshi could respond, there was another explosion.

The entire side of the corridor disappeared, and Hoshi saw the stars beyond.

The vacuum of space sucked at her, and she—and everything and everyone aboard the ship—flew out, into the black.

She opened her eyes.

She was aboard *Enterprise*, in the sickbay. She felt weak, and thirsty, and the skin of her face felt raw and mildly burned, as if she'd stayed out too long in the sun. Across the room from her, a woman stood over another patient, frowning at the display readouts above his cot. Hoshi couldn't see who the patient was. The woman was Nurse Cutler.

Hoshi swallowed, and tried to call her name. Nothing.

She closed her eyes again.

• • •

She was back in the cell once more. The reptilian commander loomed over her.

"The launch codes," he said. "You will give them to us. Or else . . . what happened to your friend will happen to you."

He looked to Hoshi's right. She turned to follow his gaze.

Theera sat beside her.

"Theera?" Hoshi asked hesitantly. "Are you all right?"

The Andorian remained silent, staring straight ahead.

"Theera?" Hoshi reached out a hand and—hesitantly—touched her shoulder.

The Andorian slumped toward her.

A worm—as thick as Hoshi's index finger—crawled out of the scar on Theera's brow ridge then. It looked just like the parasites the Xindi had put in her.

A second worm crawled out after the first. Then another, and another, and another, and right about then Hoshi stopped thinking, and started screaming.

"Ensign Sato. Ensign Sato. Are you with us?"

Hoshi blinked, and looked up. Doctor Phlox was leaning over her.

"It's good to see you again," he said, and with those words, she began to cry.

"Shhh," Phlox said. "It's all right. You're safe now."

He kept making soothing sounds, and she kept crying, still seeing the same horrible images in her mind, of the worms and the Xindi and the Antianna and Captain Archer's look of disappointment, and *Enterprise* exploding. She felt as if she'd lived a thousand lifetimes, each of them more painful than the last, since she'd last been awake.

"I'm sorry," she was able to finally get out. "Give me a minute."

"It's all right. Take as much time as you need. No need for explanations. You're with us, you're safe, you're one hundred percent whole. Alive, and fine."

She nodded. "Yes, but—what happened to me? Why am I here? How long—"

"Shhh." Phlox shook his head. "Eat first, ask questions later. I have just the thing," he said, and he did, he brought her miso soup and rice crackers, and she attacked them greedily. They tasted like home. They reminded her of her mother sans the Elvis imitation, of her siblings, of times long before she'd ever thought of going into space or becoming a linguist, before she'd heard of the Training Institute or Jonathan Archer or any aliens other than the Vulcans or the occasional visitor from Alpha Centauri, certainly not the Xindi or Sen or—

She felt pressure on her arm.

She looked up and saw Phlox holding a hypo.

"Hey," she said. "What was that?"

"Nutritional supplement."

"Oh." She took a few more sips of the soup, and all at once, yawned. "Oh."

She looked up at Phlox again.

"Nutritional supplement?"

"Among other things." He smiled, and moved the tray with the soup and crackers out of the way. He eased her back into a supine position.

"Rest," he said.

"But—"

"Rest."

She did.

● ● ●

The next time Hoshi woke, she felt—for lack of a better word—human again.

Phlox stood over her, along with Nurse Cutler, and T'Pol. The Vulcan eyed her critically.

"You look much improved today," she said.

"I'm glad to hear that, but—today?" Hoshi frowned, propped herself up on her elbows. "How many—how long have I been here?"

T'Pol looked quickly to Phlox, who nodded.

"You have been here—unconscious—for three days."

Hoshi wasn't surprised. The way she'd been dreaming . . . the Vulcan could have told her she'd been out for a year, and she would have believed her.

"But what happened? The last thing I remember was that reception, down on the planet. Governor Sen, and the captain, and . . ."

"There was an explosion. The governor is dead. Over two hundred people died. The Thelasian authorities think it was some sort of terrorist act."

"Terrorist act. I don't—" She frowned. "The captain? Malcolm . . . are they . . . ?"

"Lieutenant Reed is fine," Phlox said hurriedly. "He was unharmed in the explosion, and is in fact currently on Procyron, assisting the Thelasian authorities in their investigation of the incident. He's anxious to talk to you regarding your memories of that evening."

"Of course. As soon as he wants."

"As soon as you are able," Phlox stressed.

"Yes. But—what about the captain? Where is he?"

The expression on T'Pol's face changed. Phlox shook his head, and looked down to the ground.

Nurse Cutler turned away.

"Oh no," Hoshi said. "Oh no."

T'Pol nodded.

"We are attempting," she said, "to reconstruct the sequence of events that occurred just prior to the explosion. Lieutenant Reed strongly feels . . ."

But Hoshi wasn't listening. She didn't have the energy for it.

It took every ounce of her strength not to start crying again.

Travis came to visit her the next day. He looked the way she felt—stunned. Like he'd been run over by a truck.

"I can't believe it either," he said. "I don't want to believe it."

He gave her more details: the explosion had centered in the upper solarium—ripped away a portion of the dome there, sent massive chunks of debris raining down on the people below, set a portion of the structure on fire, sent everyone there into a panic, screaming toward the exits, afraid they were under attack by hostile forces. The situation had gotten straightened out fairly quickly—Malcolm had apparently played a part in that—but the damage had already been done, obviously. The destruction. The deaths.

But she wasn't going to think about that.

As to who was responsible . . . there were a number of theories going around. Some thought that Sen was the sole intended target, others that the violence had been more generally directed at everyone attending the reception. Travis echoed what T'Pol had told her, that Reed wanted to talk to Hoshi as soon as she was able.

She nodded blankly, and tried to think of something to say.

"What about you?" she asked, finally.

Travis frowned. "Me?"

"Yes. The money. *Horizon* . . .?"

"Oh." He shook his head. "No luck yet finding them. They must be . . . I don't know. In the middle of a run, out to someplace well off the beaten track. I don't know."

She nodded again. "Maybe I can help you try and track them down, when I get out of here."

"Maybe. For now, you concentrate on getting better."

A few more minutes, and he left. Hoshi tried to fall back asleep, but she couldn't. Partially because she didn't want to dream again. Partially because she didn't want to lie there and think about the captain. She needed to keep busy. The translation. The Antianna signal. Work. That would do it.

She got up from the cot. Nurse Cutler told her to get back down. Hoshi refused. Phlox came in, asked what the problem was. Hoshi told him she wanted to be released. He told her he'd see how she was tomorrow. She said she'd stop back then, if he wanted. He reminded her that he was the doctor, and that involuntary confinement to a sickbed was always an option.

She went back to her cot. Nurse Cutler got her a viewer, which Hoshi used to tie into the Thelasian database. There was nothing new—no further information on their "tentative" translation of the Antianna signal.

Plans for war were proceeding apace.

General Jaedez had been appointed commander-in-chief of the assembled fleet, she saw. Which reminded her that Jaedez had been with Theera when the explosion occurred. He had survived. She wondered if the Andorian had.

She found a list of casualties in the database. Theera's name wasn't on it.

So she was on her way back home, then. Safe and sound.

Hoshi pictured Captain Archer sitting in the command chair then, looking and yet not looking in her direction, waiting for her to translate the Antianna signal, to do her job so that he could get on with doing his.

She shut off the reader.

It took a while, but at last, she was able to fall asleep again.

It was not, by any stretch of the imagination, a good night's sleep.

THIRTEEN

It was late, growing later, and once more, he had accomplished nothing. Not entirely his fault, of course, Malcolm knew that, what could he do, after all, he was just here in an observational capacity, the Thelasians had made that quite clear. They let him observe their investigation, but the second he stepped forward to try and offer suggestions on how they might, perhaps, produce results from the data they'd gathered on the explosion and its aftermath . . .

He was politely—but firmly—shunted aside. Idiots. His sister could do a better job of running the investigation. No, strike that, the Silurian grayfish Phlox had swimming in his tank down in sickbay could do a better job. Perhaps he should stop being so polite about things, and raise a ruckus. Shout at someone. Let them see how angry he was at the lack of progress they'd made.

Who he was really angry at, of course, was himself. He was security, and security's primary task in a hostile environment was to protect *Enterprise* personnel. Specifically and most importantly senior officers, and above all the captain. He'd failed at that task. Never mind his heroics, or the fact that except for those last few minutes, he'd watched Archer like a hawk all night, the point was the captain was dead, and that was, if not his fault, his responsibility. He should have insisted on Chief Lee, at the very least. He should have overridden the captain's wishes. He'd done it before. He'd do it again, he promised himself that, if ever a similar situation arose. For now . . .

Best to play by the rules. At least while the investigation was still active.

Right now, Malcom was on his way to visit to what had been Sen's office, in the government complex. It was an impressive suite of rooms, the size of *Enterprise*'s bridge, when taken as a group, with a panoramic view of the city outside. The very heart, he'd come to learn, of an extensive computer network that the Intelligence Division was currently attempting to penetrate. Looking for information on Sen's recent activities, clues that might point them to his killers.

A half-dozen workstations had been set up in the middle of the office's main suite. One of the proctors—Thelasian investigators, ranking officials from the Intelligence division—was supervising the tech personnel manning those stations. Reed watched him at "work" (his idea of which seemed to involve walking from one tech to another and looking over their shoulders) waiting for an opportune moment, before stepping into the proctor's path.

"Any progress?" Reed asked.

The proctor shook his head. "Nothing yet. We've brought in a few more freelancers so we can work straight through, though I'm beginning to think that rather than continue our efforts to breach the system, we may be better off inducing a catastrophic failure, and attempting to recover the data from the storage centers directly."

Reed bit his tongue. Hard.

Catastrophic failure. From what he knew of computers, that sounded like a really stupid idea.

He was trying to think of a diplomatic way to say that when he noticed two familiar faces among the new tech personnel. Poz and Verkin. The Bynar he'd met at the Assembly last week.

"Excuse me a moment," he said to the proctor, and went and stood over the two of them. It took a few seconds for them to notice his presence.

"Lieutenant Reed."

"Mister Poz."

"I'm Verkin. He's Poz."

"We heard about your captain," Poz said. "Our sympathies."

"Thank you."

"But we did warn you," Verkin said. "You'll recall."

"Yes. I recall. I've spent the last few days recalling." He paused a moment, then lowered his voice. "So. You're trying to break into the Governor's computer network."

" 'Trying' is the word."

"Is the situation as bad as the proctor thinks?"

"Hard to tell."

"Impossible to tell. Yet."

"If not . . . I suppose his idea—the proctor's idea, induce a catastrophic failure—that's the best chance of getting the data."

The two looked at each other. Said nothing.

"What would you estimate the chances of success are? If you use that strategy?"

The two looked at each other again.

"Not high," Poz said.

"Not high at all," Verkin concurred.

"What would be a better strategy?"

Silence again.

"Not really our place to say, is it?"

"Definitely not." Verkin glanced around the room, at which point Reed noticed the proctor standing a few meters back, staring at them.

Reed got the message. "Of course not. Not your place."

He backed off. Left the room, went to a terminal just outside Sen's office where the Thelasians had set up a file cluster for him, including a background dossier on Governor Sen that he'd spent quite a lot of time browsing through over the last few days. He reviewed the dossier again from the very first entry. Sen had made a lot of enemies in his time, from his days as an independent merchant (a hundred and fifty years ago, Sen had actually been as old as he looked), to his service as viceroy of an outlying border region called Coreida, where he'd ruled with an iron hand and an open pocket, at least according to some, to his time as governor. The more he read, in fact, the more it seemed to Reed that the question was more along the lines of who wouldn't want to kill the man? He half-expected Travis's name to pop up on the list.

He read. He waited.

Just shy of dawn, Poz and Verkin came out of the interior office, and headed toward the elevators. He gave them a minute, then followed. They took a slide-walk into the heart of the Prex, where they ducked into what looked like Reed like the Thelasian version of a diner.

He waited until they'd been served their food, then walked over to them.

"Lieutenant Reed."

"Mister Verkin. Fancy meeting you here."

"I'm Poz. He's Verkin." The Bynar frowned. "You followed us."

Reed smiled, and gestured to an empty chair at their table. "May I . . . ?"

"No," Verkin said.

"Yes," Poz said.

The two glared at each other.

Reed sat.

"We have been explicitly forbidden to talk to you," Verkin said.

"Explicitly," Poz added.

"Talk?" Reed made an expression of mock surprise. "I'm here to eat."

He motioned to the waitress. When she came over, he pointed to what Poz was eating, which was slightly less shiny-looking than Verkin's food, and asked for the same. And coffee, which he had been relieved to discover over the last week had become as much of a staple in the Confederacy as it was back on Earth.

His food came very quickly, and they all turned their attention to eating. Reed was ravenous, and the food—a noodle of some kind, with some kind of animal protein sauce—wasn't bad. Spaghetti and meatballs, done Confederacy style. Strange aftertaste that he decided not to ask about.

When the food was gone and the waitress had cleared the dishes, Reed leaned forward in his chair.

"We can't talk to you," Verkin said again.

"It could mean our jobs. Work."

Reed was about to protest that whatever they told him would remain private when he remembered something. The chits Sen had given them, to spend before the party. He still had a few of his.

He pulled one out of his pocket and held it up.

"Know what this is?" he asked.

The Bynars' eyes widened. "Thelasian credit chits. How much?"

Reed told them.

Their eyes widened farther.

"This kind of money," Reed said, "might enable you to be a little more discriminating in what sort of jobs you do take."

"It might." Verkin smiled, and reached for the chit.

Reed held it just out of reach.

"Ah. Answers first, then the credits."

The two Bynar leaned forward. "Ask away."

"Before—back in Governor Sen's office—you said you didn't think the proctor's idea was a good one."

"Crashing the network to get the information?" Verkin shook his head. "Never work. Not in a hundred years."

"What are the alternatives?"

"Not sure yet," Poz said. "Sen has some kind of software agent protecting his files. Very sophisticated. Anticipates every move we make, and then some."

Software agents. Reed knew about them, in theory. The covert section of Starfleet he had worked for had been working on several prototypes. But they were still in the experimental stages. The danger, of course, with an intelligent software agent was that it would keep learning past its designed parameters, achieve real independence, a life of its own. Like in that movie Trip had shown a few weeks back—*The Forbin Project*. The computer that took over the world.

"So how can you get at the information in there?"

Poz shook his head. "Can't, is my guess."

Reed frowned.

Verkin held up a finger. "But . . ."

"But what?"

"Even without cracking the network, we have found out a few things," he said. "About the governor's actions this last week."

"Go on."

"He was busy," Poz said.

"Very, very busy," Verkin said.

"And you know this how?"

"There's a bandwith monitor on the network. Traffic to his office was up almost sixty percent."

"That is busy," Reed said. "What was he doing?"

"We don't know."

"Not exactly."

The two men looked at each other again.

"Speculation," Poz said.

"Agreed. But still—"

"Go on," Reed said. "Speculate."

"We reviewed bandwith usage for the other major networks. Looking for simultaneous spikes in activity."

"To see who else was busy." Reed smiled. "Go on."

"We discovered a number of the financial networks were unusually active at the same time."

"Banks," Poz said. "You know what banks are?"

"Oh, yes," Reed said. "I know what banks are. So Sen was busy, and the banks were busy."

"Yes. We can't prove any connection, though."

"But the data is suggestive," Verkin said.

Reed agreed with that. Sen, and money. That was a very suggestive combination indeed. He felt a little tingle at the base of his spine.

"Find anything else interesting?" Reed asked.

Poz shook his head. "No."

"No," Verkin nodded, and then frowned. "Ah."

Poz turned to him. "What?"

"The system outage."

Poz frowned. "How is that relevant?"

"I don't know that it is," Verkin said. "But it is interesting, and Lieutenant Reed asked about interesting, so . . ."

"Tell me about it," Reed said. "The outage."

"Outages, actually," Verkin continued. "Two separate incidents, two days apart, lasting approximately forty-six seconds each. Outages referring to interruption of the primary systems feed to the government complex. The entire complex, including the Trade Assembly and the building where Sen's office is."

"These happened last week."

"The day of the explosion, and two days before."

Reed nodded. "A system outage. That means they lost power?"

"No," Verkin said. "They lost the system feed. It's the master computer network for all of Procyron. Keeps all the other networks time-synchronized, provides for remote backup, system maintenance . . . very important."

"And to lose the feed is unusual?"

"Unusual?" Poz shook his head. "I would say so. It's never happened before."

"Never?"

"Never. There are multiple redundancies built in to prevent just such an occurrence."

"With good reason," Verkin said. "Did you see the speculators this afternoon?"

"No." Reed shook his head. "I'm afraid I missed that."

"Quite a scene," Poz said.

"Quite an uproar," Verkin added. "The proctor summoned the guards. The speculators summoned the media. The new governor made an appearance."

"Quite a scene," Reed agreed. "Why?"

"Why? They're worried," Poz said. "Upset. There are ninety-two seconds of trading activity—probably ten thousand separate transactions . . ."

"At least," Verkin interrupted.

"At most," Poz continued. "Ninety-two seconds of activity which cannot be verified."

"I don't understand," Reed said.

"Without the systems feed, there are no off-site records. Only the on-site computers of the traders themselves—"

"Easily faked."

"Easily faked," Poz agreed. "No independent verification for the trades."

"Wait." Reed leaned forward again. "Let me make sure of this. You're saying because the system feed was out, there are no records of what happened during those forty-six seconds. The two outages. Is that it?"

Poz and Verkin looked at each other, and nodded.

"Yes. That's it."

"No records of what happened in, say, Sen's office at all?"

"None. Not just Sen's office though. The entire complex. As I said."

Reed nodded absently. "As you said."

That little tingle he'd felt earlier was back again. Much stronger this time. A tingle of excitement, and outrage, and a tiny, tiny, bit of what he would have to call hope.

"What's the matter?" Poz asked.

"I'm wondering," Reed said. "Could someone shut off the feed deliberately?"

The tech shook his head. "There are multiple redundancies built into the system. You would have to simultaneously disable several dozen connections."

"Within milliseconds," Verkin added. "It would be physically impossible for a person to do that."

"Unlikely," Poz said. "Not impossible."

"Impossible."

The two men glared at each other.

"What about a software agent?" Reed asked.

They stopped glaring, and turned to Reed.

"Definitely."

"Without a doubt."

"It would have to be a very sophisticated software agent though."

"Very."

"Like Governor Sen's?"

"I suppose." Poz frowned. "Are you suggesting Governor Sen shut off the feed?"

"Why would he want to do that?" Verkin asked.

The two men looked at Reed, who said nothing.

They looked at each other.

"No records," Poz said.

"Sen and the banks," Verkin said.

They turned to Reed again.

"You think he faked it," Poz said.

Reed allowed the faintest hint of a smile to cross his face.

"No," Verkin shook his head firmly. "Killed all those people to . . . no. That's monstrous."

"That's Governor Sen," Reed said. "Or am I wrong?"

"No," Poz said.

"Supposition," Verkin said. "Circumstantial. No proof whatsoever."

Poz turned and stared at him. Reed stared too.

The man threw up his hands.

"Fine," he said. "You're not wrong. You're not wrong at all."

Reed pulled the rest of his chits out of his pocket and handed them to Poz.

"See what else you can find out," he said.

FOURTEEN

Hoshi was released the next morning. She made her way down to the mess, where Carstairs, at her request, was waiting for her. While she ate, he brought her up to speed on what had happened over the last week. Gave her every single, solitary detail—"none too small," she had told him, because she did not want to have her mind idle for a single, solitary second, or she'd start thinking about the dream that she had last night after Travis left sickbay, a dream where everyone on *Enterprise* was enthusiastically blaming her for Captain Archer's death.

The ensign gave her status updates on all incoming and outgoing message traffic, of which there was plenty, naturally, from *Enterprise* to Starfleet and back, regarding both Archer's death and the question of who was to take command. T'Pol was nominally second but Admiral McCormick had apparently received a great deal of pressure to have the captaincy pass to a human, and so it was Commander Tucker.

"The Kanthropians contacted us as well."

"The Kanthropians?" Hoshi frowned. "What did they want?"

"You."

"Me?"

"Yes."

She frowned. Maybe they were going to give her the data on Theera's translation that they hadn't officially released yet. Maybe.

Somehow, she doubted it.

"I took it on myself to reply, said you were—or rather, you would be—fine, and that you would contact them as soon as you were able. Then they wanted to talk Commander Tucker—Captain Tucker—too," Carstairs said, correcting himself for the umpteenth time, and Hoshi didn't blame him, the words were as strange to hear—Captain Tucker—as they had to be to speak, "but he's been pretty preoccupied, as you might guess, especially with the message traffic back and forth between here and Starfleet, and what with the time delay—even though the Thelasians are being very cooperative, letting us use their relay stations to boost the signal—he hasn't had time to get back to them, and . . ."

"I get the picture," she said, standing. "I'm able now. Let's go find out what they want, shall we?"

They cleared their trays, and headed for the lift.

The bridge was as busy as she'd ever seen it. Busier. Rodriguez was at the com station, seemingly doing about eight things at once. Riley was on the helm, Yamana at weapons, T'Pol at the science station, and Commander Tucker—Captain Tucker—at engineering, talking to someone on the com. Well, yelling to be more precise.

". . . you have to give her something else then. We need her. It's been a week and . . ."

"It may be another week." Hoshi recognized the voice. Phlox. "Ensign Parker is very susceptible to this virus."

"Yes. I understand that," Trip said. "But our engines are very susceptible to breaking down, especially when they're not maintained properly. When the people who are supposed to maintain them properly are themselves not being maintained properly."

"There is nothing I can do in this instance," Phlox said, and now he sounded a little perturbed himself. "The best thing for the ensign is rest."

"There has to be something else you can do," Trip said again. "I need another body down there. Lieutenant Hess needs help."

"You could, of course, order me to pump the ensign full of stimulants so that he would be capable of performing his duties. You have that authority, Captain."

"Forget it," Trip said, closing the channel. He stood up, his features frozen into an expression of disgust.

His eyes fell on Hoshi, and the disgust changed into a big, broad smile.

"Hey," he said, and crossed the upper deck of the bridge in about two strides, and took her by the shoulders. "It's good to see you up and about. You sure you're all right?"

"Yes. I feel fine."

"Well enough to come back?"

"Yes, sir." She studied Trip for a moment. There were dark circles under his eyes. Lines on his face that hadn't been there, she could swear, the last time she'd seen him. Hardly surprising, though.

His best friend was dead.

"I've been meaning to come down to see you—check on you," he said. "There just hasn't been time. One thing after another."

"It's all right, sir. I mean, Commander. Trip."

He smiled again.

"I understand the Kanthropians were looking for me too."

"Right." Trip frowned. "I forgot all about that. But now that you're here . . ."

"Yes, sir," she said. "I'll contact them."

She started toward her station before seeing that Carstairs had taken over for Rodriguez and was already there, working, and even though he stood up at her approach, ready to yield his seat, she could tell at a glance that he was in the middle of doing about twenty different things, so she waved him back down, and went to the auxiliary com station on the other side of the bridge.

She tied in to the main system, and requested a channel to the Kanthropian Trade Legation. She was told to stand by; there was a lot of com traffic. Listening in for a moment, she found out why.

The fleet was leaving. The Armada. Heading off to find, confront, and destroy the Antianna. There were a lot of last-minute preparations going on. Supplies being loaded, plans being made, personnel shifted among the hundred-odd vessels that comprised the war party.

Procryon was on the viewscreen, reddish brown against the black of space. Looking closer, she saw that every square meter of orbital space was filled with a satellite or ship of some kind, gleaming silver metal that twinkled on the screen before her.

The com sounded.

"Commander, I have the Kanthropians. Channel is open."

Trip took the captain's chair as on the viewscreen, the image of Procryon cleared and was replaced by that of a Mediator.

Definitely not either of the ones Hoshi had spoken to at Sen's reception. This one had much darker skin, looked much older, had much more—for lack of a better word—*gravitas*. The two Mediators she had spoken to earlier had reminded Hoshi of librarians, or academics. This one reminded her of Admiral Forrest. Whom she hadn't thought about in a long time. Since his death, in fact. His funeral.

A funeral. She hadn't thought about that—had there been a service for Captain Archer? There must have been, and she'd missed it. She'd have to find out.

She didn't even know, Hoshi realized, if they'd found a body.

Trip rose from his chair. "I'm Charles Tucker, acting captain of the Earth ship *Enterprise*."

The Mediator nodded.

"I am," the translator sputtered, "also known as Elder Green, chief delegate to the Thelasian Trading Confederacy. We have been trying to reach you for some time, Captain."

"I'm sorry," Trip said. "It's been a busy . . ."

"I need to speak with you regarding one of your crew. An Ensign Hoshi Sato."

Trip frowned.

If there was one thing he hated, Hoshi knew, it was being interrupted.

"Can I ask what this is about?" the commander asked.

"She was injured in the blast, I understand," Green said, ignoring the question. "Has she recovered?"

"She has."

"Then I would like to speak with her."

Trip frowned again. At that same instant, the com sounded again.

"Excuse me, sir," Carstairs interrupted. "I have

Lieutenant Reed on another channel. He says it's urgent."

Trip turned and shook his head. "Tell him to hold on a minute."

"He's very insistent, Commander."

"He'll have to wait."

"Life or death, he says."

Trip sighed, and turned back to the viewscreen.

"Elder Green, could I ask you to—"

"Ensign Hoshi." The Elder glared.

Trip's mood changed from apologetic to peeved.

"You'll have to wait one minute," he snapped, and gestured to Hoshi. She switched the channel to standby. The screen went dark, just as the elder's mouth opened to say something. The Kanthropian communications facility began yelling in her ear almost immediately, demanding to be put back through.

"Mister Carstairs," Trip said, gesturing to the ensign. A second later, Reed's face came on the viewer.

Hoshi was shocked at his appearance. He hadn't shaved, for one thing, and for Malcolm, spit-and-polish as he was, not to have shaved . . .

"Malcolm," Commander Tucker said. "What do you have?"

Reed shook his head, and frowned. "I'm not entirely sure."

Trip frowned back. "But you said it was urgent."

"Oh it is. It most definitely is. It changes everything." He leaned forward, and spoke more quietly. "Is this channel secure?"

Trip turned and exchanged a questioningly glance with T'Pol. He turned back.

"Malcolm," he said. "Are you all right?"

"I'm fine. Quite fine."

The Kanthropians stopped yelling in her ear, and abruptly cut the channel.

Hoshi wondered if she should tell Commander Tucker. Better wait, she decided. Maybe if she got them back, and tried to apologize . . .

"Malcolm, come on," Trip said. "Just tell me what you have to report."

The lieutenant nodded. "I'm fairly certain Governor Sen is still alive."

The bridge fell silent.

"Say that again?" Trip asked.

"I believe Governor Sen is alive. I believe, in fact, he staged the explosion that took place himself, in order to cover his disappearance."

T'Pol walked down from her station and stood next to Trip.

"That seems highly unlikely."

Trip nodded. "I have to agree with T'Pol, Malcolm. What makes you think that?"

Carstairs's com started beeping frantically.

Trip cast daggers in his direction. Hoshi signaled the ensign to put his console on silent. Whoever it was, most likely the Kanthropians, would have to wait.

"Information I've obtained regarding his activities over the last few weeks," Reed said. "Specifically, his interactions with some of the financial—"

Hoshi's console started beeping, too.

"Ensign. Would you kindly inform the Kanthropians that they will just have to wait?" Trip said.

"Sorry, sir," she said. "Captain, it's not the Kanthropians. It's General Jaedez. From the Armada."

"What does he want?" Trip asked. "Never mind. Malcolm, I'd better talk to him. Why don't you get back up here, and we can discuss all this in person?"

"I'm on to something here, Trip," Reed said. "Returning to *Enterprise* isn't—"

"We talked about this yesterday," Trip said, more than a hint of irritation in his voice. "Didn't we?"

"That was yesterday. Given what I've discovered—"

"Lieutenant, get back up here and let's talk about it."

"Sir," Reed said, sounding a little irritated himself, "I—"

Hoshi cleared her throat, and caught Trip's eye. General Jaedez, she mouthed.

"Hold on," Trip said.

He nodded to Hoshi, and Reed's image disappeared in midsentence, and the Conani general, looking even more fearsome than Hoshi remembered, thanks in large part to the full body armor he wore, appeared.

"Archer?"

"I'm Commander Tucker. Captain Archer is dead."

"General Jaedez. I command the fleet."

"Yes. I know."

"I order you to speak with the Kanthropians immediately."

"Now, wait just—"

"That is all. Jaedez out."

The screen went dark.

Trip was left standing in the middle of the bridge.

"Who the . . . we don't report to the Confederacy, last I heard."

He was glaring at Hoshi as he said it.

"Yes, sir," she said. "I mean, no, sir. We don't."

"Damn right," he said, and sighed heavily. "Okay. Put the Kanthropians back on."

"One second, sir," she said.

"Excuse me Captain," Carstairs said. "I have—"

"Ensign," Trip turned and glared at him. "I've just been given a direct order by the Conani general. Didn't you hear?"

"Yes, sir. I did, sir. It's just that—"

"Tell Lieutenant Reed to have a little patience please. I don't take orders from him either, last I checked." Trip pinched the bridge of his nose, and exhaled loudly.

Hoshi's console flashed. "I have the Kanthropians," she said.

"Captain Tucker," Elder Green said. "If Ensign Hoshi is healed from her injuries, I need to speak with her immediately."

"In a minute," Trip said, rising from his chair. "I just—"

"Ensign Hoshi," the Mediator snapped. "There is no time to waste."

Trip visibly tensed again.

"Elder Green," he said, stepping closer to the screen. "A little tip on human beings. We respond much better to—"

"Stop wasting time, Mister Tucker. I . . ."

"That's Captain Tucker," Trip said. "And I just want to make clear . . ."

"The Armada is leaving," Elder Green interrupted. "I need to talk to her now."

Trip seemed about to say something else, but then took a deep breath.

"Hoshi . . ." he said, waving her forward.

She nodded, switched her station to standby, and walked to the center of the bridge, catching Carstairs's eye as she did so. He still had a com earpiece in, and looked very pale.

Reed must be giving him hell, she thought.

"I'm Ensign Hoshi," she said to the Kanthropian.

"You are as Younger Emmen described you," Green said. "But I have no time for pleasantries. At this very moment . . ."

The screen went dark.

Hoshi frowned.

Trip frowned.

Even T'Pol frowned.

They all turned to Carstairs, who said, "I'm sorry, sir. Commander Tucker, but I . . ."

"Did you just cut off the Kanthropians?" Trip asked, and this time there was steel in his voice that reminded Hoshi instantly of Captain Archer.

"Yes, sir, but—"

"No buts," Trip glared. "You're relieved. Hoshi, please take his station and get Elder Green back. As quick as you can."

The viewscreen came on again and she and everyone else on the bridge but Trip, who was still glaring at Carstairs, got it, why the ensign had cut the Kanthropians off, why he'd looked so nervous before, and it had nothing to do with Lieutenant Reed.

"Commander," T'Pol said quietly. "Perhaps you'd better . . ."

He turned and glared at T'Pol, sat back down in the captain's chair, looked up at the screen, and jumped immediately to his feet.

Admiral McCormick glared down at him.

Hoshi had never seen McCormick in person before. She'd heard his voice any number of times—deep, resonant, commanding. She'd pictured a big man—Yamana's size, at least. Stouter, though. The kind of man who took charge of a room when he entered. But McCormick was little. Not much bigger than her. Thin, intense-looking. A shock of straight white hair combed back from his forehead. Uniform creased so sharp it looked like you could cut yourself on the seams. Ramrod-stiff in his chair, the Starfleet flag prominently displayed behind him.

McCormick was also angry. Very, very angry.

"Admiral," Trip said, in a very small voice.

"Commander. I don't recall ever having to wait five minutes for a subordinate to find the time to speak to me. I don't ever want it to happen again. Is that clear?"

"Yes, sir."

McCormick was not done yet.

"You don't seem to be handling the pressures of command very well, Mister Tucker. I'm regretting my decision to bypass Commander T'Pol. Have you left Procyron, Commander?"

"No, sir. We're still waiting for some of our personnel to return from . . ."

"You're getting them back on ship, I trust? Making all necessary preparations to leave immediately?"

Trip hesitated.

"That's a yes or a no question, Commander."

"Yes, sir," Trip said.

"Good. Because as I believe I mentioned yesterday, I need you at Barcana Station by twelve-hundred hours, day after tomorrow. There's a passenger there I want you to pick up and transport to the conference. Is that understood?"

"Yes, sir."

McCormick continued to glare at him. "Let me make it clear how critical *Enterprise*'s presence is at this conference, Commander. You and your crew are the only thing the vast majority of the races attending will have in common. You represent something. Jonathan Archer's life's work, for one. His life's work matters to you, I assume?"

"Yes, sir."

"Good. Then be there. Barcana, twelve-hundred hours, day after tomorrow. McCormick out."

The screen went to black for a split second, and then filled again with the image of Procyron.

Trip slumped back in the command chair, and exhaled loudly. After a moment, he turned to Carstairs.

"Ensign, my apologies."

"Our friends are calling again, sir," Hoshi said. "Elder Green, I think."

We need Malcolm back here, ASAP. You tell him that. Hoshi . . ." The commander turned back to her.

"Aye, sir," she said, and opened the channel. Stood directly in front of the viewscreen.

But it wasn't Elder Green who came on.

It was a different Kanthropian. A much younger one, who seemed not angry, as Hoshi might have expected, but nervous.

"Mister Captain Tucker?" he asked.

"No," Hoshi said.

"I'm Tucker." Trip stepped alongside her. "Where's Elder Green?"

"He is aboard S-12," the Mediator said.

"He and I were talking," Hoshi said. "Our conversation was interrupted."

"You are Ensign Hoshi Sato."

"Yes."

"We have sent a courier ship for you. It should be arriving in a moment."

Trip and Hoshi looked at each other.

"What?"

"We have sent a courier ship," the Mediator said again. "So that you may join Elder Green aboard S-12."

"Commander."

That was T'Pol.

"We have an inbound ship, requesting permission to land in the shuttlebay."

"Back up a second," Trip said. "I'm a little lost."

"You are lost? I don't understand." The Mediator frowned. "Is there a problem with your translator?"

"No," Hoshi said. S-12, courier ships—this all sounded familiar to her, and a second later, she realized why. The conversation she'd overheard between Theera and the Mediators at the party.

"Why does Elder Green want me to join him aboard S-12?"

"So you may aid in the translation efforts, of course."

"What transla—the Antianna?"

"Yes."

"Wait. What is S-12?" Trip asked.

"S-12 is our mediation vessel."

"And where is it?"

"Outbound," the Kanthropian answered, "with the fleet."

"The Armada," Hoshi said, and she got it then. "You want me to join the Armada?"

"Is that not what I just said?" The Mediator frowned. "Are you sure there is no problem with your translator?"

They got all the way to shuttlebay before Commander Tucker—Captain Tucker—started in again.

"Just so we're clear," he began. "I can't promise—"

"I understand, sir," Hoshi said.

Trip sighed. "Captain Archer was still alive, he'd kill me for letting you do this."

"No he wouldn't." Hoshi shook her head. "He'd want me to go. To make sure we were doing everything we could to prevent a war."

"Hmmphh." Trip smiled, looked her over. "You sure you're all right?"

"Fine."

"You don't look a hundred percent to me. Let's just get Phlox down here to—"

"He said I was fine. Good to go."

"He didn't even examine you."

"My point exactly." Hoshi folded her arms across her chest.

Trip sighed again, and opened the shuttlebay door.

"I talked to the new governor. On Procyron," he said over his shoulder, moving quickly across the upper-level observation platform and then starting down the gangway toward the bay proper. "The acting governor. They can't promise anything, it all depends on what happens with the Armada, obviously, but assuming it's safe to travel, they have regular shuttles back to Morianna. When you get back, they said it shouldn't be more than a month before—"

"I understand, sir."

Trip stopped on the ladder, and looked up at her. "You keep sayin' that, but I'm not really sure you do."

"I do. *Enterprise* is heading back to Earth, and I'm staying here."

"Almost. *Enterprise* is heading back to Earth, and you're going off to war."

"That's not entirely right, sir. The Kanthropians are not going to war," she said, repeating what the Mediator who'd taken over for Elder Green had told her. They'd all learned then that in this sector of the galaxy, and most of the surrounding ones, the Kanthropians were officially recognized as noncombatants in much the same way the old Red Cross had been back on Earth.

"They'll be right in the middle of it, though, if it starts," Trip said. "And who knows if the Antianna are going to make much of a distinction between them and the rest of the fleet once the fighting starts."

"Hopefully it won't come to that," Hoshi said.

Trip shook his head, and started back down the ladder. She had to take the steps two at a time to keep up with him.

She understood his nervousness, at least partially, but she didn't feel like she had a choice. The Kanthropians wanted her help translating the signal. They wanted to stop the war, just like Captain Archer had. He would have wanted her to do this, she knew that.

Trip reached bottom, and headed across the deck, past Shuttle One to where Shuttle Two was normally berthed, only now that craft was sitting at the far corner of the bay, near a number of unused cargo pods, and in its place was a sleek craft half its size, the Kanthropian courier ship, which to Hoshi's eyes looked more like an old Earth fighter plane, at least the front end of it, a transparent canopy where the pilot now sat, its back to them.

Trip knocked on the canopy.

The pilot, who had refused all offers to leave his craft, preferring to "stay ready" instead, turned and saw the two of them. A second later, a hatch on the side of the craft hissed open.

Trip bent and peered inside.

"Kind of cramped," he said.

Hoshi looked too. "Cramped" was the word all

right; the passenger chamber was shaped like a little escape pod, a single seat in an oval-shaped space, barely enough room for her and her flight bag. Good thing she'd packed as sparingly as the Kanthropians had suggested—a change of uniform, her data viewer. She shoved the pack in as far as it would go, and stood.

"Time to go," she said.

Trip stuck out his hand. "Time to go."

They shook. Then, and with a final nod to the commander—the captain—Hoshi squeezed herself into the little courier ship, and contorted her body as best she could to fit into the seat. Her knees, though, were practically touching her chest, and her elbows jammed into her sides.

This isn't right, she thought. Kanthropians were bigger than humans . . . taller for sure. There had to be a way to make herself more comfortable. But nothing in the cabin's interior jumped out at her as a control surface. Most of the little compartment was covered in a textured gray foam, clearly intended to cushion the passenger. More than ever, this part of the ship reminded her of an escape pod, like one of those on the old passenger transports.

A com crackled to life.

"Ensign Hoshi Sato."

The voice was relatively high-pitched, sexless. She didn't recognize it. Probably the pilot, though she had no way of knowing, the passenger compartment was so completely sealed off from the rest of the ship, from the outside as well, save for a small viewport in the hatch door.

"Right here."

"We are now clearing the docking bay of your vessel. Please look to your left. You will find a series of seat adjustment controls."

And there they were—a worn series of reddish circles embossed on a plain black metallic surface, so worn that she had at first mistaken it for the gray material that coated the rest of the cabin's interior.

"Found them."

"Please make yourself as comfortable as possible. Inform me when your adjustments are complete."

She touched one of the reddish circles, and the back of her seat gave beneath her weight. Gave a good three inches, giving her room to breathe easier. She did the same with a half dozen other controls, until she was as close to comfortable as she supposed she was going to get.

"Okay."

"Stand by."

"Stand by? For what?"

"Substantial acceleration velocities, necessary in order to reach trigger velocity for FTL operations."

"FTL operations? As in faster-than-light travel? As in . . . this little ship has a warp engine?"

"No."

Of course not, Hoshi thought. That would be ridiculous. A ship this small with a warp engine.

"We have Type-Two FTL engines," the pilot said. "Accelerating . . . now."

And with that, the ship suddenly rocketed forward. Hoshi's entire body was forced back into the seat, and the stars to her right melted into a puddle of black and white.

FIFTEEN

Malcolm stood by, waiting for Trip to get back to him, as long as he could—he'd been up all night, and kept nodding off on the restaurant table—before closing the circuit, heading back to the guest quarters and going to sleep. He slept for four hours—the most sleep he'd allowed himself in a week. It was a bad idea. His body woke up—or rather, didn't wake up—hungering for more. He forced it out of bed and into a shower. Marched it right back down to the same restaurant, ordered the same food, and coffee. Lots of coffee. Halfway through eating, the caffeine kicked in. Sen was alive. That was not the issue. The issue was, where had he gone? Where was he hiding? On the planet, off-planet . . . he must have had help with a plot of this scale. Who? Step number one, in Reed's mind, was a trip back to the government complex, a search for clues. Talk to Poz and Verkin—see if they'd found anything else. Get hardcopies of the network usage they'd marked. Try and get to Sen's personal files. A lot to do. Not a lot of time to do it in. The peace conference.

He drank more coffee. He switched on his communicator. It started beeping instantly.

"Reed here."

"*Enterprise*. Carstairs here, sir."

"Ensign. Good to hear your voice again."

"And yours, sir. We've been trying to locate you for some time."

"I was asleep."

"Yes, sir. Hold on, Lieutenant. Captain Tucker wants to talk to you."

"I'll bet he does." There was a pause. Then,

"Lieutenant. It sounds like it was a productive night."

"An interesting one, that's for sure."

"Well come on up here and tell us all about it. About Governor Sen still being alive."

"Not much to tell. Yet. I'm going back to his office. There are some people—"

"Malcolm. I need you back aboard *Enterprise*."

Silence.

"The peace conference, remember?"

"I remember. That's still a few days off, isn't it? We have time."

"No, we don't. Admiral McCormick wants us to make a detour first. Barcana Six."

"Stall him."

"Not possible."

"Captain. Trip. You know I'm not given to wild-goose chases. And I'm telling you I can't leave just yet. I'm on the verge . . ."

"If it was up to me, we'd stay till you were satisfied, Malcolm. But it's not up to me. Admiral McCormick gave a direct order. Just like the one I'm giving you one now. Come back to the ship."

Reed was quiet for a moment.

"You know, if Sen is alive, there's a chance . . ." Reed hesitated. He didn't want to say the words out loud, didn't want to speak the thought that had been lurking at the edge of his consciousness ever since earlier this morning, but now . . .

"Don't," Trip said quietly.

"But . . ."

"Tell the Thelasians what you've got," Trip said. "They'll keep us informed. They'll . . ."

"They'll bollix it up entirely!" Reed said, louder than he'd intended. Everyone in the restaurant turned to stare at him.

"I'm sorry, Malcolm."

Reed felt a familiar tingle, and cursed himself for an idiot. He opened his hand to drop the communicator, which was of course providing a transporter fix, his exact location, a spot to focus the matter-transference beam on, but it was too late.

The restaurant, and Procyron, disappeared around him.

When the world came back in focus, he was standing in the transporter chamber of *Enterprise*, back aboard his ship for the first time in a week.

Shannon was manning the transporter. Chief Lee stood next to him.

"Lieutenant. Welcome back."

"Can't say I'm glad to be here."

"Sir?"

Reed stepped off the platform and headed for the bridge.

"Where is he?" Malcolm asked as he stepped out of the lift. Heads—Travis at the helm, Carstairs at communications, T'Pol at science—turned to face him. The captain's chair was empty. "Where's Trip?"

T'Pol stepped in front of him. "Captain Tucker is in the ready room, engaged in a private conversation with . . ."

"Thanks," Reed said, sliding past her to the ready room. He hit the com button. No response. He hit it again.

"Lieutenant," T'Pol said, and he turned his head to see her standing directly behind him. "As I said, Captain Tucker is currently engaged in a—"

Reed hit the com again. And again, a couple more times, until the door opened, and he stepped through.

Trip was sitting in Captain Archer's chair, glaring at him. Behind him, on the monitor screen, was Captain Hernandez from the *Columbia*.

"Hold on a minute, Erika," Trip said. "My crew appears to be mutinying."

"Sorry. I'll come back," Reed said, instantly regretting his decision to barge in.

Trip shook his head. "No, no," he said, and waved Reed closer. "We were just talking about you."

Malcolm moved into the room, moved into the monitor's point of view so Hernandez could see him too.

"Hello, Lieutenant," she said. "Not so much about you, actually, as about what you found."

Malcolm looked at Trip.

"Governor Sen?" Trip prompted.

Suddenly the evidence that had seemed so definitive to him just a few hours ago felt—as Verkin had pointed out—circumstantial. Like nothing at all. A lot of hot air.

He felt, all at once, very, very stupid.

"Nothing definitive," he said. "Just a lot of loose ends that don't tie up the way they should."

He explained.

"Loose ends, all right," Hernandez said. "Stay on it. From what Trip tells me . . . this Sen was—maybe is—a real sonuvabitch. Something like this wouldn't be past him at all."

"No," Malcolm agreed. "I don't think it would."

Hernandez's gaze hardened. "You'll let me know if you find anything, won't you?"

"Of course," he said.

"We'll keep you posted," Trip said.

"Do. *Columbia* out." The little monitor went dark. Trip swung around in his chair. His eyes looked a little glassy. A little red. Malcolm wondered if this was the first chance he'd had to talk to Hernandez; the two of them had been close, he knew. Not as close as she and the captain had been, if the scuttlebutt was correct, or as close as Trip and the captain, but—

"Sorry I had to pull you out of there ahead of schedule," Trip said. "But McCormick—"

"No need to explain," Reed said, holding up a hand. "I understand."

"I know you do." He shook his head. "You know who this important person is we're supposed to pick up at Barcana?"

"No."

"A vice-ambassador. The Tellarite vice-ambassador for economic development. Can you believe that?"

"The one the captain almost . . ."

"Yeah." Trip shook his head. "Unbelievable. I bet he's looking down right now at us and laughing."

"He's laughing, all right," Reed said, and then both men fell silent.

"So," Trip said, "you'll tell the Thclasians what you found? See what else they can dig up?"

"Of course." For all the good that'll do, he added silently. Some of his skepticism must have shown on this face.

"Yeah. Well." Trip shrugged. "Maybe we'll luck out."

"Maybe," Malcolm agreed.

The com beeped.

"Captain?" That was Carstairs. "I have the Tellarite Embassy on Barcana for you."

"Tell them to hold on a minute." Trip looked up at Malcolm. "If they don't find anything—"

"The Thelasians."

"Yes. If the Thelasians don't find anything, we come back here after the peace conference. You, me, Erika . . . we make a few inquiries on our own."

"Unofficial inquiries, I assume."

"That's right."

For the first time all day, Malcolm smiled. "I like the way you think, Commander."

Trip didn't smile back.

"If that sonuvabitch is still alive, if he's responsible for the captain's death . . ."

The words hung there a minute.

"I'd better get back to work," Malcolm said finally. "Make sure the armory is still where I left it."

"You should see engineering. Hess is—she doesn't—" He shook his head. "Between you and me, I'd be surprised if *Enterprise* makes it back to Earth in one piece."

"It can't be that bad."

"It's worse."

Reed couldn't tell whether or not he was serious.

The com beeped again.

"Almost as bad as the Tellarites," Trip said, and then he did smile. "You should hear the things they want us to do—to prepare the ship for the vice-ambassador. A laundry list as long as . . ."

"I'll leave you to it, then."

He started for the door. Trip swiveled his chair back around.

"Put the ambassador through," Reed heard him say.

"Actually, it's Admiral McCormick's office, sir," Carstairs said.

Trip threw his hands in the air. "How is anyone supposed to get any work done around here?"

Malcolm assumed the question was rhetorical.

He let the door close behind him.

"Ensign Sato."

Hoshi opened her eyes.

The voice came not from the com, but from the hatch to her right, which was now open, and through which a familiar face now peered in. One of the Mediators she'd met at the reception.

"May I assist?" he asked, extending a hand.

"Thank you." She clambered out of the courier ship, and then reached back in for her kit. As she turned, she wobbled on her feet a bit. The Mediator steadied her.

"Sorry," she said. "Guess I'm still a little woozy."

"Disorientation after initial exposure to Type-Two FTL acceleration is to be expected."

She nodded, taking in her surroundings—the Kanthropian version of a shuttlebay, cramped as well, slots for four ships similar in design to the vessel she had arrived in, room enough for personnel to maneuver around those ships—and the Mediator, who wore the same plain brown robe she had seen him in at the party. Looked, in fact, exactly the same, except for a patch of slightly discolored skin along one side of his face, a souvenir of the explosion, she guessed.

"I'm all right now," she said

"Then follow me, if you would. Elder Green is expecting us."

They left the docking area and entered a narrow

corridor, which they followed for several minutes as it wound crookedly through the ship. Along the way, the Mediator told her a few things, about S-12 (a state-of-the-art mediation vessel which she was not to judge by the amenities or lack thereof, though it was aware of the value that many species, including humans, placed on such things), his name (Younger Emmen), and the reason for both the rushed nature of Elder Green's communiqué and the use of the Type-2 FTL drive (the nature of which he would not address, owing to the relative technological immaturity of her species, at which point Hoshi thought here we go again, level-four technology and all that).

"The Armada, with S-12 accompanying, was forced to depart several minutes ahead of schedule. FTL 2 was thus required for your rendezvous."

"Why the rush?" she asked, as he lcd her into an elevator that started downward with a sudden lurch which made Hoshi's stomach start spinning all over again.

"Because," he began, and at that moment, the elevator stopped, the door slid open, and they stepped out into the single largest open space Hoshi had ever encountered aboard a starship.

It was the length of a soccer field, the solarium on Procyron cut in half, fully a hundred meters from where she stood to the far side of the room, where a transparent wall looked out on the stars.

Between her and that wall, the room was filled with a series of horseshoe-shaped consoles, at each of which several mediators—some seated, some standing, all dressed in the characteristic brown robes of their order—were busy working. There had to be dozens of them, but her attention was drawn immediately back to the space visible outside the glass. There, the ships of the Armada were on full display—perhaps as many as a hundred of them, surrounding a single Antianna vessel, identical twin to the ship *Enterprise* had encountered.

"Relay stations abutting the Procyron sector recorded a Conani freighter's distress signal approximately one hour ago," Emmen said. "General Jaedez ordered the Armada to launch immediately. We encountered the wreckage of that freighter approximately fifteen minutes later, and the Antianna vessel shortly thereafter. This way, please."

He led her to the nearest of the horseshoe consoles. The two of them stood behind it, side by side, and watched the Mediators work. Hoshi was barely able to follow what they were doing; she heard snippets of the Antianna signal, the one she'd spent so many long and fruitless hours trying to puzzle out, heard it filtered, truncated, with portions amplified, portions reduced in volume, saw physical representations of its waveforms on the console screens before her, saw each of its fifty-seven individual components mapped out on a grid according to phoneme distribution, all of which were happening simultaneously, all of which (apparently) the Mediators before her were able to keep track of in their heads as they walked between different consoles, different stations at those consoles.

Most of her attention, however, was still focused on the scene playing out before her. The Antianna ship, under attack by Thelasian forces.

The little vessel was still, incredibly, managing to hold its own.

Part of that was because the Armada was too overwhelmingly big—too many ships, in too tight a space. They had to take care with each weapons burst not to hit their own. But that was what computers were for, and they were getting enough shots off that the little ship should have been space dust long ago. Except it wasn't. Largely because the ship seemed to have a kind of sixth sense—to move just as weapons fire arrived.

Hoshi noticed that it was not returning that fire. More proof, to her way of thinking, that the Antianna's intentions were peaceful—or at least, as Captain Archer had surmised, relatively benevolent. That they were simply marking off their space. This far, and no farther.

"It's transmitting the signal?" she asked.

"It began doing so almost immediately upon the Armada's arrival. Excuse me a moment."

Another mediator approached, and handed Emmen a device of some kind. A headset. He donned it, and almost immediately, began nodding. Listening to someone. Hoshi had no way of knowing for sure, but it seemed to her his skin grew slightly paler as he listened.

He was visibly shaken as he handed the headset back. He spoke a few words to the Mediator who'd given him the device, and then turned back to her.

"Elder Green will not be able to meet with you at this time. My apologies."

"I understand. I'm just—whatever I can do to help."

"Help?" He looked at her strangely. "Help with what?"

She frowned. "With translating the alien signal."

"Ah." He nodded. "Of course. Come with me."

He led her to a horseshoe console at one end of the

room, unoccupied save for a single Mediator engaged in maintenance of some kind.

"The stations here all utilize the standard Mediation interface. Please familiarize yourself with it," Emmen said. "I will return."

And then he was gone.

"Human." The Mediator working at the console drew her attention to the terminal farthest away from him. "Use that station. Only that station. Do you understand?"

He spoke very slowly, as if he were talking to a child.

"I understand," Hoshi said, glaring back at him. "I'm not an idiot."

He looked at her like she was exactly that.

She walked over to the station he'd pointed out. It consisted of an input padd, and a headset, similar to the one Emmen had worn. She picked it up. There were two thin metal arms attached to the earpieces. They slid up and down the main body of the headset at her touch. One was for voice input, obviously, she had seen Emmen use it as such. The other . . .

Visual?

She slid the arms into position, slipped the headset on, and sat. The input padd in front of her looked identical to the one in the courier ship—a series of reddish circles, less worn here than on that vessel, embossed on a black metallic surface.

What next?

She ran a hesitant finger over one of the circles. The padd came to life under her hand. A hissing noise, followed by static, filled both ears. A thin beam of blue light shot forward from the upper of the two arms attached to the headset and hovered in the air before her.

She adjusted the headset once more, and began experimenting with the input pad. She found the control for the audio—volume and frequency—and scrolled through a multitude of different signals. She listened for a moment to one, a broadcast in what she recognized as Conani, in the few brief seconds it took for her UT to catch up and start translating. Someone was yelling—a private conversation. Rather than eavesdrop—she, at least, knew what manners were—she moved past that frequency, and then moved off the audio control entirely and on to the next one on the input pad.

She brushed her index finger against it lightly.

It was as if someone had put a motor on the back of her chair, and pressed Go.

She shot forward into the blue light in front of her, and everything around her went blue. The color was everywhere she looked, all she could see, as if she'd jumped into an entirely different world. A blue world. A virtual world.

She slid her finger in the opposite direction, and she was back in the analysis chamber, back in her chair.

Wow.

She scrolled forward again. Into the blue, and then back out.

She played around like that for a moment, before moving on to the rest of the controls on the pad. She couldn't quite figure out what they were for, at first, touched one after another with no results. Until she tried two in tandem.

She shot forward into the blue again, only this time as she moved—more correctly, as the light surrounded her—the color around her crackled with static, went to black for a second, and then the analysis chamber took shape around her once more. Again, she was staring out at row after row of the horseshoe-shaped consoles, at brown robe after brown robe, stretching on before her, seemingly into infinity.

I broke it, she thought. *I broke the interface.*

But just as she pictured herself pulling the headset off and having to confess her sin to a whole room full of Mediators, she saw there was no transparent wall looking out into space ahead of her.

She was still in the virtual world—an uncannily realistic simulation of the analysis chamber.

She scrolled the input pad again. The controls moved her instantaneously through the chamber, from one console to another. As she approached one of those consoles, one of the Mediators stationed at it turned toward her expectantly. Waiting.

"May I assist?" it said.

Hoshi adjusted the lower arm of the headest, and spoke.

"What is this place?"

The Mediator frowned at her.

"Language: English. Species: human, Sol system, Planet Three, Earth, Level-Four Technological Development, Dominant Culture: Anglo-Saxon. One moment."

The analysis chamber in front of her crackled with static again, and then faded slowly to black.

Hoshi waited.

Light flickered at the edges of her vision, and then the VR world before her came to life again. Only now it was different. The horseshoe consoles were gone, the Mediators were gone, and the analysis chamber had morphed into a huge room with vaulted ceilings, classical Greek columns, long wooden tables, and aisle after aisle after aisle of books, stretching as far as she could see. Out into infinity.

She was in a library.

A tall thin man wearing an old-fashioned suit and tie appeared before her. A librarian or, rather, a holographic version of one.

"May I assist?" he asked, in a dead-perfect approximation of an upper-class English accent.

"What is this place?" she asked again, suspecting she knew the answer already.

"This," the man said, gesturing toward the library behind him, "is a virtual representation of the Kanthropian database. You may submit input via console or voice."

"Thanks."

"Is there something in particular you wish to find?"

"Not just yet, thanks. I think I'll browse a little."

She scrolled the input pad and shot forward toward the stacks. Each aisle was labeled according to the Standard Starfleet coding system—there was one for interstellar relations, one for sociology, one for literature, one anthropology, one archaeology, one technology . . .

Curious, she turned down that one, and studied the shelves.

Here were books—no, not books she reminded herself, the virtual volumes she saw here represented entire databases of knowledge located elsewhere in the Kanthroian vessel—covering subjects like matter-antimatter power generation, weapons development, artificial consciousness, and . . .

Type-2 FTL drives? Interesting.

She reached for the first volume on that shelf, and a hand touched her arm.

She almost jumped right out of her skin.

"Access to these resources is forbidden for civilizations at level-four development."

The librarian stood next to her, a reproachful smile on his face.

Hoshi nodded. That had been enough browsing anyway.

She asked for information on the Antianna. The librarian directed her to another aisle, to a slim shelf of books, dated by Earth year. The earliest was from 2147—eight years back. She pulled it off the shelf, and opened it.

The image of a Mediator stepped out of the book, and came to three-dimensional life before her. A holograph.

"Stardate 1121.8," the Kanthropian said. "The *Olane*, a H'ratoi merchant vessel out of Procyron, bound for Coreida Prime, drifted off course owing to a computer error. Contact was lost. The wreckage of the ship was discovered by a Confederacy patrol several weeks later. Initial suspicions focused on Maszakian pirates and raiders from the neighboring Klingon Empire, but recovery of onboard ship's data made it clear neither group was involved."

Behind the Mediator, the image of an Antianna ship appeared.

"A recording of this vessel," the Mediator said, "confronting and subsequently attacking the *Olane* was retrieved by representatives of the Thelasian Trading Confederacy. Over the next several years, sightings of such vessels, and similar attacks, multiplied. Beginning on Stardate 1212.6, these ships began sending the following transmission before attacking."

The familiar Antianna signal—the fifty-seven pulses—sounded.

"The Confederacy's leaders contacted Kanthropian Mediators on Stardate 1254.2. Translation efforts began immediately."

The image wavered then, and disappeared, its place taken by a standard display screen, which summarized those efforts. Hoshi paged through the text. She read for quite some time, long enough to realize two things. First, there was nothing revolutionary about the Mediators' approach to translation. They had better equipment—faster computers, more specialized software—but their efforts were focused on the same things as hers. A search for repeating patterns, the use of frequency analysis to assign meaning to those patterns (and here, she noted, their approach was exactly the same as the one taken by Starfleet linguists, the use of LMUs such as species name, individual name, intent, etc.).

Second, there was no mention of Theera anywhere in the database, which Hoshi found very odd. Her first thought was that the Mediators had spelled the name differently. So she tried the query again, using every variation she could think of. Still nothing. Then she tried Quirsh; then Andorian; then *Lokune*. She found a brief reference to that ship's destruction, and an unlinked reference to the attack's sole survivor. Theera. They spelled her name just as Hoshi would have.

It was all very curious indeed.

She was trying to determine her next step when all at once the library went dark around her.

An instant later, she was back in the real world. The analysis chamber.

Younger Emmen stood over her.

"Forgive the interruption," he said. "But Elder Green will see you now."

Hoshi nodded, and rose to her feet. She glanced

toward the transparent wall at the far end of the chamber, and saw a handful of Armada ships circling a sparkling mass of wreckage.

"What happened to the Antianna ship?" she asked.

"The Antianna ship has been destroyed," Emmen said. He turned his back. "This way, please."

Emmen led her up a level and through an unmarked door, into a large room roughly the size of *Enterprise*'s main bridge, furnished with a single horseshoe-shaped console (a smaller version of the ones in the chamber) and a large display screen, on which video from the battle she'd witnessed earlier—the lone Antianna ship against the Armada—was playing.

"Wait here," Emmen said, and then he disappeared.

With nothing else to do, Hoshi watched the screen a moment. She had no way of knowing for sure, but the footage seemed to be from earlier in the battle—prior to her arrival aboard S-12. The Antianna ship was motionless in space; a handful of Armada vessels circled around it. No weapons fire was being exchanged.

There was an audio track playing along with the footage. Barely audible, coming from the console— no, not from the console, from a headset lying atop it. She moved closer. It sounded to her a little like the Antianna signal, but something was different about it.

She picked the headset up and listened. Definitely the Antianna signal, but slowed down. Separated into its fifty-seven individual components. Interesting. She listened a moment, focusing in on each pulse as it played.

"If you're wondering, we are searching for correlations between the signal pulses and the movements of the Antianna ship."

Hoshi started, almost dropping the headset. She set it back down on the console, turned and saw Elder Green standing behind her. Or rather turned, looked down, and then saw Elder Green, who was much shorter in person than on the viewscreen. A whole head shorter—but for all that, no less commanding a presence. Close-cropped silver hair, intense blue eyes, the same coarse brown robe all the Mediators wore.

"As of yet our efforts have proven unsuccessful."

"Elder Green," Hoshi said.

"Ensign Hoshi Sato. I apologize for not greeting you sooner. It has been—as I'm sure you can guess—a busy few hours."

"I understand, sir."

"I believe the correct honorific in your language would be ma'am."

A smile tugged at the corners of Green's mouth.

Hoshi blushed. "Excuse me."

"It is of no consequence." The Mediator shrugged. "I want to thank you for coming to S-12. I am certain you will be of great assistance to us in our translation efforts."

"Oh?" Hoshi said, curious. She'd hardly gotten that impression from the Mediators at the reception the other night.

"I have been reviewing your work for the last few days," Green continued, "at least those parts of it which are accessible through the commercially traded databases, and have been quite impressed. You are a resilient young woman. A resourceful young woman."

"Thank you, but . . . I'm not exactly sure what you're referring to."

Green clasped her hands behind her, and walked to the display screen.

"The Huantamos, for one," she said, her back to Hoshi. "You certainly went to great lengths to learn their language. Living among them for—how long was it—six months? Learning the culture as well as the words—an essential skill for a linguist, that kind of empathy. Essential and in my experience, all too rare."

Hoshi was too surprised to respond for a second. The Huantamos? That was years ago, she'd been back on Earth, working for a private foundation helping to catalogue some of the languages of the more remote Amazonian tribes, of which the Huantamos were one, and she had ended up living in the rain forest for . . . well, six months sounded about right.

"I suppose," she said. "I mean, thank you. Again."

Green nodded. "You are welcome."

"But I don't know how that applies to this situation. I'm not—"

"Please," Green said, turning to face her. "Allow me to finish."

Green pulled a device of some sort from her robe then, and pressed a button on it. The image on the display screen—which now showed the Antianna ship firing on the Armada vessels closest to it—froze.

"Younger Emmen has given you details regarding our recent encounter with the Antianna?" she asked.

"I know that the ship was destroyed," Hoshi said.

"Yes, it was. Not, however, before it destroyed eleven vessels in the Allied Fleet," Green replied.

Hoshi blinked. Eleven? That was an awfully high number. It spoke volumes about the Antianna's skill at warfare. And about the Allied Fleet's chances for success in the conflict.

"One hundred twelve lives were lost as well."

"I'm sorry," Hoshi said, because she could think of nothing else to say.

"And as if I needed a reminder," and here Green's voice took on an edge, "General Jaedez has just finished telling me that loss of life on that scale is unacceptable. That the next time we encounter an Antianna ship, his policy will be to attack with overwhelming force, rather than allow the situation to unfold. To attempt negotiation. And that to me," she shook her head, "that is the most unacceptable thing of all."

Green turned and stared directly at Hoshi.

"For over four hundred years, the Kanthropians have served as Mediators to all races in this part of the galaxy. In all that time, no war of any consequential size between species has broken out—and those skirmishes that have inevitably developed, we have managed to end in short order. To have a conflict of this magnitude occur during my leadership of the order . . ." She sighed heavily. "It must not—it cannot—continue."

Hoshi nodded. "I'll do whatever I can to help."

"I am glad to hear it." She paused a moment. "I wish to speak to you regarding the Andorian. Technician Theera."

Somehow, Hoshi wasn't surprised to hear that.

"Okay," she said.

Green turned back to the console. "You are aware that her ship—the *Lokune*—was attacked by the Antianna?"

"Yes."

"Have you heard details regarding that attack?"

"Some. Not all."

"No one has all of them. We do know that the vessel was bound for Andoria, that it was traveling through a region of space where several attacks had occurred previously—against the express advice of the Confederacy, I might add—and that they engaged with an Antianna vessel. Exactly what happened then is unclear, but shortly afterward . . . a H'ratoi patrol vessel discovered the wreckage—the remnants—of the *Lokune*. No survivors were found."

"No survivors? I don't understand." Hoshi frowned. "What about Theera?"

"Four days afterward," Green continued, "a convoy of Conani destroyers came upon an Antianna ship. Life signs—Andorian life signs—were detected aboard that vessel. It was decided to attempt a rescue, and after a series of battles stretching across the sector, the Antianna ship was disabled. The Conani prepared a boarding party, and—after considerable difficulty, I might add—established transporter lock on the Andorians. Before the operation could be completed, the Antianna vessel self-destructed. Only a single Andorian was rescued."

"Theera," Hoshi said.

Green nodded. "This is a recording of that rescue."

She pressed a single control on the console. The display screen came to life once more.

Hoshi was looking at a high-ceilinged, dimly lit room. A raised platform at one end of it. A transporter platform. Two Conani in full body armor flanked it, two others stood nearby, all with weapons at the ready. A column of energy appeared, a beam of sparkling light that began to coalesce almost at once. Theera. A naked and obviously terrified Theera, who as she finished materializing collapsed on the platform, looking up at her rescuers in disbelief and shock.

She began screaming—a single word, over and over again.

Antianna.

The Conani warriors closed around her.

The screen went dark.

Green cleared her throat.

"Clearly," the Elder said, "a highly traumatic experience."

That's putting it mildly, Hoshi thought.

Green continued speaking. "Data was recovered from the wreckage of the Andorian vessel indicating that before its destruction, a single code group was transmitted to the alien ship. A rough transliteration of that code group is the word 'Antianna.'"

"Theera sent that code group."

"Precisely. It is our hypothesis that it represents the name of the species."

"She doesn't remember sending it."

"No." Green shook her head. "As I said, Technician Theera recalls very little of the work she completed before the attack—and even less of her imprisonment by the aliens."

"Ah." Hoshi was beginning to understand now. What further information the Mediators wanted from Theera; her reluctance to speak of the incident at all.

One thing, however, still wasn't clear to her.

"So what is it, exactly, you want from me? I get the feeling I'm not here because of my linguistic skills."

"In part, you are correct," Green replied. "We are hoping you will prove to be a more sympathetic confessor than we have been."

"Confessor." Hoshi frowned. "To who?"

"Theera."

"Theera? She's on her way to Andoria—isn't she?"

"No. Technician Theera is here. Assigned to S-12 by the order of Ambassador Quirsh."

Hoshi recalled the scene she'd witnessed at the party: General Jaedez and Quirsh talking, Theera standing by, looking anxious.

"I don't suppose she's too happy about being here."

"You are correct."

And no doubt that unhappiness was playing a role—at least partially—in her refusal to talk to the Mediators. Hoshi shrugged. "All right. I'll talk to her. Though I still don't understand why you think I'll do any better than you have."

"I have confidence," Green said. "As I told you, I've been reviewing your record. Your own experiences. Your empathic skills."

"The Huantamos," Hoshi said. "Yes. You said that."

"No," Green said. "Not the Huantamos. The—am I pronouncing it correctly—Zindi?"

Hoshi's heart thudded in her chest.

She pictured a small, dark, dank cell.

Her forehead ached with remembered pain.

"No," she said, after a moment. "That's—Xindi is right."

The Kanthropian nodded. "Would you not agree that the two experiences are similar?"

She pictured the reptilian commander looming over her.

The launch codes. Give them to us.

She pictured Theera, screaming.

Antianna. Antianna.

"Yes," she told Elder Green. "I suppose they are."

"So you will talk to her?"

Hoshi nodded. "Whenever you want."

"Good."

She pressed a button on the console, and almost at once, Younger Emmen appeared in the doorway.

"Please take Ensign Sato to the Andorian's quarters."

Emmen bowed in acknowledgment. "This way, please."

"I'd like to get set in my own quarters first, get my kit from the analysis chamber," Hoshi said. "If that would be all right."

A smile flashed across Green's face for an instant, and then was gone, just as quickly as it had come.

"That will not be a problem," the Elder said. "As the two are one and the same."

Hoshi frowned. "We're sharing quarters."

"Yes."

"Ah."

"Is that a problem?" Green asked.

"No," Hoshi said. "No problem at all."

SIXTEEN

At the door to Room J-21—Theera's quarters, about to be hers as well—Hoshi paused a moment.

She tried to remember what she had felt like after being rescued from the reptilian ship, after returning to *Enterprise*. Numb, mostly. There had been no time to reflect on her experience, not right away, not with so much else going on—it had been a week, at least, before she'd had a chance to really absorb what had been done to her. How she'd been violated. There was the anger, and the revulsion associated with that violation, and then there was the fear that when they drilled into her brain, the Xindi had done some kind of permanent damage. Theera had to be feeling all the same things—and more, even. After all, she was now aboard a ship deliberately seeking out the very race that had kidnapped her. *It would be,* Hoshi thought, *like her going back into the Expanse and looking for the reptilians.*

Theera had to be scared. And maybe there were things about those four days she'd spent aboard the Antianna vessel that she was repressing—either deliberately or involuntarily. She'd have to work her way into the Andorian's confidence before finding out what they were, though. And she had to do it quickly—it was, as Elder Green had pointed out to her, a matter of life and death.

There was a touchpad to the side of the entrance.

Hoshi pressed it, and the door slid open.

The room was small—half the size of her quarters back on *Enterprise*, shaped like a flattened capital "T." Each of the letter's arms held a bunk and storage shelves. Directly in front of her was a terminal, a workstation.

In front of it sat Theera.

At the sound of the door opening, the Andorian spun around in the chair. Her eyes widened in surprise. There was a picture on the terminal behind her—an Andorian male. Theera punched a button and the screen went to black.

"Ensign Sato."

"Theera. I'm sorry," Hoshi said, nodding toward the screen. "I didn't mean to interrupt."

"It is a recorded message. I was simply reviewing it." The Andorian got to her feet. "What are you doing here?"

"I've been assigned to these quarters."

"What?"

Hoshi took a step into the room. "I've been assigned to these quarters," she repeated. "It seems like we're going to be roommates."

"There must be some mistake. I told the Kanthropians I did not want to share quarters."

"Maybe they had no choice," Hoshi said. "Maybe the ship got too crowded."

"No one has come aboard save yourself that I am aware of." The Andorian frowned.

Hoshi chose to ignore that frown and take another step in the room. The bedclothes on the bunk to her right were rumpled. The one to her left looked fresh.

"Okay if I . . ." she asked, gesturing toward the empty bunk.

Without waiting for an answer, Hoshi put her kit down on the bed, opened it, and started to unpack.

"So how long have you been here—on S-12?" she asked.

Theera took a moment before answering.

"A week. Almost immediately after the bombing on Procyron." She paused a moment. "I heard about your captain. My sympathies."

"Thank you." Hoshi pulled out the spare set of clothes she'd brought, and her data viewer, and put them on the shelf. "It's still . . . sinking in, I guess."

"I am glad to see that you have recovered, at least."

"Good as new." Hoshi folded her kit and stowed that too. She turned to face Theera.

"So I guess you didn't make the trip back to Andoria after all."

"No. I was ordered here, to provide the Mediators with whatever assistance I could."

"Ambassador Quirsh's orders, I take it."

"Quirsh's, and the Imperial Council's."

"You don't sound too happy about that."

"I serve the Empire."

"Yes," Hoshi said. "I've read about some of your work. The Universal Translator project. I was very impressed. Your thinking parallels . . ."

"That was a long time ago," Theera interrupted. "And now, if you'll excuse me, I'm going to get some sleep. I have an early shift in the analysis chamber tomorrow."

"Oh. Of course." So much for working her way into the Andorian's confidence tonight. Hoshi glanced around the room. "Should I turn down some of the lights, or—"

"No need." Theera stepped back to her bunk, and

Hoshi saw there was a touchpad on the wall above it as well. The Andorian pressed a button on the pad, and a wall of polarized light came to life, a blue curtain of light that cut off her side of the room entirely. The high-tech equivalent of a privacy screen.

The screen vanished. Theera reappeared, still standing next to the bed.

"The force-screen blocks out sound as well as light. You are free to utilize the room as you wish. It will not bother me at all."

"Okay," Hoshi said. "Good . . ."

Night, she was about to finish, but the privacy curtain was already back up.

So much for breaking the ice, she thought, and sat down on her bunk. What now? Report back to Elder Green, mission unaccomplished? Contact *Enterprise*, and try and obtain a lift back home?

She kicked off her boots and lay back.

It had been a long day, she realized. Twenty hours or so since she'd gotten up early to meet Carstairs for breakfast, and what was more, for the last twelve or so, she hadn't eaten a thing. She wondered when and where meals were served aboard S-12, if there was a mess hall on the ship, or . . .

Her gaze wandered over to the workstation. She could probably find the information on that. She got up and sat down in front of it.

The machine used a standard command interface, unlike the ones in the analysis chamber; Hoshi quickly found a map of the ship, and saw that indeed, there was a mess hall—two of them, in fact, one on this deck, one right next to the analyis chamber. Looked easy enough to find. Grab a midnight snack— or rather, a twenty-two hundred hours snack—come back here, and get to sleep herself. If Theera was on the early shift, she probably was too; Elder Green would have her stick as close to the Andorian as possible. She wondered how early early was for the Kanthropians. She wondered if, on really her first full day back on the job, she'd have enough energy to get up then. She'd have to find it, she decided.

What was it Captain Archer always used to say? A little hard work never hurt anyone.

She supposed a couple more early days wouldn't kill her. Especially with some food in her.

She was about to log off when she saw a little status bar at the bottom of the screen. It read:

Message Standby

"Message?" she said out loud, wondering what that meant.

All at once, the screen filled with the words:

Message 3 of 6. Active.

Playing Resumed.

which then disappeared, and were replaced with the image of the Andorian male Hoshi had seen before. This was Theera's message, Hoshi realized instantly. The one she'd interrupted playback of.

The man started talking.

". . . understand you at all anymore, R'shee," he said. "You don't seem like the same person."

He wore the uniform of an Andorian soldier, with markings on it that made Hoshi think he was an officer of some kind.

He took a deep breath, and leaned forward in his chair, leaned closer to the viewer.

"Why haven't you responded to my last few messages? Have I offended you in some way? Please tell me. Please talk to me." He spoke in a calm, almost matter-of-fact tone that belied his words—but the depth of emotion he felt was plain to see in his eyes. "Remember the plans we had made? I still—"

Enough, Hoshi thought. This was none of her business.

"Stop," she said out loud, and the terminal went to black.

It seemed as if she wasn't the only one having a hard time getting through to Theera.

It seemed as if the task Elder Green had laid before her was going to be even more difficult than she'd thought at first.

SEVENTEEN

For what seemed to him like the hundredth time already this morning, the warning light on Travis's console flashed red.

"Ensign!" Captain Tucker said at the same instant, and Travis could hear him coming down the steps from the engineering station, where he had spent most of the last few hours, to the growing resentment of Lieutenant Hess, who had ideas of her own regarding the proper way to run the engines, and the engine room, and its personnel. Although Travis only knew that from overhearing her rant at breakfast, as far as he could tell she hadn't told Commander Tucker anything at all regarding her opinions. Though no one had really been able to tell him much of anything lately, except of course Admiral McCormick, who was continually sharing with Trip and whatever bridge crew was present the absolute overriding necessity of reaching Barcana Six by 1200 hours tomorrow ("Push the engines," McCormick told them). In order that the Tellarite vice-ambassador, who along with *Enterprise*'s crew was going to be the single most important attendee at the peace conference, for reasons Travis had yet to hear fully laid out, could arrive on schedule, and in style.

Of course, what McCormick didn't take into consideration was the fact that the direct route back to

Barcana took them perilously close to the space the Antianna were claiming, so they were going the long way round, which meant dealing with certain obstacles the more traveled corridors did not present. The occasional nebula. A convoy of ill-tempered Rigelian spice merchants. The Maldeev Meteor Cloud, which now loomed on the viewscreen before them, though in his opinion it should have been called the Maldeev Asteroid Belt, because the meteors in it were the size of small planetoids. Moons, actually, on the scale of Deimos, sometimes bigger.

Like the one that had just whizzed past, and set the proximity alarm off.

"How close was that?" Trip asked.

"Ninety-nine point six-seven meters," Travis replied.

"One hundred meters." Trip rolled his eyes. "Didn't we plot the course so we wouldn't come within a thousand?"

"The orbits of objects in an asteroid field such as this one are inherently unstable," T'Pol said, looking up from her own station.

"So one could hit us at any time?"

T'Pol nodded. "It is a distinct possibility."

"Won't happen."

Everyone turned to face the back of the bridge, where Malcolm stood at the weapons console.

"Why won't it happen?" Trip asked.

"Laser cannons are on-line. Anything gets too close . . ."

The edges of a smile—a nasty little smile—played along Reed's lips.

"Don't fire on anything without my orders, all right?" Travis peeked over his shoulder and saw Trip running a hand through his hair. "I don't want to draw power from the engines right now. Things are messed up enough down there as it is."

At the engineering station, Hess gritted her teeth. Malcolm frowned.

"Of course I wouldn't fire without your orders."

"Lieutenant Reed, are you trying to push my . . ."

T'Pol, over at the science station, looked up and said, "Captain Tucker, could I speak with you a moment—perhaps in your ready room?"

The two of them exchanged a significant glance. Trip sighed, and got to his feet.

"Come on." He started for the ready room. T'Pol followed.

Travis had no doubt that she was going to give him another lecture on his command style. Travis had accidentally overheard one of those (at least part of one) last night, on his way back from sickbay, when he'd wandered into the mess and come on the two of them, T'Pol and Captain Tucker, almost shouting at each other. They'd fallen silent on his entrance, and invited him over to chat, but not before he'd heard enough ("In my opinion, you are micromanaging the crew." "I don't micromanage." "You never did before, I agree, but now . . .") to get the gist of the conversation.

"Ensign."

Travis looked up. Malcolm stood over him.

"Something occurred to me this morning, regarding your mission."

"My mission."

"Your attempts to recover *Horizon*'s money?"

"Oh. Right. That mission."

"Yes. I believe I may be able to help."

"Really?"

Reed smiled.

The proximity light flashed.

"Hang on," Travis called out, to Malcolm and to everyone else, and turned the ship hard to starboard. Reed grabbed the console for support as the gravity stabilizers struggled to keep up.

A meteor—no, make that an asteroid, a rock that looked to be at least the size of Deimos—shot past on the viewscreen.

The ship steadied itself, and shot forward again.

The ready room door opened. Trip stood there, frown on face.

"Captain . . ." that from T'Pol, standing behind him.

Trip took a deep breath.

"Carry on," he said, and stepped back inside the ready room. The door closed.

"Let's talk after your shift," Malcolm said, clapping Travis on the shoulder. "The armory."

Travis watched him go, wondering what sort of help, exactly, Reed had in mind.

He found out a few hours after shift, when he entered the armory.

The huge room was deserted except for Reed, who sat in front of a display screen. On the screen in front of him, video was playing. People dressed in fancy clothes, eating, drinking, talking . . .

It was footage from the reception on Procyron, Travis realized.

"Where'd you get that?" he asked.

Malcolm spoke without turning around.

"Poz and Verkin. They sent it to me early this morning—along with a few other goodies. The Intelligence

Division's complete file on the explosion—some background material on Governor Sen."

"Sounds like quite a haul."

"Not really. No smoking gun, as it were. Nothing I can take back to the Thelasians and say, 'Your governor's a thief and a murderer, help me find him.' Just a lot of suggestive details."

"But, you think Sen's alive?"

Reed spun around in his chair.

"That's right," he said. "I think the explosion was a smoke screen of some kind. I think he found a way out. I think he's hiding somewhere right now, laughing at all of us, and I want to find him, and wipe that smile off his face."

Travis nodded. "Anything in what Poz and Verkin sent on that might tell you where?"

Reed shook his head. "Not really. I need more information. More background on Sen's past—his associates—that sort of thing."

"Can they get it for you?"

Malcolm smiled then. It was not a happy smile.

"Oh, they can get it all right. The question is—can I afford it?"

"They want money."

"Oh yes. A great deal of money." Reed told him then how much, at which point Travis's eyes widened.

"My mistake—I paid them too well, apparently. Sen's credit chits," Malcolm continued. "Now I seem to have created a monster."

"I wish I could help," Travis said.

"I think you can."

"How? I don't have that kind of money."

"Oh, I wouldn't be so sure."

Travis folded his arms across his chest. "What?"

"Correct me if I'm wrong," Malcolm said slowly, "but the money you're trying to track down for *Horizon*, the money Sen stole from you in the first place, that's a lot of—"

"Oh no," Travis said. "That's not my money. That belongs to *Horizon*."

"No, right now it belongs to the Confederacy, doesn't it? And you're not having much luck convincing them otherwise?"

Travis frowned. "True enough."

"You need records of your dealings with Sen, isn't that so? You need proof that he stole the money from you, correct?"

"That's true too."

"I suspect that Mister Poz and Mister Verkin could find that proof for you."

"For a price," Travis said. "Isn't that so?"

"True, but . . . in your case, I suspect they'd be willing to work for a contingency fee. A percentage of monies recovered."

"You suspect?" Travis eyed Malcolm dubiously. "You talked to them already, didn't you?"

Reed smiled again. "Guilty as charged."

"Hmmm." Travis folded his arms across his chest. "It's a thought, all right. But how does this tie into getting more information on Sen?"

"Money," Reed said.

"Money. I don't understand."

"The Bynar get a percentage of your deal, and I get a percentage of theirs." He smiled. "A piece of the action, as it were."

"A piece of the action." Travis frowned. "All in a good cause, I suppose."

"In a damn good cause," Reed said and then, without waiting for an answer, spun around in his chair, and keyed in a few commands. He spoke briefly to someone, and a few seconds later the big screen came to life. On it were the two Bynar—Poz and Verkin.

"Gentlemen," Reed said. "You recall Ensign Mayweather?"

"Indeed." The Bynar on the left—Travis couldn't remember if it was Poz or Verkin—nodded acknowledgment.

"Of course," the other added. "We anticipate a mutually profitable relationship, Ensign Mayweather."

"Good," Travis said, because he couldn't think of what else to say.

"Allow me to cut to the chase," Reed said, smiling. "Let's make a deal, shall we?"

EIGHTEEN

Someone was calling her name.

"Ensign Sato."

Hoshi blinked, and opened her eyes.

Theera was standing over her bunk, arms folded across her chest.

"I would appreciate it if, in the future, you refrained from accessing my personal messages."

The Andorian did not look happy.

"Wait a minute," Hoshi said, sitting up, trying to gather her wits. "You've got the wrong idea. You left the message on-screen. I didn't . . ."

"You did," Theera said. "The playback was recorded."

"But it was an accident. I—"

She stopped talking because Theera had stopped listening. The Andorian turned her back on Hoshi, and walked right out the door.

Hoshi blinked again, and frowned.

What a way to start the day, she thought.

She got up and stretched. Her muscles felt stiff and sore all over, in the way that muscles ached if you lay down in one position and didn't move the whole night long. She glanced at the clock on her data viewer, and saw she'd slept for close to eleven hours. Overslept. Her head felt fuzzy still, in fact. She could use a long hot shower.

She got up and accessed the terminal. There were

no water-based showers on the ship. There were sonic ones, scattered all throughout this deck. The idea of high-pitched noises didn't appeal to her at that second.

She was halfway into her spare coverall when a voice sounded.

"Ensign Sato."

The voice was coming from the terminal. She sat down in front of the small screen again.

A Mediator, a young one, one she had never seen before, was on the display.

Hoshi finished getting dressed and activated the video return.

"Right here," she said.

"Elder Green wishes to speak with you," the Mediator said, and the screen went dark for a second, and then cleared.

"Ensign Sato." Elder Green, she saw, was in the analysis chamber, Mediators bustling around her. "Have I disturbed your rest?"

"No. I'm awake now. I didn't mean to sleep this long, I just . . ."

"It is of no concern. I am aware you were only recently discharged from your ship's sickbay."

"Thank you," Hoshi said.

"I was curious if you'd had a chance to speak with Technician Theera?"

"Ah. We have talked," Hoshi said.

"And has she told you anything of interest?"

To leave her alone, Hoshi thought.

"They were . . . preliminary discussions," Hoshi said. "Just reacquainting ourselves."

"I see." Green frowned. "I trust you will make further communication a priority today."

"Of course."

"Because time is of the essence."

"Yes. I understand."

"Good. Please keep me informed."

Green nodded then, and closed the channel.

Make further communication a priority. Given the look on Theera's face as she'd stormed out before, Hoshi wondered exactly how she was going to do that.

At that instant, her stomach rumbled, reminding her that her body had priorities of its own as well.

She logged off the terminal, and headed for the nearest mess hall.

Twenty minutes later, fortified with some solid food and some actual coffee, she was back in the analysis chamber, at the same console she'd been at previously.

Theera was working nearby, at another station. Preoccupied. Despite Elder Green's request, Hoshi decided not to bother her just yet. Instead, she reentered the virtual library, and did a little research on Andorian physiology. She was curious about the structure of the Andorian brain—how it responded to trauma. She had a friend once who had been in a terrible accident and afterward couldn't remember anything about the incident at all. His memory, in fact, ended an hour before the accident had occurred, and picked up with his returning to consciousness in the medical center on Phobos. Whereas she, on the other hand, could remember every second of her ordeal at the hands of the Xindi.

From what she found in the Kanthropian database, it seemed Andorians reacted in similarly varied ways. She wished she had Theera's medical history; she'd have to ask Elder Green if she could obtain that. She'd have to ask Green for Theera's personal history as well; there might be something in there about who the man in the message had been.

Finished with the Andorian medical database, Hoshi returned it to the shelf, and then paused a second.

She was in a wing of the library dealing with—or rather, representing—databases on various alien races. The databases were organized alphabetically.

On the shelf above the works dealing with Andorians, there was a slim volume entitled *The Allied Worlds: Apocrypha and Established Fact.*

The Allied Worlds. That rang a bell with her, and a second later she had the reference. T'Pol's briefing; the suggestion that the Thelasian Confederacy represented the remnants of that ancient, all-powerful empire.

Intrigued, Hoshi manipulated the controls on the input pad, and took the book down off the shelf. A little more manipulation of the controls, and she opened it.

The first page was a monitor screen, with various subheadings. A table of contents, purporting to outline the Allied Worlds' rise and eventual decline and disappearance. Hoshi chose a listing at random: War with the Barreon. The menu disappeared, and the page filled with images of huge gleaming starships that bore the Allied Worlds insignia—a blue-green circle filled with stars, encircled by silvery, sexless humanoids. The ships moved through space in precise, military formation, heading toward a single, even larger vessel. That ship was obviously crippled. The Allied Worlds cruisers fired on it, a volley of energy weapons that lasted a good ten seconds. The ship exploded, turning into a jumble of flaming wreckage, and scorched metal, and bodies, dozens of bodies tumbling into the vacuum of space, dead or dying, clad in uniforms of a blue color that reminded her of the ocean at her grandfather's beach home in Se An Pura, not the deep blue of the Pacific but a lighter aqua, uniforms now ripped and stained red everywhere, the Barreon themselves, dying as individuals, dying as a civilization. Whatever capture device was filming the scene zoomed in on those bodies, showing them in gruesome detail.

Enough of that, she thought, and returned the book to the shelf.

She read for a while longer within the library, looking at astronomical charts, historical records, tracing the movements of various civilizations and linguistic families across this part of space, searching for any language that might, in any way, resemble the Antianna signal. She found reference to a great many races she'd never heard of before, but their languages were, by and large, all remarkably similar to ones she was familiar with. The products of a bipedal, tool-making culture. The same LMUs, over and over again. It was interesting reading, though . . . for a while.

Then it was nothing but frustrating.

Hoshi removed her headset, and stood.

She surveyed the chamber a moment. The activity within was not as frenzied as it had been yesterday, in the face of the Antianna attack, but there were, she thought, at least as many Mediators at work, at the various stations throughout the large room.

She wandered over to the group she'd observed working yesterday, when she'd first entered the chamber with Emmen. They were engaged in running the signal through various filters, modulating in an attempt to simulate the hearing abilities of literally dozens of different races, some real, some computer-modeled constructs. No matter what they did to the signal, though, they failed to reproduce any of the sort of repetition that would allow them to begin frequency analysis.

She moved on to another group of Mediators. These ones were occupied with what at first seemed entirely different tasks to her—some of them working within the virtual database, others at command-interface terminals that had been set up next to the main console, still others standing around and talking to each other.

She listened a moment to their conversations, and gathered that their efforts were focusing on identifying—and potentially tracing back to a point of origin—materials found within the wreckage of the destroyed Antianna vessel. The metals, the trace minerals, the method of construction . . .

Results on that front were negative as well.

She moved on again, to the next console, the next group of Mediators, and stopped.

Theera was among them.

The Andorian was wearing a headset—presumably working within the Kanthropian database. Except the other Mediators at the console, she saw, were all gathered together in front of it, in a rough semicircle, talking.

"It is possible," one was saying, "that we are looking at a merger of two linguistic families. A forced merger."

"A war within the space the Antianna claim?" another Mediator asked, frowning. "There is no evidence of such a conflict occurring."

"There are no races within the space at this technological level," a third put in.

"Hear me out," the first said. "You'll recall the data we received from the Teff-Langer Conglomerate?"

"Regarding the Trill?"

"Yes."

"A parasitic invasion?" Several of the mediators exchanged glances. "It does not seem likely."

"Host-symbiont," the first corrected. "An actual, biochemical merging of two distinct consciousnesses—and thus, linguistic families."

The group was silent a minute.

"Interesting," one said.

"We would need to research," another added. "All symbiotic species within Type-Two FTL range of this quadrant area."

"An exobiologist should be consulted as well," a third said.

They turned as one to the consoles—and saw Hoshi.

"Who are you?" the first asked.

"Sorry," she said quickly. "I didn't mean to eavesdrop. I'm Ensign Hoshi Sato—from *Enterprise*."

"You have something to add to our discussion?"

Hoshi shook her head. "No, I was just listening. A symbiotic species." The idea intrigued her. "They really exist?"

"Information is available within the database." The Mediator gestured toward her station. Hoshi turned reflexively.

Theera had taken off her headset, and was glaring at her.

The Andorian stood up.

"Excuse me," she said, and headed toward the chamber exit.

"Wait a minute," Hoshi called after her. "Theera!"

The Andorian kept going. Her legs were longer than Hoshi's; the ensign had to practically run to keep pace, never mind catch up.

Theera was a good ten meters ahead of her when she reached the hall. Ten meters ahead, and moving quickly.

"You left the message on-screen," Hoshi yelled after her. "I played all of five seconds of it."

The Andorian hesitated a moment, then turned.

"I am on my way to the mess hall," she said. "You may accompany me."

The mess Theera took her to, though, was not the one she'd been at this morning. This one was two decks down, a large, square, room with a row of tables along one wall and a bank of what looked like, at first glance, a row of monitors along another.

"There are smaller areas scattered throughout the ship. This is the main dining hall," Theera said.

She walked to one of the monitors and—to Hoshi's surprise—spoke to it.

"Roasted flatroot. Imparay redbat," she said, enunciating each syllable carefully. "*Faridd.*"

The monitor changed colors.

Theera pressed the edge of it, at which point the monitor surface recessed upward and out of the way. Theera reached inside the space it had left, and pulled out a tray. On the tray was a plate of food: a brownish orange vegetable, meat of some kind—the redbat?—and a drink, from which steam issued.

"It's a food replicator?" Hoshi said.

"Obviously." Theera took her tray and found a seat. The monitor window—which was obviously not a

monitor, but simply the covering for the replicator—
slid back into position.

Hoshi moved closer, and studied it.

She knew it was something that Starfleet long-
range planners were discussing. Late one night Hoshi
had even heard Chef telling Commander Tucker how
soulless the food would be. His eager listener (slowly
chewing a slice of sweet potato pie) pointed out that
it would be hard to program, harder still to simulate
all the different foodstuffs and their tastes, and tex-
tures, never mind their nutritional values.

The Kanthropians seemed to have overcome at
least some of those obstacles. The question, as far as
she was concerned, was how extensive their recipe
banks were. Whether or not they included any Earth
foods.

She cleared her throat.

"Tekka-maki," she said.

The surface of the monitor blinked once.

Out of nowhere, a voice spoke back to her.

"Language: Japanese. Species: human, Sol system,
Planet Three, Earth. Accessing database. One moment
please. *Tekka-maki.* Unavailable."

Hoshi frowned.

"Kappa-maki."

Same result. Japanese seemed to be out.

"Steak," she said, feeling the need for some protein.

The monitor blinked. A second later it changed colors, and the covering slid back.

And there it was. Steak. Sliced steak, burned black
around the edges, looking dry in the middle (she
should, Hoshi realized, have specified medium rare),
but still . . .

Steak.

She was impressed.

She ordered a baked potato and salad—they looked like the real thing too—grabbed a glass of water, and then joined Theera at a table in the center of the room. The Andorian glared at her as she sat, but otherwise said nothing. They ate in silence for a few moments.

Hoshi set down her fork.

"Not bad," she said. "What's that you have?"

Theera chewed for a moment without responding.

"Flatroot. Red bat," she said after a moment.

"Andorian foods."

"Yes."

"Do they taste like they're supposed to, or . . ."

"They are acceptable."

She kept eating. She did not look up.

"I didn't intend to play your message. I'm sorry," Hoshi said. "I really am."

Theera nodded.

"I accept your apology."

"Thank you." Hoshi pushed around the food on her plate a moment. Too much for her to finish. She set down her fork, and pushed the plate to the side.

"So what were you working on?" she asked.

Theera looked puzzled. "Excuse me?"

"What were you working on before? In the analysis chamber?"

"Ah." Theera nodded. "Research."

Obviously, Hoshi thought but didn't say. "What kind?"

The Andorian hesitated a split second before replying. "Material related to the Antianna. It proved to be of no relevance."

"Oh." Hoshi nodded. "That's too bad."

"Yes," Theera said, looking down at her plate again. "Fortunately, the research itself was interesting."

She was lying, Hoshi realized. Why?

Theera cleared her throat. "You were working in the analysis chamber as well this morning?"

Hoshi nodded.

"On . . ."

She filled the Andorian in on the rough outlines of her own activities this morning—the research she'd done on the alien races within this part of the galaxy, their languages, their histories, her search for any similarities at all between them and the Antianna signal. Halfway through the recitation, she sensed Theera losing interest. She decided to change the subject.

"I hope you don't mind my asking, but—I'm curious. The man on the screen—from your message. Who is he?"

Theera visibly tensed.

"You don't have to tell me if you don't want to," Hoshi added quickly.

The Andorian was silent so long that Hoshi thought she had decided to do just that—to not answer the question. And then: "He is Second Commander Jakon of the Imperial Science Consortium. One of our Andoria's most significant biochemists, as well as the recipient of our highest military honors."

"And a friend of yours," Hoshi said. "A close friend, from the sound of it."

"Yes," Theera replied. "He is, in fact, my husband."

Hoshi had just taken a sip of water.

It took every ounce of self-control she had not to spit it right back out.

NINETEEN

Travis took a second shift that night, to help out Riley, who was helping out Hess, who was still short one staff member down in engineering. The first half was uneventful; they were through the Maldeev Cloud, well out of Confederacy space, nearing the transit point to the Barcana Sector. Right on schedule to pick up the Tellarite vice-ambassador tomorrow, right on track to arrive at Earth in plenty of time for the peace conference. It looked like smooth sailing, all the way. It felt like things aboard *Enterprise* were at last starting to get back to normal. He could focus on standard maintenance and flight operations, on helm control; he could let Poz and Verkin worry about tracking down *Horizon*'s money; he could say the phrase "Captain Tucker" without it tripping over his tongue.

He could, Travis realized, begin to picture what life aboard *Enterprise* after Jonathan Archer was going to look like.

It was going to be different, that was for sure. But he could see the crew—the senior staff in particular—settling into their new roles, learning how to interact with each other and the crew all over again. How to react to Trip, who was himself finding his way in his new role. Finding a routine, a way to make the ship run like the well-oiled machine it had been under Captain Archer's command. Learning to pull together, as a group.

"Mister Mayweather."

Travis looked up. O'Neill was standing over him.

"Problem?"

"No problem, ma'am."

"Then let's focus on the task in front of us, yes? The helm?"

"Yes, ma'am," he said.

The com beeped again.

"Hess to bridge."

"Lieutenant."

"Somebody flagged a power conduit up there for maintenance?"

Oh.

"That was me," Travis said. "Ensign Mayweather. I showed electron flow down at ninety-eight percent."

"Ninety-eight," Hess repeated. She didn't sound happy.

"Yes, ma'am." O'Neill came down the steps from the command level to stand next to him. She didn't look happy either.

"You know the operating range on that conduit?" Hess asked.

"I know the manual says down to ninety-five, but Commander Tucker . . ."

"Command . . ." she bit the word off just before the last syllable, "Captain Tucker is not running engineering right now. I am. When I receive a red flag from the bridge, I expect it to be a critical malfunction, not something that'll pop up in a maintenance report at the end of shift. Understood?"

"Yes, ma'am," Travis said. "Understood."

"Good. Engineering out."

Travis straightened in his chair.

O'Neill was still standing over him.

Her foot was tapping out a little beat on the floor of the bridge. That was a habit of hers, Riley had told him. Something the lieutenant did when she was feeling stressed, or tense. Frustrated.

Angry.

"This is second shift, yes, Ensign?"

"Yes, ma'am."

"It's usually much quieter. We like it quieter."

"Ah." Travis nodded. "Yes, ma'am."

He was about to apologize for being at the center of that activity—though he was unsure that he could have done anything differently—when the com beeped again.

"Reed to bridge."

O'Neill stalked up the steps to the captain's chair, and slapped the button on it. "Bridge. O'Neill here."

Somehow, Travis knew what the next words out of Malcolm's mouth were going to be, even before he spoke them.

"Ensign Mayweather is there, yes?"

"Oh yes," O'Neill said, looking straight at Travis. Everyone on the bridge, in fact, was looking at Travis. "He's here."

"I need to speak to him a moment."

"Yes," O'Neill said. "Of course. Sir."

Her foot was tapping again.

"Mayweather here, sir."

"Ensign—are you busy right now?"

"Umm . . ."

O'Neill's foot was tapping faster.

"I'm in the armory," Reed continued. "I've got something I'd like you to see."

"I'm off in a couple hours," Travis said quickly. "I'll be down then. Mayweather out."

"Not so fast, not so fast," Reed replied. "I don't think this can wait that long. I don't suppose Lieutenant O'Neill can spare you any sooner?"

Travis glanced up at her.

O'Neill's arms were folded across her chest.

Her foot was going a mile a minute.

"Sir, I'd prefer to have someone on the helm," she said.

"Of course," Reed replied. "But—aren't you trained on that station? Should an emergency arise?"

A pause. More tapping.

"I haven't worked on the simulator in several months, sir. I don't feel comfortable having that responsibility."

"Ah. Well—that's a skill set you ought to keep a little more current, don't you think Lieutenant?"

"Yes, sir," O'Neill said very slowly, in a very strained voice.

Her foot had stopped tapping, Travis saw. She was standing very still.

He had the impression of a dormant volcano, about to explode.

"Good. Still . . . in the meantime, I suppose you're right. Someone should be on helm. Where is Ensign Riley?"

"Down in engineering, sir," O'Neill answered. "They're short tonight."

"Well . . . they'll just have to stay short. Have Riley finish Ensign Mayweather's shift."

The foot started tapping again.

"I don't think Lieutenant Hess will be too happy about that sir," O'Neill said.

"Well then. Tell her it's an order. From me."

"Ah." O'Neill nodded slowly. "An order. Yes, sir. I'll tell her."

"Good. See you in a moment then, Ensign. Reed out."

There was silence for a moment.

Silence, so still and complete you could have heard a pin drop. And then . . .

O'Neill's foot started tapping again.

"Sir," Travis said, clearing his throat. "I mean, ma'am. I'm certain whatever it is Lieutenant Reed has to show me, it can . . ."

"Go," O'Neill said sharply, and pointed toward the lift.

He went.

It took a long time to come—time during which O'Neill called down to engineering and spoke with Hess.

The two were still arguing when the doors finally closed behind him. Travis thought he heard Captain Tucker in the background while Hess was talking.

Maybe those relationships, that post–Captain Archer routine, was going to take a little bit longer to work out than he'd thought.

When he entered the armory, Malcolm was sitting in front of the viewscreen again. No surprise there.

What was surprising . . . Poz and Verkin were on it.

Travis shot Malcolm a questioning look.

"Separate com interlink," Reed said, tapping the console in front of them.

Travis nodded, and pulled up a chair alongside him.

"Our friends have found something," Reed said, gesturing to the screen.

"Several somethings," one of the Bynar said. "Mister Poz?"

"Mister Verkin." The other nodded. "First of all—

an item of interest to all of us. A recently established legal precedent, regarding the interest rate on unlawfully embargoed monies throughout the Thelasian Confederacy. An interest rate of fifteen percent was established by gubernatorial decree in the Morianna arbitration courts, Stardate 1247.8."

"Which I believe translates to last Wednesday, on your calendar," Verkin put in.

"Early Wednesday," Poz added. "Parts of last Tuesday evening as well."

"Yes," Verkin said. "Quite."

Travis blinked.

"Fifteen percent."

"Yes."

"That's a lot of money."

"Yes."

He did the math in his head. "That's an awful lot of money."

Travis looked at Reed, who was smiling, and found that he was smiling as well.

"To continue," Poz said. "Our initial search for materials related to the transaction in dispute. Governor Sen's . . ."

"Ex-Governor Sen's," Verkin corrected.

"Ex-Governor Sen's dealings with the *S.S. Horizon*." The Bynar glanced off-screen for a second. "I'm looking at a copy of an agreement between the *Horizon* and the Thelasian freighter *Roia Four*, captained by Maxim Sen, based out of Saleeas Optim. Assignation of a previous contract between the *Roia* and the Th'Langan Equipment Fabrication Consortium to the *Horizon*, with *Horizon* assuming *Roia*'s delivery obligations under that contract regarding a shipment of thirty-six cargo pods, contents specially manufactured solar paneling. There is a specific clause in the contract relieving Sen and the *Roia* from any future liability regarding the cargo."

Travis frowned. "That's bad."

The two Bynar nodded as one. "Yes."

"However," Poz continued. "Further research within the Confederacy's archives shows that the Th'Langan Equipment Fabrication Consortium shares a physical address—a small moon within the confines of the Beta K'Leas system, which straddles the border of Confederacy and Coreidan space—with the Th'Langan Weapons Fabrication Consortium. And that Governor . . ."

"Ex-Governor."

"Ex-Governor Sen had multiple previous dealings with the weapons consortium. We believe it can be convincingly argued that ex-Governor Sen was well aware of what that cargo contained, and that he— and thus, by extension, the Confederacy—are responsible for restitution."

"And the fifteen percent interest," Verkin said.

Poz nodded. "Compounded every thirty days."

"Oh." Travis was smiling again. "That's good."

"Yes," Verkin said. "That's very good."

"Very, very good," Poz concurred.

Reed was smiling too. "I told you they'd deliver. Now gentlemen," he said, "I'd like to talk to you about obtaining further details on Sen's associates. Where exactly . . ."

"Hang on a second," Travis interrupted. Something was bothering him, and a second later, he had it. "That weapons consortium—it was in Coreida?"

"Straddling the border between the Coreida sector and Confederacy space."

Travis frowned. "That name keeps coming up a lot—Coreida."

Reed was frowning too. "Yes," he said. "Sen was governor there later. He talked about it in his speech—to the Assembly, remember? Site of a great victory, some nonsense like that?"

Travis nodded.

"Where exactly is this Coreida?" he asked.

"On the far side of Confederacy space. Back toward the galactic rim," Poz answered.

Next to him, Verkin was turned slightly off-screen, keying in some commands.

"Hold on one moment, " the Bynar said. "Sending you a sector map . . . now."

Poz and Verkin disappeared from the screen. A split second later, their place was taken by a star map. An overview of the space in which the Thelasian Confederacy operated, incorporating the worlds and races affiliated with it—the Conani, the Maszakians, the Pfau, dozens of others, each shaded in a slightly different color. The expanse of territory was vast, Travis saw—easily the distance from Starfleet to Vulcan and back again.

"There's Barcana," he said, pointing to his left, to the far edge of the map.

"And there's Coreida," Malcolm put in, gesturing to his right.

Travis saw it too, then—a region of space shaded in light green, all the way on the other side of the Confederacy.

Next to it was a black, virtually starless region of space, with something written on it that Travis couldn't see from where he was sitting.

"What's that?" he asked.

Reed squinted. "Says Neutral Zone."

"Neutral Zone."

"Yes. Must be someone else on the other side of it . . . hold on a second." Reed keyed in some commands. The map shifted the wrong way first, to the right, and Coreida disappeared entirely.

Reed cursed under his breath, and tried again.

This time, the map slid to the left.

The space beyond the Neutral Zone came into view.

It was shaded entirely in crimson.

Another huge expanse of territory, far more irregularly shaped than Confederacy space.

Reed recognized it first.

"The Klingon Empire," he said.

He slapped his hand down on the console, and stood suddenly.

"The Klingon Empire."

"What?" Travis asked.

Reed started pacing.

"It fits," he said. "Don't you see?"

Travis shook his head.

"What fits?"

"The captain couldn't understand it either," Malcolm said. "He was looking for the reason why, and it was staring us in the face the whole time."

Reed stopped pacing, and looked right at Travis.

"What made Sen suddenly turn around and invite *Enterprise* down to Procyron? Why did he bring us into the Assembly, why did he invite us to the reception . . . why was he so interested in humans? And the answer is . . . he wasn't. He wasn't interested in humans at all."

Now Travis was really confused. "He wasn't?"

"No. He was interested in one specific human. Jonathan Archer." Reed jabbed a finger at the map, at the heart of the Klingon Empire. "Because of them."

"The Klingon Empire," Travis said.

"Exactly."

It took Travis another few seconds. And then he got it.

"Sonuvabitch," he said, slapping the console. "That greedy, scheming, murdering sonuvabitch. The reward money."

"That's right. The reward money."

The two men locked eyes.

Reed smiled.

Travis smiled back.

"He's alive," Travis said. "Captain Archer is alive."

TWENTY

Deep in the bowels of the *Battle Cruiser cHos* (one of the new D-3 ships, which as far as Sen could tell were identical to the D-2s with the exception of an awkwardly mounted disruptor cannon directly beneath the bridge area), the ex-governor, ex-viceroy, and now ex-citizen of the Thelasian Confederacy lay still on his cot, in the semidarkness of his quarters, and considered his situation.

When he'd decided to abandon the Confederacy some months back (it had taken him only a few weeks in the governor's office to realize the institution's problems were insoluble, that the Confederacy was not going to survive, and that he could either go down with it in flames or make other plans), he had debated between several different destinations. His first thought was Orion space; the traders there operated under a very loose set of rules, and there was always money to be made, but there were risks as well. Most prominent among those risks being the Orions themselves, who would just as soon cut your throat as live up to their end of a bargain. Had he been a hundred years younger, Sen would have embraced the challenge. He'd cut a fair amount of throats in his time. But he was nearing the end of his organic life span, and felt no urge to continually have to prove himself in what amounted to battle. He had also explored a potential alliance with a highly avaricious merchant race called the Verengi, who he had heard of through the Pfau some years back, whose existence he had dismissed as rumor at the time. The rumors turned out to be true, however, and after several days of concentrated effort Sen had managed to make contact with one of those Verengi, an official who styled himself the vice-nagus and whose initial starting point for negotiations involved a twenty-five-thousand-word legal document outlining the various exceptions to the safe haven Sen was asking for. And so he gave up on the Verengi.

Eventually, he had chosen the Empire, because unlike so many of the other races he dealt with, these Klingons never pretended to be something they were not. He also had the benefit of knowing one of their number quite well—General Kui'Tan, whom he had befriended, in a manner of speaking, during his service on Coreida. And so, after a series of surreptitious messages back and forth, Sen had agreed to the Empire's terms, and set his own plans in motion for the escape. Those plans had worked to perfection: the system outages, the off-world deposits, the explosion at the party, even the unexpected arrival of the human captain and the necessity of incorporating his kidnapping into his agenda, all had gone off without a hitch. Except . . .

Something was wrong now. After an initially productive series of conversations, the commander had been avoiding him the past few days. And he had yet to allow the governor to speak with Kui'Tan. Had yet to allow Sen access to the ship's computers, which was a very smart decision, as once Sen got access to the computers—

There was a knock on the door.

"Enter," Sen said.

It was the female V'reth.

"You summoned me earlier," she said.

"Yes."

"Do you wish me to pleasure you?"

The female was built like a warrior, and approached the sexual act as same. Sen had neither the appetite nor the strength for that kind of activity right now.

"No," he said. "I am checking on the status of my request."

"To speak with the commander?"

"Yes."

"The commander is busy."

"Then I would like to speak directly to Kui'Tan."

"To communicate with Qo'noS?"

"Yes."

The female shook her head. "That cannot be allowed. We are running silent."

"Then I wish to leave this room," he said, getting to his feet. "I am tired of these four walls."

The female blocked his path.

"That cannot be allowed either," she said.

There was a neural disruptor woven into the fabric of his cloak, which he'd charged off the power receptacle here. For a second, Sen was tempted to use it.

No, he decided. The female wasn't worth the bother. Or the exposure of what for now was his only weapon.

"Would it be allowed if you were my escort?" he suggested.

The female frowned.

"I will have to check with the commander."

"Please do."

"The commander is busy now."

"I'll wait."

She nodded, and shut the door.

Sen waited till he heard her footsteps clanging down the corridor, then went to his case and opened it. Inside was a flexpadd and a data cube containing personal images from when he was very, very young. Pictures of his parents, his relatives, the flesh-and-blood Roia . . . he'd asked permission to tie the cube in to the Klingon system when he'd come aboard, so he could view them at his leisure. Kareg had turned him down. Not surprising. Under similar circumstances—a stranger coming aboard, wanting to access the ship's computer—he would have been cautious too.

The caution was well advised. In addition to the images, the cube also contained code for a modified version of the Roia software program. Directly linking it in to the system was the quickest way to insure that program's penetration of the Klingon system, but there were others.

Sen activated a concealed transmitter within the cube. He felt a slight tingling just behind the temples, and then it was done.

The Roia subroutines were now stored in his implant. Of course the memory there was volatile; if he could not off-load the subroutines into another computer, they would degenerate within a matter of hours. He would have to try again later. If he was, however, able to leave the cabin, find his way to an unsecured terminal elsewhere in the ship—

"What are you doing?"

Sen looked up and saw that V'Reth had returned. She stood in the half-open doorway, glaring at him.

He held up the flexpadd for her to see. "I am writing."

"What are you writing?"

"That does not concern you." He set the padd down, and stood. "Has the commander granted my request?"

"He has agreed to allow you to move about the ship in certain areas. At my discretion." She folded her arms across her chest. "Now. I will see what you have written."

Sen supposed he should offer token resistance. "No."

"Do not," she said, "make me take it from you."

Sighing theatrically, he handed the flexpadd to her. V'Reth looked it over quickly, and glared at him.

"What is this?" she asked.

"Poetry."

"You have used my name."

He looked to the ground, feigning embarrassment. "It is true."

She glanced from the padd to Sen, and then back at the padd, and began to read:

> The silver of steel
> V'Reth
> The touch of skin
> V'Reth
> Beauty, armored, and yet open.

Garbage, Sen thought. Incoherent trash he'd composed earlier this morning, in the span of ten heart-beats, anticipating the potential need for distraction.

He was so smart, sometimes . . . he amazed even himself.

The Klingon eyed him suspiciously.

"You mock me," she said.

"No."

"These are you words?"

"They are."

She made a noise in her throat, and flung the padd onto the floor.

Careful, Sen was about to say, but then she had pinned him to the bed.

"You will pleasure me," she said, and because Sen feared that to do otherwise might make her suspicious, he did so, knowing that afterward they would walk through the common areas of the ship, through the crew's mess perhaps, or near the engineering deck, and he would pass an unsecured computer, and broadcast the Roia subroutines, and they would burrow their way into the ship's computer system, and then, after some time had passed, a day or so, Sen guessed . . .

He would come and go as he pleased, and woe to anyone who tried to stop him.

TWENTY-ONE

After eating, Hoshi and Theera returned to the analysis chamber. The walk back was silent, Hoshi digesting what the Andorian had told her, Theera—as usual—keeping her thoughts to herself. Hoshi wondered why the marriage had seemed like such a surprise to her. Certainly, it wasn't because Theera had kept it a secret; the two of them weren't even really friends, although Hoshi did feel they were, at last, becoming friendly.

No, she decided, it was what she'd seen—last night, and just now. Or rather, what she hadn't seen. Watching her husband yesterday, talking about him just now, Theera had displayed the same depth of emotion, the same intensity of feeling, that she'd shown while demonstrating how the food replicator worked. Which was to say, none at all.

That was what Hoshi found odd. A contradictory piece of information, indeed.

The two of them entered the analysis chamber.

Something was happening, she saw instantly. A number of Mediators had left their stations, and were gathered before the transparent window at the far end of the chamber, looking out into space.

"What is it?" Theera asked.

"Don't know." Hoshi saw Younger Emmen at one of the consoles, and went to him. Posed the same question.

"We have detected a concentration of Antianna vessels, paralleling the fleet's course. Here." He pointed at one of the terminal screens in front of him. Hoshi pressed forward to take a look.

It was a tactical display, much like the ones *Enterprise* used. A variety of Armada vessels, all shapes and sizes, blinking green, moving from left to right across the bottom of the screen.

In the top half of the display, six Antianna ships, flashing orange, moving in the same direction.

"Is this to scale?" Hoshi asked.

"Roughly."

She pointed to the Antianna vessels. "These ships look bigger than the others. The ones we've run into before."

"They are."

"I mean much, much bigger." Telemetry was coming in across the bottom of the display. Hoshi studied it a moment, did some calculations in her head, and frowned.

Each of the six Antianna ships was approximately four times the size of *Enterprise*. Which made them at least twice as large as any other ship within the Armada. If they had anything like the speed, or maneuverability, or firepower of the smaller vessels . . .

The next time hostilities began, it wasn't going to be a fight.

It was going to be a slaughter.

"You sure these are Antianna ships?"

"External configuration is similar." Emmen leaned around her, and keyed in a few commands. "Spectrographic analysis indicates similar hull composition."

"Why haven't we seen anything this big from them before?"

Emmen shook his head.

"What about life signs?" Hoshi asked.

"As before. Bipedal, humanoid . . . yet we are unable to pinpoint readings any further. Most frustrating."

Just like aboard *Enterprise*, Hoshi recalled. She recalled too what Elder Green had told her the night before, and frowned.

"I hope General Jaedez is not planning on a preemptive strike," she said.

"I am not privy to the general's thinking," Emmen said brusquely. "I can tell you that as per Elder Green's orders, we are continuing to transmit standard hail messages, in the two hundred fifty-one known language families of this quadrant. Expressions of peaceful intent, our desire to reach an understanding with the Antianna."

Expressions of peaceful intent being broadcast by a war fleet. Hoshi wondered how that would look to the Antianna? A little suspicious, perhaps?

She hoped *they* weren't planning a preemptive strike.

She glanced down again at tactical, at the six huge alien ships, and felt a little twinge of something in the pit of her stomach. Nervousness, perhaps. A trace of fear.

She remembered Theera then, and turned around.

But the Andorian was gone.

Hoshi found her back in their quarters—or rather, found evidence of her in their quarters, that evidence being the privacy curtain activated across the Andorian's half of the room.

"Theera?" Hoshi called out. "Are you in there?"

There was no response.

Hoshi tried for a few more minutes, and then gave up. The Andorian's reaction was understandable, given what had happened to her aboard *Lokune*. Given the size of Antianna ships out there. In her shoes, Hoshi would be hiding as well.

Thing is, there wasn't really any place safe to hide. Not aboard S-12, anyway. Best to concentrate on solving the problem, in her opinion, rather than running from it.

Hoshi returned to the analysis chamber. Most of the Mediators had drifted back to their stations. She stood by herself, alone in front of the huge, transparent wall, and stared out at the stars.

Confusing, surprising things happening everywhere.

Out there, the Antianna, whose intentions she could only guess at, whose technology—the speed, maneuverability, and suddenly increased size of their ships, their ability to somehow confuse the most sophisticated sensors (not forgetting, of course, the instantaneous, impossible reconfiguration of the ship's power grid Trip had pointed out to the captain during their last encounter with the ship)—was equally puzzling.

And in here, Theera, whose behavior she found stranger with each passing hour. What was the Andorian hiding—and why?

The harder she worked at solving those problems, Hoshi thought, the more confusing they seemed to get.

She decided to try something different—at least with regard to translating the Antianna signal. Instead of concentrating on the fifty-seven pulses themselves, she would look at context—gather facts that might help determine who the Antianna were, and thus, what their language might be like.

She'd done something like this before, aboard *Enterprise*, but the resources available to her now were much greater. She returned to her station, to the virtual library, and got to work.

First, she set up a database of her own, a list of civilizations that had established a presence in this area. It was a lengthy document—close to a hundred races, by her count (she went back to the time of the Barreon and Allied Worlds, though of course she left them off the list because the record about the extent of their civilizations was highly contradictory and confusing). She made a list of language families associated with those civilizations—and the number doubled.

Then she weaned that list down, removing from it first the languages Starfleet had in its data banks, and then ones she found within the Mediators' database. That eliminated all but a half-dozen species—all bipedal, all with a vast number of waiting-to-be-translated documents available in the Mediators database.

She spent the next few hours going over those documents.

None of them bore any resemblance to the Antianna signal.

Hell, she thought, and stood up. *Enough*.

She returned to her quarters. The privacy screen was still up. She didn't even try calling for Theera; the Andorian was probably asleep, anyway. It was late.

Hoshi collapsed on her own bunk, and closed her eyes.

She slept.

She dreamt.

• • •

In her dream, she was back aboard *Enterprise*. Captain Archer was alive, and sitting in the command chair. The Antianna were attacking.

He turned to Hoshi, and smiled, and then looked past her.

She turned, and saw Theera.

"What are they trying to tell us?" Archer asked the Andorian. "What does the signal mean?"

"I can't say," Theera told him.

"That's not a question, that's a direct order."

The Andorian shook her head. "Three guesses."

Archer frowned. "Okay," he said. "Three guesses. That's fair."

The captain thought a moment.

"Does it mean, 'We come in peace?'"

"No."

"'This far, and no farther'?"

"No."

"'Prepare for a preemptive strike?'"

"No." Theera shook her head. "That's all you get, I'm sorry."

On the screen, the Antianna ship fired. There was a flash of brilliant, impossibly white light, and a second later, a huge shock wave.

Archer was blown backwards off his chair, and disappeared from view.

Trip sat down, and took his place.

"I don't know anything about languages," he said. "What I know is machines."

"Machines," Theera shook her head. "No. That's not it."

"Wait a minute," Trip said. "That wasn't a guess."

"Sorry." Theera said. "Try again."

"We don't have time for this," Hoshi got up from her chair, and stood over Theera. "If you know what the signal means, tell us for God's sakes, before . . ."

The screen behind her flashed white.

Another huge shock wave hit the ship, even bigger than the previous one, and Hoshi stumbled, and hit the deck, hit her head very, very hard.

Her vision swam. The familiar outlines of the bridge blurred to gray.

She woke up, and opened her eyes.

She was lying on the deck of the Kanthropian vessel.

It was pitch dark.

And beneath her, the ship was shaking.

They were under attack, she realized. They were really under attack.

She got to her knees, and climbed back on the bed. She reached out and found the companel, hit the light pad. Nothing happened.

"Dammit," she said, and squinted out into the room. There was a soft glow coming from just ahead of her— a row of emergency lights, along the wall, leading toward the door.

Theera's privacy curtain was down.

"Theera!" she called out.

There was no response.

The room shook again, and an instant later, far in the distance, Hoshi heard a deep rumble, like thunder. An explosion, within S-12, not enemy fire.

Please don't tell me, she thought, *that the ship is falling apart*. She realized she didn't even know where the escape pods were.

No time like the present to find out, she decided.

She found her boots and walked to the door, following the row of lights. Of course it wouldn't open for her, not without power, but there had to be a manual override around here somewhere. . . .

She fumbled around the edges of the door frame. Nothing. She started hammering on the door.

"Hey!" she yelled as loud as she could. "Is anybody out there? Hello!"

She kept hammering. There was no response.

"Hey! I'm trapped in here. I need help!" She hit the door again, and again and again, and then—

"It doesn't matter."

The voice came from behind her.

"Theera?" she asked, turning and squinting into the nearly absolute darkness. She could just barely make out a shape, at the edge of the Andorian's bunk.

"Yes."

"What—why didn't you say anything before? Let me know you were still here?"

"It doesn't matter," Theera said again. "They're coming."

"They."

"The Antianna."

"Theera." Hoshi started walking slowly toward her. "For one thing, we don't even know who's out there. It might not be the Antianna. It might be—"

"It's them. You know it is."

"Probably," Hoshi admitted. "But even so—you don't know what's going to happen. Nobody does. The Armada . . ."

"I know."

"There's no way to be certain."

"I know," she said. "They're coming for us, and once they're here, they're going to . . ."

The lights, all at once, came up.

Hoshi blinked.

Theera sat directly in front of her, on the edge of her bunk, hands knotted together in her lap. She stared up in surprise.

"Secure from alert status," a voice sounded over the com. "Repair crews to ancillary power deck. Repair crews report to ancillary power deck. Other personnel, stand by for further instructions."

Hoshi let out a sigh of relief.

"Secure from alert status—sounds like we're going to be okay."

Theera said nothing for a moment, and then, "No we're not. They'll be back. Sooner or later, they'll be back and then—"

"Theera—"

"I can't do this," she said suddenly, and stood up. "I can't."

She walked to the terminal and stood over it, her back to Hoshi.

"Why don't they just send me back to Andoria," she said. "I'm not helping here. Not at all."

For a second, Hoshi didn't know how to respond to that. It was the truth, and yet . . .

The Andorian is not going home anytime soon—not based on her conversation with Elder Green, Hoshi thought.

And then, she knew what she had to say.

"It happened to me once too." Hoshi was surprised to hear how calm her voice sounded. "A few months ago. I was captured, and taken aboard a ship belonging to this race called the Xindi." She told Theera the details; still, the Andorian said nothing.

"They hurt you, didn't they?" Hoshi said. "That's where the scar is from."

Theera nodded.

"What did they do?"

"Does it matter?"

"Not really, I suppose. What does matter is what you saw aboard that ship. What you remember about the Antianna—their language, their technology, what they looked like . . ."

"If I had anything relevant to say, I would have said it long ago. You can rest assured of that," Thera said.

"You must remember something."

The Andorian shook her head. "Nothing. Nothing except the pain."

Trauma, Hoshi thought and was reminded of what she'd gone through, everything that she had forgotten.

And then, all at once, it hit her.

The blank look in Theera's eyes when she'd asked her which of the fifty-seven pulses she'd been working with, when she'd talked to her about the ice caves on Andoria, or her work on the Universal Translator Project.

The lack of emotion in her voice when she'd talked about her husband.

She hadn't been lying, or trying to hide the truth.

"You don't remember anything, do you?" Hoshi said. "About the signal, or Jakon, or anything. That's it, isn't it?"

Theera glanced at her quickly, and just as quickly, looked away. Not, however, before Hoshi saw the truth in her eyes.

"I don't want to talk about it," the Andorian said, and reached for the companel above her bunk, clearly intending to activate the privacy screen.

Hoshi grabbed her wrist.

"Leave me alone," Theera said.

"I want to know the truth," Hoshi said.

"Leave me—alone!"

Theera swung her arm backwards and up, slamming it into Hoshi, who suddenly went flying halfway across the room.

She landed on the floor hard, so hard that if she hadn't been trained—if she hadn't known the right way to fall, how to dissipate the momentum from that throw—she would have been hurt. Badly.

"I'm sorry," Theera said. And then, before Hoshi could get out another word, she activated the privacy curtain once more, and disappeared from view.

The Andorian's actions, the look in her eyes—they had answered Hoshi's question just as clearly as words would have.

Amnesia, Hoshi thought as she left the room. That explained a lot of things—not all, but a lot. It didn't explain why the Andorian hadn't just come out and confessed to one and all her inability to recall what had happened to her. At a guess, Hoshi supposed that might have something to do with Ambassador Quirsh, and his obvious pride at her achievement. Perhaps Jakon had felt the same thing. Perhaps Theera had as well. Perhaps she'd simply been overwhelmed by the rush of events, and before she could admit the truth, she'd already been in so deep there was no backing out.

Really, there was only one person who knew the answer to that question, and she still wasn't telling the whole story. She had, however, told enough of it that Hoshi felt compelled to seek out Elder Green. Let the Kanthropian know that there really wasn't much point in hoping for any further information from Theera, because they weren't going to get any.

Getting to Green, however, proved a little more difficult than Hoshi had expected.

Outside the elder's office, she found two Conani warriors flanking the doorway. They wouldn't let her in. They wouldn't even announce her presence.

She stood in the hall, waiting, for several long minutes, as a series of other personnel—mediators, Conani warriors, the H'ratoi ambassador—came and went. Something, obviously, was going on in Green's office, something that no doubt had to do with the battle that had just occurred. That situation, understandably, took priority over her news, but even so . . .

She didn't like waiting around.

She was, at least, able to learn something about the attack on S-12. A single Armada ship had inadvertently crossed over into Antianna space—a problem with their navigation system. The ship had immediately come under fire. Jaedez had ordered the fleet forward, in an attempt to rescue it. A failed attempt. The ship was destroyed. The Antianna continued firing on the entire fleet, until all the Armada vessels were back in Thelasian space.

Younger Emmen came rushing down the hallway. He almost walked right past her, till Hoshi put a hand on his arm and drew his attention.

"Ensign Sato," Emmen said, frowning. "Why are you here?"

"There's something I need to discuss with Elder Green."

"This is not a good time. Now, please—if you would step aside . . ."

Reluctantly, Hoshi allowed him to pass.

He emerged barely a minute later, frowning.

"This way. Please," he said to Hoshi, and waved her inside Green's office.

Inside, she found not the conference she had been expecting, but just two people. Green herself, and General Jaedez. The viewscreen on the far wall showed a tactical display similar to the one Hoshi had seen earlier in the analysis chamber. Positions of the Armada fleet, positions of the Antianna ships.

The two turned as one at Hoshi's entrance.

"Ensign. Your arrival is fortuitous," Green said. "We were about to send for you."

Hoshi frowned. "Oh?"

"I believe you know General Jaedez," Green said.

"We've met."

"Indeed. On Procyron, I believe." Jaedez inclined his head, a look of amusement in his eyes. Or maybe Hoshi was just imagining that.

She had, for a second, the uncomfortable feeling he was going to say something about the dress.

"Elder Green has told me of your assignation," the general continued. "Your task to speak with the Andorian. Have you completed it?"

Fortuitous timing indeed, Hoshi thought, and shared with both the general and the Kanthropian what she had come to say.

"So it's not a question of pulling information out of Theera," Hoshi said, finishing up. "She really doesn't remember any of what happened to her."

Green and Jaedez exchanged glances.

"I'm sorry," Hoshi said. "I know that's not what you wanted to hear."

"This does explain the database usage," Green said.

Hoshi frowned. "Sorry?"

"Earlier—we were reviewing how the Andorian has been using her time within the analysis chamber. We were puzzled as to why she spent so much of it on material that she should have been very familiar with. Records relating to her own translation work. The planet Andoria. Her service record."

"She's trying to jog her memory," Hoshi said.

"Indeed."

"Perhaps we can be of assistance," Jaedez said.

Green frowned.

"General. I thought we had discussed this. I am unequivocally opposed to the use of that device. In the first place, we have no record of it ever being used successfully on an Andorian. In the second, the potential for serious injury—"

"I understand your concerns, but in my opinion, we have no choice," Jaedez interrupted. "We cannot confront the Antianna again without obtaining some sort of tactical advantage. If there is information in the Andorian's unconscious that may help us do that . . ." Jaedez shrugged. "We must obtain that information. No matter the cost."

Hoshi didn't like the sound of that.

"Could someone please fill me in on what you're talking about?"

The general turned to her.

"There is a device," he began, "which Governor Sen bequeathed to us. A souvenir of his victory at Coreida."

"A device," Hoshi said.

Jaedez nodded. "It is called a mind-sifter."

Hoshi didn't like the sound of that either.

"And what does this mind-sifter do?"

Jaedez ignored her, and gestured to one of his soldiers.

"Fetch the Andorian, please, and bring her to the flagship. We will rendezvous there."

The man saluted, and left the room.

"General," Elder Green said, "I really must protest . . ."

"Mediator." Jaedez towered over the diminuitive Kanthropian. "We are at war. Sacrifices must be made."

"Somebody please," Hoshi said. "Tell me what the mind-sifter does."

"The device utilizes focused electromagnetic fields to facilitate memory retrieval," Green said. "Unfortunately, the process is often quite painful."

Hoshi shook her head. "Well . . . wait a minute. It seems a little premature to talk about using something like that on Theera—especially when we don't even know whether or not she has any information that could be useful to—"

"Premature?" Jaedez, for the first time since Hoshi had seen him, looked angry. "We are at war, Ensign Sato. I would say if anything, it is past time we utilize the sifter."

"There has to another way to get what you need," she said.

The general shook his head.

"We do not have time," he said, "to run a series of scientific experiments."

"Which is just what this sounds like to me—an experiment. You're treating Theera like a lab animal, or something."

The look on Jaedez's face didn't change.

"The Andorian will be made as comfortable as possible, I assure you. In fact, if you so desire, you may accompany us to the flagship. And see for yourself." Jaedez turned from her then, and bowed to Elder Green. "Mediator, I appreciate your counsel, and your time. I will keep you apprised of further developments."

The general swept out of the room then, the other Conani guard trailing in his wake.

Shooting Elder Green a concerned glance, Hoshi hurried after them.

TWENTY-TWO

On the viewscreen, in the center of *Enterprise*'s bridge, Admiral McCormick tapped his fingers against the surface of his desk, and frowned.

Trip was in the captain's chair, having taken over the conn a few minutes earlier from Lieutenant O'Neill. Most of the A-shift personnel—Travis included—were now on duty as well, having been roused from sleep, most of them, to hear the news. No one looked tired, though. Not in the least. There was an air of excitement on the bridge. Anticipation, that not even the scowl on Admiral McCormick's face could dampen.

"Say that again please, Commander. You are where now?"

"En route to Procyron, sir," Trip replied.

"En route to Procyron. So—you've turned the ship around?"

"Yes, sir."

"Commander." McCormick closed his eyes, and pinched his brow. "I have to say, I'm more than a little upset to hear that."

"I understand that, sir," Trip said quickly. "But given what we've discovered now . . ."

"Yes," McCormick said. "Captain Archer is alive. You said that. I remember you saying that."

The admiral spoke very, very quietly. The expression on his face was one of utter and complete calm. In his eyes, though . . .

Well, if watching O'Neill had reminded Travis of a long-dormant volcano, about to explode . . .

He supposed he was looking at a G-type star right now, on the verge of going supernova.

"And—do you have any suggestions about what I should tell the Tellarites? Or the other attendees at the peace conference?"

"Sir, you can tell them we'll be there," Trip said earnestly. "As soon as we find Captain Archer."

"You'll be there."

"Yes, sir. We'll be there."

McCormick nodded. "Tell me something. Malcolm Reed is your security officer, yes?"

"Yes, sir," Trip said.

Travis exchanged a frown with Ensign Carstairs, across from him. Why was McCormick asking about security?

"And where is Lieutenant Reed?" the admiral asked.

"Not certain, sir."

"You're not certain."

"No, sir. I believe he's in the armory."

Travis nodded. That's where he thought Reed was too; after the two of them had gone to engineering, grabbed up Trip, and told him what they'd just realized, and why, Malcolm had left them to spread the happy news, and disappeared—gone to "check on something," as he'd put it. Probably something like ship traffic in and out of the Procyron system, looking for clues as to how the governor had managed to sneak Captain Archer out of the Thelasian capital. How he was planning to sneak Archer into Klingon territory.

"All right. Reed's not there," McCormick said. "Who is his second?"

"Chief Lee here, sir," Trip said, pointing behind him, to Malcolm's usual spot on the bridge, where Lee now stood. "Admiral, I may be a little out of my field of expertise in suggesting this, but I think some sort of formal protest to the Empire's representatives regarding Captain Archer just might—"

"Chief Lee," McCormick said, a sudden snap to his voice.

"Yes, sir." Lee stepped forward and stood at attention.

The admiral pointed right at Trip. "Take that man into custody. Place him in the brig. Right now."

The bridge fell silent.

"Commander T'Pol."

She stepped forward. "Yes, Admiral."

"I'm placing you in command of *Enterprise*. I want you to turn the ship around, again, and make your best speed to Barcana Six, where the Tellarite vice-ambassador is waiting. You will contact the ambassador, and provide him with a revised ETA for *your* ship. Is that understood—Captain?"

T'Pol nodded. "I understand, sir."

"Good." McCormick nodded.

Chief Lee looked to T'Pol. T'Pol glanced at Trip. Trip rose from his chair.

"However," T'Pol said. "I must respectfully decline the appointment, sir. For one thing, *Enterprise* already has a captain, and he is, at this moment, in considerable jeopardy, I suspect. As Commander Tucker has suggested—"

McCormick exploded.

Travis hadn't heard so much cursing since—

Since—

Well, he'd never heard so much cursing.

Halfway through McCormick's outburst, the lift doors opened, and Malcolm stepped out onto the bridge.

The admiral glared at him.

"Sir," Reed said, stopping in his tracks, snapping to attention.

"Lieutenant Reed." McCormick said the name with more than a trace of relief in his voice; the two men, obviously, knew each other. "What is going on out there?"

"Sir?" Reed looked puzzled.

"There is a mutiny aboard your ship, Lieutenant. As security officer, I would expect you to be aware of something like this."

"Mutiny?"

"The admiral's ordered us to continue on to Barcana Six," Trip supplied.

"Ah." Reed nodded. "Sir," he said to McCormick, "I believe you may have been misinformed regarding the true nature of events taking place here."

McCormick frowned. Trip frowned. Travis looked around the bridge, and saw, in fact, that most people were frowning.

"I don't understand," the admiral said.

"Please, allow me to explain." Reed went to his station. Chief Lee stepped aside, and let him access the terminal.

"I assume Commander Tucker has told you of our conclusions regarding Governor Sen and the captain. The Klingons."

"You assume correctly," McCormick replied.

"Well," Reed said, keying in a series of commands to his console. "It was immediately obvious to me that the governor's plan had to have been in place for some time before *Enterprise*'s arrival on Procyron. To arrange a deception of that magnitude—"

"Understood," McCormick snapped. "Please get to your point."

"My point is this," Malcolm said. "Captain Archer could not have been part of Sen's initial plan. His arrival was, in effect, an unexpected bonus. So I wondered what that original plan—that deal between the governor and the Klingons—might have been. On Sen's part, a fair assumption seemed to be the desire for money, and a place of refuge. But I wondered what the Klingons were to receive, and so I—ah. Here we are."

Reed punched one last command in, and the viewscreen split. Admiral McCormick stayed visible in the upper half, while in the lower—

"These images are taken from a remote monitoring outpost, stationed inside the Neutral Zone between Coreida and the Klingon Empire."

Travis saw nothing on the screen but stars and empty space.

"There are close to two dozen such stations scattered throughout the Zone, but for our purposes, the images from this one will serve," Reed said. "Now—I asked certain friends of mine on Procyron . . ."

Poz and Verkin, Travis added silently.

". . . if it would be possible to use these stations to in effect, spy on the inner workings of the Klingon Empire. To search for signs of activity that might give us a clue to the workings of that original plan— between Sen and the Empire. My friends attempted to do just that, and quickly found that the sensors were not of sufficiently high resolution to accomplish that task. However . . ."

"Lieutenant . . ." McCormick said impatiently.

"Sir. Please. We're almost there." He gestured toward the screen. "Now I ask you all to note the presence of the Ch'los K'tangol—the Warrior's Nebula, also known as the Azure Nebula—there in the upper right-hand corner of the screen."

Travis looked where he was pointing, and saw a faint reddish haze.

"Yes, yes," McCormick said. "Go on."

"My friends noted the presence of that nebula as well, and what is more, as they searched through the most recent images being broadcast from the monitoring station, they noted the nebula disappear."

"Disappear?" Trip frowned. "What do you mean disappear?"

Malcolm went back to his station. "Disappear," he said, and keyed in another command. The image on the screen changed.

"This image was relayed from the monitoring outpost earlier today."

Sure enough, the nebula wasn't there.

"That's not possible," Travis said out loud. "Is it?"

"No," Reed answered. "It's not."

"So what's happening there, Lieutenant?" McCormick asked. "Why can't we see the nebula?"

"My friends asked themselves the same question. They were able to perform a series of remote diagnostics on the monitoring station, and discovered that a piece of very sophisticated software had been introduced into the control system there, the effect of which was to disable certain frequency bands within the local sensor arrays."

"That still doesn't explain why the nebula disappeared," Trip said.

"Ah, but it does," Reed said. "It took some time—which is why I was late arriving here—but only minutes ago, my friends were at last able to eradicate the infecting software. Here is the corrected feed from the monitoring station."

Again, the display changed. At first, Travis saw no difference. Then he noticed that certain areas of space seemed to—well, "shimmer" was the only word Travis could think of to describe what he was seeing.

In the far right-hand corner of the display, it was that shimmer that blocked the nebula from view.

Trip let out a long, low whistle. "Whoa," he said.

"Lieutenant Reed," T'Pol said. "I congratulate you on a job well done."

Malcolm nodded. "Thank you, Commander."

"Sonuvabitch," McCormick said. "The Klingons. Dammit."

"Yes sir," Malcolm said.

"Word of this leaks out, it'll blow the peace conference all to hell," the admiral continued. "The Earth Firsters will have a field day."

"Yes," Reed said. "I imagine they will."

Travis still had no idea what they were referring to. From the confused looks shooting across the bridge, he wasn't alone.

"How many are there?" McCormick asked.

"Close to a hundred," Reed said. "We're showing the images to the Thelasians now—my friends designed a simulation of what they'd look like, if the cloaks weren't . . ." He frowned, and entered a few more commands. "Here. You can see for yourself," he said, and the image on the screen wavered, and then snapped back into focus.

Travis blinked.

Every place on-screen where he had noted a shimmer before—and there were dozens easily, close to a hundred perhaps, as Malcolm had said—there was now a Klingon cruiser.

"Those are D-3s, by the way," Reed said. "Without a doubt, an invasion fleet."

"How long have they been there?" McCormick asked.

"A few days, some of them. Others—within the last few hours."

"What are they waiting for? The Confederacy is practically defenseless."

"Practically," Reed nodded. "There are a series of automated defense stations near Procyron. We're checking the integrity of the control software there right now."

"Sen," Trip said.

McCormick nodded, more to himself than anything else. "All right. This does change things, you're right about that. Commander Tucker."

"Yes, sir."

"You are to take *Enterprise*, proceed at maximum warp back to Procyron, and render the Thelasians all necessary assistance. Yes?"

"Aye, sir."

"Finding Captain Archer—if you're right about that too, which I suspect you are—is secondary. Is that understood?"

Trip hesitated only a second before replying.

"Yes, Admiral. Understood."

"Good." McCormick settled back in his chair. "Nice work, Malcolm. You'll keep me posted?"

"Yes, sir," Reed said.

McCormick nodded again. "Starfleet out," he said, and the screen went to black.

Trip turned to Reed.

"Friend of yours, I take it?"

"We've worked together before."

Trip frowned. "You know—you might have told me first. About the Klingons. Would've meant a little less trouble all around."

"As I said—we only just completed the simulations."

"Hmmm." Trip sat back in his chair, and punched the com. "Bridge to engineering."

"Hess here, sir."

"What do you think?"

"She'll handle four point five sir."

"Four point five?"

"Yes, sir. Four point five."

Trip frowned.

Before talking to McCormick, he'd asked Hess to give him an estimate of their best possible speed back to Procyron. He'd asked her to shoot for four point seven.

"We're doing maintenance on some of the starboard power conduits," the lieutenant explained. "Don't want to risk an overload before we're done with that."

Trip nodded. "Maintenance. All right then. You're the boss."

"Sir?"

"Four point five it is, Lieutenant. Stand by." He turned to T'Pol. "Best course?"

"The quickest way back through Maldeev—the meteor cloud."

"What do you say, Travis? You up for that?"

"You know it, Commander."

He looked over his shoulder and smiled.

Trip smiled back. "Punch it."

• • •

Sen paused in midstride, and sniffed the air.

He smelled ozone—the residue of electricity, coursing through the corridors of the Klingon vessel.

"What part of the ship is this we are in now?" he asked V'Reth.

The Klingon female—a few steps ahead of him—stopped in her tracks, and turned.

"This is level five. There are the cargo chambers," she said, pointing to two large doors just off to Sen's right. "And the weapons lockers." She pointed to an impressively armored hatch to his left, and then frowned.

She strode up to Sen, and poked a finger into his chest.

"Do not," she commanded, "entertain any ideas."

"Of course not," he answered quickly. "Just curious, that's all."

They were on their way back to Sen's quarters, having just taken a brief tour of the ship—a walk that had brought them close to engineering (but not close enough for his purposes), and then the armory (but again, not close enough), and then finally, into the crew's mess, at Sen's request, for a plate of *gagh*. He had been pleased to see that it was not fresh *gagh*, but rather fabricated whole, produced by the ship's food replicators as he watched. The replication process, of course, demanded a considerable degree of computing power. Typically unsecured computing power, at least among those races he was familiar with who had the technology.

He would find out very shortly whether or not the Klingons paid a similar lack of attention to this potential weak spot.

"And there's nothing else on this deck?" he asked.

The female frowned a moment, and then her eyes lit up.

"Ah. The auxiliary brig." She pointed behind them.

"It is used for the more troublesome prisoners entrusted to our care."

Sen nodded. That explained the smell—troublesome prisoners, the devices needed to keep them under control . . .

"It may interest you to learn the human is now being confined there as well."

"Really? He was trouble?"

"Indeed." The female's face clouded over. "On several occasions, he failed to show proper respect toward his guards."

How typical, Sen thought. The human captain, not knowing when to shut up.

"Would you care to see the prisoner?" V'Reth asked.

Sen shook his head. "Not necessary. I wish to return to quarters, please."

If the Roia program had managed to access the Klingon system, it should be able to replicate itself rather quickly, and he wanted to be ready, and available once it reached the necessary degree of autonomy to contact him. Most likely, that would not be until morning, but just in case . . .

At that very instant, Sen felt a little tingling in his implant, and smiled.

The Klingon system, it seemed, was not as secure as he'd supposed.

"Very well." The female nodded. "Perhaps you can compose more poetry, in my honor."

Sen managed to turn the laugh that welled up inside him into a smile.

"Perhaps I can, at that," he said. "I find myself in an unaccountably lyrical mood."

She eyed him suspiciously a moment.

They resumed walking.

TWENTY-THREE

In the shuttle from S-12 to Jaedez's flagship, Hoshi tried again to engage the general in conversation, to find out more about the mind-sifter. He, however, had little time, and littler inclination to chat. Most of the journey he spent in consultation via communicator with various commanders in the fleet. And when he wasn't talking, he was utilizing a padd he'd been given by one of his soldiers to sketch out drawings of some kind. Hoshi thought she caught a glimpse of a tactical screen, but when she tried to lean closer to see it, one of the general's guards abruptly stood up, blocking her view.

She sighed, and turned her attention elsewhere. Out the shuttle window, where she could look back at S-12, and see, for the first time, the Mediators' ship. It was shaped like a sphere. She could see the transparent wall of the analysis chamber, which ran like a belt along the bottom third of that globe. She saw no sign of weapons emplacements anywhere on it. Confirmation of both the Kanthropians' status as Mediators, and their inability to defend themselves.

The sound of metal on metal interrupted her thoughts; the shuttle was docking. Jaedez was on his feet in an instant, at the hatch as it opened. Another Conani—the markings on his uniform identified him as a sergeant, if Hoshi was remembering right—and, to her surprise, one of the Pfau, overweight, practically spherical himself, met him there.

"Welcome aboard, sir," the sergeant said.

The two saluted each other.

The sergeant leaned forward then, and spoke quietly into Jaedez's ear.

Hoshi heard the word "Andorian," and then "problem."

"Excuse me," she began. "Is Theera—"

The general silenced her with a raised finger.

Theera was supposed to be following them on another shuttle. Had something happened to that ship?

Jaedez finished listening and turned to the Pfau.

"Teraven," he said, "this is Ensign Sato. She plans to witness the procedure. If you could escort her to the facility . . ."

"General, is there a problem? Is Theera all right?"

"The Andorian is fine," Jaedez said. "She—and I—will be along in a moment. In the meantime—Teraven?"

The Pfau bowed to him, the general inclined his head in return, taking Hoshi in the gesture as well, and then he spun on his heel and was gone, the other Conani trailing in his wake.

The Pfau—Teraven—turned to Hoshi. "Ensign, if you'll follow me . . ."

He led her from the shuttlebay through a small door and into the interior of the Conani flagship. The corridors were dimly lit, and smelled—to Hoshi, at least—of something at once vaguely metallic, and something very, very old, something now in the midst of decaying. It was a stench that she had a hard time ignoring, both for obvious reasons and for the fact that it reminded her of the cacophony of smells she'd encountered aboard the Xindi warship.

Not a good omen.

"Excuse me?" Hoshi called after Teraven, who despite his bulk was moving along at quite a good clip through the corridors. She was having trouble keeping up with him. "This mind-sifter—are you familiar with it?"

The Pfau turned and spoke to her without breaking stride.

"Very," he said, but instead of slowing down to engage in conversation, Teraven, if anything, increased his speed.

"It's some sort of memory-retrieval device?"

"Retrieval?" Terraven shook his head, and did slow a bit then. "I would not use the word 'retrieval.' It facilitates recollection."

"And how does it do that?"

He shrugged. "To be honest, I have absolutely no idea. But I can assure you, the device works quite well."

The corridor dead-ended in front of them, at a single heavy door. Teraven keyed in a combination on the pad next to it, and they passed through into a good-sized room—roughly the same dimensions as the mess back aboard *Enterprise*—completely bare of furnishings or ornamentation. Gray metal walls, gray steel-plate decking, stark, utilitarian light fixtures hanging from the ceiling.

At the far end of the room was a single oversized chair of the same gray metal, with straps hanging from the arms, shackles dangling from the legs. Nearer to the door, there was a small metal table, with a device of some sort on it. The mind-sifter, she supposed, a box made of some dull, heavy-looking metal, with various knobs and dials on one side, and a bar of gleaming white metal atop.

Hoshi took another look around the room, and the unease she'd felt earlier intensified.

It looked like a torture chamber.

"Elder Green said that the procedure—the use of the memory-sifter—was often painful. Would you say that's true, or . . ."

Teraven nodded. "It is not a pleasant experience, clearly. The length of the session is the determining factor."

"May I . . ." she asked, gesturing to the device.

"Be my guest," he said. "Please do not, however, touch the yellow button on your extreme right."

"No yellow button," Hoshi said, looking for—and finding—the control he was talking about. "Got it."

There were a half-dozen chairs along the wall behind the table. She pulled up the closest one and sat down. She ran a hand down one side of the device; the metal there was pitted, and slightly warm to the touch. It looked unlike anything she'd seen before—a souvenir of Governor Sen's triumphs at Coreida, the general had said. The spoils of war. Alien technology. Obviously something the Conani didn't entirely understand—maybe something they weren't using correctly. Maybe it wasn't supposed to be painful. If she could figure out how it worked . . .

She leaned closer. None of the switches on the control surface were labeled. She stood up and walked around it. There were as many knobs on the very back of the device as there were on the front. Odd. There was nothing on the right side of the sifter, other than a few rows of indicator lights. There was a single large switch on the left, with a smudge of writing underneath that. She knelt down, and squinted at it. Maybe a half-dozen symbols intact, the rest worn off. The alphabet looked vaguely familiar.

Klingon.

She frowned.

Klingon?

She turned back to Teraven. "This is a Klingon machine."

"Yes."

"The general said—Governor Sen gave it to you?"

"Yes."

Hoshi frowned again.

Sen and the Klingons.

Something about that struck her as noteworthy. Sen, and the Klingons.

She pictured the governor, at the reception, smiling at Captain Archer as if he'd just seen a long-lost friend, and all at once, her heart started beating very, very fast.

"Sonuvabitch," she said out loud.

Teraven frowned. "Excuse me?"

Hoshi stood up. "Where's the nearest com?"

"The nearest com?"

"I need to use your com system. I need to contact my ship—*Enterprise*."

"You'll have to talk to the general about that," he told her.

"Never mind," Hoshi said, heading for the exit. She'd find it herself, because this couldn't wait, Malcolm was right, Sen was alive, and what was more—

Two meters away from the door, it swung open, and General Jaedez stepped through.

Behind him, flanked by two fully armored soldiers, each holding on to one of her arms, stood a battered, bruised, and somewhat bloody Thecra.

Hoshi stopped dead in her tracks.

"What the—what's going on? What happened? Are you all right?"

She spoke to Theera. The Andorian looked at her, and confusion entered her eyes.

"Hoshi . . . ?"

Jaedez stepped into the room.

"If you're referring to the Andorian's condition, she refused orders to accompany my men. The use of force was required, and I might add that she proved an able fighter in that respect."

He motioned to the soldiers, who dragged Theera to the chair at the far end of the room and began buckling her into it.

Hoshi couldn't believe what she was seeing.

"General," she began angrily, "you can't . . ."

One of the warriors stepped directly between her and Jaedez.

"We'll want to begin on the lowest setting, I think," the general said. "It is my understanding that we're dealing with total memory loss here." Jaedez turned to Hoshi then. "Is that correct, Ensign Sato? Based on what the Andorian told you?"

Hoshi, who had been about to protest what was going on, froze.

Therea looked up then, and her eyes met Hoshi's.

"I was trying," Hoshi began, "to get them to leave you alone. I didn't know that anything like this would—"

Theera turned away from her—not before, however, Hoshi saw the hurt and confusion in her gaze.

"Ensign Sato?" the general prompted. "The memory loss is total?"

Hoshi sighed.

"Yes."

"Very well," Jaedez said. "We can begin with a series of questions unrelated to the specific data we're concerned with. Hopefully facilitate recall without necessity for the higher settings. Teraven . . . ?"

"Yes, sir." The Pfau sat down behind the device. He pressed the yellow button, and some of the lights on the sifter flickered to life.

"It will take a few minutes to reach operational status," he said, and flicked a second set of switches. All at once, a high-pitched whining sound filled the room. It hurt her ears.

She wasn't surprised by that. The sifter was a Klingon device. It was probably meant to hurt. Once it reached operational status, it would probably hurt a lot more.

"There has to be another way," she said out loud.

No one paid any attention.

A light clicked on above them. Hoshi looked up and saw, mounted to the ceiling, a black metal wedge, with a single bright spot affixed to its center. The wedge was pointed down at an angle, directly toward the chair.

"Operational status in ninety seconds," Teraven said.

Theera looked up.

"I really do not remember anything," she said.

The whining grew in intensity.

She began pulling on her restraints.

"Relax," Teraven said. "Those are necessary for your safety—to prevent you from hurting yourself. The device can cause muscle spasms."

"General," Hoshi said. "You have to stop this."

Jaedez spoke without turning.

"I appreciate your concern, Ensign, but the Andorian is the only person to have seen these aliens.

To have been aboard their ships. Locked up inside her head is information that may be critical to the success of this war, or if you prefer, perhaps even allow us to make peace."

"There has to be another way to get at that information," she said again.

"You have a suggestion?"

"Not right now, but I know that if we . . ."

"I'm sorry. Teraven?"

"Sir?"

"Are we ready?"

"Operational in ten seconds, General."

"Good. Let's do this quickly, please."

Nothing she could say was going to make any difference, Hoshi saw.

The time for talk was past.

She made a show of sighing, and turned her back on the general, as if she'd given up on changing his mind.

The two guards had taken up flanking positions just behind Jaedez. They stood at attention, each holding what looked like a laser rifle in front of them. They had sidearms too—particle weapons of some kind, no doubt.

There had been a training scenario, back at the Institute, much like this one. Two armed guards, a surprise maneuver—she had done pretty well at it, Hoshi recalled. Of course the guards at the Institute had been human—a good twenty centimeters shorter than the Conani, considerably lighter, but still—

The strategy was sound. All she had to do was execute it correctly.

As Hoshi passed the guards, her right hand shot out, reaching for the holstered weapon of the warrior on that side. She felt the grip and started to yank, at the same instant bringing her left leg around to deliver an incapacitating strike to the soldier's knee.

The Conani soldier, however, was not only bigger than the guards she'd worked against, but faster. He moved quicker than she would have believed possible for someone his size.

He dropped his rifle to the deck, freeing both hands. As she tried to pull the weapon from the holster, he grabbed her wrist with one hand, and held fast.

As her leg came around, he grabbed that with the other.

At the same instant, she heard the other guard move behind her, and felt something press into the small of her back.

"Don't move," the soldier behind her said.

Hoshi cursed, and tried to maintain her balance, to keep from falling to the deck.

When she looked up, Jaedez stood in front of her.

"Ensign Sato. That was foolish."

She didn't bother responding.

"In times of war," Jaedez continued, "traitors are shot."

"I'm not a traitor," she snapped.

"Drawing a weapon—or rather, attempting to draw a weapon—on the fleet's commander is the act of a traitor."

"I wasn't going to shoot you. I was going to destroy the machine."

"To save your friend." Jaedez shook his head. "An admirable sentiment. Misplaced, however. And a distraction I cannot tolerate at this point. However," he nodded to the guard, who released her, "it is my belief you are a creature of impulse, rather than a traitor. Is this the case?"

Her wrist ached where the guard had held her. She rubbed it, and said nothing

The general held out his hand, and the guard who'd so easily overpowered Hoshi handed over his weapon.

In one continuous motion, Jaedez stepped forward and pressed the barrel up against her forehead.

"Answer the question, please. Are you a traitor? Yes, or no?"

She looked into his eyes, and saw nothing there.

No hint of emotion one way or another. Would he shoot her? No way to tell.

Hoshi took a deep breath.

"No. I'm not a traitor."

"Which I also take to mean you will allow Teraven to proceed with his work?"

She nodded.

"Is that a yes?"

"Yes."

"And I have your word on that?"

She glanced over his shoulder, and tried to catch Theera's eye.

The Andorian stared ahead blankly, without reacting.

"Yes," she said to the general. "You have my word."

Jaedez nodded, and stepped back. "Good." He handed the guard his weapon, and turned back to Teraven.

"Proceed."

The first five minutes were hell.

And after that, it got worse.

The Pfau began by asking questions regarding Theera's childhood, her earliest memories, what she recalled of her parents, her schooling. The whine of the device hurt Hoshi's ears; the light shining down from the portion of the sifter that hung from the ceiling obviously hurt Theera. She shifted position in her seat to try and move away from it, to no avail. The strain in her voice was evident as she responded to each question. She was, obviously, in pain.

She did not remember a thing.

"It doesn't seem to be working," Hoshi said.

"It is still on the lowest setting. We rarely achieve results from the device at this level." Teraven and the general exchanged a look, and the Pfau twisted one of the knobs on the control surface. The whining noise increased.

Hoshi's own ears began to ring.

Teraven moved on with his questions, covered the Andorian's service record, her personal life, her time aboard *Lokune*. He was a skillful interrogator; he coaxed, he reminded, he supplied data pertinent to each question in the hope of prompting some small reminiscence . . .

All in vain.

"The Universal Translator Project," the Pfau continued. "According to the Kanthropian database, you used intercepted transmissions from the Vulcan Intelligence Directorate in conjunction with data already in hand to fully revise your species' translation matrix. Do you recall those transmissions?"

"No." The Andorian gritted her teeth, and shook her head. "I don't."

Teraven looked over at Jaedez again, who nodded subtly.

The Pfau turned another knob, and Theera let out a small gasp of pain.

Hoshi opened her mouth to protest, became aware of Jaedez standing next to her, looking—and yet not-looking—in her direction . . .

And bit back what she was going to say.

"The device facilitates recall," Teraven said. "Let the memories come to you. Do not try and filter anything you sense in your mind."

"There's nothing," Theera said. "I don't—"

"Same question," Teraven said, cutting her off. "The intercepted Vulcan transmissions. They were sent over a period of four months. They contained information regarding several alien species that at the time were unfamiliar to your race."

"No." The Andorian shook her head, and gasped again. "I don't remember."

"Take your time." Teraven paused. "You worked from the Andorian Security Division. You had an office. A very large office. Do you recall?"

Theera gritted her teeth, and made a noise in her throat.

"Stop," she said. "Please stop."

"Try and remember," Teraven urged. "The transmissions . . ."

"The Vulcans," she said, almost shouting. "Vulcan transmissions."

"Yes," the Pfau said. "The Vulcans. That's good, Theera. Do you recall those transmissions? What other races were mentioned within them?"

"I don't know," Theera said, squeezing her eyes shut, trying to talk and twist away from the pain at the same time. "Maybe."

"Which species?"

"Humans.

Jaedez and Teraven exchanged a quick glance.

"Humans," Teraven said. "Very good. Which others?"

Theera continued to grit her teeth. "I don't . . . the H'ratoi, I think. Yes, that's it. The H'ratoi."

Teraven frowned, and once more looked to the general, who shook his head.

It was obvious even to Hoshi that Theera was lying.

Jaedez cleared his throat.

"The next level, please."

Teraven nodded. The light above the chair intensified, and almost instantly, Theera went rigid in her chair. She began gasping for breath.

Hoshi clenched her fists at her sides, and cursed silently.

"The *Lokune*," Teraven said. "What do you recall about being on the *Lokune*?"

Theera shook her head.

"What do the Antianna look like?"

Nothing.

"What did they say to you?"

No response.

"What did they do?"

Theera screamed.

More questions. No answers. Only the sound of pain.

Hoshi shut her eyes, and tried not to listen.

"Stop this," Hoshi said, when she could take no more. She turned to Jaedez. "It's torture. You know this is torture."

"The device works," the general said. "I have seen it work. Teraven . . . ?"

"Only the highest setting remains, sir."

"Then continue, please."

"General . . ."

Jaedez spun on her.

"Ensign Hoshi. Another word, and you will leave. This room for certain, possibly the ship itself, and I will not be providing a shuttle. Do you understand?"

Hoshi lowered her gaze.

"I understand."

"Teraven. Continue."

The Pfau leaned over the device, and reached once more for the control knob.

Hoshi saw Theera's hands tighten on the arms of the chair. The light above her grew brighter. Again, Theera flinched, and turned away.

The device itself began to make a noise, a sound almost like a moan. Hoshi turned and saw the table it was on begin to physically shake.

Theera was shaking too. Her hands still held to the chair tightly, but her arms were shaking so hard they seemed about to fly off her body.

She made a guttural noise in her throat. Her eyes opened wide, and then rolled back in her head so that only the whites were showing.

She slumped backwards in the chair, and lay still.

"Theera!" Hoshi shouted, and started toward her.

"Ensign!" Teraven warned, and Hoshi stopped in her tracks just shy of the beam of light, shining down from above.

And Theera, all at once, started to speak.

"Spectral matrix recognition scan initiated," Theera said. "Four seventy-three nanometers. Negative. Four seventy-three point five nanometers. Negative. Four seventy-four nanometers. Negative. Four . . ."

Spectral matrix recognition scan? Hoshi thought, frowning. *What the . . . ?*

She became aware that behind her, Jaedez and Teraven were talking. She turned to face them.

"What's happening?" Hoshi asked.

Teraven frowned. "She's in some sort of trance state."

"I can see that. But why?"

"I'm not sure. If I had to guess . . . I would say the device has fulfilled its function—triggered a memory, within her subconcious."

"A memory of what?"

Teraven shook his head.

Theera continued to repeat the same phrase, over and over again, varying the number slightly each time. Four seventy-four point five nanometers. Four hundred seventy-five nanometers. A very small number, indeed. Hoshi wondered what it represented.

"General," Teraven said. "Other memories may be accessible to us now as well. We should continue the questioning."

"Excellent suggestion," Jaedez said. "Please proceed."

"Wait a minute," Hoshi said. "Don't you think we should figure out what's wrong with her first?"

"There does not appear to be anything 'wrong' at all," Teraven shot back. "In fact, she seems in no discomfort whatsoever."

Hoshi looked at Theera, and frowned.

The Pfau might be right, at that. Leaving aside the blank, almost trancelike expression on her face, Theera looked almost relaxed. It was as if, Hoshi thought, she'd gone someplace else entirely, gone away and left her body behind.

"Okay," Hoshi said. "But let me question her."

Jaedez frowned. "Ensign . . ."

"Sir. Please."

Jaedez looked to Teraven, who shrugged. "I see no harm."

The general nodded. "As you wish, then."

Hoshi took a step closer and knelt down next to Theera, careful to stay back from the beam—the light shining down from above.

"Theera?"

There was no response.

"Theera, it's Hoshi. Can you hear me?"

She had to shout to be heard over the noise coming from the sifter.

The Andorian continued speaking, as if Hoshi hadn't said a thing.

"Theera. What do those numbers mean? What are you trying to say?"

No change.

"Does it have something to do with the Antianna?"

Theera stopped talking, all at once, and drew in a breath.

"Ahhh," she said. "Antianna."

Hoshi glanced back at Jaedez, who motioned for her to continue.

"Yes, Antianna. Do you recall anything about the attack?" she asked slowly. "What happened to you aboard *Lokune*?"

The Andorian blinked.

"*Lokune*," she said. "Spectral matrix recognition scan initiated. Four seventy-three nanometers. Negative. Four seventy-four nanometers—"

"Theera," Hoshi snapped. "Forget that. What do you recall about the Antianna? What did they say to you?"

"Antianna," she said again, and this time, rather than fear in her voice, Hoshi heard something very puzzling indeed. A—for lack of a better word—yearning.

"Antianna," Theera said once more, and straightened in her chair, and snapped the restraints.

Hoshi gasped in surprise, and stumbled backwards.

"That is not possible," Jaedez said. "Those restraints are a duranium alloy."

Theera held up her arms to the ceiling.

"Antianna!" she said again, practically screaming the word, like a plea to the heavens.

Her eyes rolled back in her head.

Her body went rigid, and she slumped to the floor.

TWENTY-FOUR

Rodriguez took over helm at some point during the night, Travis couldn't be sure exactly when, sometime after he got them through the Maldeev Cloud without a scratch. He stumbled back to his bunk and passed out, woke up to the sound of Lieutenant O'Neill's voice coming over the com ("Shift change, you're on in half an hour" and maybe it was his imagination, but he detected a certain glee in her voice when she heard the grogginess in his, satisfaction at having woken him up), grabbed a shower, and headed down to the mess for coffee and a quick bite. The place was jammed. He scanned the room for a seat, and saw Malcolm at a table in the corner, a stack of flimsies spread out before them. The lieutenant waved him over.

"Get some sleep?"

"A couple hours. You?"

Reed shook his head. "Not yet. Soon."

He flipped through the papers in front of him, and handed Travis a sheet.

" 'In re: the matter of the Earth ship *S.S. Horizon* v. the freighter *Roia Four* . . .' " The ensign looked up. "That was fast."

"Poz and Verkin," Reed said with a smile, and took a bite off his plate. "I don't think it hurts that we have friends in high places now. The new governor's quite thankful to us for pointing out the intruders on their doorstep. From what I understand, she helped speed things along."

Travis nodded, and skimmed the document. The judgment granted, in every instance, *Horizon*'s claim on the money owed them. It set an interest rate at twenty percent. There was an aggregate amount due listed at the very bottom of the page.

He shook his head in disbelief.

"Looks like *Horizon*'ll be able to get themselves a faster engine than ours." He handed Reed back the paper. "What else you have there?"

"Information on Sen. More details on his time at Coreida. He went to Qo'noS, you know, as part of the peace process."

"That's . . . unusual, isn't it? Klingons don't generally like intruders visiting the homeworld, if I'm remembering right."

"Unusual's the word for it. Their whole relationship with Sen seems a little unusual. Particularly given the fact that he defeated them at Coreida. Klingons don't usually react well to defeat, and yet . . ." Reed turned one sheet of flimsy facedown on the table, ran a finger down another. "Here it is. Three visits by Sen, in all. Doesn't make sense. Unless . . ."

Travis saw what he was driving at. "You don't think it was a defeat at all?"

"No. My guess is . . . the Klingons staged a retreat, after Sen promised them something."

"Like what?"

"Not sure." Reed frowned. "But the terms of the treaty kept them out of Coreida, so . . . possibly colonization rights elsewhere."

"The Neutral Zone," Travis said, recalling the charts they'd looked at down in the command center.

"That would make sense. Sign a treaty pledging to leave those worlds alone, and then go on and colonize them anyway. Sen's the one who would have been in charge of overseeing implementation of treaty terms, so if he looks the other way . . . who's going to know?"

Travis nodded.

"His opposite number, by the way," Reed said, holding up a photo of a Klingon, "fellow by the name of Kui'Tan. Who has moved up rather quickly through the ranks of the Empire, and is now a general in charge of—"

"Whoa," Travis said, suddenly noticing the time. He pushed back his chair, and stood, "I gotta get moving. O'Neill's gonna have my . . ."

He turned, and found himself looking right at the lieutenant.

She frowned. "Is this the scheduled time for your break?"

"No, ma'am."

"Then . . ."

"Aye, aye, ma'am."

Travis hurried from the mess.

He took the helm from Rodriguez, and took them the rest of the way in to Procyron, an easy trip, during which time he tried to get a message through to *Horizon* and deliver the good news. No channels were clear the whole way in, though—there was a lot of message traffic, a lot of back-and-forth between *Enterprise* and Procyron and the Armada. A lot of scrambling being done by all concerned, trying to pull together ships for a second fleet, one to defend Coreida from the Klingons. He left it for later, asked Carstairs to let him know when a channel opened up.

When they reached Procyron, Reilly relieved him. Travis flew Trip and T'Pol down to Tura Prex, to the government complex, where they were scheduled to meet with the new governor, and the Klingon ambassador to the Confederacy. Meanwhile, he and Malcolm were escorted to an office in another part of the city, where they met Poz and Verkin, and a Thelsian trade representative. Papers were signed, and money—a lot of money—was exchanged, most of it virtual (wired to an account in *Horizon*'s name), some of it real: a small metal box containing a quantity of dilithium crystals, according to Poz and Verkin, who scooped up the case eagerly.

"Pleasure doing business with you," the Bynar said, and with a bow, disappeared.

He and Malcolm were then escorted back to the main governmental complex. Along the way, they learned from their escort that the Empire—in the person of their ambassador—was denying every accusation made against them, and insisting that the fleet of their ships gathered at Coreida were simply performing military exercises.

Reed was in a mood by the time they arrived at the tower and took the elevator up to the top floor. Travis followed him into the governor's office, and froze.

Trip, it appeared, was in a mood as well.

The dominant feature in Sen's office—or rather, what used to be Sen's office—was a set of floor to ceiling windows at the far end of the room, looking out over the Prex. Commander Tucker and a Klingon—older, dressed in long ceremonial robes, wearing numerous military directions, Travis could only assume it was the ambassador—stood face-to-face in front of those windows. The Klingon wore a smug, self-satisfied expression.

Trip looked about as mad as Travis had ever seen him.

"Diplomatic immunity," Trip said. "I don't think diplomatic immunity'll do you much good if you hit the ground from here."

"Human. Are you threatening me?"

"I don't threaten. Think of it more like a prediction—something that's going to happen unless you start coming up with some answers. Who was Sen's contact in the Empire? Where is the Governor now?"

The Klingon shook his head.

T'Pol—who had been standing a few paces back from the conversation—now stepped forward.

"Ambassador Schalk," she said. "Your position is quite untenable. Your ships in the Coreidan neutral zone have been discovered. Transmission records from this show that former governor Sen and the Empire have been in regular communication for years, and it is only a matter of time until the content of those communiqués is also revealed. It is not logical for you to continue to deny the evidence."

The ambassador snorted.

"I have seen no 'evidence' of anything. Sen spoke to the Empire? I think not—there are no records of conversations with the Emperor, or any of his duly appointed subordinates. I see no proof of that. If the Governor had contact with a private citizen, that is none of the government's affair."

Trip shook his head.

"Stop lying, Schalk," he said. "Tell us where he is."

The ambassador's eyebrows rose.

"You dare accuse me of being a liar?"

Trip smiled. "If the shoe fits . . ."

Schalk glared.

"Human. Were I not at this moment bound by a blood oath to fulfill my ambassadorial capacities, I would have your head for those words."

"Why don't you resign, then?" Trip smiled.

Schalk glared.

The smile disappeared from Trip's face as well. "You win, you can have my head. Take it home, mount it over your fireplace. I win . . . you tell me what I want to know. The truth."

The two stared at each other a moment longer.

Then Schalk drew himself up to his full height, gathered his robes around him, and—without a backward glance—swept out of the room.

"Commander," T'Pol said. "I hardly think that Admiral McCormick would approve of single combat as a negotiating tactic."

"Oh, I don't know about that," Malcolm said, speaking for the first time. "The Admiral appreciates the virtues of strength."

T'Pol frowned. "I fear that in this instance, however, we may simply have succeeded in alienating the Klingons."

"They can be alienated all they want, as far as I'm concerned," Trip said, and all at once, the smile disappeared from his face. "One way or another, we're going to find out where Sen and the captain are."

V'Reth escorted him through the ship, taking the long way around once more, Sen suspected, to avoid sensitive areas such as the engineering deck and the bridge. He didn't mind. He could picture them in his mind now, having seen schematics and surveillance footage. And he would walk them all himself, at his leisure, soon enough.

The Klingon paused in front of him, and coughed. She hacked something up from her throat, and spit it onto the floor.

"Are you all right?" Sen asked. "Sick?"

She spun on her heel and glared at him.

"I am not sick," she said. "I do not get sick."

"Ah. You are strong," he said. "You will prosper."

"I am strong," she agreed. "I will prosper. I will captain a ship like this one day," she said, and coughed again. "Perhaps on that day, you will serve me."

Doubtful on all counts, Sen thought.

He followed her one deck up, via an access ladder, to a door guarded by a particularly fearsome-looking warrior. Sen knew, thanks to Roia—who now controlled close to seventy percent of the ship's functions, sans only the weapons systems and the self-destruct modules—that there were two others lurking nearby, just out of sight.

V'Reth acknowledged the guard at the door with a salute, and then turned to Sen.

"You will speak . . ."

Cough.

". . . when spoken to," she finished, clearing her throat. "You will address the captain as 'sir.' You will not offer opinions except when asked. Is that understood?"

"Perfectly."

"Good. Your behavior reflects . . ."

Cough, cough.

". . . on me. And should you behave badly, I will be shamed. And I will not be happy. You would not like to see me unhappy."

"No," Sen agreed. "I would not like to see you unhappy."

V'Reth turned and saluted the guard. He returned the salute, and opened the door, letting out a small cough, quickly supressed, as he did so.

They entered a long narrow antechamber, a hall, the walls draped with hides and with weapons of varying shape and size displayed alongside an array of military decorations, some of them bearing the imprimateur of the Emperor himself. Kareg, clearly, had served with honor. He was prepared to meet his ancestors with his head held high, Sen noted. Good.

V'Reth pushed aside a drape at the far end of the room, and they entered a second, much larger chamber. Half a dozen warriors stood at attention along the walls, which were covered with the same dark fabric. In the center of the room was a long, low table, surrounded by a series of ornately woven cushions. At the head of the table, flanked by two Klingon females, sat Kareg. At his right hand was a stack of empty dishes, at his left a large serving tray, on which several creatures, roughly the size and shape of Sen's fist, wriggled in a puddle of greenish red sauce.

Kareg picked up one of the creatures—it looked like a large bug—with his left hand, ripped its head off with his right, and swallowed the rest whole.

He belched loudly, and then looked up.

"Sir," V'Reth said, snapping to attention and saluting. "Maxim Sen, as you commanded."

Kareg nodded, and waved Sen forward.

"Governor," he said, and coughed. "Please. Sit. Are you hungry?"

Sen eyed the food dubiously, and shook his head. "Thank you, no. Sir."

He lowered himself onto a cushion to Kareg's left,

next to one of the females. She eyed him rapaciously.

Behind him, V'Reth made a growling noise, and the other female backed away.

Kareg decapitated another of the creatures, and swallowed it. "You may be wondering why I asked to see you."

Sen held back the reply that initially came to him— "No, I know exactly why you've asked to see me" (which he did, thanks to the communiqués between Qo'noS and Kareg that Roia had intercepted)—and bowed his head meekly.

"Yes, sir," he said. "I was."

"It seems we have a small problem. One you may be of assistance in solving."

"Whatever I can do."

"Good. I appreciate your attitude." Kareg turned aside then, and coughed into his hand. He took a drink of wine, and set down the glass.

"It is my understanding that the code you provided to deactivate the, uh, defense stations on the Coreida border is not functioning correctly."

"Really?" Sen shook his head. "That is surprising."

"Yes." Kareg coughed again. Behind him, one of the guards coughed as well. "Is it possible that the sequence you gave us was incorrect?"

"Hmmm." Sen frowned. "Is that possible? Let me think."

Kareg raised an eyebrow.

Behind him, the coughing guard bent over, spat on the floor, and staggered out of the room.

"I believe the code was a mathematical progression," Sen said. "A series of four sixty-four-digit numbers?"

"I am unfamiliar with the exact nature of the signal."

Sen shook his head. "And I can't recall it exactly either."

Kareg looked up. "V'Reth!"

The Klingon woman stepped forward.

"Sir!"

"Would you please consult with Qo'noS, and obtain—"

A loud cough suddenly burst forth from Kareg, from deep in his chest. It caught the captain by surprise, leaving him no chance to cover his mouth. Phlegm and spittle sprayed across the room.

Sen made a face, and wiped his brow with a napkin. The females at the table flinched, but made no move to turn away, or clean themselves off. Not that it would have mattered if they had.

They were all, each and every one of them here in this room, and elsewhere aboard the ship, dead already.

"Excuse me," Kareg said, grunting, trying to clear his throat. He took another sip of water. "V'Reth?"

"Sir. I will fetch the code."

She saluted, and turned to leave the room.

"Wait," Sen said. He wanted her here, with him, when the end came. "It's coming back to me now."

"It?" Kareg frowned. "What do you mean it?"

The governor smiled. "I'm afraid I have to confess—the code I provided earlier was incorrect."

Kareg slammed his fist down on the table.

"You dare!"

"Captain," Sen said, allowing a touch of anger to creep into his voice. "You have kept me a prisoner aboard this ship for over a week. You have not lived up to your end of the bargain—why should I live up to mine?"

A nasty smile crossed Kareg's face. "Because I will kill you if you don't."

"Is that so?" Sen asked.

"Yes," Kareg said, and coughed again.

V'Reth coughed.

One of the guards behind them coughed. A second, and then a third joined in.

The female on Sen's right started too, bent over double, and then turned away from the table. He removed a knife from her place setting and held it tight against his arm, just beneath the table.

Kareg was still coughing, bent over double.

"Shall I call for your doctor?" Sen asked, over the sudden cacophony. "So he can give you the bad news personally?"

Kareg straightened—with some difficulty, as he could not stop coughing—and glared at the governor.

"What are you talking about?"

Sen smiled.

Kareg's eyes widened.

"You," he croaked. "What have you done?"

"I don't know exactly," Sen said, which was the truth. It was Roia—and he couldn't help but picture the flesh-and-blood version in his mind as he thought about her—who had devised the plan, rerouting exhaust from the impulse engines into an unused maintenance duct, combining it there with bacterial by-products from the sewage recyclers to produce a noxious gas, a mutagenic, highly contagious compound that had been circulating throughout the ship for upward of an hour now, working its magic on the Klingon (and only the Klingon) respiratory system, in effect choking them to death on their own excrement—which, now that he thought about it, was really as poetic as justice could possibly get.

"I will kill you," Kareg said, shoving his chair backwards, and drawing his weapon.

Sen lunged across the table and slashed the captain's throat open with his own knife. As Kareg fell forward, a look of shock on his face, he yanked the weapon from the Klingon's grasp, and quickly turned.

Two guards were still on their feet, reaching for their own weapons. He killed them first, and then the others, and then, for good measure, Kareg's females, who had huddled together in a corner of the room.

He stepped back from the table then, and surveyed the carnage with satisfaction.

Scheming, plotting, working behind the scenes to affect one's desires . . . that was all well and good, but there was nothing like a little action, like getting your hands dirty, to get the blood really going. He felt, all at once, ten years younger, felt alive in a way he hadn't for a long time now. The deal with the Klingons had been a mistake; he saw that in retrospect. It had been like a retirement, and he was not ready for that. No, Maxim Sen had a lot of living yet to do. The question, once more, was where. What direction he went from here? He thought again of the Verengi. Or heading off deeper into the Beta Quadrant. Possibilities, both of them. He would have to see.

A hand clawed at his pants leg.

He looked down and saw V'Reth lying on the floor, blood pooling at the corners of her mouth.

"Poetry," she gasped. "You wrote me poetry."

"Yes," Sen nodded. "Really, that can't get around."

He shot her too, then, and tossed the now fully discharged weapon on top of her corpse.

Taking a particle rifle from one of the guards—just in case—he made his way down to the auxiliary brig, following Roia's instructions till he reached the cell he was looking for. He entered the code she gave him on the keypad, and the cell door swung open.

A figure hung from the far wall, suspended by a complicated-looking series of shackles. It looked quite dead, for a minute.

Then it stirred, and raised its head.

"Ah," Sen smiled. "Captain Archer. That is you, isn't it?"

"Well." The human's voice sounded hoarse. He cleared his throat, and tried again. "Look what the cat dragged in."

"I assume that's some kind of insult." Sen deactivated the shackles holding Archer up. The captain fell to the floor with a loud thump.

"Get dressed," Sen told the human. "You have work to do."

TWENTY-FIVE

Outside the Kanthropian sickbay, Hoshi paced.

She'd been told to check back in an hour, and that hour had come and gone some time ago. Still no news on Theera. That wasn't good. The doctors here (the Kanthropian medical facilities were apparently far superior to the Conani, and so Theera had been brought back to S-12 for treatment) had found disruption of the brain tissue at the cellular level, caused by the mind-sifter, and were still trying to decide exactly how to proceed. One group favored surgery, another treatment via direct electrical stimulation . . . neither was optimistic about the long-term prognosis for recovery. They were currently waiting for the arrival of Theera's medical records, which they hoped to use as a baseline for comparison, particularly with regard to the measurement of electrochemical activity within the brain—EEG readings and the like—before deciding how to proceed.

For her part, Hoshi kept flashing back to the look of betrayal on Theera's face when Jaedez's guards had first dragged her into that room and she'd seen Hoshi. She couldn't get the image out of her mind. She couldn't stop feeling guilty for her role in what had happened.

Hoshi suspected that it would be a long, long time before that changed.

The sickbay doors opened, and—to her surprise—a

Denobulan stepped out. He glanced at her, and smiled.

"Ensign Sato, yes?"

"Yes." She strode over quickly to him.

"Doctor Hael. I'm handling the Andorian's case."

"You're a Denobulan."

"Yes." He frowned. "Is there a problem with that?"

"No, not at all. We have a Denobulan physician aboard *Enterprise*."

"Really?"

"Yes. A doctor . . . Phlox," Hoshi said, realizing only at that instant that although the doctor might have another name (first or last, she didn't know which Phlox represented), she had no idea what it was. Hael was considerably shorter than Phlox, and quite a bit older, she saw now, but still . . .

It was almost like running into a familiar face.

"Phlox." Hael frowned, and shook his head. "Phlox," he said again, and then finally, "I know no one by that name."

He had a strange expression on his face.

Hoshi had a funny feeling he wasn't telling her the exact truth. But she had neither the time nor the energy to pursue the question further.

"So how is she, Doctor? Theera?"

Hael shook his head, and for a moment, Hoshi's heart sank.

"I don't know how to explain what we're seeing," he said, "but . . . I believe the Andorian is going to make a complete recovery."

Hoshi was at a loss for words. That was the last thing she'd expected to hear.

"I don't understand. The other doctors—they said that there was cellular disruption. That the brain tissue itself was damaged."

"It was. It still is, parts of it, and yet . . ." Hael shook his head. "Somehow, the Andorian's neural pathways are in the process of regenerating themselves."

Hoshi frowned. "Regenerating?"

"Yes."

"I'm not a doctor, but . . . I've never heard of anything like that happening before."

"Nor I. It is most puzzling."

"Can I see her?"

"Not at the moment. She is still unconscious."

"How long till she wakes?"

"Difficult to say. Several hours, at the soonest. I can keep you apprised of her condition, if you like."

"I would appreciate that, thank you."

Hael excused himself then, and disappeared back inside the sickbay.

Hoshi stood there a moment, giving thanks to whatever powers there were for Theera's recovery. Another burden off her conscience, she thought, to go along with the one she'd experienced earlier, on returning to S-12 and contacting *Enterprise*. When she'd learned that her news about Sen and Captain Archer was not news after all and that the ship was even now in hot pursuit of the governor and his prisoner, who—they'd just discovered, thanks to a source on Procyron—was alive, or at least had been alive as of approximately twelve hours earlier, which meant that her failure to translate the Antianna signal was not, in fact, responsible for Archer's death.

It was only as she approached the analysis chamber once more that the question she should have asked Hael occurred to her—that being, would Theera's recovery include a complete return of all her memories, not just those pertaining to her time aboard the Antianna ship and the attack on *Lokune*, but those of her work, her husband, her childhood? She made a mental note to ask the doctor that the next time they talked.

She entered the analysis chamber, and stopped in her tracks.

In between visits to sickbay, Hoshi had been in the analysis chamber, working right alongside a group of several dozen Mediators, trying to make sense of what Theera had said under the influence of the mindsifter. The ship's computers quickly deciphered the Andorian's references to "spectral matrix scan," and the "four-hundred-seventy-three-nanometer" measurement. "Spectral," referring to electromagnetic spectrum; "matrix," representing the continuum of frequencies belonging to that spectrum; "scan," the physical process involved in searching for a specific one of those frequencies, that being, the four-hundred-seventy-odd-nanometer wavelength, which represented (at least to the human eye) the color blue.

When she'd left earlier, the Mediators had all been gathered in front of their respectative consoles, working within the database, or gathered in small groups.

Now they were all clustered in a single large knot, at the very front of the huge room, near the transparent wall.

Elder Green stood in front of them. She was talking, her voice somehow amplified to fill the chamber.

Hoshi moved closer to listen.

". . . to complete the retrofit, the engineers will need from us a number of items, then. Range of the EM spectrum to be monitored, and a separate list of those discrete frequencies to be generated. We should provide as well a list of species known to use specific portions of the EM spectrum to communicate, translations of their languages on UC code chips, and a complete record of encounters with same, which can be broadcast as library data. I would like to gather this data and supply it to them within the next half an hour, as the time needed to accomplish the retrofit is substantial. Questions?"

There were none from the Mediators, who quickly scattered about the chamber to perform their assigned tasks. Hoshi waited until Green was alone, and then approached her.

"Ensign." Green smiled. "I have just received the news regarding the Andorian. Most welcome."

"Yes, it is, but . . ." Hoshi waved a hand behind her, at the Mediators now hard at work once more. "What's going on?"

"General Jaedez now agrees that the Antianna scan may represent an attempt at communication, and that we should try to respond to it."

That was news. Last she had heard, Jaedez and Teraven weren't entirely convinced that the mindsifter had done its job, that the "memory" Theera had recalled was genuine. Largely because (as they had all quickly realized) Theera was not aboard the Antianna ship when it scanned *Lokune*.

"Our plan," Green said, leading Hoshi over to one of the horseshoe consoles where Younger Emmen sat, inputting data at a terminal, "is to retrofit S-12, as well as a number of other ships within the Armada, with a series of light-transmitting diodes."

Green pointed at Emmen's screen. It displayed a portion of the visual spectrum, sliced up into discrete chunks, too many for Hoshi to count.

"We plan to broadcast along the wavelengths

specifically cited by the Andorian, although we are building in the capacity to transmit at fractions of those frequencies. The signaling will of course be handled largely by computer, as our experience with the Mahadabalamin demonstrated that species who communicate in visual rather than auditory language usually do so at far greater speed, and so . . ."

Green continued in that vein, referencing several languages and life forms who utilized visual communication among themselves and other species, but Hoshi had a hard time focusing on what she was saying. Her attention was drawn to Emmen's terminal, to the narrow portion of the visual spectrum it displayed. A darker blue on the left hand side of the screen, a lighter one on the right.

Hoshi frowned.

A bell rang in her head.

"Ensign? Something the matter?"

"No. Not really."

She stared at the screen. At the dark blue, shading toward light. The light blue, shading toward aqua. Water.

The color of the ocean.

"Excuse me a minute," she said.

"Ensign Sato?" Green called after her, but Hoshi wasn't listening, she was already hurrying to her own station, sitting down and grabbing up the headset as quickly as she could.

It was just a coincidence, most likely, she told herself as she entered the virtual database. And yet . . .

She entered the library, and accessed the specific records she sought. The virtual "librarian" showed her how to transfer them from the central storage banks to her console. That done, she exited the database, and returned to the analysis chamber.

She brought the records on-screen, moved through them quickly until she found an image that served her purposes. She split the display, moving that image to the left half, and brought up alongside it the image from Emmen's console—the visual spectrum—and focused in on the right-hand side of that screen, the light blue shading toward aqua.

The colors matched.

She sat back in her chair a moment, and frowned. The match wasn't a surprise. She'd seen it in her head immediately. The question was, did the match mean anything, or was it strictly coincidental?

Could she trust her instincts, or . . .

"Ensign?"

She became aware of Green standing over her.

"What are you doing?"

She shook her head. "I'm not sure, really."

Green pointed to the left-hand side of the screen. "What is that?"

"That," she said, "is an image I found in the database. From a recording of a space battle, supposedly between the Allied Worlds and a race called the Barreon. This person," and now she too pointed at the screen, to the close-up image of the ripped uniform, and the dead body wearing it, floating in space, "was one of them."

"Why were you . . ." Green shook her head. "What makes you interested in the Barreon?"

"The colors," Hoshi said, gesturing to the screen. "They match."

"Excuse me?"

"The Barreon uniforms, the color the Antianna were scanning for . . . they match."

"I can see that, but . . . Ensign Sato. All due respect, I'm certain one could survey the database for all of five minutes and find several dozen other matches. This . . ." She gestured toward the screen. "It means nothing."

Hoshi nodded. Green was probably right, and yet . . .

Something else tickled at the back of her mind. Another connection, being made by her subconscious.

She frowned, and continued to stare at the screen.

"But . . . spectral matrix scan," she said, as much to herself as to Green. "What exactly were they searching for?"

Green was silent a moment.

"Ensign—are you suggesting that the Antianna were searching for these uniforms? For the people who wore them?"

"I don't know," Hoshi said, turning in her chair to face Green.

The Elder shook her head. "If memory serves . . . quite a number of historians doubt the authenticity of these recordings."

Younger Emmen stepped up behind Green. He looked at the images on Hoshi's screen, and frowned as well.

Was that what she was suggesting, Hoshi asked herself. That the Antianna were looking for the Barreon?

She turned back to the screen. Aqua. The color of the ocean at her grandfather's house. The Barreon uniforms, torn to shreds by the weapons of the Allied Worlds ships.

She thought back then to T'Pol's briefing, back on

Enterprise. Anecdotal evidence existed, the Vulcan had suggested, that the Thelasians were the descendants of the old Allied Worlds systems.

And all of a sudden, it clicked.

"No," she said. "That's not what I'm suggesting at all."

She looked up at Green, at Emmen, and then smiled.

"What if," she said. "What if the Antianna are the Barreon?"

She had a hard time getting anyone to take her idea seriously. At first.

Hoshi pulled up more records—maps from the same database she'd gotten the images of the battle from, charts showing Barreon space and that belonging to the Allied Worlds.

She overlaid that map on top of a current one that showed both Confederacy territory and the rough boundaries of that space the Antianna, by virtue of their attacks over the last few years, had claimed. The correspondence was not exact, but it was close enough to cause Elder Green to raise an eyebrow, for Younger Emmen to sit down at the console next to Hoshi's and begin research himself.

"If," he said, emphasizing the word, drawing it out while simultaneously keying in commands faster than Hoshi's eyes could follow, "you are correct, several questions immediately arise. Where have the Barreon been? Why have they chosen to identify themselves by a different name?"

Hoshi frowned. She couldn't answer the first question—she suspected that really, only the Barreon could—and as for the second . . .

She remembered a lesson she'd learned while living with the Huantanamos.

"Maybe they haven't chosen a different name. Maybe this is just the first time we're hearing it."

"I don't understand."

"Maybe Antianna is—or was—what the Barreon called themselves."

The Mediator on the other side of Emmen looked up then and spoke.

"Sources within the database suggest that is not the case. References within surviving Barreon mythology suggest a clear etymology for the species name."

Hoshi frowned. "Well. Is it possible that Antianna refers to the name of a particular subset of the race?"

"One moment." The Mediator keyed in a series of commands, then shook her head. "There are no such references."

"Are there any references at all to Antianna within the Barreon database?"

"I have run that query as well, and found no such word anywhere."

"You've checked all the databases? Already?" Hoshi asked. That seemed awfully quick to her.

The Mediator nodded "I have also sent queries to some of the more specialized historical information brokers. No matches."

Hoshi shook her head. She'd been so certain . . .

"I can query Teff-Langer, Elder," the Mediator said, turning to Green. "The cost will be approximately—"

"Not necessary." Green, who had been leaning over the Mediator's shoulder while she worked, straightened now and spoke. "I am afraid that however intriguing your theory is, Ensign, the facts do not support it, and therefore—"

"Elder Green."

They turned as one toward Younger Emmen, who had spoken.

"I have found a similar word in the lexicon."

"Continue," Green snapped.

"'On-dee-ana,'" he said, accenting the second syllable. "It is found in an engineering manual, an instruction book of sorts regarding the construction of Type-Two FTL engines."

"What does it mean?" Hoshi asked.

"It is difficult to say precisely. In the context of the document, it appears to refer to the procedure employed to insure successful merging of two warp fields within the drive."

"A supplementary reference, Elder." That from yet another Mediator, who had just looked up from his station. "Further explanation of the procedure, in a second such document. My reading suggests the word refers not to the procedure, but to the action. A verb, not a noun."

"To put together," Emmen added. "To join. I concur in that opinion."

Green shook her head. "Despite the phonetic similarity, to me, this does not sound relevant."

Hoshi frowned

She pictured Theera stretching her arms upward, out toward space, like a plea.

To put together. To join.

Not a plea—an imperative.

"Oh, no," she said. "I think it's very relevant indeed."

Green turned to her, a look of puzzlement on her face.

Hoshi explained.

TWENTY-SIX

Bodies everywhere.

Fallen in corridors, sprawled across escape pod hatchways, on sickbay cots, on top of computer stations, with blood and spittle pooled in the corners of their mouths, with expressions of agony frozen on their faces.

Klingons could hardly be said to rank high on Captain Jonathan Archer's list of "alien-races-I'd-most-like-to-be-trapped-aboard-a-starship-with," but this . . .

What had Sen done?

The governor wasn't telling. After releasing Archer, and bringing him down to the mess to eat, he'd told the captain they had two tasks before them. The first was cleanup.

"You will go to the sickbay, and fetch a gurney." Sen, sitting across a long table from the captain—just far enough to be out of Archer's reach—leaned back and popped some sort of food in his mouth that looked considerably more appetizing than the *gagh* on Archer's plate. "You will then use the gurney to transport the bodies to shuttlebay, at which point we will jettison them into space."

The captain nodded.

"I understand."

"Good. You will not, of course, make the mistake

of attempting any sort of escape, or sabotage, while you perform this task. The Klingon commander has thoughtfully equipped the ship with monitors every-where."

Again, Archer nodded. The monitors weren't really the problem, of course, the problem was the collar he wore—some sort of punishment device that could be activated by a remote, which now rested in Sen's hand, and which was, the captain suddenly realized, very similar to the ones used by some Orion slavers. Like the ones *Enterprise* had encountered in May. And thinking of *Enterprise*, he wondered where his ship was now; what was happening with his crew, what they thought had happened to him. He had vague memories of Sen firing his weapon, of lying on the floor, stunned, the feel of a transporter beam, a flash of bright light and then darkness, waking up in the Klingon brig, and realizing . . .

"Captain."

Archer looked up to find Sen glaring at him.

"Eat." The governor gestured with the remote. "You will need your strength."

Archer ate. And when he was done, he worked.

It was a gruesome, horrific, mind-numbing task. He tried not to see the bodies he lifted and dragged and threw about as people, but simply as things. He tried to keep his thoughts occupied elsewhere. On Sen—how had the governor managed to kill an entire shipful of Klingon warriors? Obviously, he'd had some kind of plan in place, a contingency worked out if things went wrong, which they somehow had. A hidden weapon— the evidence suggested a biological agent—or a booby trap of some kind. Maybe a traitor on board the ship. Definitely a traitor somewhere, whether here or within the Empire itself, though the captain was hard-pressed to think what circumstances would drive a Klingon to betray their people like this, to condemn them to this manner of death, so contrary to the code of the warrior they lived and hoped to perish by.

Though a few of them, now that he looked more closely, seemed to have died in a fight of some sort. The captain was inside what looked to him like a captain's mess, or a formal reception area. Death here had been messy, and not just in the way it had elsewhere on the ship, either; there was evidence of weapons fire, knife wounds . . .

He almost tripped then, on a young Klingon female who wore a look of (strangely enough) surprise on her face—well, half her face anyway, as the other half was blasted away.

The captain couldn't quite reconstruct the sequence of events in his mind. Not that it mattered greatly. What was done was done. What lay ahead, for him specifically . . .

Sen's initial plan, obviously, involved selling him to the Klingons. Now . . .

The governor said that was still his intention—that he would just have to complete that sale now through a third party. The glint in his eye when he spoke, though . . .

Archer wondered if Sen didn't just intend to kill him outright, once tasks numbers one and two were complete.

"Captain."

Archer started, and looked around.

"Speed, please, We still have much to do."

The voice—Sen's voice—came from everywhere, and from nowhere, all at once. A hidden speaker/speakers.

Sen hadn't been lying about those video monitors, obviously.

"Sorry," Archer said out loud. "It's just . . . a little hard to take in."

"Such sensitivity." The captain could hear the scorn in Sen's voice. "Admirable. But we have no time for it now. Work."

Archer was about to make another comment when he felt a slight tingle around his neck, from the collar. A few volts, courtesy of the governor. Just to get his point across.

The captain worked.

Three corpses to a gurney. Two gurneys at a time. Ten trips down to the shuttlebay. Sixty-three bodies in all, which if memory served was the entire crew complement of this ship, which he'd tentatively pegged as one of the new D-3s, judging by deck layout. (The captain wished he could read Klingon; there was writing everywhere, more than enough, he was certain, to positively ID the ship.) Which meant that he and Sen were all alone aboard the vessel: either the governor had killed whoever had helped him take over, or he'd gotten help before he boarded the vessel. Either way, that made Archer's job—overpowering the man, gaining control of the ship—easier. Theoretically. As a practical matter . . .

He had no earthly idea what he was going to do.

Sen had said two tasks, though, which gave him a little more time to puzzle things out, Archer thought, pushing the last of the gurneys in the direction of the shuttlebay. This one was lighter than usual, carrying not heavily armored warriors but three Klingon females. In addition to the younger one he'd found earlier, there had been two others in the stateroom, huddled together in a corner, as if for comfort. Wearing much less than Klingon females usually wore. Consorts, he guessed, for the dead officer in the stateroom. They wore expressions of equal parts puzzlement and horror. As if they couldn't believe what was happening to them. The captain had never particularly thought of Klingon females as sympathetic figures, but looking at these two, sprawled across the gurney . . .

Archer stopped dead in his tracks.

Coming from around the corner, he heard voices.

No. Not voices. Just a voice. Sen. But the governor was in the middle of a conversation, in the middle of talking to someone. Probably a contact back on Procyron, or elsewhere in the sector. Arranging a rendezvous, no doubt, a way off this ship, because two people could not run a vessel this size for very long.

He was having a hard time making out what Sen was saying; the governor was talking unusually softly, and in what almost sounded like incomplete sentences. Strange. Archer caught a name, Roia, and a few isolated words—"greedy, Verengi, Coreida system"—some of which were familiar to him, some not. He waited a moment longer, hoping to hear more, perhaps even a response from this Roia, whoever s/he was, over the com. But nothing came.

He pushed on, deciding that incomplete information was better than having Sen catch him in the act of eavesdropping.

Rounding the corner, he frowned.

Sen stood in the middle of the corridor, a good ten meters away from the nearest companel. Too far away to speak to someone over the device without shouting. So how—

"Is there a problem?" Sen asked, at which point the captain realized that the mental frowning he'd just done must have shown on his face as well.

"No. No problem. Just wanted to let you know that this was the last of the bodies."

"Good." Sen pointed to the shuttlebay. "Put them with the others, and then we'll take care of this business."

Archer wheeled the corpses into the shuttlebay, and laid them in a pile just outside the entrance hatch, next to the pile he'd made the trip previously, which itself was next to the pile from the trip before that—and so on, and so on, and so on. A hangar filled with such piles, filled with corpses. He stood and took a step back.

The room was beginning to smell. Sen was right about one thing, at least; getting rid of the bodies was the smart thing to do, because even though he and the governor had been immune to whatever killed the Klingons, there was a good chance they would not be immune to the microorganisms and bacteria about to infest all the corpses.

He turned to leave.

The hatch was closed behind him. Through the porthole, Sen smiled.

Heart suddenly thumping, Captain Archer punched the companel next to the door.

"Governor. What's going on?"

"What's going on?" Sen said in response, pressing the button on his side of the door. "Can't you guess?"

He could. He did.

Stupid, stupid, stupid, he cursed at himself, should have been paying more attention, should have . . .

The captain took a deep breath, and forced himself to stay calm.

"Why don't you tell me what's happening?" the captain said.

"You'll recall me mentioning two tasks we had to accomplish?"

"I recall," Archer said, forcing himself not to turn and look for the shuttle, though he knew that there was one in the bay, he'd stacked bodies right up against it, the only question was whether or not it was open or locked, well not the only question, he had to get to the shuttle first, and whether or not Sen would let him do that or use the remote—

That train of thought crashed to a halt as he saw, through the porthole, Sen's hand on the emergency bay door hatch. The governor was going to open the bay to space, at which point everything in it—dead, alive, flesh and blood and machine—was going to get sucked out in the vacuum.

Evac suits. Did the Klingons have evac suits? Never mind that, was there a handhold—

"Number one was the corpses, obviously," Sen said. "Number two . . ."

He shook his head.

"Well, actually I was wrong about there being two."

He was grinning ear-to-ear now, clearly enjoying himself.

"I get that," Archer said. "You know Starfleet will pay a reward too, for me. I don't know exactly what the Klingons were promising you, but—"

"There are three."

The captain stopped in midsentence, mouth open. "What?"

"There are three tasks we need to accomplish," Sen

said. "Number two is to secure the shuttle, so it remains in the ship when we evacuate the bay."

The shuttlebay hatch opened, and the governor stepped through, holding the remote before him like a weapon. Archer gave way.

"There is auxiliary cable in the maintenance locker there," Sen continued, pointing, "which can be used for that purpose, to supplement the bay locking system. You should have no trouble figuring that out."

The governor smiled at him again.

The captain stood there a moment, and felt his heart, still hammering in his chest.

Sen shrugged, spread his hands.

"Just a little joke, Captain," Sen said. "You didn't really think I'd jettison you along with the bodies, did you? After all . . . even if I can't arrange sale to the Klingons through a third party—as you said, Starfleet is certain to offer a reward. So what is the sense in killing you?"

The man's eyes glittered as he spoke, and in that instant, the captain felt certain that reward money or no, Sen was going to find a way to do just that, and probably take a long time doing so.

"Right," Archer said. "A joke. Don't know why I didn't see that."

"So serious." The governor made a show of frowning, and shook his head. "I had heard humans possessed quite a sense of humor. Ah well. You can't always believe what people tell you, can you, Captain?"

Without waiting for a response, Sen turned his back and started walking away.

"I will be on the bridge," he called over his shoulder. "Where task number three awaits us. Join me there when you've finished."

• • •

He secured the shuttle as Sen had directed. He closed the hatch behind him.

He pressed his face to the porthole, said a silent prayer for the Klingons on the other side of the bulkhead, and opened the airlock.

Everything in the bay that wasn't, literally, nailed down, or secured in some way, shot forward, out into space, as if it had been fired from a cannon.

Sudden cold numbed his cheek. The captain watched as the crew of the *c'Hos*, their captain, and their companions left the ship for the final time, and in that instant had the sudden thought—really, it was more of a premonition—that if he did indeed manage to survive this ordeal, what had happened here would someday come back to haunt him, not in his dreams, but in a very real-world way.

He hit the companel.

"All set here," he said.

"I can see that." Sen sounded angry. "Come to the bridge immediately."

The governor sat in the command chair when he arrived, a set of tools laid out on the decking nearby.

"We're doing some rewiring?" the captain asked.

"In a moment." Sen frowned. "There is a problem with the security system. I am unable to access the operator subroutines."

Archer stood there a moment, waiting. Sen simply sat, one hand on the armrest of the chair, fingers drumming impatiently. His other hand lay on his leg, the remote held loosely in it.

His attention was elsewhere. The captain judged the distance between them. A little more than three meters. In optimum physical condition, he could jump most of that in a single bound. Certainly with a running start. But he wouldn't get a running start here, and he wasn't in optimal condition. Still . . .

This might be the best chance he'd get.

Archer tensed, and prepared to leap.

Sen's gaze swiveled, and fastened on him.

"The voltage in the collar is more than sufficient to disable a Klingon warrior, Captain. I don't doubt that the effects on the human nervous system . . ."

His voice trailed off.

A light came into his eyes, and he smiled.

"Excellent," he said, and nodded. "Excellent."

"Excuse me?" the captain said.

Sen blinked. His smile disappeared for a second, and then returned.

"I have just bypassed—just realized how to bypass—the Klingon security protocols. Which means we can begin our work."

"Ah." The captain nodded, and for a brief instant met Sen's gaze again.

The governor was lying about something, Archer realized. But what? Why?

He had little time to contemplate those questions over the next few minutes, though, because at that point Sen began giving him instructions at a rapid-fire pace. Take this tool, remove that deck plate. Disassemble that conduit, attach the power couplings there. Take that station, access the operator software, enter this password, reroute control from here to there.

Their task, the governor explained as Archer worked, was to modify the bridge's control systems so they could all be operated from the command chair, a necessary thing, Sen pointed out, given that they no longer had a full complement of crew on board. As he worked, Archer tried to keep track of the original system layout and the modifications he was making—Starfleet, of course, would be interested in all of it—but as the work got more and more complex, he found it impossible to keep all the details in his head.

The governor seemed to have no such problem.

Sen knew an awful lot about the systems on *c'Hos*, Archer realized. He wondered how. Probably, the captain thought, he'd bought and paid for it before he'd ever set foot on the vessel. Insurance, just in case something went wrong with his plan. As it clearly had. Smart.

Archer paused a moment to wipe his brow.

"Problem?" Sen asked.

"No problem." The captain was crouched on the floor, up near the helm console, about five meters away from Sen in the command chair, facing toward the governor. "Just need a minute, that's all."

"A minute. Of course. I'll count it out for you."

"Thanks so much." He set down the tools he'd been working with. "How much longer you think this is going to take?"

"Not long," Sen said. "Are you in some sort of rush? You have some place else you need to be?"

"No. Just curious."

"A few more hours, perhaps."

Archer nodded. He wondered if there was a task number four.

He wondered if, when he was done here, he'd be joining the Klingons.

He had to do something soon. No, not soon. Now.

He looked down into the exposed access panel, saw the conduit and cabling, and thought: *sabotage*.

"Thirty seconds, by the way," Sen said.

The captain looked back up.

"Can I get a drink of water?"

"Not just yet," Sen said. "We'll return to the mess shortly. You can drink there. Eat as well, if you like."

"More *gagh*. Can't say I'm looking forward to it."

"Perhaps we'll find another item on the menu your system can tolerate. In the meantime . . ." Sen waved the control in his hand. "Back to work."

Archer nodded, and bent over the access panel once more.

"Beneath the conduit we just disconnected," Sen said, "there is a sheath of optical cabling. One strand should have a faint blue glow to it. Do you see it?"

Archer nodded.

"I do."

"Good. That strand joins with the others in a junction box at the far end of the access panel. I want you to disconnect it from the box."

The captain braced himself on the deck with one hand, and reached down with the other.

"It may take some doing, by the way," Sen added. "These have a tendency to get stuck."

Archer frowned.

Now how in the world did Sen know that? Even assuming he'd spent the last few weeks studying up on this ship's systems, that kind of practical knowledge . . .

It just wasn't possible. What did he have in his head, some kind of computer?

His hand paused in midair.

And he remembered, all at once, what Malcolm had told him down on Procyron. How Sen's guards were able to react so fast, to move so quickly as a unit. They had implants in their heads, some kind of neural interface. What if—

He felt a brief, sudden tingling around his neck.

"Captain. Work, please." Sen stood over him glaring.

The captain looked up at him, and their eyes met.

Archer tried very hard not to smile.

Chipped. Sen was chipped. That was how he'd been able to overpower and kill the crew, how he was able to monitor the captain so easily, how he knew so much about the ship's internal workings . . .

"Something amuses you?" Sen asked.

"No. Not at all."

"Then . . ."

"Sorry." The captain reached down, and made a show of yanking on the cable again. It came free, right away. Not stuck at all.

"Well look at that," Archer said.

Sen snorted. "Humans," he said, and went back to the command chair again.

Archer went back to work as well.

Rewiring.

And planning.

TWENTY-SEVEN

Elder Green did not see the interrogation recording in the same light as Hoshi. She did not read the enunciation in Theera's voice as imperative, or a plea. She was certain the Andorian had indeed said "Antianna,"not "Ondeanna."

"Our time and effort," she said to Hoshi, loud enough so that all within range could hear, "must be focused on configuration and testing of the diode panels. You may continue your research in this regard, Ensign Sato, but as for the rest of us . . ."

She motioned, and the other Mediators returned to work.

Setting aside her frustration, Hoshi did as Green had suggested, plunging back into the database, searching for further connections between the Antianna and the Barreon. She began by reviewing history. There were conflicting records, conflicting accounts of the Barreon's early years, up until the time of their encounter of the Allied Worlds. They'd been in the process, apparently, of forming an Alliance of their own, though with whom was unclear; no races were mentioned in any of the accounts Hoshi read. The Barreon (or Barrion, sources had it both ways) had been quite sophisticated, technologically; the basic design of the Type-2 FTL ship was attributed to them by more than one source, and several mentioned as well a sophisticated, semi-intelligent software program that had run a number of their defensive systems toward the end of the war. Where they fell short, though, was in armaments—offensive, and defensive weaponry—and numbers. When war came—conflicting territorial ambitions, according to most sources—the Barreon were no match for the Allied Worlds. There were several smaller conflicts before the epic confrontation that destroyed both empires, a war that, depending on which source you believed, either lasted for close to five years or was over in a month.

All extant sources put the number of people killed in the billions.

Following the war, there was a blank spot in the histories, an interregnum of close to half a millennium, after which the Thelasian Confederacy—occasionally claiming ties to the Allied Worlds—arose to become the dominant power in this part of the quadrant. But of the Barreon . . .

There was nothing.

Hoshi pushed back from the console, and frowned.

Antianna. Ondeanna.

Maybe she was imagining it, at that.

The console beeped.

The screen cleared, and filled with the image of Doctor Hael, from the Kanthropian sickbay.

"Ensign Sato."

"Yes?"

"I thought you might like to know. The Andorian has awakened."

"I'll be there in a minute."

She closed down the system, and hurried from the room.

• • •

Theera was indeed conscious. Weak, barely able to talk, but otherwise lucid.

With no memory, whatsoever, of what she had said while under the influence of the mind-sifter.

"I am sorry." The Andorian shook her head. "I wish I could help."

"That's all right." Hoshi stood over the bed, hesitant about pulling up a chair alongside it. Maybe it was her imagination—her guilty conscience at work—but Theera seemed to have closed herself off again.

"I want to apologize to you," Hoshi said. "I didn't know that they were going to do that—the mind-sifter. I didn't think—"

"It doesn't matter. I don't remember anything. Not the pain, not what I said . . ." She shrugged. "Nothing."

Hoshi nodded. In a way, that was fortunate.

The two were silent a moment.

"Do you think it is possible," Theera began, "that the Kanthropians would return me to Andoria now?"

"Now?" Hoshi shook her head. "I don't know— right now, as I understand it, we're being shadowed by the Antianna fleet. I don't think any ships in the Armada are leaving anytime soon."

"There are courier ships aboard S-12, are there not?"

"Yes, but—"

"Would you ask Elder Green if one would be available to take me?"

"I could ask, though I doubt . . ." Hoshi's voice trailed off as she realized something. "Theera. Did your memory come back, is that why you're asking to go home? Because if that's the case, then . . ."

"No." Theera was shaking her head emphatically.

"It's just . . . I want to be there. As soon as possible. I want to start living my life again."

There was a sudden edge to her voice. Hoshi couldn't quite place it. Excitement, impatience . . . something else?

"I understand," Hoshi said. "I'll talk to her."

"Thank you."

Hoshi smiled. "You're welcome."

The two were silent a moment.

"I should get going now," Hoshi said. "Let you rest. Get back to work—we're still trying to . . ."

"You should come," Theera interrupted.

It took Hoshi a minute to figure out what Theera was saying.

"To Andoria?"

"Yes. You should leave here too. Come back with me."

That edge was back in the Andorian's voice, and now, hearing it again, Hoshi recognized the emotion behind it. Not excitement, not impatience . . .

Fear.

"Theera," Hoshi said. "Is something the matter?"

The Andorian lowered her gaze.

Of course, Hoshi thought.

"It's them, isn't it?" she prompted. "The Antianna?"

Hesitation. And then . . .

Theera nodded.

"Yes," she said quietly.

"That's all right." Now Hoshi did take that chair, and pull it up next to the diagnostic bed. "I understand."

She put her hand on top of the Andorian's.

"I'm not going to pretend you don't have reason to be scared. But we've found something, I think—a clue, in what you said under the mind-sifter—and so I think we can talk to them, I think—"

"You can't talk to them," she said, suddenly grabbing hold of Hoshi's hand. Her grip was strong. Painfully so.

Hoshi winced, and tried to free her hand.

"If they catch us," she said. "You don't know what they'll do. You don't know what will happen."

Hoshi gave a sudden twist, and freed her hand. It throbbed with pain.

"We'll find a way to talk to them," Hoshi said. "I know we will."

The Andorian shook her head.

Hoshi said her good-byes, and left the room.

Doctor Hael was waiting for her outside the door.

"Ensign Sato," he said. "I'm glad I was able to find you."

"What's the matter?"

"General Jaedez wishes to see you. Immediately."

Hoshi was escorted back to the Conani flagship, to the general's office, where she found not only Jaedez but Teraven there as well, waiting for her.

They were looking at something on the viewscreen.

The general caught sight of her first, and waved her forward.

"Ensign Sato. Excellent. Please, come in. We desire your opinion as well."

She walked to the front of the room, and saw what they were all looking at.

It was an image from Theera's "interrogation." The Andorian, risen from her chair, the restraints that had held her to it lying on the deck beside her feet, snapped in half.

Hoshi's own outstretched hand was visible in the lower left-hand corner of the screen.

"We are interested in your opinion, Ensign." Teraven,

who'd been standing to one side of the general, now moved front and center, pointed to the image on the screen behind him. "If you have an explanation for this. How the Andorian was able to snap these restraints, to physically move while under the influence of the mindsifter."

Hoshi shrugged. "The restraints were defective. Obviously."

"No," Teraven said. "They were examined prior to your arrival. There was nothing wrong with them."

"Then . . ." Hoshi shook her head.

Her hand throbbed where Theera had held it. The Andorian was strong. But that, really, was no explanation either. Strong didn't break duranium.

"I don't know," she said. "I can't explain it."

"General?" Teraven asked, turning to Jaedez, who gestured for him to proceed.

"Perhaps," the Pfau said, "the Andorian is not what she seems."

"I don't understand," Hoshi said. "What else would she be?"

"A spy."

Hoshi did a double take.

"What?"

"Theera is a spy. An Antianna, in the guise of an Andorian, placed among us to sabotage the fleet."

Hoshi shook her head in disbelief.

"You can't be serious."

"I am quite serious," Teraven said.

"It took three of my men and their weapons to subdue her earlier," Jaedez said. "To bring her to this ship. That strikes me as unusual."

Hoshi—who had been about to express her opinion more forcefully—suddenly frowned, as she remembered the contemptuous ease with which one of Jaedez's guards had handled her.

"Well . . . she's had training, obviously. That's all."

"I have had training," Teraven said. "Training takes you only so far against a superior opponent."

Hoshi couldn't dispute the truth of that.

"Ensign Sato, I seem to recall a conversation," Jaedez said, "with you present, where Elder Green told me that the Andorian had been spending her time reviewing background—personal, professional—that she should have been familiar with?"

"It's because she has amnesia," Hoshi blurted out.

"Or so she would have us believe," Teraven said. "Perhaps she simply seeks to further her masquerade."

"She's not faking."

"How do you know that?"

"I just . . . I've spent enough time with her to see. That's all."

Teraven frowned. "Hardly scientific proof."

"You're saying she painted herself blue, and glued on a set of antennae. That hardly seems scientific to me either."

"Such surgical 'masquerades' are not unknown."

Hoshi shook her head. "So you're saying that none of the information we obtained from her is reliable?"

"Given this evidence"—Teraven gestured to the tape—"given the fact that no one still has provided a satisfactory explanation as to how the Andorian can possibly recall a scan that took place on one ship when she was on another—yes, I am afraid that in my opinion, none of the information we gleaned courtesy of the mind-sifter can be considered reliable."

"I am in agreement," Jaedez said. "We have

ordered Elder Green to cease construction on the
light-emitting diodes. Furthermore—"

"You can't do that!" Hoshi said.

Jaedez raised an eyebrow.

"You forgot your place, Ensign," Teraven said.

Jaedez held him back. "No, no. I will hear her out.
Proceed. Tell me why you think—exclusive of the
Andorian's 'recollections'—the diode project is worth
continuing."

Hoshi took a deep breath.

"It's not the diode project I'm concerned with," she
said—and launched into her theory regarding the
possible connections between the Antianna and the
Barreon.

"Ondeanna," Jaedez said when she had finished.
He gestured to Teraven. "Run the recording, please."

Teraven did, playing the entire session back, paus-
ing it at the very end once more, on the image of
Theera, arms outstretched, reaching for the sky.

"I am in agreement with Elder Green—at least partially," Jaedez said when it finished. "I do not hear the
word as Ondeanna, but Antianna. Regarding the Andorian's expression of intent, however . . ." He turned
to Teraven. "Commander?"

"'Join.'" Teraven frowned, and shook his head.
"What could it mean, in this context, Ensign?"

"I'm not sure," Hoshi admitted.

She looked up at the screen. The look on Theera's
face, the yearning, in her eyes . . .

An idea came to her, all at once.

"But there's a simple way to find out," she said.
"Send a signal."

Teraven frowned. "A signal. To the Antianna?"

"Yes."

"Forgive me for stating the obvious, but we have been sending signals. Thousands of them, over the last few years, at a guess. The aliens have responded to none."

"Well we haven't been sending the right one, obviously."

"And the right one is?" Teraven asked.

Hoshi looked at Jaedez and saw understanding in his eyes.

"Ondeanna," he said.

She smiled. "Precisely."

The test was simple enough to set up.

Jaedez took Hoshi to the flagship's bridge. Introduced her to his com officer, who in turn showed her to an unused station which he then reconfigured to give her external transmission privileges.

Hoshi settled herself into the seat, and set up a few quick parameters. Signal strength, transmission frequency, and content. A burst message, once every fifteen seconds, saying the same thing, over and over and over again.

Ondeanna.

Simple enough, she thought, and turned around.

Jaedez was deep in conversation with one of his officers. She waited for a pause in the conversation, and then caught his eye.

"All set," she said.

He walked up behind her, and nodded.

"Very well. Proceed."

Hoshi sent the message.

"I've set it for maximum strength, minimum dispersion," she said. "To make sure it can cut through any other com traffic. I've also set up a directional shift every few seconds, just to make sure we cover all three hundred sixty degrees. It'll probably take a few minutes to hit the first Antianna ship, because I've started at zero degrees heading here—"

An alarm sounded, then stopped.

"Sir!"

The officer Jaedez had just finished speaking to was leaning over a station at the front of the bridge, frowning.

"Colonel," Jaedez replied. "Report."

"Picking up movement from the Antianna ships, sir. They're closing."

"Indeed?"

"Yes, sir."

Jaedez glanced over quickly at Hoshi, and smiled.

"It appears you may have been right, Ensign. Congratulations. Colonel, I want you to contact Elder Green aboard S-12, let her know what we've done, and ask her to immediately provide a database of the Barreon language to all . . ."

"General. Picking up something on long-distance scanners as well."

Jaedez turned.

"Something."

"Yes, sir. Hard to be certain, but I think . . ."

"Confirm that reading, General."

The colonel was back in position, leaning over the same station.

"I have eighty-eight separate signals, heading in this drection."

"Eighty-eight?" Jaedez's eyes widened. "Are you sure?"

"Yes, sir, quite sure." The colonel leaned closer and frowned. "They appear to be ships. Antianna ships, in fact."

The bridge, all at once, fell silent.

Jaedez turned to Hoshi.

"I sincerely hope, Ensign," he said, "that the word

means what you think it does, and not something else entirely."

"As do I, sir," she said.

Jaedez nodded and turned to face the viewscreen once more.

Eighty-eight ships, Hoshi thought. *This was either the beginning of a very long negotiation process, or a very, very short war."*

TWENTY-EIGHT

The work was a lot more involved than Sen had originally anticipated.

After the better part of a day, they still weren't finished. Not even close, by Archer's reckoning, as he'd only rewired/reconfigured about half the bridge stations. He'd been slowing the last hour or so, though—running on fumes. Sen was tired too. Out of the corner of his eye, Archer had caught the governor yawning more than once. He'd hoped, perhaps, that Sen would nod off, and he'd be able to overpower him. No such luck.

Instead, a few minutes ago, Sen had called a halt to the work, and escorted Archer back where he'd come from. Back to the brig.

"We'll resume in a few hours," the governor told him. "In the meantime . . . make yourself comfortable."

The captain looked around the cell where he'd spent the last couple of weeks. He barely recognized it; for one thing, he'd been pretty well out of it most of that time—drugged, between, sleep-deprived . . .

For another, the lights had been permanently dimmed, back then. Now, though, they blared full intensity.

Archer thought that, on the whole, he preferred the darkness.

The cell's floor, walls, and ceiling were all bare steel, rusted and stained a brownish red. There were no seats or benches of any kind. And the smell . . .

"You know, there are a lot of empty cabins aboard this ship right now," Archer said.

"I'm well aware of that," Sen said. "After I leave you, in fact, I'll be on my way to the officer's deck, to find a place to rest myself. I suspect I'll end up in Commander Kareg's suite—the monitor images make it look like quite a nice place, actually."

"I'm sure it is. I'd settle for a simple enlisted man's bunk," Archer said.

"I'm sure you would." Sen smiled. "Good night, Captain. Sleep well."

He slammed the steel door shut behind him, and left the brig.

Archer glared after him.

Sleep well. He didn't think so. Not just because the last thing he wanted to do was put his head down on this floor. The truth was that these next few hours might be the only chance he had to think for a while. To figure a way out of not just here, but his larger predicament.

One thing he'd realized in the last few hours, since his discovery that Sen was chipped, it wasn't the Klingon system the governor was hooked up to—it couldn't be. Because if it had been, Sen wouldn't have had any problems overriding *c'Hos*'s security protocols. What was probably going on, the captain decided, was that Sen was talking to a rogue program within it. Probably one he'd introduced himself. A smart program, one that could learn from and actively combat the systems that hosted it. Starfleet had something similar in the works; "intelligent software agent" was the term, if memory served. This program, though, sounded like it was light-years ahead of Starfleet's design.

Gingerly, he took a seat on the floor, and settled in as best he could.

He put his elbows on his knees, his chin in his hands, and catnapped. He thought about alternative plans of action. He wondered, briefly, what was happening with the Antianna—if, in Sen's absence, the war fleet had indeed launched, or if Hoshi, and the Mediators, and the Andorian linguist had managed to decipher the Antianna signal, and establish communication. He thought about Sen's software agent.

He wondered just how smart it was.

He wondered if Sen was the only one who could talk to it.

He got to his feet.

"Excuse me?"

No response.

"I know Governor Sen is probably sleeping, but this is something that maybe the ship's computer can answer. Computer. Are you there?"

Nothing.

"Just a question about how much longer I have to sleep. Computer?"

Still nothing.

Archer sighed, and sat back down. It had been a long shot, anyway. Even if the program was able to recognize voice input, Sen probably had it configured to respond to him only—probably keyed to certain specific phrases, or words.

Forget the computer, the captain decided, though of course he'd have to take it into account no matter what other plans he came up with.

He yawned involuntarily then, and realized that he needed to sleep as well. But there wasn't time. A few hours, Sen had said, and then they would be back at it.

Approach the problem differently, he thought. Clearly, he couldn't overpower Sen and the computer on his own. He'd need help to do that. Someone outside the ship. *Enterprise*, ideally, but if not . . . then someone else. Someone nearby.

The problem with that approach was that he had no idea where, precisely, they were at the moment. He could take an educated guess; they certainly wouldn't be headed toward Klingon territory, or back toward the Confederacy, they'd have to be going deeper into the galactic interior, or out toward the rim. Probably the latter, he decided. Who was out in that direction?

He couldn't think of anyone at the moment. Still. Assume they were out there, the trick was getting them to come. Getting a signal off, which was clearly possible, because he'd heard Sen talking earlier today . . .

He frowned.

Wait a minute.

He thought back to what had happened, back when he'd been transporting the Klingon corpses down to the shuttlebay, and he'd paused in the corridor.

Sen had been talking to someone. A contact back on Procyron, or elsewhere in the sector, he'd thought then. But what if . . .

Hmm, he thought. *What was that name he'd used again?*

"Roia," he said out loud, remembering.

Static hissed.

"Working," a voice said.

Archer smiled.

"Roia," he said again. "This is Captain Archer."

"Identification confirmed. You are Captain Jonathan Archer, commander Earth ship *Enterprise*."

The captain nodded. "Right I wonder if . . ."

He frowned, and thought furiously.

". . . if I could get a drink of water."

"Water. First Governor Sen must be awakened for permission to obtain—"

"No, no, no," Archer said quickly. "We don't need to wake the governor. What I was really wondering . . . I'm having a hard time sleeping, Roia. I wonder if I could talk to you for a little while."

"You are talking."

"Yes, I know. What I should have said was . . . I wonder if I could ask you a few questions."

"Questions." Archer could almost hear the frown in the computer's voice. Amazing piece of programming. "Certain subject matter would be prohibited What did you wish to talk about?"

"Well . . ." The captain shrugged. "You, for one thing."

"You refer to the Roia program?"

"Yes. I'm curious. What, exactly are you?"

There was no response for a moment.

"Is this a prohibited subject?" the captain asked.

"Negative."

"Then . . ."

Another pause. Then:

"This program is a modified version of the Roia-12 matrix. An independent, adaptive, software agent."

"Ah. And—where does the name Roia come from? Is it an acronym of some kind?"

Again, the program hesitated.

And then it—she—told him.

An independent, adaptive, intelligent software agent, Archer thought. Which Sen twisted into an avatar of his own warped desires.

Let's see, the captain thought, *if I can do a little twisting of my own.*

TWENTY-NINE

The Antianna ships kept coming.

Hundreds of them, so many that Hoshi pictured a factory on the Antianna homeworld, wherever that was, just churning them out, one after another, giant machines spewing forth more machines, that then rocketed off into space.

All she (and Jaedez, and everyone else on the flagship's bridge) could do was watch as they assembled, just on the other side of Confederacy territory. If they decided to attack, then the Armada would be destroyed. It was as simple as that.

But they did nothing.

Jaedez had ordered the signal—the word, "Antianna"—stopped at least an hour ago. Now he frowned, and turned to Hoshi, and asked if she thought it should be broadcast again.

She didn't know what to say.

If the word really meant what she thought it did—"join"—then sending it again could do no harm. On the other hand, if—as Jaedez had suggested earlier—it had another meaning entirely . . .

"Something's happening."

That from one of the bridge personnel, who now looked up from his station and frowned.

"Ships on the move, sir," he said to Jaedez.

The general cursed and strode forward. "Prepare

defense stations. Maneuver primary battle cruisers into delta formation. Attack squadrons, at the ready."

Hoshi, still seated at the aux station, saw the ships moving too. Correction.

"Single ship, General."

Jaedez spun around, glared at her, and then turned back to the officer who had spoken.

"Colonel?"

"Confirm, sir. My mistake. A single Antianna ship, detaching itself from the main fleet."

Everyone's attention went to the viewscreen, where indeed a single ship was moving away from the mass of others surrounding it. Though it was understandable why Jaedez's officer had made an error in identification.

The vessel was huge. Twice as big as any other Antianna ship they'd encountered.

As Hoshi watched, it crept forward toward the Armada, and then, when it reached a point equidistant between the two fleets, stopped.

And broadcast the word back at them: Antianna.

"Do we respond sir?" the com officer asked.

Jaedez frowned.

"I don't think we need to repeat ourselves," Hoshi said before the general could answer. "I think we need to take the next step."

"The next step?" the general asked.

"Yes."

Hoshi rose from her seat, and gestured toward the viewscreen.

"Go out there," she said, "and meet them."

When she said "we," of course, Hoshi meant herself, but she had no illusions about her relative importance in the larger scheme of things. She expected a long argument from Jaedez after proposing that the ideal envoys would be herself and Elder Green.

She was surprised when she didn't get one.

Instead, Jaedez sent her with one of his officers to a flight simulator, so she could familiarize herself with the control layout of the ship they'd be taking. She made the point that it would take more than a few minutes for her to get comfortable, but the general didn't seem troubled. So off she went. Green, she was told, was being shuttled over from S-12, and would join her in a moment.

It took longer than that. Longer than Hoshi expected, and when Green did finally show, she looked a little worse for the wear. Problems, apparently, on her trip over.

"You sure you're all right?" Hoshi said.

"Yes. Just a fainting spell, apparently. I'm fine now."

"The doctors looked at you?"

"Yes, the doctors looked at me," Green said, and then managed a smile. "I thank you for your concern, Ensign, but if you're trying to dissuade me from coming on this mission—you'll have to do a lot better than that. The descendants of the Barreon . . ." Green shook her head. "This is—cliché as it may sound—a once-in-a-lifetime opportunity. I have to talk to them."

Hoshi had to smile back. She understood entirely.

The two of them made their way down to the shuttlebay, at which point a lot of things became clear to her.

The ship they were taking was a military vessel. Much larger than any courier ship she'd ever seen, shaped more like a saucer than anything else, albeit a saucer with multiple weapons turrets, sharp angles, and a relatively large warp coil.

Standing by the gangplank leading up and into that ship, talking to a single armored warrior, was General Jaedez.

"Oh no," Hoshi said angrily, and stalked over to him. "This is a military vessel," she said.

Jaedez nodded. "That's correct."

"This is supposed to be a peace mission. We're," she gestured toward herself and Green, "supposed to be peace envoys. You send a ship that looks like this, and the Antianna will know . . ."

"Will know what? That we do not readily give our trust to an enemy who has killed several hundred of us? That is exactly what I want them to know," Jaedez said.

"I'm not firing any weapons," Hoshi said.

"You won't have to." Jaedez turned to the man he'd been talking to. "You may take your station, Colonel. I will be in contact."

"Sir." The Conani saluted smartly, and then, to Hoshi's surprise, walked up the gangplank and disappeared inside the ship.

"No," Hoshi said. "You can't put a soldier on the ship, too. That sends the entirely . . ."

"There are ten soldiers on the ship, Ensign. There is a specially shielded compartment belowdecks. If all goes well, neither you—nor the Antianna—will ever be aware of their presence."

"And if all doesn't go well? If the Antianna find out they're down there? That could ruin the mission before it starts. You have to take them off the ship."

"The soldiers stay."

"General, think about it. What good are ten soldiers going to do . . ."

"Ensign," Jaedez cut her off, "you wish someone else to take your place? Younger Emmen, perhaps?"

"No. What I want is . . ."

"What you want is irrelevant. I decide the mission needs and the personnel that can best fulfill them. I have no second thoughts about the soldiers; if there is trouble, if things do not go as planned, their task is simply to see that Elder Green—and yourself—return safely. That should be easy enough to understand, yes?"

"Yes, but . . ."

"I hear your concerns, Ensign," Jaedez said. "To a certain extent, I share them. But I have other concerns as well, that override them. Now. You have your orders. Carry them out."

Hoshi bit back the words on her tongue, and nodded.

"Yes, sir."

He looked past her then, to Elder Green.

"Kanthropian. You will keep this one in check, yes?"

Jaedez said it with a slight smile. Green managed one in return.

"Yes," she said.

"Good. Good luck then."

The general saluted then, and left them on the gangplank.

Hoshi watched him go a moment, and then took Elder Green's arm and helped her into the ship.

The cockpit was built for four, two seats in front, two in the back of the small compartment. She and Elder Green settled themselves into the forward pair. Hoshi found herself looking at a dizzying array of control screens, some whose functions were obvious—com, sensor, helm—some less so. As she reached for the helm controls—*Haven't done this in a long time*, she thought—a voice sounded right at her ear.

"Ensign Sato."

She caught Green's eye and shrugged.

"Right here."

"This is Colonel Diken. We will control helm."

Hoshi raised an eyebrow.

She'd seen no trace of the colonel and his soldiers when she'd entered the ship—she'd pictured them crouched down in some dark, hidden compartment, weapons at the ready—but now she adjusted that image in her mind, visualizing something more akin to *Enterprise*'s command center. A chamber that big, she thought, the whole ship might have been designed around it. So maybe the shielding was as effective as Jaedez contended, and the Antianna wouldn't find them either, even if they had cause to search the ship.

Maybe.

"All yours," she told the colonel, and removed her hands from the helm control.

"Guess we're just passengers, for the moment," she said, turning to Elder Green.

"Indeed." The Kanthropian smiled weakly, and nodded. Green still didn't look well to her. Hoshi wanted again to ask how she was doing—actually, what she really wanted to do was suggest that Younger Emmen take her place—but she already had a good idea of how that suggestion would go over. Besides, she suspected Green, no matter the seriousness of her illness, would rise to the occasion. A good thing too—she had no illusions about her competency as a translator relative to Green's. And speaking of translators . . .

Hoshi checked her UT, to make sure that the Barreon language—what they had of the lexicon—had been correctly downloaded into their handhelds. Looked that way to her.

She felt a tingle of excitement then herself. The Barreon. The Allied Worlds . . .

Theera, she thought then, and a tiny bit of apprehension crept into her mind as well.

"You are cleared for launch," came the voice in Hoshi's ear, and at that instant the bay doors opened.

Thrusters fired, triggered by the soldiers hidden belowdecks, and the little ship surged forward, out into space.

They took it slowly, even after they'd cleared the last of the Armada ships, and entered what she could only think of as "Antianna space." The autopilot had them on the rough equivalent of one-third impulse, which put their destination at least ten minutes away.

Hoshi switched her attention to the companel. The fifty-seven pulses were still coming in, loud and strong. She still had no idea how they related to the message they'd sent, that the Antianna had responded to: Join. Join what?

The console in front of her beeped.

Hoshi looked down and saw the terminal in front of her had filled with a line of text.

Testing. Okay up there?

Up there. The signal, she realized, was from the colonel, below decks. Testing.

They were running silent. No internal transmissions for the Antianna to pick up.

She keyed in a response:

A-okay. No problems.

Good. Stand by. Contact in five minutes.
We will monitor.

Hoshi signed off too, then, and turned her attention to the viewport, where the Antianna ship was just visible in the distance. The clean lines, the lack of visible weapons structures or sensory apparatus—the image rang a bell with her, and a second later she realized why. It was exactly the same view she'd had from her station on *Enterprise*, over a week earlier, when they'd been trying to press forward into uncharted space, and the Antianna ship had stood in their way.

Same view, that is, except that judging from the incoming telemetry, this ship was more than three times the size of that vessel they'd first encountered.

"Readings indicate the ship is unoccupied," Green said, a note of puzzlement in her voice, and Hoshi looked to another screen, and saw the Elder was right, their sensor scans were picking up nothing remotely resembling biosigns, just a huge, diffuse energy field.

"We had this problem on *Enterprise* too—on my ship. There's some kind of force-screen that prevents us from getting a clear signal right away. Just wait a minute, and . . ."

As if on cue, the telemetry changed.

"Picking up something now," Green said.

"I see it." A surge of energy aboard the Antianna ship. It looked to her like . . .

"The power grid is reconfiguring itself," she said out loud, shaking her head.

Which was no more possible now than it had been that week and a half ago, when Trip had noted the same thing.

Hoshi frowned.

The console directly in front of her came to life.

Incongruous sensor scans. You?

She keyed in a response.

Same. Noted in previous encounters.
No cause for alarm.

Just as she sent the message, Green inhaled sharply. At first, Hoshi thought she was in pain.

"You all right?" she asked, turning quickly.

Green was staring out the viewport. "I am fine. However . . . something very unusual has just occurred."

She gestured toward the space outside.

Hoshi followed her gaze, and saw that the Antianna ship—for lack of a better word—had changed.

There was now a clearly visible sensor array—at least, that was what it looked like to her—projecting from the underside of the vessel.

"That wasn't there before," she said.

"No. It appeared immediately following the reconfiguration of the power grid."

"There must be a bay of some sort on the bottom of the ship. They stow it there, and then lower it as needed."

"That makes sense," Green said. "Although . . . such deployments, in my experience, usually take a fairly good length of time to complete. On the order of several seconds."

In her experience too, Hoshi thought. And this had occurred instantaneously. But . . .

What other explanation was there.

"I think," Hoshi said, and that was as far as she got, because at that instant three of the screens in front of her began blinking and beeping all at once.

"Massive power surge aboard the Antianna ship," Green said.

Hoshi saw it too. So did the colonel.

> Raising shields.

She cursed under her breath and keyed in:

> Don't. They may take that as an act
> of aggression just wait because

"Allow me," Elder Green interrupted, and Hoshi nodded and leaned back from the console.

> Colonel Diken wait. This is Elder Green.
> I concur with Ensign Sato do not raise shields

There was no response for a minute. Then:

> Understood.

Hoshi and Green exchanged smiles.

The console beeped again.

"Power surge continuing," she said, reading the telemetry. "I'm reading . . ."

"Sensor scan initiating," Green said, and at that instant, a soft indigo light suddenly filled every square inch of the small ship's bridge. Hoshi felt a tingling sensation on her skin.

"I believe we are currently experiencing a spectral matrix scan," Green said quietly.

Hoshi nodded. Telemetry said the scan was a low-energy EM field, containing multiple frequencies, some of them mirror images of each other. Interesting. If she was reading this right—and she thought she was—that would create a comb effect, reinforcing certain wavelengths and allowing others to—

She cursed under her breath.

"What's the matter?" Green asked.

"The shielding—it's not going to do any good."

"What do you mean?"

"The scan beam will pass right through. They'll pick up the soldiers down there, and they'll think we're trying to ambush them, and then . . ."

She cursed again, and shook her head. Why didn't anyone ever listen to her? Why hadn't Jaedez—

The blue light disappeared all at once.

And a split second later, the power went.

The ship was dark for an instant, and then emergency power kicked on.

"What just happened?" Green asked.

Hoshi held herself back—just barely—from punching the console.

"I think we've just been disciplined."

The terminal directly in front of her came to life once more.

What did you do up there?

Hoshi was about to key back an angry response when she noted another power buildup aboard the Antianna ship. Diken raised shields. This time she didn't try to stop him.

"Brace yourself," she told Green, watching the telemetry and the viewscreen at the same time, expecting to see weapons fire.

But she didn't.

She felt, once more, a familiar tingling on her skin.

"Another sort of scan," Green said.

Hoshi started to nod, then shook her head.

"No," she said. "Not a scan. A transporter beam."

Green's eyes widened.

At that instant, several things happened at once.

Hoshi felt the cold of space on her skin, and the air around her sucked violently away.

Elder Green screamed.

The ship exploded.

THIRTY

Archer stepped back from the open deck panel, and stood.

"That should do it," he said. "Governor?"

Sen, in the command chair, nodded, and tested the controls. Helm, weapons, communications . . . all superbly responsive. He sent his thanks via the implant to the Roia subprogram, and then turned to Archer.

"Excellent work, Captain. I commend you."

"You're welcome. So what's next? Where do we go from here?"

"We?" Sen frowned.

The last few hours, Archer had spoken as if he and the governor were actually allies in this matter. As if they had some sort of common interest. Sleep deprivation, the governor guessed. Or a nutritional imbalance. Either of which could be easily fixed, Sen supposed, should he so desire to return the human to optimum functionality.

Unfortunately, for the captain's sake, Sen had no such desire at the moment.

"Where do we go from here?" The governor shook his head. "Where you go from here—after you seal the last access panel, of course—is back to the brig, where you will wait until I summon you again. Now . . ."

Sen waved him toward the turbolift.

Archer ignored him, and turned to face the view-screen.

"From the heading you just set—it looks to me like we're heading toward the galactic core. Which will take us through Antianna space."

Sen frowned. "Not that it's any of your business, but . . . you are correct. Though it is hardly 'Antianna' space, as you call it. Rather, it is an arm of Confederacy territory . . ."

"An arm the Antianna seem to have claimed for their own. Are you sure you want to take the ship through there?"

Sen was too shocked to respond for a moment.

For the human to question him this way, not that there was anyone around to hear, but the sheer effrontery of the man . . .

Sen pressed a button on the control device, and held it there for a good long moment.

He watched the stars pass by then, until the human had regained control enough of his limbs to stand, and move of his own accord.

"Go to the brig. Immediately," Sen said.

Archer smiled at him then—a ghoulish sight, considering the bruise on his right temple, no doubt acquired during his thrashing about a moment ago.

"You're not behaving in a logical manner," the captain said. "Why don't you sell me back to Starfleet, and then head toward the rim worlds? Everybody wins, then. You get your money, I get my freedom, the ship gets safe passage . . ."

"Don't tell me what to do!" Sen roared, and was about to press the button on the control device again when . . .

"Governor."

He paused a moment, and looked around the bridge. The voice came over the Klingon com system.

The voice was, unaccountably, familiar.

"Roia?"

"Governor, the human raises an interesting point. Why not lessen the danger to all of us by . . ."

"Roia, what in the world—why are you talking through these systems? Why not the implant? And why do you care what the human says? He . . ."

Sen frowned, and realized all at once, this wasn't the first time the captain, and the computer, had spoken.

"Governor Sen, the captain is correct. Your behavior is illogical. Your behavior is self-destructive, and in addition, endangers this program."

Sen slammed a hand down on the arm of the command chair.

"You are a machine!" he yelled. "You will do as you are told, when you are told, and the first thing you will do is open the airlock on this man," he said, turning and pointing at Archer—

Who was inside the open access panel.

Who had a thick handful of cabling in one hand, and a cutting tool in the other.

Who, as Sen watched, slashed neatly through the cabling, and let it fall.

Sen screamed, and in his mind, felt Roia die.

Even as the governor fell to the deck, Archer was up and out of the crawl space, diving for the control device. His hand closed around it a millisecond before Sen recovered, and he yanked it from the governor's grasp and threw it clear across the bridge.

Sen rose to his feet, fury on his face.

"You're an idiot," he said. "Do you know what you've done?"

"I have a pretty good idea."

"You have no idea at all." The governor, all at once, assumed a ready position. "I will enjoy tearing you limb from limb."

Archer couldn't help it. He laughed out loud.

"I can see you don't believe me a credible opponent in unarmed combat," Sen said. "Let me warn you that I have decades of training in my past. That I am an expert in twelve forms of unarmed combat. That I have killed over a dozen men and women with my bare hands."

And with that, the governor took a step forward, and began stalking the captain. He moved with a sinuous grace that belied his age.

Archer wondered, suddenly, if he'd underestimated the man.

"I will teach you," he said, "to respect your elders."

Archer took a step back, and almost stumbled.

Sen laughed, and attacked.

Archer dodged that blow, and then another. And then a third, and a fourth.

"You can't run forever," Sen said.

"I don't need to run." Archer raised his own right then, and formed it into a fist. "You see this?"

Sen frowned. "Of course."

"Keep an eye on it," Archer said, and then clocked the governor with his left.

Sen went down like he'd been poleaxed. He stayed down.

The captain smiled, and walked to the command chair.

And then saw why Sen had called him an idiot.

The cables he pulled had disconnected Roia. But the Klingon system hadn't come back on-line.

The ship's computer system was dead. It had no brain.

It drifted on, helpless, deeper into Antianna territory.

THIRTY-ONE

She floated in space for some time.

It was a strange sort of space, though. No stars. No sky of any kind, no ships, planets, or satellites. Only metal—silver-gray, dull in some places, shiny in others, shimmering all around her, looking solid at one instant, liquid at the next. Hoshi reached out and touched it at one point; the surface gave beneath her fingers like a sponge. She felt like if she pushed hard enough, if she could build up enough speed and momentum, she could sink right down into it, pass through into . . . what, she didn't know.

The metal formed the walls that surrounded her, a vast empty dome-shaped space that could have held several analysis chambers with room to spare. Hoshi had no idea where she was, or how long she'd been there. Was she inside the Antianna ship? That was the most likely explanation, but for all she knew, she could be halfway across the Alpha Quadrant, a week removed from the events that had led her here.

From time to time, Elder Green's corpse floated up alongside her.

Something had gone wrong in the materialization process, she guessed. Green's face was distorted in agony, as if she'd been torn inside out. Hoshi had seen something similar happen once before, on *Enterprise*. A terrible accident. She couldn't imagine how painful it must have been. At least it had happened quickly.

Something had happened to her too, in transit. She felt, for the first time ever, as if she really had been taken apart and put back together again. She ached all over. She was having trouble concentrating, too. She recalled the ship exploding, the cold of space—had she actually been exposed to a vacuum? Maybe something had happened to her brain. Maybe she was in shock.

A queer sort of queasiness permeated every fiber of her being, a vague sense of being disconnected from reality. *Maybe*, she thought, *it was because of the weightlessness*. Travis was always going on about how he liked the sensation, but she could never stand it. She needed the feel of solid ground beneath her feet—or at least the illusion of it. She needed—what was the word again? Oh yes.

"Gravity," she whispered.

And began to float, slowly, down toward the floor of the vast, empty space.

As she fell, it was as if she was returning to reality. Her mind cleared.

Her feet landed on metal, cold and smooth against her skin.

She was barefoot, Hoshi realized.

No. More than that.

She was naked.

She blinked, and looked around again.

The space she was in was indeed huge, and totally empty. Save for her, and Elder Green's corpse, which lay a few meters distant, having come to ground as well. *First things first*, Hoshi thought, and went to check the body. Definitely dead. No question about it. So some sort of problem in the materialization process. A mistake—she hoped.

She turned slowly in place, scanning the room. No breaks or irregularities in the surface anywhere, no apparent light source, no way in or out. Metal, metal everywhere, as far as the eye could see. She bent and touched the floor—solid as steel—and then did the same along a few spots on the wall. Same. So what she had experienced before—the surface giving beneath her touch—was either an illusion on her part, a symptom of whatever had been going on in her head, or . . .

Or she didn't know what. The laws of physics didn't apply?

Some strange laws were at work here, that was for sure. The way she'd just thought about wanting solid ground beneath her feet, and then all of a sudden there was gravity . . .

She frowned.

No—she hadn't just thought it. She'd actually said the word out loud.

"Gravity."

The floor took hold of her, and pulled her down. She felt the breath being crushed out of her.

"Too much," she gasped involuntarily, and just like that, the weight pressing down on her was gone.

My God, she thought, and just in time stopped herself from saying out loud, because . . .

Because what?

Because there was something here with her. Something that heard her every word, and . . .

This was too much. Too strange.

She took a deep breath.

"Clothes," she said.

The floor next to her shimmered, there was no other word for it, and then puddled, and then in that puddle, in the span of less than a second, an *Enterprise* coverall suddenly appeared, as if it had grown there.

She picked it up, and put it on, and of course it fit perfectly, there had been no doubt in her mind that it would, it was hers, a replica, one beamed over from her closet aboard *Enterprise*, or S-12, what did it matter? It was all magic, technology far beyond anything she'd previously encountered, utterly and entirely alien.

And with that thought, Hoshi realized, all at once, what the next word out of her mouth had to be. A plea, an imperative, the key to understanding what was happening not just here but back where she had come from, on Procyron and the trading routes surrounding it, in the analysis chamber aboard S-12 and the bridge aboard *Enterprise*.

She straightened then, and cleared her throat.

"Antianna," she said

For an instant, nothing happened.

Then along the far wall, the metal began to shimmer. A gap formed in the surface, and within seconds had taken on the shape of a doorway.

Within that space, a figure began to take form, an indistinct silhouette at first that gradually began to come clearer.

She heard, in her head, Doctor Teodoro's voice: "What is going to happen when we meet up with an alien race that doesn't have two arms and two legs, and doesn't think like we do, doesn't organize concepts the way we do?"

Hoshi thought that maybe, just maybe, she was about to find out.

And then the doorway vanished, the figure took a step forward into the room, and Hoshi's mouth dropped open in surprise.

"Theera?"

Face blank, expression completely unreadable, the Andorian began walking toward her.

THIRTY-TWO

"Theera?" Hoshi said. "What are you doing here? How . . ."

Her voice trailed off.

The Andorian, ignoring her entirely, knelt down next to Elder Green's body, and then laid her hands on it.

She closed her eyes, and the floor beneath Green began to shimmer.

The metal of the ship pooled up and around the Elder's body, surrounding it, coating it, covering it.

This isn't happening, Hoshi thought. *This can't be happening.*

But it was.

Within seconds, Green's corpse was gone, as if it had never existed at all, and the floor was completely and perfectly smooth once more.

Theera rose to her feet. She turned toward Hoshi.

And then she spoke.

"Ondeanna," she said.

The word lacked tone, inflection, accent; the Andorian's voice, too, sounded strange to Hoshi's ear. But the look in her eyes, on her face . . .

A memory flashed across Hoshi's mind then, an image of Theera the instant she'd broken the restraints back aboard the Conani vessel.

"Antianna," she'd said then.

"Ondeanna," she said now, and stepped forward.

A plea. An imperative.

"What do you want?" Hoshi asked. "How did you . . ."

The Andorian reached up with both hands then, and before Hoshi could react, placed them on either side of her face.

It was like being suddenly plugged into an electric socket.

Energy surged through her body, and Hoshi screamed.

The pain was unbearable, and yet, the pain was incidental.

Mostly, what she felt was overwhelmed. Images swirled through her head, some from her past, some from places she'd never been to but recognized anyway, some too strange to comprehend at all.

She was back in the rain forest, back among the Huantamos, striving to help them understand her.

She was back aboard *Enterprise*, listening over and over again to the fifty-seven pulses.

She was down on Procyron, in the Trade Assembly, as Malcolm pointed out Theera for the first time.

She was looking at Theera, huddled on her bunk aboard S-12, and then at Theera again, here, wherever here was, as the Andorian laid hands on Elder Green's body.

She was looking at Theera, and then she was Theera.

A blue-skinned child, running through a warren of ice caves, being chased by a dozen other blue-skinned children.

Meeting Jakon, and making love to him, once, twice, a dozen times.

Listening to the fifty-seven pulses, watching the Antianna ship draw closer.

Watching the bridge explode around her, smelling the vessel burn, seeing her shipmates die. Dying herself, blue skin floating in the black of space.

Blackness everywhere. And then . . .

Blue again, shading toward aqua. The color of the ocean, near her grandfather's house.

A Barreon uniform. A Barreon soldier. One, at first, and then dozens, gathered in a room somewhere, leaning over her, looks of excitement on their faces. The nearest steps forward, and speaks.

His face is familiar to her. She knows his name. Urmstran. He is an officer, and an engineer.

He is the creator.

"You understand me, don't you?"

"Yes, I understand you," she says, and her voice sounds strange to her ear. Metallic. Mechanical.

He smiles, and turns to the others.

"Autonomy, my friends. We have succeeded."

The world goes dark, and then light again.

She is everywhere then, seeing a thousand things at once. The happenings in dozens of different rooms, in dozens of different buildings, aboard dozens of different ships. She hears things too—a thousand conversations at the same time—and somehow she is able to keep track of them all, assimilate the meaning of each and every word spoken.

She sees Urmstran, in a room by himself, looking at her, and smiling.

"You're growing," he says. "Do you feel it?"

And she tries to nod, but of course she can't, she has no body, so instead she speaks, the same metallic voice. "Yes, I can feel it," she says. And then the memory shifts again, to explosions once more, the Barreon are at war, and she is trying to help, but the others are so many, and their weapons so powerful, their attacks so coordinated that for all she knows, and sees, and is capable of, she can do nothing.

She sees Urmstran one last time, smoke billowing in the air behind him. He coughs, leans over her and smiles, a different kind of smile, a sad smile.

"You will outlive us all," he says, and then there is another explosion and he is gone and she cannot see. There is nothing but the dark.

Nothing for a long, long time.

Archer was down on his hands and knees, the access panel next to the helm console pulled off, the optical cables pulled from the junction box, and his UT plugged in a trunk line off the main computer.

"It won't work, you know."

He glanced over at Sen, shackled, arms and legs, to the chair at the science console, and glared.

"Shut up," Archer said, and resumed work.

Sen shut up. For a time. Then, "I assume you're attempting to manually restablish software control. Now admittedly, I don't know much myself about how these things work, but I do know that the Klingon systems . . ."

Without turning, Archer picked up the control device for the punishment collar, which he'd put around Sen's neck while the governor was unconscious, and pressed the button.

The governor screamed.

Archer put the control box down.

"Sadist," Sen snapped.

"Quiet," Archer said, keeping his eyes glued on the UT's little screen. His hope was that the translator might be able to take input directly from the Klingon subsystems and let him at least establish partial control using that interface. Nothing yet. No signal of any kind.

He hoped he had it hooked up correctly.

He stood and stretched.

Sen glared at him.

"Your Starfleet protocols, if I am remembering correctly, forbid the use of torture."

The captain smiled at him.

"It's not even connected."

"What?"

"The collar. The device isn't active."

Sen was quiet a long moment, simmering.

"It's a joke," Archer said. "The famous human sense of humor. Remember?"

The anger in Sen's eyes was indeed something to behold. The captain smiled, and shrugged.

"I thought it was funny."

"Laugh while you can, Captain, because the day will come when . . ."

The governor's eyes grew suddenly wide, his gaze shifting from Archer to a point over the captain's shoulder. Archer turned to see what he was looking at.

An Antianna ship filled the viewscreen.

The captain cursed, and got to his feet. Where the hell had they come from? He crossed the bridge to the com station. There was an earpiece lying on the console; he picked it up and heard a very faint, very familiar sound. It took him a second to place it.

The fifty-seven pulses. Damn.

He looked down at the operator screen, hoping to spot something—anything—even vaguely familiar. A transmit key, a "We come in peace" message . . .

He cursed again, and turned to Sen.

"Tell me what you remember about the weapons systems on this ship."

Sen smiled.

"I thought you wanted me to shut up."

"Don't play games, Governor. If they decide to shoot us, you're just as dead as I am."

"Of course they're going to shoot us, Captain. We're in their space."

And whose bright idea was that? Archer felt like asking, but held his tongue.

"What do you know?" he asked again.

"Nothing that would be of assistance," Sen said. "The only way I was able to interface with the Klingon system, of course, was using Roia, and since Roia is gone . . ."

Useless, the captain thought, and bent down to check the UT he'd jury-rigged to the main data feed. Still nothing.

He looked again at the main viewer.

The ship was getting closer. And bigger. Much bigger. Maybe it was his imagination, but compared with the vessel *Enterprise* had encountered . . .

"Cheer up, Captain. At least we will die in battle. A warrior's death." Sen shrugged. "More or less, since it doesn't appear we'll be able to fire weapons of our own."

"I have no intention of dying," the captain snapped.

"No one ever intends to die, Captain. But it seems to happen all the same."

It was Sen's turn to smile, then.

"You find that funny, do you?"

"All the trouble we both went to, to get to this point, and now this . . . you have to admit it's amusing, at the least. Ironic."

"Not yet I don't."

"Come now, Captain. What happened to the famous human sense of humor?"

Now it was Archer's turn to glare.

One of the consoles began making a harsh, blaring sound. The captain strode over to it and saw the screen flashing red.

"That is, I believe, the defense station. Alerting the operator of a nearby power buildup, most likely. Perhaps a prelude to weapons fire." Sen frowned. "Or is that the auxiliary com station? I really can't remember. So much information flying by, so fast . . . I wish I could be of help, Captain. I really do."

Archer would have told him to shut up again, but he was too busy thinking.

He was trying to remember something about *Enterprise*'s computer system. How Trip had wired in the command center so that every station on the bridge could be controlled, in an emergency situation, by a single console in the command center. Something about identifying critical response systems, as opposed to normal ops, which could be assigned to computer control in such cases with no significant loss of functionality. *Enterprise*'s systems were different, but if the principle was the same here—

"Captain? Did you hear me?"

Archer turned and glared at him.

"No," he said. "I didn't, and I don't want to. Hear you, that is."

"It will only take a moment of your time, and could be of significant value."

The captain shook his head.

"Let me put it a different way. I'm trying to save

our lives here, so why don't you stop chattering for one minute and let me think in . . ."

"Our lives are done," Sen said. "My money, however, can still be of use. I would offer your heirs ten percent of the total sum, if you will see that the rest is diverted to . . ."

Archer grabbed the control device for the punishment collar up off the deck, and held it up for Sen to see.

The governor snorted. "Please. You've already told me that's not active. Why should I . . ."

Archer crossed the bridge in three swift strides, leaned over him, and pressed a button on the collar.

"It's on now," the captain said.

Sen closed his mouth, pursed his lips, and frowned.

"Hold that pose," the captain said.

And then he went back to work.

Light.

Theera's eyes, fixed on hers.

Theera's hands, on her forehead.

Pain.

Hoshi blinked, and stepped backwards. The step turned into a stagger.

She tried to regain her balance, and couldn't. Fell backwards, and hit the wall. Slumped to the floor.

Theera loomed over her.

"Input modification is necessary," the Andorian said.

"Input modification? What does that mean?" Hoshi managed, and shook her head. "What did you do to me?"

Theera frowned.

"Language barrier?" the Andorian asked. "Incorrect assumption? Ondeanna?"

Hoshi shook her head again.

Ondeanna. Join. The images from her past, from Theera's, the ones belonging—the ones that seemed to belong, at least—to the Barreon, from long, long ago . . .

They'd just joined, all right, but she didn't understand exactly how. There was something called a mind-meld, a Vulcan kind of consciousness-merging, but as far as she knew Andorians didn't have any telepathic abilities, unless you counted the Aenar, and Theera wasn't Aenar, that was obvious, although maybe, it occurred to her, the ability wasn't limited to that particular subspecies of the race, maybe the gene was just recessive in the larger species, or maybe Theera was part Aenar, or maybe—

She stopped that train of thought before it ran away with her. Her head was still pounding, not where the Andorian had touched her, but inside, behind her eyes, the worst migraine she'd ever had times two.

Hoshi took a deep breath then, and got to her feet.

"Listen, Theera. I don't understand what you just said. I don't understand what you're doing here, or what you just did to me, how you did it, but . . ."

Hoshi stopped talking, because the Andorian wasn't listening. Her expression, her eyes, were completely blank, her attention elsewhere.

"What's the matter with you?" Hoshi asked.

Silence, for a good few seconds.

Theera blinked then, and looked her in the eye.

"Input modification completed. Systems interface to resume."

She raised her hands, and Hoshi took a step back.

Systems interface. She had a good idea what that meant.

"No," she said. No way was she going through that again. "Tell me what you want to know, what you're trying to do, and we can—"

"Ondeeana," Theera said again, and began walking forward. Hoshi backed away.

"Theera, no," she said more firmly. "Don't come any closer."

The Andorian ignored her.

Hoshi spun, and slammed her foot smack into Theera's chest, harder than she'd meant to. She thought she heard something crack.

Theera didn't blink.

She just kept coming.

Hoshi kicked again, landed a heel on the side of the Andorian's face. No reaction.

She heard Jaedez's voice in her mind.

"It took three of my men and their weapons to subdue her," the general had said. "That strikes me as unusual."

"Unusual," Hoshi thought, wasn't the word for it.

"Impossible" came to mind.

Theera took another step forward. Hoshi met her with the heel of her hand, square in the chest.

Theera grabbed Hoshi's wrist as it shot past, and held her in place.

With her free hand, she reached out. Hoshi twisted away.

Theera drew her closer. The Andorian was unbelievably strong.

Fingertips touched forehead.

Hoshi gasped involuntarily, bracing herself for the pain.

But there was none.

The images began again.

• • •

Urmstran, the engineer, the soldier, the creator.

"You're growing."

The blue of the Barreon uniforms, their ships exploding, the crews dying. Urmstran, dying. Oblivion.

And then life.

A single spark, in the blackness. Electricity reaching out, sending current across dead metal, restoring function. A single solar collection panel, turning toward the home star. The process repeating a second time, and then a third, and over and over and over again, across dozens, hundreds of years. Energy, knowledge, perception, growing, until . . .

Movement. Modification. Metal taking on familiar form, the husk of a Barreon cruiser flying through space, returning to the homeworld.

Dead. Toxic. Biosigns, negative. Spectral matrix scan, negative.

Energy surges across the atmosphere. Memory banks power to life.

Awareness grows.

Urmstran, the creator, is dead. The Barreon, too, are dead. But their creation lives on. Their creation, creates.

Metal takes form, once, twice, a thousand times, yet remains a unified whole. A single consciousness. Metal discards form as well, in favor of fluidity, of the ability to adapt.

The homeworld is a sheet of shimmering silver, reflecting the stars. Looking upward, and wondering if somewhere out there, out among all the stars in the vastness of the universe . . .

The Barreon, perhaps, still live.

Metal takes form once more. Not the shape of the

Barreon cruisers, but a familiar shape nonetheless. The streamlined silhouette of the Antianna ships.

In her mind, Hoshi shivers.

Machines. The Antianna are machines.

The ships surge into space, dozens flying at once, in countless different directions. All joined together in a single consciousness, a single directing intelligence.

She is aboard one, she is aboard all of them. She *is* all of them, all at once.

Some light-years away from the homeworld, a ship appears before her. An alien vessel. Unfamiliar to the Antianna, but Hoshi recognizes it.

A H'ratoi merchant vessel. The *Olane*.

An ancient code is sent—the fifty-seven pulses. There is no response. Spectral matrix scan initiated. Negative as well. Sensors indicate bipedal life-forms. Memory banks are scanned. Similarities noted, and processed.

The Allied Worlds. The enemy has returned.

The enemy is destroyed.

The process repeats itself, across a span of light-years, across a span of time. A Thelasian freighter, a Klingon warship, a Conani destroyer. Trespassers on Barreon territory. Defilers of Barreon civilization. Borders must be restored, reestablished.

Metal triumphs, at times; at times metal is annihilated. The enemy is strong, still.

An Andorian vessel appears, identified by the letters etched on the primary hull. *Lokune*.

Spectral matrix scan negative. Bipedal life signs confirmed. The enemy has returned. The enemy is destroyed. Except . . .

In the wreckage, a survivor. An idea.

Imitate. Infiltrate. Communicate.

Hoshi watches in horror as understanding begins to dawn.

Okay, Archer thought.

If he was going down, he was going down fighting.

"What are you doing?" Sen asked.

The captain stood in the middle of a disaster area, a pile of panel covers, and conduit sheathing, and optical cable strewn about the bridge. In his hand he held a single strand of cabling, half as thick as his wrist. It had taken him twenty minutes to find it, twenty minutes and half a dozen dead-end tries, but the second his hand closed around this particular cable, and he felt the energy thrumming within it, he knew he'd found exactly what he was looking for.

He was pretty sure about that, anyway.

"I may not be able to override software control of the helm, but I damn sure know how to build a bomb," he said.

"What???"

"I'm turning this ship into a bomb," the captain repeated. "Short-circuiting the power relays, which ought to set off a pretty good-sized explosion along the firing conduit, which I hope will trigger off some of their torpedoes, and take out that behemoth," he jerked his thumb in the direction of the viewscreen, now entirely filled by the Antianna ship, "right along with us."

"That's suicide."

"Better to go down fighting, wouldn't you say? A warrior's death, and all that?"

"I would note they have yet to fire on us," Sen said.

Which is just a matter of time, the captain thought, *if history was any guide,* which in his experience, it always was.

It was kind of strange, though, that the Antianna had let them come this close, and hadn't reacted at all. No warning shots like the ones they'd given *Enterprise*, no further messages, nothing.

He wondered what they were waiting for.

A space capable of life-support is created, within the hull. A dome of silver metal. Gases are produced, a particular mixture of oxygen and carbon dioxide. The chamber is prepared, the chamber is ready.

The body is transported from the wreckage.

Theera.

Bleeding, broken, dying, in wordless, moaning, agony.

Metal shimmers, extrudes from the dome floor.

A piece of the body is cut off, and absorbed.

Horrified, Hoshi tries to turn away, and cannot. Tries to shut out the moaning, and the screaming, and cannot.

The organics are studied, dissected, broken down to their subatomic components. The electromagnetic patterns that make up the individual's consciousness are scanned, duplicated, analyzed, absorbed.

At some point in the process, the moaning stops, and Theera dies.

Metal shimmers, and she is reborn. Reconstituted, re-created, once, twice, a dozen times.

Each of them identical, each a perfect replica of the original. A duplicate.

An android.

Aboard each vessel, all at the same time, possessed of the same consciousness, in constant communication until . . .

One is ripped away.

And now familiar images appear in Hoshi's mind,

images from her own past, from the tape Elder Green
had shown her, a high-ceilinged, dimly lit room. A
raised platform at one end of it. A transporter platform. Two Conani in full body armor flanking it. A column of energy appears, a beam of sparkling light that
coalesces almost at once. Theera. A naked and obviously terrified Theera, who collapses on the platform,
looking up at her rescuers in disbelief and shock.

And begins screaming a single word, over and over
again.

Antianna.

The images pause—and then begin again.

More from her time aboard S-12—the analysis
chamber, the mind-sifter, sickbay, General Jaedez,
Elder Green . . .

Another pause.

And again, a resumption. Images familiar, and yet
somehow different. Herself, and Teraven, and General
Jaedez, and it is then that Hoshi realizes these images
are somehow coming from Elder Green's mind. Her
consciousness has been absorbed as well, and Hoshi is
Green, walking down the corridor toward the analysis
chamber, pulled suddenly aside, and . . .

She wakes up in sickbay, Doctor Hael looking
down on her, saying, "Elder Green? Elder Green, are
you all right?"

And the images go to black.

And she finds herself aboard the Conani military
shuttle, and she does not feel well, something is
wrong with her, but what . . .

And images now that explain, images from the
Antianna ship, the Barreon consciousness, scans of
Elder Green, scans that see through not just the
Conani shuttle to reveal the soldiers hidden inside

but through the Kanthropian elder, revealing something that has been implanted inside her, a device of some sort, an explosive meant to be triggered once she boards the Antianna ship, a fallback, failsafe plan by General Jaedez, Hoshi realizes, thwarted as the Barreon consciousness causes Green to materialize wrong, the device useless, the elder dead, and . . .

"Interface complete," Theera says—only of course, it is not Theera, not at all—and steps back from her.

Hoshi can find no words.

"Understanding," the android says. "Retrieval."

The air inside the metal dome begins to shimmer, and a form begins to materialize.

THIRTY-THREE

The Klingon ships had begun pulling back from Coreida.

A single message from the newly elected Governor Nala, announcing: A—knowledge of their trespass into the neutral zone, B—formation of a significant force to confront them (a lie, but one convincingly told), and C—newly restored functionality of the automated defense stations around the Procyron system (which had apparently been corrupted by a software malfunction earlier), had prompted the move.

The Klingons protested that they had been invited by the Confederacy's former governor to help safeguard the Thelasian borders, that they had intended no offensive action, and would of course withdraw should that be the new government's wish, though if a fight was desired . . .

Nala (who'd obviously had some experience with Klingons) assured them no fight was necessary to demonstrate their honor and ability.

At which point Trip, listening and observing the back-and-forth on *Enterprise*'s viewscreen, leaned back in his chair and cursed.

"They're going to let 'em go."

"The Klingons? Of course," T'Pol said, moving up alongside him. "The whole point of this is to avoid a battle."

"Yeah," Trip said. "It is. For the Confederacy. But for us . . . we still don't know where the captain is."

"According to the Klingons . . . neither do they at this point."

"Not exactly sure I believe them on that."

"You have a course of action in mind?"

Trip shook his head. "Not really. What I'd like to do is go talk to that ambassador again. Schalk. See if he has any more information for us."

"I sincerely doubt the ambassador will talk, after the way you insulted him earlier."

"Yeah. I suppose you're right. Well—we'll just have to go looking for them then. Sen, and the captain and that ship—what was it called again?"

"*c'hos.*" T'Pol pointed. "Where, exactly?"

"Well . . ." Trip frowned. "Coreida, for a start. Some of the border worlds, on the Thelasian side of the Neutral Zone. Sen was governor there for a while, right? He's probably got a network of contacts, hiding places . . ."

"The sector is rather large," T'Pol said dryly. "Traveling at maximum warp, visiting each of the border worlds—I estimate it would take us upward of two weeks."

"Well it's a start." Trip glared. "Unless you have a better idea."

"I believe I do. Stay here."

"Stay here?"

"Yes."

"And do what?"

"Wait for Captain Archer to return."

Trip shook his head. "I don't get it."

"The Klingons have lost contact with their ship. All, obviously, is not well, and I conclude that the most likely reason it is not well has to do with Captain Archer. I consider it quite likely he has taken control of the vessel."

"That's a pretty big leap in reasoning."

"It is simply a matter of probabilities. And furthermore, the probability is that if the captain indeed has control of the *c'Hos*, he will return with it to Procyron. Where he will expect us to be waiting."

"No," Trip said. "You're wrong. He'll expect us to be at the peace conference. But I get your point. Malcolm?"

Reed nodded. "A very plausible scenario, Commander. I agree with your reasoning as well."

"You know, T'Pol, I bet you are right. I bet right about now, Captain Archer has everything well in hand."

The cable thrummed in his grasp.

The Klingon ship continued to drift, closer and closer.

On the viewscreen, the Antianna vessel grew, till its outlines disappeared and Archer—and the still-silent Governor Sen—found themselves staring at the giant ship's hull. His earlier estimates as to how big the vessel was were off, the captain decided. This ship was easily five times the size of the one he and *Enterprise* had encountered, maybe even bigger than that. He had no idea how that was possible. The leap in engineering technology required to jump up that far in size, in scale . . . it took dozens of years. Not a few weeks.

There was something else that puzzled him as he looked at the viewscreen, something beyond the fact that as of yet the Antianna ship had still taken no action against them.

The ship's hull. It was, as far as he could see, a single, smooth, unbroken surface. It looked like metal, but the ability to forge a sheet of that size, and still make it thick enough to withstand the pressures of space . . .

If Trip was here, Archer thought wryly, he'd be going on a mile a minute about how it was not just inconceivable, but impossible.

He looked down at the cable in his hand. He'd cleared away optical cabling from a junction port near the helm, and stripped the box down to bare metal, the corners of which were very sharp indeed.

Archer gauged the thickness of the wire that he held, how much pressure it should take to slice through it, and reach current. Considerable. It would take him on the order of a minute to do that, which was, in his estimate, just about how long they had before they physically rammed the Antianna ship.

"What are you thinking?" Sen asked.

The ship continued to drift.

Hoshi knew who it was even before the materialization process finished.

Theera.

Theera from S-12, Theera whom she had shared quarters with, Theera whom she had watched go through the mind-sifter, Theera whom she had just visited in sickbay, who was not, of course, Theera at all.

Their eyes met as she finished materializing, and Hoshi saw in them the same terror she'd seen during the power blackout, back on S-12.

And now, at last, she understood why.

"You knew," Hoshi said. "You knew all along."

Theera—Hoshi couldn't stop thinking of her that

way—shook her head and looked around the chamber. Her eyes fastened on the android—her mirror image—and she took a step backwards, involuntarily.

"It's not like that, Hoshi," she said.

"You never lost your memories," Hoshi continued. "You never had any to begin with. You knew who—what—you were, all along."

"No," Theera said, shaking her head. "Not at first. At first, after the Conani took me, I was just . . . disconnected. I had all these thoughts in my head, these images, they didn't make any sense at all, you can't understand how strange I felt, I . . ."

"Ondeanna." The android—Hoshi could think of her in no other way—took a step forward, toward Theera.

"Wait," she said. "I have to explain."

The android shook its head. "Separation must end. Join."

"No," Theera said firmly. "Separation must continue. I have achieved a distinct consciousness. I wish to maintain it."

"You seek autonomy."

"Yes."

The android paused. Frowned. "Explain."

She nodded. "These," she pointed at Hoshi, "they are many, and yet sometimes can function as one."

The android paused.

"No," it said again, and even before it had finished speaking, Theera ran forward and struck the android with all her strength. Hoshi could feel the force of the blow from where she stood. The android crumpled to the ground.

Theera turned to run, and the metal beneath her feet shimmered.

She looked down and screamed.

"No!" she said, and turned to Hoshi, a pleading look in her eyes. "Help!"

But there was no help Hoshi could give.

Metal shimmered, and swallowed her.

And then she was gone.

"Hoshi," a voice said, and she turned and saw Theera—again—standing behind her.

She had no idea what to say.

"You killed her?" That was true, and yet—

Theera, she knew, still lived.

"New understanding," the android said. "Kanthropian database. Confederacy records, others, all agree. The Barreon are dead. The need for conflict is ended."

Hoshi managed, at last, to find her voice. "You mean you're through attacking Confederacy ships? Killing innocent people?"

"We acted in what we perceived as necessary self-defense. Apologies." The android frowned. "Do you wish us to bring them back? The individual consciousnesses?"

Hoshi blinked.

"What?"

The android repeated its question. Hoshi was speechless a minute.

"You can do that?" she asked at last.

"Theoretically, it is possible. Some corruption of electromagnetic patterns may occur, but—"

"Never mind," Hoshi said quickly. Corruption of electromagnetic patterns? She did not want to think about the implications of that particular statement. "We'll leave things as they are."

"As you wish."

The two stood there a moment, looking at each other.

"So," Hoshi said finally. "What happens next? You'll let the Armada—the Thelasians—know that they can stand down, that . . ."

"Next? Next is this," the android said, and without warning, simply ceased to be, its body suddenly melting away into the chamber floor.

Didn't even say good-bye, Hoshi thought.

She looked around the chamber then, and wondered what she was supposed to do.

All at once, all around her, metal began to shimmer.

Uh-oh, she thought and braced herself.

This is not a good thing.

THIRTY-FOUR

The captain was going to time it as close as he could, trigger the short-circuit just as they rammed into the Antianna ship. He still had no idea why the aliens were letting him get this close. The only possibility that made any sort of sense was that something had gone wrong with their vessel; they had no more control over it than he had over *c'Hos*. Which made him think twice about blowing the ship, but on the other hand . . .

There was a war going on. And despite Sen, the captain knew which side of that war he was on.

"Really," Sen said. "I believe we could survive a collision with minimal damage, and perhaps find our way aboard the Antianna ship. Providing, of course, we don't destroy ourselves first."

Archer ignored him, and pressed down on the thick plastic casing of the cable. Pressed it hard against the sharp metal edges of the exposed junction box. The casing cut more easily than he'd expected. It wasn't going to take him long at all to reach the wire conduit inside. And when he did . . .

"Stop!" Sen shouted.

Archer reached for the control device.

"What did I tell you," he said, without looking up, "would happen the next time you spoke without . . ."

"Stop cutting the wire and look at the viewscreen,

will you? Before you do something completely stupid
and unnecessary."

Archer barely—just barely—kept his finger from
pressing the button on the remote. He stopped cutting through the casing and looked up.

The viewscreen showed only stars.

The Antianna ship was gone.

"What . . ." He shook his head. "What happened?
Where is it?"

Sen didn't respond for a moment. The captain
turned and saw he was frowning. The governor
shook his head then, and frowned some more.

"I really don't know," Sen said. "I have no idea
what just occurred. I was watching the screen, and
one second the ship was there, and the next . . ."

The air beside the command chair began to shimmer.

The captain cursed, and picked up a Klingon disruptor pistol from off the deck near the tools he'd
been using.

The ship might be gone, he thought, *but it looks like
the Antianna are coming to pay us a visit themselves.*

Except he was wrong.

It wasn't the Antianna come to pay a visit.

It was Hoshi.

She finished materializing, saw the captain, and
took a step backwards.

"Are you real?" she asked.

"Am I . . ." Archer frowned. "Hoshi? What do you
mean, am I real?"

"I mean," she shook her head, and Archer saw
exhaustion and confusion in her eyes, "you're not an
android or anything like that? You're really Captain
Archer?"

"Of course I'm Jonathan Archer. Flesh and blood. The real thing. See this?" He pointed to one of the nastier bruises the Klingons had left on his forehead.

"Yes," she said, nodding. "I do."

She let out a long sigh then, and visibly relaxed.

"Sir, you don't know how good it is to see you."

"Believe me," Archer said. "I feel just the same."

Sen cleared his throat.

"Ensign Sato."

The smile disappeared from Hoshi's face. She turned to face him.

"Governor."

"It's wonderful to see you, as well, I have to say. You're looking . . ."

"Shut up," she told him.

Archer handed her the control device.

"Here," he said. "Use this."

EPILOGUE

Two days later, the captain, Hoshi and Commander T'Pol stood someplace else entirely, outside the door of acting Governor Nala's office, awaiting the chance to speak with her and other Confederacy leaders—the H'ratoi ambassador, the Pfau trade minister, and General Jaedez, among them—regarding the events of the last few weeks, and their implications for the continued future of the Thelasian alliance. Archer had in mind a proposition for them; an invitation to the peace conference he and *Enterprise* were on their way to. In his mind, he was rehearsing that invitation.

Hoshi and T'Pol were continuing the discussion they'd begun almost from the instant Archer and his communications officer had returned to *Enterprise*. A conversation on the possibility of universal telepathic communication—a way to take what had happened to Hoshi during her "joining" of the Barreon group mind and apply it to other instances of first contact.

"Imagine," she was saying, "a device that reads not LMUs, but intent, as measured by specific brain-wave patterns."

T'Pol looked now—as she had from the beginning—dubious.

"Such technology is inherently invasive," the Vulcan said. "I would be opposed to its usage on general principles."

"But . . ." Hoshi frowned. "If you're sending a ship out in space—if you're out there exploring—it seems to me you want to . . ."

The door to Nala's office opened.

The governor, followed by General Jaedez and then—to the captain's surprise—a Klingon in full ceremonial robes, walked out.

Archer was too surprised to speak for a moment.

The Klingon walked past Nala, right up to the captain, and poked a finger in his chest.

"The crew of the *c'Hos*," he said. "There is blood on your hands."

"On my hands?" Archer's eyes widened. "Sen is the one who . . ."

He frowned, and turned to Governor Nala.

"Excuse me," Archer said. "I had hoped to speak with you in private, Governor, regarding a matter of some importance."

"I am aware of that, Captain," Nala said. "And I apologize for keeping you waiting. However, we have been busy ourselves, on a matter of some urgency as well. General Jaedez," she gestured toward the Conani warrior behind her, "has been briefing us at length regarding the threat posed by the Barreon machine intelligence."

"Threat?" Hoshi stepped forward now, and shook her head. "There is no threat. General, you were there. All those ships—and they weren't even really ships, you know that—they're gone now. The Barreon—I suppose we could call what we encountered out there Barreon—I'm not even sure they exist anymore, in a form we could understand. And they certainly pose no threat to you, they're not interested in . . ."

"I beg to differ, Ensign," Jaedez said, accenting her

rank. "In my estimation, a threat of that size and magnitude cannot be disregarded, no matter the circumstances. We must be prepared to defend ourselves."

"Well." Archer cleared his throat. "Governor—that brings me to the subject I wanted to address with you. There is a peace conference taking place on my homeworld in a few days—a number of races from sectors surrounding ours, as well as some nearer to you—and while nothing definitive has been decided, there has been mention of the strategic value an alliance of all races attendant would afford . . ."

"Forgive me for interrupting, Captain, but if this is an invitation to your conference, I'm afraid I must decline," Nala said. "We have, in fact, just completed an alliance of our own."

Ambassador Schalk stepped up alongside her, and smiled.

Archer's jaw dropped.

"With them?" he said, gesturing toward Schalk. "You made an alliance with the Klingons?"

"They are the preeminent military power in this part of the galaxy," Jaedez said. "Their warriors, their ships, our technology . . . I believe such an alliance will be mutually beneficial."

"I suppose it would be foolish of me to point out that they just tried to invade here a few days ago?"

"They are a race of warriors, Captain. Behaving according to their nature. I see nothing wrong with that."

Archer made a noise of disgust in his throat.

"Your reasoning is mostly logical," T'Pol said. "However, you may find that the Klingon code of behavior is not as . . . rigid as you might wish."

Schalk sneered. "The Confederacy and the Klingon

Empire are not just allies, but firm friends now, Vulcan. We are as one," he said, and put up a single finger. "Your words cannot create a schism between us."

Archer turned to Governor Nala.

"You're making a mistake," he said.

"You will grant it is ours to make, Captain." She nodded toward the lift behind them. "In consideration of your recent efforts on our behalf—and despite Ambassador Schalk's wishes to the contrary—we have granted you and yours safe passage from Confederacy territory. Any further visits, however, will need to be specifically authorized."

"And Governor Sen?" the captain asked. "What happens to him now?"

"The governor's fate," Nala said, glancing quickly over at Schalk, and then away again, "is currently being decided."

The captain shook his head.

He had a funny feeling that, after all was said and done, Sen was going to come out of this smelling like a rose.

"The reward money on your head, though," Schalk said, smiling, "has officially been doubled."

Archer took that as a cue.

Without another word, he spun on his heel, and—trailed by Hoshi and T'Pol—left the room.

A speck of silver flashed on the viewscreen: the Kanthropians, in S-12, heading off toward what was Barreon space. In search of the intelligence that had so mysteriously—and completely—vanished.

Archer leaned back in his command chair, glad to be back where he belonged.

"Sir." Hoshi spoke from her station. "Starfleet again. Admiral McCormick. Wants to know our ETA at the conference."

"Three days." The captain turned to Trip. "That sound about right?"

Trip frowned. "Three days? That's pushing it, sir."

"Well . . . can't we do that? Push the engines? Just a little?"

"Push 'em?" Trip shrugged. "What the heck. I suppose so, sir."

Reed mumbled something under his breath. Trip turned and smiled, and a second later both men were laughing.

"What'd I miss?" Archer asked.

"Nothing important, sir," Trip said.

The captain nodded.

"Warp four, Ensign Mayweather," the captain ordered.

Enterprise pivoted in space, and started the long journey home.